Praise for *Winner Takes All*

"Sandra Kitt is back with an emotional punch, delighting us with two strong but somewhat mismatched people. Along with falling in love, they each must deal with family issues and the complications of a huge lottery win. It's a page-turner you don't want to miss!"

—Lori Foster, *New York Times* bestselling author

"A warmhearted story of old flames, new loves, and a clever and nuanced plot reflecting current issues with sensitivity, warmth, and wisdom."

—Susan Wiggs, #1 *New York Times* bestselling author

"Skillful, silky writing, interweaving Jean and Patrick's past mistakes with hopeful futures. I especially loved the twist at the ending and the generosity of Kitt's characters."

—Nancy Thayer, *New York Times* bestselling author

"Sandra Kitt is a writing legend, and *Winner Takes All* proves that when it comes to great storytelling of the most romantic kind, she has the gift."

—Brenda Jackson, *New York Times* bestselling author

"*Winner Takes All* is heartwarming, life-affirming, page-turning romance at its best!"

—Brenda Novak, *New York Times* bestselling author

"[A] charming, multilayered, thoroughly entertaining tale, in which readers are the real winners. Prepare to fall in love."

—Farrah Rochon, *USA Today* bestselling Author

"[A] delightfully entertaining and deliciously romantic story of second chances and family drama!"

—Debbie Mason, *USA Today* bestselling author

"Sandra Kitt writes beautiful stories about fascinating characters I would love to know in real life. *Winner Takes All* is romantic, tender, emotional, and compelling."

—RaeAnne Thayne, *New York Times* bestselling author

"Sandra Kitt is always a must-read! One of the original trailblazers of Black romance is back!"

—Kwana Jackson, *USA Today* bestselling author

"Sandra Kitt delivers a tender, love-conquers-all romance. Complex interracial couples, past and present, show how things have changed— and stayed the same—but finding the *one* is all about fighting for each other. Emotional, impactful, heartwarming."

—Jennifer Ryan, *New York Times* bestselling author

"From the first page to the last, this book is a reminder of why I love Sandra Kitt's writing: her words are poised, elegant, perfection."

—LaQuette, award-winning author

"Heat, heart, and the importance of family define Sandra Kitt's wonderful stories. She navigates the complexities of real-world relationships with a radiant, positive energy that satisfies and inspires."

—Jayne Ann Krentz, *New York Times* bestselling author

"Sandra Kitt's storytelling takes you on a soul-satisfying journey to what really matters in life. The perfect combination of fun and heart."

—Susan Elizabeth Phillips, *New York Times* bestselling author

"Sandra Kitt creates a satisfying tale of sudden wealth, family ties, and not one but two second chances at love. Fans of Debbie Macomber will enjoy *Winner Takes All*. A story to warm the heart."

—Christina Dodd, *New York Times* bestselling author

WINNER TAKES ALL

SANDRA KITT

sourcebooks
casablanca

Published by Sourcebooks Casablanca, an imprint of Sourcebooks
P.O. Box 4410, Naperville, Illinois 60567-4410
(630) 961-3900
sourcebooks.com

Library of Congress Cataloging-in-Publication Data

Names: Kitt, Sandra, author.
Title: Winner takes all / Sandra Kitt.
Description: Naperville, Illinois : Sourcebooks Casablanca, [2021] |
   Series: The millionaires club; book 1
Identifiers: LCCN 2020047355 (print) | LCCN 2020047356 (ebook) |
   (trade paperback) | (epub)
Classification: LCC PS3561.I86 W56 2021 (print) | LCC PS3561.I86 (ebook)
   | DDC 813/.54--dc23
LC record available at https://lccn.loc.gov/2020047355
LC ebook record available at https://lccn.loc.gov/2020047356

Printed and bound in the United States of America.
SB 10 9 8 7 6 5 4 3 2 1

*When some things go wrong, take a moment to be thankful
for the many things that are going right.*

"In ordinary life, we hardly realize that we receive a great deal more than we give, and that it is only with gratitude that life becomes rich."

—Dietrich Bonhoeffer

CHAPTER 1

For a moment, when the text notification lit up the screen on her cell phone, Jean Travis considered ignoring it. But it was her work phone, and the incoming message meant it was from someone official, i.e., her boss, Bradley Clark.

Where are you? the message began.

About to leave, she texted back, heading down the corridor toward security and the exit.

Meet me at the pressroom. I'm on my way.

She knew this didn't bode well for the end of her day and the start of her weekend. Jean's silent response was to do as she was instructed.

Brad Clark was already waiting for her when she reached the converted conference room that also doubled as the pressroom. He appeared anxious, and Jean guessed that whatever was going on was important. The door to the pressroom was open, and there was a lot of activity inside.

"What's going on?" she asked, her attention drawn to the flurry of movement, equipment, and orders coming from inside the room.

"Press conference and brief broadcast in about thirty minutes," Brad said. "The mayor agreed to the broadcast of the current lottery winners. You're making the announcement and introducing the winners."

Jean frowned. "It's almost six thirty…"

"I know, I know. Someone dropped the ball, and everyone's gone for the day. You have to step in and do it. Local reporters and their crews are already here. The winners are in the greenroom. We already know who they are, but this is a big deal because of the Mega Million winning ticket. It's huge…" he said.

"Not funny," Jean murmured, accepting several pages from him.

"It's easy, should take less than an hour. I wrote up some guidelines. Here's a list of the current winners…" He gave Jean another page. "Make sure you emphasize that the mayor's office wanted to share the news with people in the city, letting them know that their neighbors really do become winners. They can, too, blah, blah, blah."

Jean grinned at Brad. "Have you ever bought a lottery ticket?"

"I don't gamble," he chortled. "My wife would kill me for throwing away money like that. Odds are too high. But…you can't win if you don't play. Wonder what ESPN's gonna do now?"

She was confused. "What do you mean?"

"One of our winners is a TV personality…almost famous…" While he spoke Brad's cell buzzed a notification. "I gotta take this."

"How much time before we broadcast?"

Brad looked at his watch. "Down to twenty-five minutes."

"Where will you be?"

"On my way home." He smirked, walking away and reading his text. "Do whatever they need you to. Stay until it's over. Call me if there are problems, and *only* if there are problems."

"Overtime, right?"

"Night. Have a good weekend…"

Jean watched him hurry away. She entered the pressroom to find that the reporters and film crews were pretty much set up. She then made sure the podium had a functioning mike.

She dug out a pocket mirror, checked her lip gloss, and absently fluffed her hair, then began to introduce herself to the reporters waiting to meet the lottery winners and tape the announcements.

The local networks no longer did a weekly five-minute drawing of lottery numbers. Everything was digital now, which cost less money and production time. For these occasional announcements, the winners were already known to the lottery commission. Only the public would be surprised when the names were called. Jean knew that all she had to do was interject excitement into the proceedings. She only had a minute to scan quickly through Brad's notes, to figure out an agenda for the announcement, to fashion an introduction—something cute and humorous—so that no one would suspect this was her first time.

Jean signaled to the security guard standing just outside the door. "We're almost ready. Please bring in the guests. Tell them to take seats in the front two rows quietly." She checked her smartphone clock. "Five minutes, okay?" she said to the waiting press crew.

She glanced around to find about thirty or forty people gathered in the back of the room to witness the announcement. They were fillers, like movie extras, there to lend authenticity to the moment. No doubt many were family members and friends, but mostly they were general public who enjoyed saying *I was there when*, Jean guessed. She got a signal from the reporters that they were all set. Jean took up a position at the front of the space, and camera lights suddenly flashed on. Just then, a side door opened and a number of people trooped in, momentarily creating a disruption. The bright lights for the cameras prevented Jean from seeing a thing beyond the podium. Then it went quiet.

"We're live," someone signaled.

Jean smiled into the cameras and began to talk.

"Hello! I'm Jean Travis, assistant director of Public Affairs at the mayor's office. I'd like to…to…" She fumbled and hesitated when she was distracted by another person making what could only be described as a perfectly timed grand entrance into the room.

Jean could detect a tall figure, a man, but couldn't see much else. He managed to create a stir and a brief buzz of whispering, taking his seat. Jean tried to cover her lapse.

"So much excitement," she said with a bright smile. "Thank you for being here tonight as we recognize the latest winners in our state lottery. And, of course, everyone wants to know—and see—who will walk away with the Mega Million prize that has grown over the past two drawings when there was no winning ticket."

Jean then had a chance to catch her breath while she read an official statement from the State Lottery Commission about the rules governing the program. Her attention was briefly caught again by the latecomer, who, incredibly, appeared to be giving her a covert hand wave. She ignored it and continued.

"So let's get to it! Like all of you, I'm excited to meet the lucky ones who will walk away with checks from the State Lottery, with numbers ending in a lot of zeros."

A cheer went up through the room. One camera turned to capture the seated group demonstrating their enthusiasm.

Jean smiled, and then she suddenly gasped.

The list!

She had not yet even looked at the winning names on the list Brad had given her. As smoothly as possible, she pulled the list from the other announcements. She briefly glanced at the names. The last name grabbed her attention. She recognized it. But from where?

"And now, our winners!"

Jean called the first name, including where he was from and the amount of the winnings. Shouts and applause erupted from the audience as an elderly man and woman came forward, broad smiles and clasped hand-pumps denoting their victory. Jean kissed the cheeks of the woman and man to interject a little human connection. A giant cardboard sign was passed to her, a replica of a check with the amount the couple had won. Jean asked them a few questions about how they planned to use their winnings. The gushing, excited reactions from the couple evoked laughter and shout-outs around the room. Then they retook their seats to another round of applause.

And so it went, down the list of names for the next forty-five minutes. By the time she called the fourth winner, Jean had her comments to a science, and everything went smoothly. But there was a heightened energy and anticipation, as everyone clearly wanted to know who had won the Mega Millions. Who was going to be set for life? She looked at the name again, and recognition finally sunk in. Jean knew this name. An unexpected catch lodged in her chest. She had to quickly swallow to get her next breath.

"Will Trick... Will, er... Patrick Bennett, please come to the front to accept your check."

She joined in the clapping for the winner, as she'd done for all the others. But this time she was more interested in who came forward. Out of the bright lights, a tall figure emerged. He was casually but smartly dressed in dark charcoal cargo pants, a black Henley, and a collarless, short black leather jacket. *Great presence*, Jean thought, keeping her attention on his approach, her smile fixed as her gaze widened with recognition. Jean reached out with her hand to touch his arm so that he'd face the camera in the right position. But he stunned her by taking hold of her hand and giving it a subtle squeeze...and not letting go. And he knew exactly how to position himself in front of a studio camera.

Jean made a discreet attempt to pull free, but Patrick Bennett wasn't having it. She gave in and tried to relax. Catching her off guard even more, he brought their clasped hands to his mouth and planted a light kiss to the back of hers. The audience loved it, cheering and whistling. Jean played it through and gave a faux blushing gaze into the cameras.

"Many congratulations to...to Patrick Bennett," she said with the right amount of enthusiasm and professionalism. "Mr. Bennett is the grand winner today of—are you ready?—*seventy-five million dollars!*"

There were whoops and gasps, and one audacious request from a female in the back of the room.

"I love you! Will you marry me? We're already here at city hall!" The room erupted into wild laughter.

"*Do it, do it, do it…*" went up the boisterous chorus.

Patrick Bennett, still holding Jean's hand, raised both in a kind of victory wave. He grinned broadly but didn't respond to the proposal. His free hand swept through his hair in a gesture that had Jean momentarily transfixed. Then she was able to extract her hand when she was handed the last cardboard check. Cameras flashed, dozens of cell phones were poised in the air, the glow of their blue-lit screens scattered throughout the audience.

Jean started the applause again, gazing openly at Patrick Bennett. It was an unavoidable sign of recognition between them. And then Patrick winked at her and murmured so that only she could hear, "Surprised?"

The quiet drawl of his voice made her stomach tense. That word, his tone, seemed much too intimate for the setting. She couldn't think of a thing to say. She just kept clapping and smiling.

Jean was so glad when it was finally over. She made a few concluding remarks, thanking everyone for coming and congratulating the winners again. As people got up and began moving around, many, if not most, headed to surround Patrick. She was curious about the familiarity with which people approached and spoke to him, as if they knew him. She covertly watched Trick. *Pa*trick. Jean had known him by the former moniker from the past. *Trick*. Jean gathered her things, absently chatting with some of the camera crew and making arrangements with the maintenance and security staff to have the room put back to rights.

She could just hear Patrick's deep voice off to the side, the easy way he chatted with everyone, even posing for selfies, which completely mystified Jean. He didn't know any of these people. What came across was a confidence and vibrancy to him, so unlike the other winners…just regular everyday folk who'd had a stroke of extraordinary luck. Perhaps this was one of the biggest, if not *the* biggest, moment of their lives. Patrick answered questions and accepted the good wishes of those around him with humility and a surprising grace, Jean considered. She kept stealing little glances at him, once catching Patrick doing the same to her. Her curiosity betrayed her once more.

Reporters continued to ask *How do you feel winning so much money?* questions, looking for cute, amusing, moving quotes for their profile pieces. She thought there might be an opportunity to use some footage for promo or marketing later on from her office.

The room finally began to empty out. She took a deep breath and approached the last few people, including Patrick. There was no way to leave without acknowledging him. Without remembering. Was he doing the same?

Patrick—formerly known as Trick—Bennett killed time letting perfect strangers take photos with him. But he was really waiting for Jean to be finished. He saw her in his peripheral vision, not wanting to be too obvious and stare. But it was *her*!

She'd cut her hair.

She used to have an incredible mass of thick, wavy hair. It was a light brown with lighter, almost blond tendrils at her hairline. Her hair had been a great accompaniment to her tawny skin, a creamy beige that could have identified Jean as almost anything nonwhite. Her eyes were exotic, a bit amber in color, and could hold a person's gaze with catlike intensity.

Back in high school, he'd only ever seen her in pants. This was the first time he'd seen her legs! Lean and shapely below the hem of a functional black skirt that hit slightly above her knees. She was all professional, classy, and grown up. In school, Jean looked very young, very small. She was still small, but the development since he'd last seen her was decidedly fully adult. She'd become a very pretty woman.

He spoke first as they stood momentarily alone near the door.

"I sure didn't expect to see you here," he said with a grin.

"Ditto," Jean responded with a nervous chuckle. "I think my surprise is greater than yours. Congratulations on your big win."

He shifted his gaze, shrugged. "Yeah. Thanks."

She seemed surprised by his response, the lack of excitement. He didn't think an explanation was necessary.

Patrick quickly recovered, studying her. "So, you work here?"

She nodded. "Public Affairs. I'm the assistant director."

He studied her, his grin growing wider. "I always knew you'd go on to great things."

"It's local government. Not really great things," Jean said, demurring.

He didn't answer directly, instead considering Jean as if to re-familiarize himself. He was trying to see, to hear what else may have changed about her.

"How long has it been?" he asked in quiet disbelief.

"Since high school. You graduated and moved on."

"Do you live in the city?"

"In Brooklyn."

Patrick thoughtfully assessed her answers.

Jean fidgeted, as if she was uncomfortable. Maybe she was trying to pull herself together. Did she feel odd? A little off? Like they'd fallen into the rabbit hole? He suddenly felt like the past was reclaiming them. Time was shrinking, and the strangeness of seeing each other again was fading. But neither of them could think of much more to say. The circumstances really didn't lend themselves to chatting and getting reacquainted. And she was on the job. Jean didn't suggest that they exchange information. Should he?

"Well…it's been…"

"Real? Fun? Unexpected? Weird?"

She laughed quietly. "Yes to all of the above, I think."

"Yeah, me too." He fell into step next to her as they slowly left the room and started toward the front of the building. "I'm sorry if I embarrassed you when you called my name. I couldn't believe it was you making the announcements. To be honest, I wanted to grab you right then and there and plant one…but I thought better of it."

"Thank you," she said, her gaze horrified by the possibility.

"So I did the next thing I could get away with." He suddenly stopped to stare down at Jean. "Did you know it was me?"

"Almost right away," Jean confessed. "But I wasn't expecting you to hold my hand. Kiss it."

He frowned, considering. "No, you're right. I overplayed my advantage."

"I…am…surprised to see you," she said carefully.

He grinned. "I'll take that." He straightened. "Are you done for the day? Headed home? To a date?"

Jean raised her brows. She knew he was fishing, but she did seem pleased by his curiosity. She neither confirmed nor denied it.

"I was recruited at the eleventh hour to host the announcement today. I think I'm still on call until…"

"Great!" Patrick said with sudden enthusiasm. "Some of my friends are throwing an after-party. Someplace called Filmore's."

"It's a bistro across the street from city hall."

"Come join us."

Jean shook her head. "Sounds like a private party."

"For me. I think I can invite who I want. I'd like you to be there. We could catch up. You can't say no."

Jean seemed to consider what she should do. "I need to go back to my office, check for any important messages."

"Does that mean yes?"

Jean smiled at his persistence. "It means maybe."

"And if you can't?"

"It was nice seeing you again, Trick."

The name no longer sounded right. It certainly no longer fit. "It's Patrick now. Only you and a few hundred former high school classmates have ever heard anyone call me Trick."

"Cute in school, not so much now?"

"You got it."

"Sorry I reminded you."

"Not at all. I liked it in high school. Made me stand out. I find I do much better in life when I act like an adult."

Jean laughed outright.

Behind them, a maintenance worker hurried to catch up, carrying a large sheet of cardboard. He gave it to Jean. It was the giant check made out to Patrick with the amount of his winnings. She then turned to him.

"This is yours. Don't you want it?"

He was actually embarrassed. "It was a great gesture but...I don't know what I'd do with it."

"Then I'm going to leave it in my office. My boss can figure out what to do with it on Monday. You should go. Your friends are probably wondering what happened to you."

"Will you come over when you're done?"

"Maybe I'll surprise you. Don't you like surprises?"

He shook his head. "Not really."

"Then, you'll have to wait and see," Jean said quietly with a parting smile.

Jean still felt a bit awkward with the idea of being in a social setting with Patrick. They'd never socialized in high school. And now her official city hall duties had drifted into something else. She crossed the street to Filmore's with that feeling of stepping back in time. Patrick was the last person on earth she would have expected to see that afternoon. Or ever.

They had not seen each other since high school, and he'd been two years ahead of her. He had been a standout back then. Memorable. He didn't have to work at it, or even accept it as his due, in her experience. But the benefits had always been great, and he seemed to enjoy every one of them. Patrick was always in the center of a wide circle of friends. Girls predictably trailed after him for his attention. Yes, Jean remembered ruefully, there were always a *lot* of girls. That his path had ever crossed with hers at all now seemed unbelievable, pure happenstance. But Trick—*Patrick*—had been the only white boy in school who hadn't treated her like she was a curiosity, who didn't ask dumb questions like "What are you? Where are you from?"

By the time Jean finally left city hall, she was experiencing equal degrees of excitement and apprehension about the party. Filmore's was one of the local haunts frequented for lunch, birthday celebrations, rendezvous, small group meetings, and after-work drinks to chill. When she entered, the place was busy with the after-work crowd. She continued to the back room. It was a fairly small space, boisterous and lively with some twenty men and women in laughter-filled talk. Jean spotted Patrick, in the center of it all, holding court with a half-finished beer in hand.

———

Patrick saw Jean enter right away.

He'd been watching for her. But, in fact, he hadn't expected Jean to accept his invitation to come to the party being held for him. Here she was, and he felt a crazy sense of relief. He politely excused himself from several men and women who were rehashing their shock about his lottery payout. He started toward Jean, trying to interpret her calm demeanor and the wide-eyed regard with which she watched his approach. A tiny uncertainty mixed with…what?

He'd only gone a few feet when he was stopped literally in his tracks. A squealing young woman had brushed past Jean and launched herself against him, locking her arms around his neck.

He caught her to prevent falling off balance and carefully but firmly peeled the excited woman away. She was no stranger to Patrick, but her action was definitely over the top. They had never been *that* close. Two other very attractive women, flipping their hair and covertly smoothing down the spandex material of their form-fitting dresses, quickly crowded around him as well. Patrick finished his beer, and someone promptly passed him another. He could see that Jean felt the festive vibe of the gathering, and she grinned at the happy mood of the occasion. But she stood all alone.

These people liked him. He was comfortable with them. Admired. Unable to get away from them, however, he shrugged and grinned at Jean in apology. He raised his beer bottle in greeting.

And then he watched as one of his friends, a colleague, ambled over to Jean to introduce himself and chat her up. Jean laughed lightly at something he said and gave him her attention. Patrick arched a brow.

Damn!

Was he hitting on her?

CHAPTER 2

We heard you were doing some sort of press thing today, so we had to come say hello," one of the young women said to Patrick with a coquettish smile.

"Are you here alone tonight?" another woman asked him with obvious intent.

He took a good swallow of his beer, noticing Jean over the raised bottle in conversation with not one but two of his guests. He shook his head. "My mother couldn't make it," Patrick said smoothly.

The three women exchanged confused glances.

"That's not really what we meant," the third said. "I guess we're surprised no one special came to cheer you on, help you celebrate," she fished.

"Then I'm grateful that you three are here."

In unison, the three young women giggled. The first reached out and lightly brushed her slender fingers across the back of Patrick's hand, tilting her gaze to his. "My pleasure," she murmured.

With practiced ease, Patrick was engaging and responsive, without promising anything or showing interest in choosing among them. Finally realizing that they were going to be unsuccessful in their game plan, the women drifted away to eventually be replaced with a new round-robin of beauties vying for his attention.

And there was Jean Travis, her laughter quietly carrying across the room. Patrick thought she was probably having a better time than he was. He recalled that Jean was less social, more cautious and quiet in high school. Especially around people she didn't know. Never rude or indifferent, she simply withdrew. She'd never been that way with him. At least, that's what he remembered.

She was sipping from a cold glass of something, but he knew instinctively it wasn't alcoholic. This party was a nice surprise, but he was hoping for a chance to say a proper hello, to have a conversation with her. Maybe she didn't care to renew or rehash their past relationship. Jean had been a private person back then, but not a loner; she had her own set of friends. But there had been one topic of gossip at the time—about her background, her family. He never knew what was true and what was made up by the rumor mill. He never cared. He'd had a chance to get to know Jean a little bit. Her truth had been enough for him.

"You lucky dog!"

Patrick winced as a hand clapped firmly onto his shoulder and a solidly built Black man stood in front of him, blocking his view of Jean, and pumped his hand vigorously.

"Hey, Pete. Good to see you, man."

"Is it too early to hit you up for a loan?" Pete laughed uproariously, his loud outburst drawing attention.

Patrick grinned good-naturedly at his friend. They'd known each other since their early farm days down in the minors. "I haven't cashed the check yet. Matter of fact, I haven't even gotten the check."

"I can wait," Pete responded, laughing again at his own audacity.

—

"Is there a reason why you're not circulating?"

Jean turned to a handsome Black man smiling down at her. He towered over not just her, but the two men she'd been speaking with. The new arrival held out a glass of wine. She hesitated but accepted it with a careful smile. The other two men drifted away.

"I'm really working. I was hoping to remain anonymous."

The man swiftly looked Jean up and down and took a sip from his own drink. "No chance of that."

"All of you here seem to be good friends with Patrick. It's nice that you're helping him celebrate his lottery win."

"He's a great guy. How often do you get to hang with a multimillionaire? Brian Abbott."

Jean took the offered hand. "Jean Travis."

"Are you also a friend?"

"I'm with the mayor's office. I handled the announcements of all the lottery winners today."

He nodded. "And you're here for the party? Still on duty or…" He let it trail off.

"Still on duty." Jean hesitated before revealing, "Patrick and I went to the same high school."

"Interesting," Brian murmured.

"Is it? It was pure chance that we met up this afternoon."

"You have history. Are you planning to catch up? Talk about old times?"

Jean chuckled nervously at his innuendo. She put the wineglass down on the table. "I had no idea I'd be invited tonight, or that I'd be expected to attend. I had no idea Patrick was a winner until I called out his name today. It was a big surprise…"

"I bet," Brian murmured. He took another swig of his drink, finishing it, and glanced around the room.

Jean followed his gaze. There was still a lot of drinking going on. Several die-hard women continued to eye Patrick silently, making their presence known, ever hopeful that perhaps he would still select one of them for after the after-party. Patrick finished his beer and put the empty bottle on a nearby table already crowded with discarded glasses. He took a just-opened bottle from a passing waiter.

"This could be a while," Brian said, turning back to her. "Can I interest you in a late dinner? We don't have to stay here."

Jean hid her stunned surprise, quickly formulating a response that wouldn't come across as an insult or a rejection.

"Who are you, exactly?" she questioned politely.

"I'm Patrick's producer at the station."

"Station?"

"Yeah. For his weekend sports wrap-up on ESPN. A local affiliate."

She shook her head. "I didn't know. I have no idea what Patrick's been up to since he graduated."

Brian held her gaze, grinning his interest. "Some guys have incredible luck. He wins a shitload of money, and you come back into his life."

"I don't think I understand what you mean."

Brian pursed his lips, considering her. "I think Patrick's been hanging out with the wrong crowd. He could do better. You are definitely a step up or, at least, in the right direction."

Jean still didn't get it, but it didn't matter. Seeing Patrick that afternoon was a fluke. The evening was out of the blue. Beginning and end of the story.

Someone called out Brian's name, and he turned to identify the caller. "I'll be back," he said. "You and I have more to talk about." He walked away with a confident grin.

"Jean?"

She did an about-face to find Patrick approaching her. His walk had a natural grace and ease, athleticism. He seemed in control. It wasn't so much predatory as sexy. And then her wayward thought was distracted. How many beers did he drink? Patrick stopped in front of her. Maybe a tad too close, but with surprising concern.

"Are you okay?"

"Why wouldn't I be?"

He blindly waved a hand. "They're all good people, some great friends. But if any of these guys...got out of hand..."

Jean shrugged. "They were being friendly. Nothing more."

He chortled quietly. "That's what you think. I shouldn't have left you for so long."

"I'm fine. I'm actually enjoying myself. Don't worry. I can take care of myself. I am still working. I think I made that clear a number of times."

"Well, that must have helped," he drawled, amused.

Unexpectedly, Jean found herself blushing under his regard. She'd never seen this side of Trick even in high school. Focused on her and concerned.

Patrick suddenly took her arm. He let his hand slide down until he could grab her hand. Automatically Jean wrapped her fingers around his to hold on. He started walking back to center court, where most of the guests were still clustered, gently pulling Jean with him. She went willingly.

"Stay with me. There are a few folks here I want you to meet."

Patrick introduced Jean to a handful of people. To a person, they were clearly curious about her, but friendly and inclusive. At some point, she felt less like she was working and more like she was part of the celebration. Jean could totally sense Patrick next to her, a little watchful. A little protective. She found it thoughtful and kind of sweet. But also bewildering.

While he was still as attentive as at the start of the party, Jean could see Patrick was becoming exhausted. But as long as anyone seemed interested in chatting, he stuck with it. The trio of giddy girls had given up and left, probably hoping to salvage the rest of the night somewhere else and with someone else.

Brian was in conversation off to the side but, ever hopeful, he held up a hand as if to signal *Give me a minute; I'll be right there.* Jean really hoped not. He was attractive and very masculine, but a little too slick for her tastes.

It was, incredibly, a little before 1:00 a.m. when Patrick hugged and shook hands with the final guests, and they left. The restaurant was closing for the night, the lights out in the front and tables already reset for the next day's business. Patrick and Jean were the very last to walk out the door, and then it was locked behind them.

He turned to her and shrugged his shoulders. "What can I say?"

Jean smiled slightly. "You were the guest of honor. You played the role very well. Glad it's over?"

"Yes, I am," he murmured, running his hands through his hair.

An old habit.

Jean watched him carefully. He wasn't drunk. He'd walked a pretty straight line to her before, but his eyes were bloodshot. His speech was careful and measured, although not slurred.

He suddenly stood still and stared at her, his brow creased. "Did Brian come on to you?"

Jean chuckled. "What happens if I say yes?"

"I'll have to have a few words with him. It could involve a meeting in the parking lot after work," he said dryly but seriously.

"Don't. I saw it coming and warded it off."

He slumped in relief. "Good. He's a terrific guy, but he has a two-track mind. Work and women. Not in that order."

She grinned, ignoring his comment and continuing to study him. "How much did you have to drink tonight?"

"Only beer. Anything else leaves marks." He grinned at his private joke. "Five. Six. I can make it home. I'm not drunk."

"No, I don't think you are either, but…"

"But what?"

"Well, it's been a long afternoon and evening. I'm not sure it's a good idea for you to get behind the wheel of a car."

"It was only seven beers."

"You said six."

"I've done it before."

"Not on my watch," Jean said with quiet firmness.

He raised his brows at her response. "Look, I appreciate the concern, but this isn't my first rodeo."

"Okay, but it's mine. I'm sort of responsible for you, Trick."

He leaned in to her. "Patrick."

"Sorry. Look, when my boss texted it was okay to accept your invitation and for me to be here, I understood that I was still working. I had a good time, but this was not a social evening for me."

"My party. My rules."

"I'll put you up for the night, and you can drive home in the morning."

He silently blinked at her, trying to judge her sincerity. She could see he was momentarily without a response but maybe was considering the offer.

"Jean, you don't have to do that. I'll be okay. Promise."

"If I'd never met you before, I'm not sure I would even make the offer. I'm not sure how I'd handle something like this if it were anyone else. We don't really know each other...but you're not a stranger."

For a few moments, they stared at each other, assessing the situation in a silent standoff. Jean had surprised herself with the spontaneous offer, but she wasn't uncomfortable having made it. Patrick's gaze was very intense. Finally, he let out a long breath.

"Okay. Okay, I accept. I can drive myself home, mind you. I think I'm relieved I won't have to."

"You're welcome," Jean said easily, turning to walk ahead of him. Honestly, she just wanted to get home.

Patrick's SUV was in a guest spot in the exclusive lot designated for use by the mayor's office. His was the only one left. Jean showed her ID to the night attendant, and Patrick clicked the door open. The headlights blinked and the car beeped twice. Then the engine started. It was a man's vehicle with all the bells and whistles. Jean stopped by the driver's side door and held out her hand to Patrick for the keys.

"Oh, no. No one drives my car," he said.

She waited, hand out.

"Jean…"

"Keys," she said firmly.

"This is ridic—"

She snapped her fingers, waiting.

"Fine." Resigned, he dropped the keys into her palm.

Getting in was a challenge for her, however, the shape of the slim skirt calling for her to hitch the fabric up her thigh to give her enough room to step up on the running board. A quick glance at Patrick indicated he was enjoying the display.

But once she drove out of the lot, he immediately relaxed, apparently comfortable that she could handle a vehicle a number of sizes bigger than she was.

Jean's high-rise was on a quiet, residential, tree-lined street just on the edge of Park Slope, less than a mile from Red Hook and the feed into the East River. They found a parking spot a block away from the building. Patrick seemed fascinated with the neighborhood as he looked around, finally commenting as they approached her building.

"Nice neighborhood. Seems a bit dark. There should be more streetlights. Especially when you're coming home this late. Do you have a doorman?"

"Yes, there is a doorman."

"Good," he said, satisfied.

"I'll take up your observations and complaints with the mayor's office," she said.

"No need to be sarcastic. Just thinking about your safety."

By the time they got into the elevator, Patrick had fallen thoughtfully silent again. She didn't try to fill the void. Neither one of them was up for conversation.

Jean unlocked the door and walked into the darkened space. Straight ahead, light from streetlamps shone through the living room windows. She hit a wall switch, brightening the entrance. Patrick blinked and walked into the center of the room, looking around. She watched his reaction.

"There's only one bedroom," she explained. She pointed to the love seat that was positioned to divide the length of the space into two, creating a living room and dining area. "The love seat opens out into a full bed. I've never slept on it, so I don't know how comfortable it is."

Patrick looked at Jean with a tired but satisfied expression. "I'm not going to complain."

Suddenly nervous and feeling awkward, Jean began showing him around, pointing out the bathroom and kitchen. She kept up the patter while pulling out fresh linens from a narrow hall closet, finding extra pillows. Together they pulled out and made up the convertible sofa, and Jean realized that Patrick was no longer listening. They finished, facing each other on either side of the love seat, opened between them with fresh sheets.

"Good night," Jean said, turning to her bedroom.

"Night," Patrick said behind her.

"You can sleep as late as you like in the morning. It's Saturday."

"I don't want to get in the way. You probably have plans."

Jean turned away, hand on the doorknob to the bedroom.

"Wait a minute," he called out behind her.

Jean turned back as Patrick shrugged out of the leather jacket and advanced toward her, arms spread. For an instant, she was caught off guard and was cautious. Patrick pulled her into an embrace that curved her against him, but then he did nothing more than hold her close for a long moment. Jean raised her arms to circle him as well.

Her sigh of pleasure was inaudible.

Then he stepped back, as did she, not meeting each other's gaze.

She heard "Thanks" as she closed the bedroom door.

Jean had had a crush on Trick Bennett in high school. She had been careful not to let him know. He was so out of her league, and they seemed to be polar opposites, which made tutoring him so much easier than it might have been otherwise. But seeing him again was like a jump through time and space. The changes in him were dramatic and very attractive. Jean found herself responding to them.

Now what?

CHAPTER 3

Jean lay awake, staring into the spinning blades of the ceiling fan over her bed. It was almost hypnotic. Every nook and cranny of her head seemed to be filled with images of Trick Bennett. Patrick. Several times the day before she'd called him by his high school handle. But he'd been clear that he didn't go by the name he'd used when he was a kid. He'd laid claim to his full name, and she respected that. And she liked that. She was probably the only person at his party who went back far enough to even recall the nickname from high school.

He was no longer the lanky youth with a lopsided smile and inquisitive gaze. He'd given up on the messy, too-long, dark hair that he'd habitually swept from his forehead with both hands…a signature move much copied by other boys but lacking his casual flair of spontaneity. His face had filled out, too, and was now heart-stoppingly masculine in its angles, jawline, and sharp, gray eyes. Jean remembered all of that early stuff. And even though she'd spent only three months, twice a week, secretly tutoring him for senior finals, she'd committed to memory every physical thing about Patrick Bennett she could make herself aware of. By virtue of their grade levels in school and the imposed school hierarchy that she had no say in, they were platonic friends by special arrangement and without benefits.

He'd sought her help through the recommendation of a teacher, and they had an association that they'd both managed to keep secret, for fear of the social consequences and unwarranted gossip.

Jean sighed and closed her eyes, but she couldn't go back to sleep. As was her normal inclination, she'd fallen into a deep sleep the minute her head hit the pillows. As was also her inclination, she came instantly awake a few hours later because something was on her mind. It was Patrick. If he'd never recognized her during the press announcements, she would have remained silent and never hinted that they were acquainted. But he had noticed and remembered her first and acted on it. Mouthing silent greetings, grabbing her hand and holding on, smiling at her with a light in his eyes that she had not seen, at least for her, in high school.

What was up with that?

Jean slowly sat up on the side of her bed, staring at the closed bedroom door. On the other side, Patrick was a guest on her pullout sleeper. Was he naked beneath the top sheet? She could hear nothing, but wondered if he snored. Or was Patrick a peaceful sleeper? Was he dreaming about her?

Jean went to the door and carefully opened it. She had a flash of second thoughts about what she was going to do and then tiptoed to the living room. She approached the back of the love seat and peered down onto the prone, sleeping Patrick. She could hear his rhythmic breathing, and see the rise and fall of his chest. He was long and lean. One leg was stretched out beyond the end of the mattress. The other bent at the knee, partially exposed. Even in the dark, she could detect the hair on his leg.

Jean walked slowly along the back of the sofa to the end. Her perspective of a sleeping Patrick changed with her position. At one end, she stopped again, afraid her movement had been detected as he made a subtle adjustment with his hips and upper thigh. She continued around the sofa to the front and stared through the dark at Patrick, unable to see his facial features, but that didn't matter. She knew exactly every facet of his face. She couldn't believe he was actually in her home, peacefully asleep. And here she stood, wide-awake with wild, erotic fantasies dancing in her head.

Jean was reliving the way he'd pulled her unexpectedly into his arms, just to hold her before they'd separated for the night. It stunned Jean that she wanted so much more. She desired to be pressed against him again and feel the hard width of his chest, the solid pressure of his arms, the columns of his legs. She wanted him to know how he made her feel. Jean stood and daydreamed, and Patrick slept.

She stood there only a moment. Patrick let out a deep exhalation and started to change his position, taking the top sheet with him. Jean wondered what she would do if he suddenly awakened and found her watching him. Would she hasten back to her room, embarrassed? What if he made a move for her, inviting her to join him on the bed? What if she accepted?

Her intense thoughts and wishes began to wear Jean out, until she wanted to return to her bed, go back to sleep. Just as quietly as she'd come in, she crept back to her bedroom, again putting the closed door between them.

———

Patrick winced at the stab of light through his eyelids that pulled him from sleep. He was awake. It was almost 11:00 a.m. He was alone in a strange apartment. Jean's place in Brooklyn. He stretched with abandon, yawning wide from a deep and restful sleep. He felt very relaxed. But he was not one to languish in bed. Patrick was very much the get-up-and-hit-the-ground-running type. His twenty-four-hour days were actually twenty-five.

He got up, glancing toward the still-closed bedroom door. Curiosity guided him around Jean's living/dining room combo space. The unit was neat, comfortably furnished, and bright. She favored framed posters on the walls, meaningful printed slogans, and lots of photographs. Patrick scanned every one, trying to guess at the connections between the diverse group of men, women, and children that made up family and friends.

He looked to identify Jean in images that showed her as a very young child with, presumably, her parents. A handsome, boyish white man and a petite African American woman with one of the brightest smiles he'd ever seen. It was open, drawing you in. If these were Jean's parents, they were an incredibly good-looking couple. And now Patrick absolutely understood what the supposed controversy had been about Jean circulating through school. He couldn't understand any significance to her being biracial.

Then there was a series with Jean as she grew older, photographed with one or the other of her parents. Photos of her in her cap and gown, from her high school graduation. And then from college. But no pictures from a high school prom. Finally, there were more recent pictures showing how she'd evolved into the very attractive woman he'd encountered the day before. A scattering of framed pictures he presumed to be cousins, aunts, and uncles from both sides of her family, judging from the ethnicity and hair, skin, and eye colors. He smiled to himself with a kind of *Wow* response to the display.

Jean Travis was very twenty-first century. He did not have that distinction.

Jean Travis had most definitely come of age.

Jean quietly opened her door so as not to disturb the sleeping Patrick. Except he wasn't asleep. The bed had been folded up, the linens folded neatly. There was not a sound anywhere.

"Patrick?"

Immediately there was movement from the kitchen. "In here."

She walked toward the kitchen, and Patrick appeared in the doorway, somehow looking much taller than he had the day before. He was barefoot. He was dressed in his slacks…and nothing else. Jean's gaze shifted to stare at the silky covering of dark hair on his chest.

"Sorry," he muttered, rushing around her to the living room. He returned moments later with his pullover Henley shirt on.

"You're already dressed," he observed.

She'd pulled on slim, jean-like leggings and a boxy, tangerine-colored top that complemented her complexion. She was also barefoot. She'd done something to her hair to make it look fuller, gathering it up in the back so it was bushy and curly.

"I tend to strut around in jammies or very little when I'm home."

"I could have handled jammies," he said.

She smiled broadly at his humor. "How did you sleep?"

"Like it was going out of style. The pullout was more comfortable than I thought it would be. But…"

Her stomach roiled. Had Patrick heard her, seen her staring at him in the dark?

"I know. Not long enough for your legs."

"I wasn't complaining, Jean. And you?"

"Me? I always seem to sleep well."

"Ah…the sleep of the innocent."

Now she did laugh. "I don't know about that."

There was a moment of awkward silence.

"Thanks again for putting me up last night. It was really an awesome gesture."

"I'm glad I thought of it. Were you rummaging around my fridge?" she asked, joining him in the kitchen.

"Actually, trying to figure out how your coffee maker works. Mine, you just add water and coffee and plug it in. Yours has a digital timer, a light that blinks, a buzzer… I'm a simple guy. Your machine defeated me."

"I'll do it. You'll want to get started for home…"

"I'm not in a hurry."

"I could make a little breakfast."

"You say that like you don't usually eat breakfast."

"Something light."

Patrick grunted and made a face. "That sounds like berries and oatmeal. Or yogurt with granola."

Jean laughed.

"Don't you know breakfast is the most important meal of the day?"

"Well, what would you like?"

"Do you have eggs? Cheese? Tomatoes? Bread? Butter?"

"Yes to all but tomatoes."

"Then we're having cheese toast with an egg over easy. Where's your skillet?"

"Under the cabinet to your right."

"Do you mind? Since obviously you don't cook."

"I do, but…"

"Not breakfast."

"Let me get the coffee started, and I'll get out of the way."

"There's plenty of room. I like it. It's cozy," Patrick observed.

Jean imagined that there were probably plenty of women more than willing to cook and feed him. And if the women of last night's party were any clue, they were all like heat-seeking missiles. They knew where to find him.

But the strangeness of their situation did not completely wear off just because they were seated opposite each other for breakfast. Jean covertly watched Patrick before speaking up about something that had been on her mind since the party the night before.

"I noticed that you haven't said anything about your lottery winnings. Do you have a short list of what you're going to do with the money? Are you happy about it? Are you in shock that you even won?"

"Tell you what," Patrick began after a moment of considering her questions. "When I actually get the check and can cash it, then I'll start seriously thinking about what I'm going to do with seventy-five million dollars. Right now…I'm not sure it really happened."

"It's real, Patrick," Jean murmured.

Patrick put down his fork and leaned toward her across the table. "Jean, right now I can only say I'm not ready to talk about it," he said quietly as he shook his head. "I don't know what I'm going to do. Let's do a rain check on this discussion, okay?"

She raised her gaze to his. She was surprised to detect a worry frown between his gray eyes.

"Fair enough," Jean said. "To be continued."

But she was curious about how uncomfortable Patrick appeared. Jean wondered what could be causing his reticence. Why would he have purchased a lottery ticket if he wasn't going to be happy about actually winning? The most important aspect of Patrick's win, hands down, was that it miraculously brought them together again, here in her home.

Jean sighed quietly. This had been a fortuitous interlude, and they would separate with warm memories of their mini reunion. She used to daydream about Trick asking her out. She used to imagine him kissing her like he really cared. Maybe she would have gone all the way, if he'd asked. He never did get fresh or bold. She'd imagined dozens of iterations of the possibilities in full Technicolor detail after he'd graduated and there was no chance of them seeing each other again. For several years, she'd built a very rich fantasy life around him. Over time, it faded...and she grew up. Now she could say she'd finally gotten to sleep with Trick Bennett.

Sort of.

The night also fell into the categories of the most natural thing in the world and a dream come true.

Sort of.

Jean loved being with Patrick in the Saturday-morning messiness of him unshaven, hair tousled, in bare feet, seemingly at home in her home.

They finished breakfast, and Patrick piled up their used dishes and went right to the sink to wash them.

"You don't have to do that," Jean said, removing condiments and flatware from the table.

"My parents didn't raise any slackers. They both worked. My sister and I had chores."

"I have a dishwasher."

He finished and dried his hands on a dish towel, turning to face her, amused. "I don't mind getting my hands wet."

The comment was simple enough, but Jean felt heat rushing to her face. Patrick was standing right in front of her. Her sight line was only a little higher than the opening of his Henley and his bare chest. She couldn't pull her gaze away and hoped he didn't notice.

Suddenly he asked bluntly, "Did we kiss last night?"

"No. No, we didn't," she said on a breath. She turned away from him.

"Did I try to kiss you?"

Jean faced him again, keeping her expression flat. "Don't you remember?"

A very slow, decidedly wicked grin lifted a corner of his mouth. "Good response," he drawled. He headed into the living room to finish dressing and gather his things. "I better get going. Don't want to overstay my welcome. You might not ask me back."

The idea of *asking* was intriguing.

"What are your plans for the day?" He collected his jacket and wallet as they prepared to leave her apartment together.

"My cupboards are bare. I have to do some marketing. Run a few errands. Come back and do laundry…"

"Bor-ing," Patrick singsonged.

"You probably have a housekeeper. I don't." She grinned with meaning.

He nodded. "I concede."

Jean opened the front door. Patrick pushed it closed again.

"Wait a minute," he said, putting a hand on her waist. He gently pulled her forward. Jean didn't resist, curious. "I don't want to make the same mistake I did…we did…last night."

Patrick encircled Jean in a light embrace, sliding his hands around her back but not pulling her too close, their torsos barely touching. Then he kissed her, getting as close as was needed to seal the deal. The kiss was a warm and tender melding of their lips. Their tongues briefly, gently dueled. He took his time and Jean let him, loving the thoughtfulness of Patrick's kiss as he explored.

They slowly withdrew, regarding one another with the sweet caress of their gazes.

"I hope it's not going to be another fifteen, twenty years until the next time," Patrick murmured.

"I think something can be arranged."

"I'll call you?"

"Yes."

His hands grew restless on her waist, like he wanted to do more. Patrick looked earnestly into her eyes.

"I'm really glad it was you yesterday."

Me too, Jean thought.

CHAPTER 4

Patrick laughed at the joke made by the man sitting next to him. But he was distracted.

It was Monday evening, and he'd hoped to hear back from Jean by now and was concerned that she hadn't returned any of his attempts to reach her since the weekend. Patrick wasn't yet sure why it had become urgent. Maybe because the overnight at her place had been so comfortable, so easy, he wanted very much to keep the good vibes alive. What did it mean that there was radio silence? Had he been mistaken that there had been a new connection between him and Jean? It had been less than forty-eight hours since they'd been together. To Patrick it seemed longer.

He forced his attention back to the group around him, seated in a corner of their usual noisy Midtown haunt, where they came together every couple of months to shoot the bull, rag on one another, eat wings and drink beer, and have a great guys' night out. Everyone except Patrick and Brian would soon be headed for home by car or commuter train. They were former colleagues and homeboys from the days of being in the game when they all expected fame and glory. Most of the five men had not reached their goal of going pro, had not even come close. They were now living middle-class lives, with aging, soft bodies. Most had moved on to other careers, had wives and kids and suburban homes. But they'd all remained in touch for the sole purpose of remembering the good old days, and now congratulating Patrick, one of them who'd made it big in another way. He was grateful that no one harped on that, and treated him as they always had. Just one of the team.

"I'm not sure I'd want that kind of win," Brian said at one point, shaking his head as if he'd given the prospect a lot of thought.

"Bullshit," one of the men growled, and the others burst into knowing laughter.

"Not kidding," Brian said. "I know for a fact that our boy here has had some serious weirdness thrown at him. And it's only been about a week since the announcement."

"Like what?"

Brian looked at Patrick, who didn't want to repeat some of the things that Brian was alluding to. He gave a dismissive wave of his hand, and Brian leaned forward to recount one of the more amusing and touching stories about a youngster who'd reached out to ask if Patrick would adopt him.

Patrick pulled out his cell and checked for text messages, voicemail… anything that might have come through from Jean.

"Mr. Bennett? Sorry to bother you. There's someone at the front who wants to talk to you. I told her you were with a private party, but she was insistent."

Patrick stood up. "Who is it?"

"Sorry, she didn't give her name."

She.

"She said you'd know."

Patrick turned to his friends. "Guys, excuse me for a moment. I'll be right back."

There was no chance that Jean would know where he'd be today, and he was forced to abandon the thought. There were a few other possibilities, Patrick considered, but they were all professional contacts or acquaintances, and no need for all this mystery. When they reached the maître d's desk, Patrick was pointed to a small area next to the entrance where people waited to be seated. There was a tall blond pacing tensely, stylishly dressed in tapered black slacks, a blouse that artfully exposed one shoulder, and open-toed, high-heel booties. Her expensively dyed hair was a calculated tangle of long, softly curled locks that fell around her shoulders, obscured her forehead and her eye, requiring her to either shake her hair aside or carelessly brush it away, the better to focus bright blue eyes on her audience. It always worked for getting attention, and it worked now.

Patrick slowed his walk once he identified the unexpected visitor. He quickly glanced around to make sure they were alone. When he turned to her again, his gaze was steely. Hers was a combination of haughty bravado and rage.

"What are you doing here, Natalie?"

"It's that whole Mohammed-comes-to-the-mountain thing. Obviously you have no intention of calling me, so I tracked you down."

"I think that's called stalking."

His response infuriated her, and she glared, her mouth pinching for restraint. "How dare you suggest that!"

Patrick took a step closer so they wouldn't start to shout at each other. His teeth were clenched. "I dare because you don't seem to get it. We're done, Natalie. What is there about 'We need to move on and go our separate ways' that you don't understand? I didn't want to hurt you when we broke up. I simply wanted out. And it's not like you were lacking for suitors. The way I see it, you worked pretty damn hard to try to make me jealous."

"I didn't! It's not my fault that men—"

Patrick cut her off. "Right. I don't call your flirting an attempt to push back and get even. But that's okay. I'll take the fall for ending the relationship. I realized we weren't a good match. We didn't want the same thing. Frankly, I was surprised when you still left voice messages and showed up at events I was attending."

"I thought we were great together, Patrick. Everyone said so. Being together was great for my business, and it certainly didn't hurt you."

He groaned softly and briefly closed his eyes. "This is about the card and the ticket, isn't it?"

"You didn't even tell me you'd won. It wouldn't have happened, Patrick, if *I* hadn't sent you the lottery ticket!"

Natalie's voice had raised several decibels as she let her anger gain control. Guests entering or leaving the restaurant hesitated to eavesdrop on the exchange. The maître d' discreetly ignored them, distracting customers with a cheerful greeting.

"I called you more than a year ago and told you it wasn't a good idea to keep calling me and sending me cute greeting cards. What do I have to do to make you stop? I don't want to embarrass you. I just want you to stop."

Now Natalie took a step closer. She blinked at him, making him look into her eyes, her face. She didn't have a soft, comfortable beauty. Natalie was bold, strong, and used to getting her way. The fact that Patrick had been the one to walk away had been an infuriating affront.

"You want me to stop bothering you? Fine. I can make that happen. I sent you the lottery ticket. You won. The way I see it, you owe me. You would not be seventy-five million dollars to the good if it wasn't for me!"

"I didn't want you to send me a card, or a lottery ticket, or anything. I don't owe you anything. But here's the deal. I turned your card *and* a copy of the ticket over to my attorney. He warned me I might hear from you."

"Good."

"You'll hear from him, and he'll deal with this. I'm really disappointed that it all now comes down to money. Are we finished?" Patrick asked, controlling his anger.

Her smile was both coquettish and menacing. "We'll see."

Jean was headed out of her office, carrying a tablet, her smartphone, and the cell issued by the department when her desk phone rang. She turned back to stare at the instrument, puzzled. Very few of her contacts ever called the landline, and even fewer were given the number. But it was maintained because so many of the city's constituents still were not tech savvy or had access to digital devices when they needed help from the city. She returned to her desk, briefly noticing the time on the wall clock as she answered the call.

"Jean Travis," she said.

"Hi. Can you talk?"

"Not really, Mom. I have a meeting and—"

"Okay, I'll be quick. I wanted to thank you for sending me that picture."

Jean slid into her desk chair. "What picture?"

"It's from your office, Jean. The one of the lottery winners, about a week or so ago."

"Lottery… Oh. Did I send that to you?"

"Well, not you personally, but it's from your office. I'm on your public PR email list."

"Okay…"

"The one with you and that boy. When you were in high school."

"Patrick Bennett?" Jean murmured. "You remember him?"

"I don't think you called him Patrick at the time. He had some weird teenage name…"

"Yeah. Trick."

"He was the one you tutored, right? Grown man now. Did he really win thirty-five million dollars?"

Jean shifted in her seat, began to stand again and gather her things. "Seventy-five million dollars. Mom, I really have to go. I have a meeting…"

"Okay, okay. I wanted to make sure I had it right. Seeing you two together in that image… Well, it's interesting how you both turned out.

Now he's a millionaire!" She chuckled. "If I had any idea when he asked me if he could take you to his prom how he was going to turn out…"

"His prom? Patrick? Patrick asked you if he…"

"Could take you to the prom, yes. I told him no, I couldn't agree to that. You were barely sixteen."

Her mother went on, but Jean had zoned out, trying to process news that she was hearing for the very first time. Patrick had actually asked her mother if he could take her to *his* senior prom?

And she'd said no?

"Jean, did you hear what I said?"

"I… No…no," she muttered, lost in a memory time warp.

Behind Jean, someone hissed for her attention. She glanced over her shoulder and found a colleague pointing to a page with *Agenda* printed across the top. For a meeting. She was late. She stood up.

"I have to go. Call me tonight…"

Jean hung up on the one person in life she could do that to and not be disowned. She hurried after her coworker to the meeting called by Brad.

It was just as well that she had little to no need to participate since the subject of the meeting had nothing to do with Jean or her sector of the department. Which was also just as well, as she barely listened to what was being said, trying to wrap her head around what her mother had, probably innocently, revealed. She couldn't believe it.

It was way too late to be angry that her mother had flat-out said no to Patrick's invitation without telling her about it. But why hadn't *he* asked *her?* Would she have accepted?

Jean was, to put it mildly, distracted for the rest of the afternoon. There was local press to coordinate with on the best way to publicize a community protest about the possible closing of a branch post office. There was the high school sophomore who was being recognized for placing first among the top five in the regional science fair. There were a half-dozen organizations that were requesting that the mayor provide and sign proclamations declaring…whatever.

Through all of the professional and work chatter, Jean continued trying to parse information from her history with Patrick. The very last time they'd seen each other while in school was when he'd waited before classes one morning to let her know he'd passed the state exams. And to thank her. He was pleased, of course. She'd felt oddly empty. No more Tuesday and Thursday clandestine after-school meetings between the two of them as she coached Patrick through the high points of a semester's worth of schoolwork. She'd figured out early on that he very likely would have passed the tests without her help, but she never let on. Jean liked that she might have been responsible for his successful senior year and graduating. They had been connected in a way that other students in their school had not been. It made her feel special.

She got through work, managing to assign her mother's revelation to a corner of her brain labeled *Review*, and made her way uptown to a reception. Early evening get-togethers were the mainstay of New Yorkers connected through work or personal interests. Tonight it was a music thing in Harlem, a gathering at a branch library. It was in recognition of a major archive donation from the estate of an artist who'd lived under the radar of fame and fortune, but whose work was now being lauded. The event was already filled with guests and loud conversation when she arrived. There were many small clusters of people chatting over wine, all well known to each other, and many to her.

Jean accepted a glass of wine from a waiter standing near the entrance. She tried not to let her eyes roam the crowded room, an obvious sign that there might be someone present she was hoping to avoid. It was a very diverse gathering. In navigating her way through, Jean exchanged brief words with everyone she knew. Still, her goal was to make a slow circuit of the room until she reached the entrance again and could quietly leave.

She heard a female voice call her name and tap her shoulder.

"Jean! I didn't know you were going to be here. How've you been? How come you don't call me?"

Jean turned to the woman, shorter than her...and wider. A pair of oversize, black-framed glasses drew attention to an attractive, slightly above middle-aged Black woman. She was adorned in an original, one-of-a-kind, kimono-style silk cover, over a black draped-neck top of polka dots and black harem pants. It was an outfit calculated so that the wearer was sure to stand out and be noticed. Jean gave and received an affectionate air kiss as their cheeks touched, and stood back to admire her former mentor's attire.

"Belle, you look fabulous. I love those pants."

"Thanks, sweetie. Off the rack in a Middle Eastern shop on Atlantic Avenue."

Annabelle Hampton had been a manager at the Department of Cultural Affairs for the city and was now the interim acting director, hoping for permanency. When Jean had first met Belle, she was known as the unofficial den mother for many young African American women just out of college trying to build careers. She'd been particularly kind to Jean when she ran into roadblocks in the Black cultural heartbeat of the city. Jean had not grown up in an all-Black community or gone to a Black college. Her biracial background was still an oddity at that time, and her authenticity as a Black person had been suspect growing up and into young adulthood. It had taken time to demonstrate that she wasn't playing at being Black. Her mother had warned her. It had taken Belle Hampton and being out in the world and away from home to help Jean recognize that being who she was was enough, no other justification necessary.

"It's good to see you. I wasn't sure I was going to make it tonight," Jean said, keeping her focus on the woman for whom she'd once interned as an undergraduate. "I've been crazed, as usual."

Belle chortled. "Oh, please. Like, who isn't? That's what happens when you put yourself in the fast lane to becoming a Mistress of the Universe."

"Not interested in the title."

"Maybe, but people know who you are. You get things done, and that matters. And you've been smart about not making enemies. Huge props for that. Not easy when you're backing up the mayor."

Jean grinned. "No enemies that I know of." She glanced around, still trying not to focus on any one person. "Nice turnout."

"It's the usual. Everyone's here to say they were here. Suzanne is around; you know her. And I know I saw Mel and Bunny..." Belle leaned in closer to her. "And you-know-who is here. Alone."

Jean was proud of the fact that neither her stomach nor throat tightened with the sudden impact of that announcement. But in that moment, she knew that her response to Belle's alluding to someone from the past did not compare to the newer, pleasurable reactions she'd experienced surrounding Patrick Bennett's reappearance. She exhaled slowly in relief, her expression passive as Belle searched her features for reaction.

"I'm not surprised. Ross knows everyone. He's smart, charming, knows how to work a room."

"A damned fool," Belle said with a smile that suggested a touch of empathy.

Jean shrugged, as if to shake off the aura of the man in question. "I'm not losing sleep, Belle."

Belle grimaced at her. "You better not be wasting your time doing that."

Jean spoke softly, trying to move the conversation to a safer subject. But she was aware that Belle's focus had shifted somewhere over her shoulder, and her smile became fixed and cool.

"Hey, Ross," Belle drawled, this time overly bright.

Jean appreciated Belle's warning. She could feel the male presence behind her. She turned to gaze with nothing more than curiosity at the tall, handsome Black man whose gaze focused just on her. His features were fine but also masculine. A killer smile that he now brought into play for her. With his bearing and confidence, he could easily have been mistaken for a former officer in the military or member of the Secret Service. Ross Franklin got attention and held it. Jean met his gaze without blinking, without returning the smile. She'd long ago gotten over the discomfort that arose when there was an unexpected encounter between her and Ross, her former fiancé. Fortunately, there had only been a few.

"Nice to see you, Jean."

"Hello, Ross," Jean responded smoothly.

Uncharacteristically, Belle remained silent, adding nothing to ease the slight tension between her and Ross, but she was watchful.

Ross broke his gaze and scanned quickly around. "It's nice that the artist is finally getting his due. Sorry he didn't live long enough to enjoy the attention and rewards."

Jean said nothing.

"I'm glad I was smart enough to buy his work years ago. Didn't know much about art then."

"Early investment?" Jean asked.

Ross's brows shot up, and a muscle tightened in his jaw. He shook his head. "I happen to admire the work."

"So then, you aren't looking to sell now that the market value of his work is going up, even as we speak?"

Belle also raised her brows at Jean's sudden tartness under all her calm and pleasant demeanor.

"Well, if you'll excuse me, I see the library director, and I want to congratulate her on the new acquisition for the archives. Good to see you both." Belle beamed and disappeared.

Left alone, silence rose between Jean and Ross for an awkward few moments. She conceded first, taking a deep breath.

"Sorry. That was…very unlike me."

Ross nodded, gently swirling the wine in his glass. "We're not there yet," he said.

"There?"

"Where we can behave like we're over it."

"You mean like *I'm* over it. I am, Ross, but I guess I couldn't help taking the dig."

"It struck home, and I know I deserve it. I'm still hoping we'll arrive at a point where our past relationship is not the elephant in the room."

"Where we'll kiss and make up?"

"Maybe not the kissing part," he said dryly.

"Definitely not that. I have moved on, despite what I said to you. But it did feel good," Jean boldly admitted.

He nodded, accepting the punishment. "It could have been worse."

"I'm not looking for revenge. I believe what happened was your loss."

"You could be right. We'll see."

There was no mistaking the regret in his tone, and Jean found that very satisfying. But it wasn't going to change her mind.

"I should congratulate you."

"For what?"

"I heard you got a promotion at your firm. You're now a vice president or something like that."

"Close, but not yet. I'm doing well. Very well, thanks. You know your dad stuck with me."

"Yes, he told me after you and I broke up. It was a smart move, and I don't blame him. I wouldn't say he had no loyalty to me and what I went through, but his attitude was 'If it ain't broke don't fix it.' You made a lot of money for him. My mom? Not so much. She wanted to stab you in the throat for what you did. She especially wasn't happy that a Black man did what you did to her baby girl. Know what I'm saying?"

Ross chuckled. "Totally. Your mom was all over me. If she ever changes her mind…"

"She might, once she can forgive you. Like I did."

Ross's look was one of admiration. "I appreciate that. Thanks."

Jean looked around for a place to set her glass. Ross carefully took it from her. "I'll take care of it."

"Thanks. I'm going home." Jean turned again, making her way slowly through the crowd. She didn't say good night.

"I'm glad I got to see you," Ross said as she walked away.

But Jean kept walking, not acknowledging that she'd heard. Forgiveness was one thing. Forgetting was going to take a bit longer.

———

Jean made it a hard-and-fast rule not to leave her cell phone on the nightstand next to her bed when she retired at night. She broke her own rule if her mother was traveling out of state for a conference, or if the mayor's office had some big event in the works and Brad needed her to be on call. Her father's calls were completely unpredictable, and she caught them when she could. So when she heard the ringtone coming from her living room, Jean had to rush to grab the device before the call went to voicemail.

"Hello?"

"You sound out of breath."

It was Patrick.

"Hey…"

"Did I wake you?"

"No."

"I didn't think so. I should have warned you I don't always stand on ceremony or abide by the rules. I can be pretty spontaneous."

"I assume you're busy. Traveling, still celebrating…recovering." She heard him laugh quietly.

"Yeah…I've been busy. You won't believe the crazy stuff that… Well…I won't go into that now."

"It's nice to hear from you. And thanks for the lovely flowers. They were at the front desk when I got home on Monday. How's everything going?"

"I want to see you again."

It was a simple declaration that immediately infused her with a warm, quiet surprise.

"I'd like that," Jean said honestly.

"My life has gotten complicated these days, more so since the lottery announcement."

"I bet."

"I thought I could persuade you to come to me."

She hesitated, unsure of the implication.

"I don't suppose you've ever watched *REPLAY* on the weekend?"

"No, I haven't. I know you're part of it, but…"

"It's a sports update program. The other co-hosts and myself review… and *replay*…highlights of games from the previous week. We recognize outstanding plays or rip into terrible moves and unfair ref calls. We joke around a bit, talk about players, make predictions…joke around a bit."

"I get the idea. To be honest I had no idea what you do for a living. So I Googled you."

He chuckled. "Fair enough."

"What you've done since high school is pretty impressive."

"What did you find out?" Patrick asked.

Did she hear a little concern in the question? Jean mentally organized what she'd learned by browsing the internet and kept her response brief. She didn't want to come across as a newly minted groupie. Or someone looking for dirt on him.

"After college you were recruited to the minors for one of the league's farm teams."

"I came to the game late. I played on a team in college. It was meant to be for a semester but I turned out to be pretty good."

"The bio said that was unusual for someone who didn't come up through Little League or was sponsored by a club."

"You say that like a pro," he teased.

"Not. I had to look up what all that meant. I read that you made it to the majors and played for several years…until an off-season accident ended it all. I'm so sorry."

"Don't be. I was a twentysomething bonehead who took a lot for granted. I was careless and *boom!* It was all gone."

"You seem to have come through really well. Now you're in broadcasting."

She heard him sigh, grunt. Jean was starting to suspect that Patrick was not comfortable talking about himself. Was it really modesty? Or secrets?

"You do know you can't hide on the internet, right? Wikipedia is notorious for putting your business out there. I hope that doesn't sound like I was prying."

Patrick didn't respond right away. Jean waited him out.

"What else did you find out?"

"That you were married. That you're divorced."

"Now you know everything."

"I'm sure not everything. It's life. It happens."

"Yeah. But I can promise I've never been to jail. I don't do drugs. I'm good to my family…"

"And I think it's fair to say you're a good person."

"My ex might not agree."

"Maybe not. I don't think divorces are pleasant no matter the reason. Marriage takes work like everything else."

"We tried to reconcile at the eleventh hour. Just before the legal separation was due to run out."

"A last-minute attempt to save it?"

Patrick chuckled without humor. "It was more like a lost weekend. A very brief moment in time when we both looked good to each other again. The attraction exploded. Big mistake. We were right the first time when we decided to end it all. We haven't been in touch since."

"I'm sure it was tough. But you seem to be doing well."

"I appreciate the vote of confidence. I've been lucky. And I know I shouldn't complain."

He went quiet again.

"But?"

"It's nothing."

He sighed heavily in her ear, although Jean wasn't sure he was aware. "I didn't call to rehash my past history or failed marriage. Can I persuade you to come out to the studio to watch a taping? I can give you a tour of the station. We have an amazing collection of signed footballs and baseball jerseys. Not to be missed."

Jean laughed. "Wow. I'm speechless."

"Maybe not the collection. It's real but dusty. And all the original owners are dead and…"

She kept laughing.

"Two shows are taped and then aired later. We do a live broadcast on the weekend. I don't know how much you know about sports…"

"Almost nothing, but I like watching tennis."

"Good enough. Will you come?"

"I'd love to," Jean responded, her heart rate slightly elevated. "When?"

The rest of the call was spent comparing calendar dates and schedules, finding one that worked for both of them.

"I'll make all the arrangements. I'll have a car come pick you up."

"I can do that, Patrick. The mayor's office has official vehicles. I know I can sign one out."

"This isn't that kind of invitation, Jean. It isn't about publicity or your job in the mayor's office. This is about you and me getting together again. I'm glad I have a chance at a relationship with you beyond high school."

A relationship.

"Thank you," Jean murmured, catching her breath and surprised by her reaction.

"The taping is impersonal and, frankly, not all that interesting. You might even zone out as soon as we start talking. There's a lot of stat slang and dude-like terminology. Consider this a half date. For now, okay?"

A half date.

"Sure. I'd love to see what you do."

CHAPTER 5

Jean paid no attention to the scenery, such as it was, after the luxury midsize SUV sped through the Lincoln Tunnel and made its way south on the Jersey Turnpike. She was still processing the local morning news account that a woman had gone public with her story of having been cheated by Patrick Bennett of part of his lottery win.

Jean had been catching up on city news on her tablet when the text messages and calls started coming in from her office, from her mom. Just the headline was enough to make her stomach churn, a sudden heat rushing over her as she wondered if the story was true. There were not enough details to come to any conclusion on her own, and she wasn't going to try. But she hated to think Patrick might have done something so questionable.

The ride from city hall was under an hour. As the Porsche Cayenne was turning into a gate with a single-storied nondescript building in the background, Jean noticed half a dozen vehicles outside, with a handful of men and women milling about. Two vans with call letters printed on the side doors identified them as being from a local network and had transmission towers mounted on top. Media outlets had obviously gotten wind of the story and were circling, hoping for a glimpse of Patrick...or anyone from the station willing to make a statement. Jean was used to reporters aggressively chasing after a hot tip and staking out city hall for comments from the mayor, but somehow it felt very personal that the people here were in pursuit of someone she knew. She was still mulling over the morning report and hoping there was more to the story.

Jean didn't believe for a second that Patrick was the villain he was being portrayed as.

She hoped not.

———

Having been summoned by security that the Cayenne SUV had been cleared and was at the entrance, Patrick reached the building doors as Jean was climbing out of the back seat, aided by the driver. Patrick watched her thank the driver with a brief exchange of words and a smile. Then she turned to him.

He knew right away Jean was a little nervous. But there was something else. Maybe to another person, her wide-eyed inquiry might appear a little aloof, doubtful, cautious. Patrick's guess was that she was trying to decide whether to be the professional Jean or the one who knew him back in the day and who had hosted him one night at her apartment. Patrick hoped it was the latter but erred on the side of caution.

"Jean, hey. Really glad you could make it."

Patrick took her hand, squeezing briefly as he looked into her eyes. Understanding the subtle signal, Jean seemed to relax and tentatively smiled.

"Thanks for inviting me. I love field trips out of the office."

He grinned. "How was the ride out?"

"Luxurious. Smooth and comfortable. The car smelled like it was brand-new."

"It is. I picked it up a few days ago."

"It's your personal car?"

He chortled. "ESPN might have a fleet of Toyotas or Nissans for company cars...not Porsche. It finally sunk in that I have a *lot* of disposable income. The Porsche Cayenne is the first thing I've bought myself since the win. I can tell you it felt weird not having to finance."

They'd been walking along a lengthy corridor with small offices on either side. They finally turned a corner, and Patrick opened the door of one that was bigger and better appointed with a desk, two chairs, and a small love seat sofa. There were lots of promo merchandise and sports paraphernalia on nearly every surface. Framed photos on the walls of him with star athletes. He positioned a chair for Jean. She sat, looking around.

"And you hired a driver?"

"He's not my driver. He works behind one of the cameras. When I asked how he felt about taking my car into the city to get you, he jumped all over it. I warned him that if anything happened to you or my car he was roadkill."

Jean smiled warmly at him.

Patrick sat behind his desk and gazed at Jean. It fully registered that they had not seen each other since the night of the lottery announcement and the party afterward. Or, more accurately, the next morning after Patrick slept over at her place. He thought about that a lot. He thought about kissing her before leaving. For now, he was trying to read what Jean was thinking. He couldn't quite get a handle on it, and it bothered him. Was she glad to see him?

"You know, you blush."

Her hands went right to her cheeks. "Do I?"

Patrick nodded. "It shows through the tan of your skin. Beautiful," he murmured.

He knew he'd gone too far. Jean averted her gaze and shifted in her chair.

"Is this…the inner sanctum, your man-cave?"

Patrick settled into his high-back chair. "We got the memo. This is an equal opportunity workplace. We have our share of jockettes as well…or is that sexist?"

"No comment." Jean arched a brow.

"Like man-cave?"

She nodded. "Touché."

There was a quiet buzzing sound, and Patrick dug out his smartphone. He looked at the screen and answered, his expression inadvertently signaling the call, and caller, were inopportune.

"Hey…yeah, everything's good…thanks. Look, I meant to get back in touch…" Patrick chuckled, trying to avoid meeting Jean's gaze. He knew she was trying not to listen, but was impossible to avoid in a thirteen-by-sixteen-foot space. He began nervously swiveling back and forth in his chair. He stopped and leaned forward over the desk. "Can I get back to you? I have a taping in a few minutes… Yeah, that will work. Bye."

Patrick put the smartphone aside, as if something about it had offended him. And he sensed a bit of withdrawal in Jean. She clearly knew the nature of the call. He was about to launch into an apology.

There was a rap on the door. It opened and a tall Black man appeared, filling the frame.

"Hey! You made it."

Patrick sat back and silently waited as the man joined them, giving his attention to Jean.

"Remember me? Brian Abbott, from the party."

"Yes, hello again."

Brian placed a broad hand over his chest, his gaze feigned sadness. "You know, you broke my heart. You left before we could finish our conversation that night."

"You mean you left before you could finish the conversation," Jean said. "I was still on the job. And I was one of the last to leave."

"I didn't think I'd drunk that much. My bad." Brian sent a sly glance to Patrick but continued to address Jean. "Are you still working, or is this a playdate?"

"I invited Jean out to watch a taping," Patrick said, looking at the time. "And I need to get ready. We're on in fifteen."

"Right. I'll take Jean to the set, get her a prime seat where she can see everything. Lynn is waiting for you in makeup."

Patrick exchanged a look of regret with Jean at both interruptions. His silent expression to Brian said more as the producer led Jean away. Like… *Don't even go there.*

The darkened space of the set hid the smile of wonder fixed to Jean's lips. Watching Patrick interact with his fellow commentators, playing to the cameras, was so strange. He was *on*, a persona she was unfamiliar with. Somehow his broadcast presence seemed out of character, but also so natural. The other co-hosts were also bright, good-looking former jocks who each brought their own perspectives and personalities to the program. But the only person Jean was interested in was Patrick.

She couldn't take her eyes off him. Every now and then, she imagined he focused his attention in her direction but was pretty sure that he couldn't see much of anything beyond the bright set lights. His attempt to silently communicate as she tried to process the call he'd received just before Brian arrived was still with her. Jean couldn't shake the feeling that the caller was female. Colleague? Former flame? Current one?

There were timed breaks for commercials, but the three men on the set stayed in place, chatting among themselves, comparing notes. Brian appeared with quick instructions, or the men got updates or news on their tablets. It was very high-tech, and things moved quickly. Jean was impressed by how smartly the commentators coordinated their participation and how super quick they were with their responses and humor.

Once or twice, there was a playful reference to Patrick's lottery win, but Patrick never took the bait and quickly got the conversation back on point. There was no hint at all of the morning news story about Patrick and a former girlfriend and the winning lottery ticket. Jean was sure they all must have heard or read about that by now. And he'd said nothing about the problem when he'd called to invite her to his workplace.

Jean was riveted by Patrick's obvious knowledge of sports. Right now, it was primarily basketball, and baseball since the spring season had recently began. Football was over until training started again in the fall…along with hockey, and the trials and meets in prep for the Winter Olympics.

Patrick was well versed in each one. He was focused, but easy and confident, and Jean especially liked his ability to make funny observations for what would be the viewing TV audience at a later time, but now causing laughter on the set. The production crew off to the sides could be heard chuckling at the verbal play among the three men.

It was also odd for Jean to see Patrick polished and ready for prime time in a suit and tie. He looked like a youthful CEO, a lawyer, or hot director of something or other. Corporate, but not officious. It was another aspect of Patrick being grown-up that was very appealing…and very sexy. That attraction was most definitely pulling her in, as her mind replayed their parting kiss a week ago. She wanted a replay. Like his show title.

"What do you think? Does our resident millionaire have a future in broadcast?" Brian stage-whispered close to her ear during one of the breaks.

"I think he's very good."

Brian smiled ruefully at her response. "Yeah, he's very good. And he's popular. To be honest, I'm surprised he hasn't announced that he's leaving."

Jean turned to stare at Brian. "Why would he do that?"

Brian chortled. "Are you serious? He has seventy-five million reasons not to have to work anywhere ever again."

He studied her silently for such a long moment that Jean became uncomfortable. "What are you thinking?" she asked, trying to keep her tone merely curious.

His smile did nothing to make her feel that this was an inconsequential conversation. "I'm thinking you and I might yet have a…er…conversation."

"About what?"

"Getting to know one another."

"You're a friend and colleague of Patrick's. I think we know each other as well as we have to."

"For now," Brian said with a suggestive grin that was hard to misinterpret. "Don't shoot me down so fast. You never know."

Jean grew instantly cautious, protective. She was struggling for a way to respond that wouldn't put her on the defensive. But there was a bell, and the lights began to dim again in the studio. She turned to watch the camera crew take up their positions and hand signal a countdown to the start of the taping once again. She turned to Brian to find that he was back in his work state of mind. She was relieved.

"Can I get you anything? Coffee?"

"No, thank you."

Brian responded to a call coming through his headset and walked away abruptly. Jean ignored his innuendo about the two of them and was very taken by Brian's speculation about Patrick possibly leaving the station. To her way of thinking, Patrick had yet to show that the lottery win had made any significant impact on his life.

Beyond a brand-new, very expensive luxury SUV.

Beyond whatever the morning's news report was all about.

When the taping was over, the studio lights came up, and the magic of the set and the program vanished. Jean stood as Patrick left the set desk and headed toward her. He was intercepted by Brian, who immediately launched into a discussion. Patrick listened but never broke his stride until he reached her side.

"That can wait until tomorrow," Patrick said to Brian.

"Good enough. I left the details on your desk. You can review them tonight, and we'll go over everything tomorrow before the taping."

Brian turned his attention to Jean, the look in his gaze unmistakable.

"What's up on your agenda?"

"I'm driving Jean back to the city with me after the next taping."

Brian was, if nothing else, charming and persistent. He carefully took Jean's hand and, ignoring Patrick, kissed the back of it. Then, with a little tilt of his head to her, he began backing away.

"I'm sure I'll see you again."

Jean said nothing but forced a smile in return before facing Patrick.

"I think he likes you," he said sarcastically.

"Brian seems nice enough. I think he just needs clear boundaries, otherwise…"

"Otherwise?"

"He assumes his friendly personality and good looks will take him anywhere and get him anything he wants."

"Or anyone. He's been pretty successful so far."

Jean blinked, focusing on Patrick as he silently looked down at her, waiting. Suddenly it came to her that Patrick was not just being protective or merely proprietary because of their history. His skepticism of Brian's interest in her might very well be because he saw Brian as competition.

"Not with me."

Patrick's squared his shoulders, his gray eyes bright with satisfaction.

"We have a little time before the next taping. Let's go back to my office."

"Have you had time to think about the money you've won? Do you have plans? Or have you spent it all?" she teased, prepared to be shut down again.

Patrick didn't answer right away. He didn't take the seat again behind his desk, but sat on the edge of the desk next to Jean. His outstretched leg was casually pressed against her knee. She, at least, was very aware of the contact and the instant reaction she had to his touch.

"I've been trying not to think about it. But it's pretty clear now that I'm going to need some professional advice on how to manage that much money. Remember when a million dollars was a big deal? Now it's chump change. Seventy-five million is… I still can't get my head around it," he murmured. "I mean, one day, my biggest concern is can I afford to fly my sister and her family back east for our mother's birthday. The next day, I can buy the damn plane and hire a crew. I'm starting to see that having that kind of stupid-rich money is...scary."

Jean was surprised by Patrick's confession and moved by his fear and uncertainty. It was genuine and so understandable.

"I've read accounts of past winners who blow through their money quickly or lose it all through bad decisions. Is that the kind of thing you're talking about?" she asked.

"And then some," he murmured. "I never thought about the downside of being rich. Do rich people worry about being rich? Suddenly within days of the lottery announcement, there were all these people reaching out to me. *Congratulations, that's so cool, but can you spare a dime?* There are charity requests, deals, the no-fail business opportunities. Outreach from relatives I'd never met, former school pals trying to reconnect. Friends of friends of friends. Complete strangers who tracked me down. At first I was overwhelmed."

"I'm so sorry," Jean whispered.

Patrick smiled at her, his gaze filled with warmth.

"Jean, I don't deserve or want sympathy. But I need a plan. Right now, I don't have one. I don't think my accountant is the one to direct me. I now realize that I need to be careful. I want to be smart. I've spoken with my lawyer. I think what I need is sound financial management advice."

"I'm glad to hear that. So you haven't gone out and bought an island in the Mediterranean? Or multiple Lamborghinis in different colors?" Patrick began shaking his head, his smile widening with each ridiculous example. "You did get that one marriage proposal at the lottery broadcast. Any more of those?"

His smile slowly faded, his brows drawing together in thought. He looked sharply at her. "A few. Unfortunately, other things are surfacing every day."

"Want to tell me about it? But you don't have to," Jean quickly added.

Patrick glanced off in the distance for a moment, gnawing the inside of his mouth. He looked back at her. "I'm guessing you heard the story behind the lottery ticket."

"I know what I read this morning. I don't know any of it to be true."

Patrick pursed his lips and thoughtfully smoothed down his tie. He absently ran his hands through his hair, now an endearing and familiar gesture.

"Okay. I dated this woman a few years back. It was good for a long time, but…we had different expectations, and I finally broke it off. But I kept hearing from her every three, four months. I wouldn't call it stalking, but it went on for a while. I think she was hoping we'd get back together."

"If this is too personal…"

"It's very much your business. Right now you're probably the only person I really care about believing me.

"I met her in the Hamptons. She owns a restaurant out there. It was the hot place that summer, so there were tons of people, many well-known, with summer beach homes."

The thing that occurred to Jean as Patrick thoughtfully recited personal history was exactly how open he was being with her. She was practically holding her breath, so caught by the trust he was giving her.

"After the breakup, she would unexpectedly show up wherever I was, uninvited. That eventually stopped, and she started sending cards about how much she missed me. The last card I got a few months ago was for April Fools' Day. In it, she'd placed a Mega Million lottery ticket. She wrote a message inside, a line that went, 'If you win, you'll owe me a big thank-you. We'll celebrate together.'

"And when I actually won, I felt that maybe I did owe her. But I wasn't sure what to do. I gave the card to my attorney, and he said I didn't owe her anything. The card and ticket were a gift. You can't legally make demands on a gift freely given. But I felt the only way to handle it fairly was to give her something. I wouldn't have bought a lottery ticket myself. And if she hadn't sent me one, I wouldn't have been in the game to win. See what I mean?"

"Yes, I do," Jean said.

"Through my attorney, I suggested a settlement. Believe me, it was more money than she'd ever make running a restaurant, no matter how popular. She accepted the offer. I thought, *Finally, the end.*"

"Then what about the report this morning? It didn't sound like she'd been offered anything."

Patrick sighed. "Her complaint now is not really about the money. It's about publicity. The more controversy, the more she comes across as a victim, the more people will show up at her restaurant. Curious and wanting to see the woman who got done wrong."

Jean watched him, seeing his confusion and annoyance and appreciating the situation. *Damned if you do, damned if you don't.*

The buzzing began again. Again, it was his phone. This time his response was quick and succinct.

"Can't talk right now. I'll call you back." And he hung up. "Sorry," he muttered.

Patrick stood up abruptly. "Okay, enough. I didn't bring you out here today to listen to my pity party. Anyway, I really don't have anything to complain about. Brian told me recently that I live a pretty charmed existence. Maybe he's right."

Jean stood as well, carefully stepping in front of him to get his attention. "Maybe he is. That doesn't mean you give up your right to anger if you feel you're being taken advantage of."

Patrick stopped fidgeting and blinked at her until he was focused on her face, with its expression of empathy and concern. He took a step closer.

"You don't think I'm being an ass?"

Jean slowly shook her head. "No. I think you're trying to be fair."

He studied her silently, Jean hoped reading the sincerity in her eyes.

"Thank you," Patrick said.

Patrick moved to gather her against him. He hugged her close, enveloping her in an embrace while resting his chin against the side of her head. Jean instinctively wrapped her arms around him as well, and they stood like that, with no words spoken. She liked that Patrick was drawing some sort of comfort from her. She certainly was getting a lot out of his caress.

It was a tender moment of giving and receiving, not between strangers. Jean knew that something had bonded them that had magically swept them out of their high school past and into the present moment. It was an adult moment, with grown-up emotions. She could feel the shift in herself. And she was sure she felt it coming from Patrick, his body pressed against hers, emitting a gentle heat that held them together like a sensuous glue.

There was a sound from the back of his throat, and Jean simply waited until he moved, drew back as his chin grazed against her cheek. Effortlessly, his mouth slid into place over hers as they kissed. It began as a teasing brush of their lips. Simultaneously their lips parted and pressed together. It was so easy to ignore the twinge of doubt that had earlier bubbled up in her head with the phone call and the troubling exchange with Brian.

This was different.

Jean was stunned by the degree of yearning that coursed through her, swirling about her stomach and gut…and groin. But neither of them pressed any closer. Their mouths and lips did everything they needed. For now. Patrick tilted his head, his kiss growing into something more urgent, and Jean melted into it as well, aware that this was something she'd always wanted Patrick to give her. Himself. His full, undivided attention.

Jean was faintly aware of a buzzer sounding beyond the office and spreading throughout the entire studio. Like some sort of a signal.

Patrick leaned back, slowly separating their lips, raising his hands to cup her face and regard her as if he were seeing her for the first time and was mesmerized.

"That's the signal we're wanted on the set for the taping," he murmured, nevertheless pulling one more kiss from her with his warm mouth. He sighed, releasing her.

"In your words," Patrick said softly, "to be continued?"

Jean nodded, looking into his slumberous gaze. He'd made that a question. "Yes," she confirmed. "To be continued."

Now, it was a given.

CHAPTER 6

Patrick finished reading the contract for the third time and finally signed his name to the bottom. He dropped it on the table and sat back with a sigh.

"Done," he announced.

His mother appeared to peer over his shoulder at the now-signed document. She patted his shoulder. "Honey, thank you. You know you didn't have to do a thing for me."

"But I wanted to. You've been complaining for years about redoing your kitchen and the bathroom down here."

"Yeah, but I didn't mean that you should be the one to pay for it, Patrick."

Patrick swiveled on the dining room chair and placed his arm around his mother's waist. She accepted the hug, leaning into him for a brief exchange of affection before gently pulling herself free. "The good news is that I can now afford to pay for it. And the good news is that you'll finally get that kitchen upgrade you've been wanting."

Ellen Bennett kissed the top of her son's head before moving away. She picked up the multipage contract, glanced at the last page with a signature, and carefully folded the document.

"When do you think the work will start?"

"Well, I'm still deciding on tile colors, and I'm going to look at sinks and faucets this weekend. You know you really didn't have to do this, Patrick."

Patrick stood, checking the time. "It would have been a *lot* simpler if you'd just let me buy you a new house, Mom."

She chuckled, shaking her head. "It seems to me you're too busy trying to find ways to spend money, just because you have so much of it now. A month ago, you wouldn't have objected to my plan of cashing in some of my bonds to pay for the renovation. They'd already reached maturity anyway."

Ellen turned to walk into her kitchen. Patrick followed.

"I know I didn't have to pay for the renovation, but I'd rather spend on people I love, rather than fend off the hundreds I don't know. Everyone's got a sad sob story."

Patrick was suddenly reflective about growing up in this comfortable house that now seemed so small. The bright but old-fashioned kitchen held so many memories from his youth, of the breakfasts and light meals eaten there, the cookie- and cake-baking at Thanksgiving and Christmas. Birthdays. It was the final checkpoint each morning as he and his sister left to catch the school bus at the corner. It was also true that his mother, widowed for almost fifteen years, had never wanted to sell the home in which she'd raised her children. She said she reveled in all the stories that had been created here. The death of her husband was just another part of the long story.

And Patrick remembered that Jean had lived less than a half mile away. So close, although he'd never seen her in the neighborhood, only in school.

Patrick felt his phone buzzing, and he pulled it from his pocket to answer.

"Yeah, what's up? How are you?… I'm good… No, I'm not in town at the moment. I'm headed into the city in a few minutes… Finishing up some personal business." He chuckled quietly, discreetly stepping out of the kitchen and earshot of his mother. "I didn't know you were coming into New York today... Sorry, not tonight. I have someplace to be. It's business."

The caller, a casual friend of the female persuasion, had been pursuing him for months. They'd met at the start of the spring at a baseball game in DC. She was a sportswriter for a local free weekly there. Things had moved fast between them, but Patrick had no expectations of the hookup going anywhere, and neither had she. Or so she'd said. As a matter of fact, he'd soon learned that she was actually dating someone else.

He looked at the time again. "Sounds like you're busy yourself... Please don't change your plans for me. I can't get away... Everything's good." He chuckled silently again, not in amusement. "I think it's fair to say becoming an instant multimillionaire takes some getting used to..." He was pacing. When he turned, Patrick found his mother standing in the doorway to the kitchen, regarding him curiously. Her half-frame reading glasses perched on the bridge of her nose allowed his mother to glance up over the edge for distance.

"Eh...yeah, yeah. Listen, don't mean to be rude but I really have to go... Okay, bye."

"Is that the lady with you in the photograph?"

Patrick absently shook his head as he reached for his jacket over the back of a dining room chair. "Photograph? No. That was someone I met in DC almost six months ago."

Ellen Bennett raised her brows. "She's already yesterday's news?"

"Mom..." Patrick growled in mild warning. "Let me know if you need me to talk with your contractor. Don't let them talk you into *anything*. All the bills will come to my accountant, and I'll review them and talk with you before any checks go out."

"Yes, sir," Ellen said laughing, half saluting him.

Patrick kissed his mother on her cheek and headed for the door. He stopped and turned back, frowning at her.

"Did you say you saw me in a photograph? With a woman?"

"Yes, that's right. It was right after the lottery announcement. I can't remember the caption. I just assumed she was someone new in your life."

Patrick started to say something, but stopped. He shook his head. "It's complicated. I do know her. From high school."

"Really?" Ellen responded, curious. "You dated her in high school?"

"Well, no. Nothing like that. I'm sure I told you about her."

Ellen sighed and shook her head. "Well, I certainly wouldn't remember if you had. There was a revolving door for your girlfriends as soon as you started high school. I stopped counting in your sophomore year. There were probably little broken hearts all over the county by the time you graduated."

"Funny," he groused, kissing her once more. "Talk to you soon. Love you."

"Ditto." Ellen Bennett grinned as her son breezed out the door.

Once in his SUV, Patrick sat to think about what he would say to Jean if he could reach her. He'd already tried to temper his interest in her. In being with her. He knew he was moving a little too fast, but what was the point in denying he enjoyed being with Jean? She was calm and centered. She was caring and thoughtful. She listened. It had not been hard or a leap of faith to discern the difference between Jean and many of the women he'd dated, bedded, and the one he'd ultimately wed.

Patrick was doubly glad for the introduction that had brought them together in high school. Now, as they were getting to really know each other as grown-ups, their history cut to the chase, erased at least a year of testing the waters, dancing around each other to figure out how they ticked. He'd sensed right away that this new relationship with Jean already had the makings of something special. But it needed time and nurturing. He wanted Jean to trust him.

Patrick clicked on her number. She picked up immediately.

"Hello?"

"Hi. It's Patrick."

"I know who it is," Jean said smoothly.

"Am I interrupting something important?"

"Thanks for asking. Yes."

He laughed. "Okay, I get it. My station is holding a dinner this evening to recognize my program. It's been killing the ratings, and of course, that means sponsorship and ads are up. In other words, they're making a lot of money."

"They're going to crown you prince of daytime sports?"

Patrick laughed at her ready humor. "Something like that. I'd like you to come to the dinner." He hesitated only a second before spontaneously adding, "Will you come as my date?"

Jean didn't answer right away, and Patrick's stomach churned unexpectedly. She was going to turn him down.

"Of course, I'll take you home afterward. That's in the small print of the invitation," he teased.

Still Jean said nothing.

"Unless… If you have other plans, of course I understand. I know this is last minute…"

"No, I don't have other plans. Well, not really. There's an opening at the Brooklyn Museum tonight I was going to…"

"Oh. Sure."

"I can miss that. But I'm with the mayor right now. He's giving the commencement address at City College in about an hour. Then there are two other meetings, including one at Yeshiva University in Washington Heights. Then…I think that's it."

"Where can I pick you up?" Patrick asked immediately, not giving Jean a chance to beg off.

"I can meet you at the dinner venue. Where is it?"

"I'm picking you up," Patrick said firmly.

"That doesn't make sense, Patrick. Are you coming from New Jersey, the station?"

"I'm coming from my mom's house."

"Oh. Are you sure? You may have to wait until I can get away."

"I'll wait."

———

Patrick was distracted not only by the late-afternoon rush-hour traffic, but also by the drizzle that had begun once he and Jean were on the road. And he was aware that he was feeling a little nervous beside her. Picking her up from an important academic environment, where city hall staff and mayoral security were present, had somehow let it sink in that Jean held not only an exacting position in the mayor's office, but that she held the mayor's ear. It had been daunting to watch her in action, as the mayor and his entourage were leaving the meeting and heading for their official transport back downtown. He suddenly realized maybe he was being entirely too cavalier in expecting Jean to drop everything when he wanted—needed—to see her. What if she'd said no to the dinner party? He could think of no one else he'd want to ask. Except in a pinch depending on the event, his own mother.

Jean was no busier than other professional women he'd dated since his divorce, but Jean's job rose to the top of the list in terms of importance and influence. He had to be careful not to treat that lightly.

Another thing: Did she understand that they were dating?

"Is your mother okay?"

He frowned. "My mother? She's fine. Why do you ask?"

"When you said you were with her earlier, I guess I thought something may have been wrong."

Patrick stole a glance at her, a grin playing around his lips. "Thanks for the thought. You know, one of the first things I thought of was buying my mom a new house. And I was going to arrange for a housekeeper and someone to help her with the property in seasonal weather. She didn't want any of that."

"Really? What did she want?"

"Nothing. She didn't want another house. She said the very thought of moving gave her 'agita'… I don't even know what that means," he murmured dryly.

Jean laughed. "I know what it means."

"Then, on second thought, my mom only wanted to renovate her kitchen and bathrooms, and she wanted some decent landscaping in her backyard. That's it. I said, 'Mom, can't you dream bigger than that? I can get you anything you want.' She said, 'I already have everything I want. You and your sister, and two beautiful grandkids.'"

"That's so sweet," Jean said in quiet awe.

"I'm still in discussion with my sister. She said, 'As long as you're asking, I would *love* a bigger house.' The kids are going to need bigger rooms; she and her husband want to add a one-bedroom apartment over their garage. That will give them rental property, if they choose. Or an Airbnb. I worried a little about her husband and how he'd feel about me giving all those little extras to his family. It's not settled yet. I want to have a man-to-man talk with him about it. I'm not looking to cause trouble."

"That's all good stuff, Patrick. Of course you want to help your family."

"Yeah, but I don't think I'm out of the woods yet. I might have to hire an assistant just to deal with the email and text requests."

"Are you really considering giving money to people you don't know?"

"What I'm thinking about are the people I do know that I might want to help. Remember Pete from the party? He asked me for a loan the minute he walked through the door, before he even said hello. And he wasn't kidding."

"Do you know what the loan is for?"

"I guess that it's for his son. Pete and the boy's mother aren't married, but he's very hands-on and involved in his son's life. The kid, according to Pete, has grades that could get him into one of the Ivy League colleges. He graduates high school in another year. He'd have to take out massive student loans if he doesn't get a scholarship or other financial aid. Now

Pete's son is a cause I can go for. If I can supply him with a running start with college tuition, I will."

Jean let the tale seep in as she silently watched the rush-hour traffic around them, the rain hitting and dripping down the glass. The repetitive action of the windshield wipers was hypnotic, and she felt relaxed and strangely safe, cocooned with Patrick in his luxury car. Pete had a worthwhile cause, the circumstances not unfamiliar to her.

She turned to look at Patrick's profile as he focused on his driving and the traffic. She was impressed that he was seriously considering a very modest request. But he was also demonstrating far more about himself to her. Jean took that revelation to the next step by making one of her own.

"My parents never married either," Jean murmured.

Patrick shot her a quick glance. "I didn't know."

"There were a lot of kids like me in school, Patrick. It's funny how we all managed to find each other, glomming on to each other like this weird private club. I was lucky, if you want to call it that. I always knew my parents both loved me, even if they weren't together. I had everything I needed. But what I *wanted* was for all of us to be together every day, like a real family."

"Do you know why that couldn't happen?"

"My parents never told me the whole story. I'm sure the elephant in the room was their interracial relationship. There was probably a lot of pressure on them to think about what kind of life they'd have, where they'd live, about kids. You know…et cetera, et cetera."

"That obviously didn't stopped them from being in love. They had you," Patrick suggested.

"Yes. But there were consequences." She and her parents had never had *that* conversation. "I just want to say that Pete asking you for money, as loud and over-the-top as it might seem, is because of his son. It must have taken a lot for him to come to you with his hand out."

Patrick glanced at her again. "I never thought of it that way."

"Do what you think is right, what feels right. Let's face it. The kind of money you won is ridiculous."

He chuckled quietly.

"Have some fun. This SUV is a good start. The money could also become a nightmare."

He nodded. "Like I said, I'm going to need some advice."

Jean looked out the window while she considered her next comment. "I think I know someone, if you're interested."

"That will be great. Thanks."

They both grew silent. Reflective. It was not uncomfortable at all.

"Did either of your parents ever marry someone else?" Patrick suddenly asked.

Jean was surprised by that particular question, that he should wonder about her parents' standing with each other, let alone that he would care. She rested her head back and sighed, feeling oddly dreamy and conjuring up her own youthful daydreams.

"My father has been in a few relationships over the years, but no, he never married." Jean stopped for a moment to think about her next words. "My mother…I think she waited until I was away at college, but I know she sometimes dated. Neither one of them seemed particularly interested in committing to marriage. I think she's never stopped loving my father. But I also don't think she ever hated him, or anything like that, because they never married. It must have been a tough decision, but neither of them seems bitter, or even unhappy. They just sort of moved on with their lives. With me in the middle."

For long moments, there was just the quiet sound of rain falling. Soothing. Patrick reached out for Jean's hand, threading his fingers with hers, resting them on his thigh. Connecting and holding on.

"Thanks for sharing."

Jean felt like she'd been here before.

Not the place, exactly, but a lot of the same people surrounding Patrick and congratulating him for the umpteenth time about his lottery win. And, as before, Patrick was gracious and chatty, yet held a part of himself in check. Jean now understood why.

The celebratory dinner was held in a private function room of a Manhattan hotel, gilded and formal, and out of keeping with the kind of folks who'd gathered here. She recognized a number of people from the lottery after-party. Brian was there but, beyond briefly greeting Jean again, he made no effort to get her attention or engage her in conversation. And he had not come alone, a fact that confused Jean, given the conversation between them at the studio. Was Brian just a player, going after any female who grabbed his attention?

The behavior among the guests this time was not quite as boisterous as the lottery party, which had been fueled by a lot of laughter and an open bar. This was a real sit-down dinner with several top management folks from the station speaking earnestly about how the win couldn't have happened to a greater guy. And happily sharing the latest ratings for the program *REPLAY*, where viewership had increased by almost 20 percent, a major growth spurt in so short a period of time.

There was applause and toasts and genuine affection for Patrick as he patiently accepted the accolades. He was attentive, taking both ribbing and praise in stride. Jean was coming to realize, he was a more private person than these public displays recognized. During the celebratory evening, Patrick never actually had a chance to eat, barely lifting his fork before he was interrupted by conversation, as each course was eventually taken away and replaced with the next. Despite the fact that the evening was supposed to be downtime, it wasn't. There was a lot of business on the table, the new ratings having upped the ante on what was going to be expected of Patrick.

Jean couldn't eat either. Not for the same reasons as Patrick, seated almost directly opposite her at one of three tables set up for the gathering.

She was still the subject of curiosity. Yes, she was a representative from the mayor's office, but not tonight. How well did she know Patrick? They weren't surprised he'd brought someone—he never came alone to these events—but they hadn't been expecting to see her again. Jean could only guess what that was supposed to mean.

"Are you two dating?" someone boldly asked.

"We're very good friends" became her standard response. Until she believed it herself.

Apparently, Patrick had been very closemouthed around the station, but Jean quickly got the sense that Patrick's colleague had already paired them and created a whole story around their relationship. She might have found it amusing if all the talk and fishing for confirmation wasn't striking so close to home and her own wishful thinking.

"You were at the station earlier this week. Hanging out with Patrick."

"Yes. He invited me."

"Right, right." The middle-aged man seated to her left nodded as he continued to eat with gusto. Jean attempted a sectioned asparagus spear and some grilled salmon, but it never made its way to her mouth.

"Unbelievable luck. I don't know anyone who's won seventy-five dollars, let alone millions."

"I think it's fair to say Patrick was surprised as well."

The man chortled, taking a healthy sip of his drink. "Well, that woman who came forward about the ticket was the real surprise. Do you think the story's true?"

Jean stiffened but smiled openly at the man. She shrugged faintly. "You have to ask Patrick."

The conversation continued for another minute but fortunately shifted to another topic. The woman on the other side of Jean captured her attention. They'd only had time for a quick hello and introduction at the start of the evening. Marin Phillips was African American, about the same age as Jean, and very poised and attractive. She was an account executive with ESPN. They'd exchanged business cards.

"Poor Patrick," she now said with a rueful shake of her head. "He still looks shell-shocked, don't you think?"

"I guess so. It will all die down eventually."

"Has he said anything about leaving the program and the station? There are people waiting for an announcement."

"Does the station want him to leave just because he won so much money?"

"It's not unreasonable. Then again, this whole dinner is because the ratings for REPLAY have gone up recently. I guess you could say he's like the goose that laid the golden egg. Top management is very happy with the outcome, but Patrick was popular even before the lottery. Now he's even more so, for more reasons."

"Then it's just gossip," Jean suggested, quickly casting her gaze across the table to Patrick. He was thoughtfully listening to an older gentleman who was speaking intensely to him, making notations on a paper cocktail napkin to illustrate some point, jabbing his finger at Patrick's chest.

"Who's the man talking with Patrick now?" Jean asked Marin.

"He's the top gun at the station. He's answerable to corporate, and Patrick is answerable to him." Marin shook her head with a grin. "I don't think Patrick is having fun yet."

"I agree. But I feel like everyone is hounding him. His program is doing well; the ratings have led to increased sponsors. When is enough enough?"

"It's never enough," Marin said calmly. "The pressure will be on for Patrick, but I think he can handle it."

The final course plates were removed. Patrick's wineglass was refilled.

"Patrick's a good guy," Marin said to Jean. "Not like some of the former athletes who end up with a TV deal after they can't play anymore."

"Yes, everyone seems to like him."

"Especially the ladies. But he's not a player. He's too smart for that. I know it all looks glamorous, but this business can suck the life from you."

Jean looked at Marin. Was that just an observation…or a warning? Were there a lot of ladies?

"Are people taking bets on what he'll do?"

Marin chuckled in genuine amusement. "No, there's none of that going on. But it's possible Patrick could get another offer from another network, an offer he can't refuse. Like, maybe his *own* program, no co-hosting. A higher salary or fabulous benefits. He certainly doesn't need the money anymore, but money would be on the table as the incentive."

Jean again glanced at Patrick. She met his gaze briefly as he stood up, ending the conversation. The man who'd held his attention through dinner shook his hand and walked away with a friendly slap on Patrick's shoulder.

"I don't know what his plans are," Jean said honestly, mildly bewildered by the truth of that. She was thinking purely in terms of what she was to Patrick…and what he could be to her. Jean hadn't thrown their careers into the mix. It was complicated as is.

"We're not going to find out tonight. Let's see how things go in the coming weeks." Marin stood up to leave, turning to Jean with a smile. "You know, I'm sorry the whole conversation was about Patrick. I'd really like to get to know you better."

Jean stood as well, shaking her hand. "Me too. Why don't we plan lunch sometime?" she asked with genuine interest.

"Yes, let's. I'll email you," Marin promised.

With a pleasant good night, she left, saying a casual goodbye to other guests on her way out. The evening was winding down. Many of the guests had already said their goodbyes to Patrick, shook his hand, and congratulated him on the ratings for his show.

Jean also was approached with several good-night-great-to-see-you-again comments.

As she and Patrick were leaving the dining room, they passed the maître d' in discussion with the head of the waitstaff who had served the dinner party. They'd reached the front lobby of the hotel and the valet's desk when they heard behind them, "Sir! Sir, before you leave…"

They turned as the maître d' hurried to Patrick, holding out a black leather folder. Jean stepped aside, away from the exchange that went on for long moments. A few moments later, she watched the man walk back into the hotel.

She glanced at Patrick, but his expression was closed, his brows drawn together. In fact, Jean thought Patrick seemed very annoyed. Angry. What was that all about? The valet returned with Patrick's SUV, immediately drawing attention from a passerby who stopped to admire the Porsche.

Jean was quickly guided into the passenger side by the valet.

"Hey, mistah. You famous?" a bold voice shouted from a small cluster of young Black teens who'd slowed their walk to circle the car for a closer look.

"No, I'm not," Patrick responded, about to climb in behind the wheel. "The car's a rental."

"You lie. Tryin' to play your girlfriend-in-training, man."

The group cackled.

So did Patrick, appearing amused that they'd seen right through him.

Girlfriend-in-training? Jean wondered why the boys had come to that conclusion.

One of the teens tried to peer into the front seat on Jean's side. "Oh man! This is *sick!*"

"Straight up," another added.

"Can we get a lift?" the third teen asked, causing his friends to crack up.

Jean turned silently to Patrick, surprised that he actually seemed to be considering the request.

"Where do you live?"

"Brooklyn," the teens said in unison.

Patrick started the engine. "You're in luck. We're headed to Brooklyn. Get in."

"Gucci!" the teen shouted as he and his two friends piled into the back seat and slammed the door.

Patrick pulled away into traffic. "Seat belts," he ordered. The teens complied, chattering between them over the features of the SUV. "Make sure you wipe down the seats when you get out." The boys promised.

It was quickly apparent that there was no need to be wary of the three teens. They were so excited to be in the Cayenne, so grateful not to have to make their way home on the subway, wet and uncomfortable.

Jean was content to sit quietly and let the conversation take place around her. She learned the boys had been in Central Park for a soccer workshop but had stayed to wander around Midtown for the rest of the day. Their exploits and comical experiences and observations kept her and Patrick entertained for the twenty minutes it took to deliver them to Red Hook. And as the trio was thanking Patrick fervently for their ride, Patrick presented the boys with comp tickets to a baseball game, seats on the field, the next time a New York team was home. After that, Patrick could walk on water as far as the teens were concerned. They didn't seem to mind getting wet again as they stood on the curb yelling and frantically waving a goodbye.

Patrick blew the car horn in answer as they drove away.

Despite the comical interplay, Jean was aware that Patrick seemed pensive for a full minute. She didn't question him, instead offering comments on the many people at the dinner. This seemed to focus him, and the talk on the drive to her neighborhood became more fluid. As the SUV approached Jean's building, she abruptly spoke up.

"Don't turn off the engine," she instructed Patrick. He gave her a puzzled look but obeyed, turning to her.

"What's up?"

"I want you to drive where I direct you."

"Wait...what? Why?"

Jean looked squarely at him. "Because I ask you to," she said quietly but earnestly. Patrick searched her face, considering the command. He put the car in gear.

"Okay."

Jean gave him directions and Patrick silently followed them. His gaze searched beyond the streaked windshield into the dark, rainy night of slick streets and a neighborhood that was unfamiliar to him. Less than ten minutes later, Jean had him pull into the parking lot of a small restaurant with a bright yellow neon sign: *Jimmy's Pizza Palace*.

"We're here," Jean announced, preparing to get out. Patrick's expression was still bewildered. He reached out to grab her arm. "Wait a minute. Why are we here?"

"To get you something to eat."

———

Patrick finally sat back, with a big sigh. He looked at the round metal platter with the last slice of the house special, All or Nothing, but he was done. He carefully wiped his mouth and hands on his napkin and dropped it onto his plate. He'd eaten more than half of the pizza and was still processing what had given Jean the idea to go for pizza right after the sumptuous spread served to them at the hotel dinner.

And, for the moment, he didn't know if he should be embarrassed or grateful that this unassuming neighborhood restaurant had given him the most satisfying meal he'd had in days. Nothing fancy, and maybe that was the idea. He was full…and contented.

Across the laminate table, Jean was quietly watching him, a peaceful, knowing smile on her lips. She'd eaten a couple of slices but mostly enjoyed watching Patrick scarf down nearly all of it. He placed his elbows on the table and leaned toward Jean, his clasped hands covering his mouth and chin.

"What just happened?" Patrick said, laughter in his voice.

Jean leaned in as well, her amber-colored eyes mischievous and bright. "I just made sure you don't go to bed hungry tonight."

"Okay. Want to give me a hint? Did I look like I was going to pass out from lack of food?"

"Let's just say you were giving off the signals that pretty much said, 'Feed me.'"

Patrick was curious and amused, but his brow furrowed slightly. "What kind of signal?"

"Well, you had a serious case of the 'urri upps' after we left the hotel and were headed to Brooklyn."

He silently shook his head.

"The 'urri upps' is your stomach letting you know you need to eat. You know. It growls."

Patrick watched Jean hesitate for a moment before she quietly added, "I think you had something on your mind and didn't even notice."

He lowered his gaze, a gesture indicating that Jean was right. "Okay, I'll bite. What exactly do…'urri upps' sound like?"

Jean sat straight, blinking rapidly and preparing herself. And then she took a deep breath and emitted an unbelievable, rude guttural noise that seemed to be rolling from the back of her throat. And to emphasize what was happening, she added gestures, her hands tumbling and twisting together. Patrick, totally caught by surprise, stared at Jean for a moment and then burst into a deep laugh that came straight from his belly and transformed his face. Jean continued for a few seconds more and then stopped, but Patrick couldn't deny how funny it sounded and, shamelessly, let his amusement rip until he was done. Jean grinned, pleased that she got the reaction from him she intended. He was, too, as weird as it all seemed. In that moment he felt, unexpectedly, so happy to be sitting in a tiny pizza place somewhere in Brooklyn, laughing with her.

Finally, Patrick got ahold of himself. He studied Jean, her calm presence, her abundant hair curling from the humidity. His eyes brimmed with laughter.

"You got me. I never heard of that before."

Jean shrugged, a little smug. "I'm not surprised. But all the Black kids know it."

He was really surprised now. His brows shot up. "Really? So this is a Black thing?"

"Might be. I got it from a cousin growing up. But I knew a lot of kids who made up language like that. They incorporate sounds. The 'urri upps' was my favorite. You have to admit, it's pretty original, right?"

Patrick shook his head, amusement overtaking him again. "Yeah, I do. I'll never be able to ignore that noise from my stomach again without seeing and hearing you demonstrate what it sounds like." He signaled for the one of the employees behind the counter and reached for his wallet.

Jean reached across the table to grab his hand. "I took care of it."

Patrick slowly put his wallet away, considering the gesture. "Okay. Want to tell me why?"

"Because it was my idea. I asked you. I have to tell you, Patrick, you're a cheap date." She winked at him.

He grinned broadly, enjoying the moment, enjoying her. He didn't even attempt to come up with the name of any woman he'd ever known who had done something so simple for him, so thoughtful. Jean had been paying attention to the events of the evening and put him first.

"I'll have to do something about that."

After considering for a second, Patrick reached into his jacket pocket and pulled out a piece of paper. He unfolded it, read it carefully. Silently he passed the paper to Jean.

Jean silently accepted it as she glanced with curiosity at him. It was a receipt, with all the details for the dinner at the hotel.

"How did you get this?" Jean asked, handing it back to him.

Patrick returned it to his pocket. "Apparently whoever organized that soirée this evening never gave a credit card when making the arrangement and left without paying the bill. The maître d' caught up to me while we were waiting for the car."

Jean was speechless, her eyes wide in disbelief. "So...you're telling me you settled the bill?"

He nodded.

"For the dinner that was being *given* in *your* honor?"

He nodded again.

Jean clamped her mouth closed, and Patrick could see the astonishment, but also something deeper, like she was silently coming to his defense.

"What are you going to do?"

"That is—excuse my sarcasm—the million-dollar question. The thing is, no matter what I do, there's a downside. I could come off as a conceited jerk or a petty jerk. This could be some sort of strange payback."

"I don't understand. Payback for what?"

"I have a great job. I get a lot of offers and attention and perks. I won the lottery. In other words, I have everything. Isn't that unfair?"

"That sounds like blaming you because you're successful."

Patrick sighed. "Maybe. But I have to deal with the possibility. Don't worry. I'll take care of this."

"Everything okay, Miss Jeannie? You want a little ice cream? I got your favorite." The short, rotund worker directed to Jean as he interrupted the conversation to clear the table.

"Not tonight, Julio. Thanks for making that delicious pie for my friend here. He was starving," she teased, indicating Patrick.

Patrick pointed to his oily-napkin-filled paper plate. "You both saved my life."

"I happy to make for Miss Jeannie. She special lady," Julio stage-whispered to Jean. "He no good to you. I take care of him," the man said without an ounce of fear just because Patrick was almost two feet taller.

"Thank you, Julio. I'll remember that."

"We might come to blows. There will be blood on the floor," Patrick threatened back, grinning.

Julio chuckled amiably as he waddled away to dispose of garbage and wipe clean the serving platter. They got up to leave. Patrick made note that Jean clearly was a regular here, or at least had Favorite Person status.

He shook his head at the "friend" status he had achieved...but he definitely intended to raise the bar higher than that.

CHAPTER 7

Torrential rain met Jean and Patrick as they left the Pizza Palace.

"Wow," Patrick said as they stood under an inadequate awning trying to figure out the quickest way to his car before they both became soaking wet.

"Let's go back inside for coffee and wait this out. It will slow in a few minutes."

"Or not," Patrick murmured, calculating his next move. "You wait here. I'm going to make a run for it and bring the car up in front."

He didn't wait for a response but pulled his suit jacket up from his shoulders and covered his head as best he could. From where she stood, Jean could see the rain quickly darkening the fabric. She heard the double click of the car being electronically unlocked and the instant start of the engine. In seconds, Patrick had reversed out of the spot and drove up in front of her. Jean quickly got in but was not saved from getting wet.

When they reached Jean's building, it was apparent that there would be no magical spot right in front either. Patrick again ordered Jean out at the building entrance and drove away to find parking. By the time he returned to her, Patrick's hair was plastered to his scalp, water running down his face, from his chin and the end of his nose.

It was a biblical forty days and forty nights kind of rain.

They left wet footprints from the lobby right up to her apartment door, forming a small pool of water on the doormat. Inside they kicked off their shoes behind the door, and Jean directed Patrick to the bathroom.

"There are plenty of towels. Dry off as best you can."

She disappeared into her bedroom to strip everything off and towel herself dry. She pulled on a short, black T-shirt shift and pulled her hair into a messy ponytail at the top of her head, tendrils curling riotously. Her hair cascaded about her head in tight ringlets. Jean grabbed another garment from her closet and brought it back to the living room with her. Patrick had not yet reappeared. Leaving the garment over the back of the sofa, Jean went into the kitchen and pulled several bottles and glasses from a cabinet. She also prepared a pot of coffee.

"I should hang these things up. I'm leaving water all over your place. Sorry."

"Everything will dry," Jean said.

She turned to face Patrick and stood transfixed, unprepared to find him virtually naked, with nothing more than a bath towel wrapped and secured around his waist by a twist knot. It could come loose at any moment...with the slightest movement of his hips or thighs. His damp hair was spiky and shiny. A second towel was draped around his shoulders, his chest bare. An alarming churning of her stomach signaled Jean's response.

"I'll... Let me get some hangers."

She squeezed past him, heading for a closet, swallowing to catch her breath. His physical presence was suddenly overwhelming, bringing to life far too many daydreams and wanton desires, not even counting the girlish ones she'd fashioned in high school. She handed Patrick the hangers and, avoiding his gaze, returned to the kitchen...but forgot what she was doing.

This is not going to work, Jean thought to herself, her sudden yearning growing like a live thing within her, making her feel vulnerable...and foolish.

She had *never* felt this way with Ross.

Ross always had a manly, take-charge way with her that she'd found attractive and very virile. But he'd played that card elsewhere, stepping out on her, devastating and disappointing her, until his charm had completely died. Until she withdrew her love and her heart. Until she no longer wanted him.

Patrick was not trying to play her. If he were, he would have gotten her, successfully, into bed that first time. But then there would have been nowhere for them to go, and they would have parted again, still just former high school friends. Now, Jean lived for the potential. The uncertainty was exciting and frightening. But she was very sure about what she was coming to feel for Patrick Bennett. The foundation had been there for a long time.

"I guess this means I'm staying the night."

It was a statement of confirmation. No question, no doubt.

Jean took a deep breath and turned to face him again. She avoided letting her gaze ride down his chest...to the inadequate towel cover...to his still-damp hairy legs. "I guess so. I can't send you out there. It's a dark and stormy night."

He chortled. "That sounds like a bad opening of one of Snoopy's books. I don't have a toothbrush."

That made her smile. "I have extras. My mother is notorious for never bringing one when she stays over."

"I'll be back," Patrick said, accepting the hangers from her.

He headed to the bathroom to hang up his clothing, navigating her apartment as easily and comfortably as if staying over was natural.

While he was gone, Jean made up the sofa bed. When he returned, Patrick watched silently for a moment. As she finished the last of tucking in the top sheet, he fluffed the extra pillow Jean had gotten from her own bed.

She glanced at him, his eyes smoky in the dim light of the room. "Coffee, tea, or a drink?"

A wicked grin curved his mouth, and his brow arched up. "I thought you were going to say—"

"I know what you thought," Jean said, turning away from that warm, sultry look.

"A drink. I could use something strong."

"Okay, coming right up."

———

Patrick turned away, back to the living room. He was a little surprised to find himself in Jean's apartment, apparently for the night, again. What did catch his attention was how glad he was that it worked out this way. His place was bigger, more slick and modern, thanks to the superior tastes of his mother and sister…and a former girlfriend who was an interior designer. His apartment in Jersey City was almost *Architecture Digest* quality, except for the placement of his Peloton and rowing machine. Jean's place was all about cushioned chairs, and pillows, and bookcases, and photographs of people who were important to her. It was like a real home…not a showcase for brand names. It was so…Jean.

Patrick absently wiped his chest with the towel from around his neck. He was feeling a little restless. More than that first night staying with Jean, he felt the smallness of her comfortable apartment but in a very good way. Now it felt intimate. He checked the knot holding the towel in place but wished that at least his underwear had stayed dry. He didn't want Jean to think…or did he?

The space around the open sofa bed was tight, and he now wondered how he'd managed not to kill himself in the dark the first time. He saw the navy blue material draped over the back of the sofa and held it up. It was a robe. A man's robe.

"Is this robe for me?" he called out.

"I thought you'd be more comfortable wearing it." Her voice carried from the kitchen.

Reluctantly, Patrick slipped the robe on. It didn't fit, the sleeves and length a little short. He took it off, unhappy that he'd even tried.

He sat in a club chair, leaning forward to scowl at the garment. Jean came in carrying two glasses. She passed a tall tumbler to him with a cola-colored liquid. She had a glass of wine and sat in a chrome-and-leather modern rocker adjacent to him. He watched as she effortlessly curled her legs and bare feet up onto the seat. Her damp hair appeared to be sprouting from her head like Medusa's snakes. She looked very young. In that moment, Patrick caught a glimpse of the pretty girl she had been at sixteen, now mature and filled in. The shift she was wearing didn't allow him to follow the curves and outline of her slender body, but his imagination and an educated guess hinted strongly at Jean's shape, her breasts and thighs. Patrick shifted, fighting back his body's response to being this close to her with only a suggestion of cover between them. Suddenly, he wanted to free her hair, to let his fingers comb through the curly strands. He wanted to pull her close until their bodies finally touched, and he could hold and kiss Jean, lose himself in the safety of their history, and take them both to the next level.

He took a large sip of his drink. The vodka hit him in his chest.

"Didn't the robe fit? It belongs to my father."

"I'm good," Patrick said, satisfied with the explanation.

"I got it for him when he used to visit, back when I first got the apartment. But he only stayed here a few times. He said my sofa bed was killing his back and he couldn't sleep."

Patrick nodded. He'd slept soundly on the pullout himself.

The ping of a cell phone text tone broke in, grabbing their attention.

"That's me," Patrick said, getting up to retrieve the phone from the bathroom. He returned reading the text message and took his seat again.

"Is everything okay?" she asked.

"Yes. And no." He grinned at Jean. "The interview taping for tomorrow is canceled. But I'm booked on an early flight to LA in the morning."

"Does that mean…" She stopped.

"It means I have to leave here at the crack of dawn, get home to pack. A car will pick me up and drive me to Newark International. It means I'm going to be in another studio or at a game. The Dodgers are playing Arizona. Then I might be accompanying them to Chicago to play the Cubs."

"You don't sound happy or excited about it."

"No, no, that's not it." Patrick looked squarely at Jean. "The timing is bad. Don't you think?"

She studied the wine in her glass, shrugged slightly. "It's work. The mayor isn't particularly tuned in to his staff's personal lives either. Things happen; you roll with it."

"You have a very clear understanding. In my line of work, I'm always dealing with someone else's schedule, travel, missed appointments, last-minute cancellations. Right now I'm not sure when I'm flying back. Want to come with me?"

Patrick surprised even himself speaking before thinking. He thought Jean's expression brightened for an instant before she calmly shook her head.

"I'm not a groupie, Patrick. I do have a job. As a matter of fact, tomorrow I'm accompanying the mayor to Fieldston for another commencement speech."

"That private school in the Bronx?" Patrick asked, finishing his drink. He felt the buzz from the vodka.

"I think the program starts at noon."

"Then I'll be quiet leaving in the morning, and you can get some sleep," he said.

Jean stared at him.

"Don't worry about me. I'm good at sleeping on planes."

"Okay."

The small talk wound down, and Patrick knew the next step was Jean saying good night and closing herself off in her room. He would say good night and shift around until he found a comfortable spot on the love seat. But he struggled with an awareness that was light-years beyond that first night together with her, and there wasn't going to be time to make it happen.

Did she sense it too?

Were they possibly on the same page?

She stood up to take their empty glasses to the kitchen, placing them in the sink. Patrick waited until Jean returned and stood to block the path to her room. This forced Jean to stop in front of him, waiting. He examined her makeshift hairstyle and spontaneously fingered strands of her curls. He slowly took hold of her arms, running his hands up and down a few times on her soft, smooth skin. He could feel she was relaxed.

Patrick knew then that Jean trusted him.

"I bet you weren't expecting the night to end this way. Again," she said.

"No, but it's fine. You could have sent me on my way and told me to be careful driving home. Maybe with a good-night kiss for good measure," Patrick hinted.

She smiled. "I heard this is only a half date, remember? I think I'm going to hold you to the promise you haven't made yet."

"Consider it said. I can do better." He bent to kiss her, and Jean tilted her head to meet it. "Good night," he said against her lips, pressing against her mouth.

Gentle, like the first time. Exploratory, like the first time. Not as deep and moving as when she visited in his office. But filled with expectation that they'd grown into, that still hung in the air. There was no question that the tension was mounting between them.

"I'll try not to wake you when I leave."

"Don't worry about it. I'll be fine. Have a good trip."

Patrick stepped aside to let her enter her room. The door closed quietly. He stood considering the barrier between them. And, turning out the light, settled on the sleeper.

But he never went to sleep.

Instead, Patrick twisted and turned, his mind flitting from one scenario of him and Jean together to another and another. It wasn't that the bed was uncomfortable. It was that he was uncomfortable. No. Edgy. There were any number of things he could have done about it, but truly, there was only one that he wanted. The sheets had become too warm, limp, and soft with his body heat and agitation. Impatiently, Patrick threw the top sheet off and swung his legs to the floor, sitting up. He leaned forward, resting his elbows on his knees, and massaged his hands through his hair, sighing deeply. He snatched up his smartphone and pressed the home button. The clock lit up in the center. 12:23 a.m.

Patrick put it aside and turned on the lamp. He caught sight of the small bookcase positioned between the club chair and rocker, on which the lamp was set. His gaze aimlessly browsed the titles, settling on the vertical boldface name of a high school with the class year. It was Jean's yearbook. Their high school yearbook.

Patrick pulled the book out and examined the cover with the school seal embossed over the school colors. He switched to sitting in a chair and began to leaf through the book, first going immediately to the alphabetical catalog of senior portraits until he came to Jean's. Unexpectedly, he was back there, in school with her. He was aware of the talk, the teen speculation about her, her parentage, seeing her as "other." What the hell did that mean?

In the portrait, her gaze looked right into the camera with confidence. A closed-mouth smile that was friendly, that protected Jean from too much familiarity. Her hair, more curly then, framed her face and shoulders.

Everything Patrick had learned about Jean during his final year came back to him, reinforced in a major way by reuniting with her recently. He settled in the chair, lifting his legs to rest on the foot of the sleeper, his ankles crossed, and went back to the beginning of the book to see what Jean's senior year had been like.

Jean did eventually fall to sleep. But now she jerked suddenly awake. She didn't hear anything but detected a light from the living room shining dimly beneath her bedroom door. Either Patrick had never turned it off, or he'd never gone to sleep. Her bedside digital clock read 12:41 a.m. She could still hear the rain outside, no longer torrential but steady. Jean turned on the light and slowly got out of bed. She hesitated for a moment, frowning at her own decision, her heart racing, but nonetheless feeling strongly about what she was about to do.

She carefully opened the door, in case Patrick was indeed asleep. She stepped out and saw immediately that he wasn't. It was several seconds before he realized she was there, watching him. Their gazes connected and held. Patrick slowly closed a book he'd been reading and set it aside. Jean realized he was waiting for her to speak first…or make the first move.

"You can't sleep," she said simply.

His chest heaved with a sigh. "No, not really."

"Is it the bed?"

Patrick waited a beat, finally shaking his head. "No."

There were any number of things Jean knew she could have suggested. But she went straight to the top of the list.

"You might be able to catch a few hours on the flight tomorrow, but you'll do better if you can get some sleep now."

"I don't disagree."

"Okay. Then…I think you should come in with me. I think we can… We'll be fine sleeping together until the morning. My bed is far more comfortable than the pullout."

Patrick kept his gaze absolutely riveted to her. "I'm sure. Do you think that's a good idea?" he whispered.

"I think we can make it work," Jean said just as quietly.

But still Patrick sat, watching, assessing. She wasn't sure how she'd feel if he instantly jumped up to accept her offer. Instead, she was pleased that he was running her invitation over and over in his head. He wasn't going to take the suggestion of actually sleeping together lightly. Good.

Jean took Patrick's frowning consideration to mean the outcome was going to be as important to him as it most certainly was to her.

And she didn't think any further explanation was needed. Either Patrick understood her or he didn't.

He nodded. He slowly stood up…a towel wrapped around his loins still in place. "Okay."

Jean turned back to her room. She felt overly warm, a little apprehensive. She climbed back into her bed and settled down as comfortably as she could. Patrick appeared very slowly in the doorway, his gaze traveling to her and how she lay in bed. Still trying to pick apart her offer, no doubt, but it was nothing more than a thoughtful offer and not a solicitation. When Patrick moved toward the opposite side of her bed, Jean reached and turned out the light.

Patrick got into the bed next to her so carefully Jean barely felt the mattress give under his weight. She closed her eyes and smiled slightly. He was nervous. So was she.

He settled down somewhat stiffly. Jean knew he was practically holding his breath.

"My mother once told my sister that cuddling can relieve anxiety. She had a new boyfriend and was trying to convince him to not…you know."

"Did it work?"

"I don't know. She never said. My mother also said it's good for your immune system."

Jean gnawed her lip, trying not to laugh. Not because it was funny, but because he was so worried about doing the wrong thing…with her. *He'll figure it out*, she thought, letting out a deep sigh.

Jean turned her head toward the window, away from him. "Good night."

She heard his exhale.

"Night."

Patrick lay, waiting. It was just minutes before he could detect Jean's even, light breathing.

He closed his eyes and chuckled silently. He'd had no idea what to expect when he'd followed Jean to her room. But, apparently, the invitation was sincere. They were going to spend the night…rather, the rest of the morning…together in her bed. Sleeping. Nothing else. Patrick didn't know if he was relieved or disappointed. In the end, he simply felt his body finally relaxing, finally letting go. He stretched out one leg, bent the other at the knee, and felt sleep beginning to engulf him. When Patrick laid his arm at his side, his fingers encountered Jean's. Without hesitation, he carefully captured her hand, holding it. She was already asleep and barely responded to the movement. That was okay. He sighed again, totally comfortable now. He turned his head toward the door… away from Jean. And went to sleep.

A few hours later, Patrick turned on his side. His eyes dragged open long enough to read the time: 4:17. He groaned and pushed himself into a seated position, swinging his feet to the floor. He quickly remembered where he was and turned to the quiet, curled figure next to him in the dark. He stared until his night vision brought Jean more into focus. He reached to finger a curl near her ear. He bent and very carefully left a kiss on her cheek. Then he quietly left the room.

When Jean awoke, it was early but not quite dawn, and it was very quiet. She got out of bed. When she left her bedroom, it was obvious that Patrick had not only managed to get up and dressed without her acting as an alarm, but he'd already left. Quiet, as he'd promised, so as not to awaken her.

Jean's disappointment squeezed tightly around her, constricting her heart for…a beat. He'd been so neat, so careful not to leave any hint of his presence from the night before: linens folded, as was the pullout. How did she not hear him moving about? How did she not hear him close the apartment door with its distinct structural *click* sound?

How could he not awaken her anyway, to say goodbye?

She'd only gotten about three hours of sleep, but there was no chance of her going back to bed now. She walked through her living room and spotted her yearbook on the rocker seat. She was taken aback. Her yearbook?

Jean picked it up and sat down in the chair, wondering what he'd seen, what he might have been looking for. She flipped through the pages, and it automatically opened to the portrait page that held her image. There was a torn piece of paper with text that looked like part of some internal notice from the station, marking the page. Jean turned it over. It contained a brief message. *A*—followed by a rough outline of lips forming a kiss, followed by—*for you.*

A (kiss) for you.

CHAPTER 8

Okay…I need someone to volunteer to stay a few extra hours today. I know it's Friday, but the deputy mayor is doing a stand-in for the mayor for a last-minute meeting at police headquarters. We work at the pleasure of the mayor. Jean, I know I can count on you."

Brad Clark was about to move on to the next item on his must-do list.

"I can't."

He turned back to Jean, genuinely surprised. "What do you mean you can't?"

"I know this meeting is last minute and things happen. I'm sorry, but I have confirmed plans for tonight. I have to get home."

"If it's for a hot date, it won't count."

"I'm having dinner with my father. He's in from out of town."

Brad sighed dramatically. "You're forgiven."

There was mild laughter among the half dozen other staffers, but someone else did speak up to accept the last-minute assignment. It had been a particularly difficult day that included an unexpected demonstration outside city hall and a fight breaking out between two opposing factions of the demonstration. Crowds, traffic, and madness ensued, and a dozen or more police officers were needed to restore order. It was only in the last few hours that the situation had been dealt with and things were pretty much back to normal.

Jean had her own last-minute surprise developments to deal with. Her father was coming into the city and wanted to take her to dinner. They had not spent any time together since the previous March, when she'd flown out to LA for his birthday. That had been special because it had been just the two of them. No sharing of Seth Travis's time with a current girlfriend or important last-minute work.

When she'd gotten the voicemail earlier that day, she'd hoped it was Patrick. His business trip out west had gone on for three days, two days longer than he'd expected, and now he wasn't sure what his schedule was going to be like once he got back. But they had exchanged a few text messages, and Patrick had called twice.

She also didn't want to admit that she had been rattled once when, catching a brief sports update on the news, there was a video clip showing Patrick being interviewed before the start of a game somewhere, standing with a pretty brunette sports reporter. She shared with the audience that she and Patrick used to work together…and it had been an exciting, fun working relationship.

Jean wondered how close a working relationship. But also was not sure if she and Patrick had now known each other long enough for it to count as a relationship. What was it now? What did she want?

Her cell phone toned, and she answered on the first chords.

"Hey, Daddy."

"It's me."

"Mom. Hi. Sorry about that."

"Have you heard from your father?"

"Yeah. He contacted me that he was coming into the city. We're supposed to have dinner tonight. But it's getting late and I haven't heard from him."

"I was calling to tell you he might be in the city."

"You knew that? How come?"

"Your father and I do keep in touch, Jean. We've always been on good terms."

"Because of me."

"Well, of course. That's part of it. I don't have much else to say. I just wondered if you'd heard from him."

"Any reason? What's going on?"

"Nothing, Jean. Have a nice dinner with your father. We'll catch up soon."

Her father had not said exactly when he would arrive or where they might go for dinner. Jean knew he was just as likely to call and have her meet him somewhere…or be late. But by seven thirty, she had still not heard from him, and he wasn't responding to her texts. She was more concerned than annoyed. Two hours later, she was vegging in front of a news magazine program, ready to bag the idea of dinner, ready to go to bed, when her intercom buzzed. The front desk announced a visitor.

"Tell him I'll come down."

"He says he wants to come up."

"Fine. Send him up."

Perhaps this was better. She and her father could have a chat for a little while, and she might persuade him to forget dinner. She no longer wanted to go out.

Jean was ready with a tart but amusing greeting for her dad when the bell rang and she opened the door.

Patrick stood on the other side.

He had luggage and looked like a weary traveler. Jean's mouth fell open, and she stared as if he was an apparition. And her stomach roiled.

"Maybe I should have called first?" he said with a charming but hesitant smile. His smartphone was in his hand.

"Hi. What are you doing here?" Jean breathed out, her gaze locked on his.

He looked exhausted.

Patrick stepped into the doorframe. Jean took a step back, unable to find her voice.

"I should have made a reservation," he joked weakly. "Is there room at the inn?"

Jean's brief laugh sounded strangled, even to herself.

"I…I…" She shook her head, bewildered.

His smile began to fade. "Bad move. No problem. My car is still waiting out front…" He began pressing buttons.

"No, no. You don't have to do that. Come on in."

Jean moved, giving Patrick space to enter. But he continued to stand and stare at her, judging if she was sincere.

Jean blinked, clearing her head. "It's okay, Patrick. I'm sorry I seem so…so…"

"Surprised? That's what I was hoping for. But maybe this wasn't such a great idea."

Jean's shock was wearing off, to be replaced with a heady rush of joy. That Patrick was here rather than there, or anywhere else, was enough.

"Cancel your car," she said.

"Are you sure?"

Oh my god…Daddy!

Jean's mind whirled through a number of ways the evening could end. She quickly picked the one she most wanted.

She nodded. "Yes."

Patrick connected to a number on his phone. "You can go. I won't be needing you."

There was a leather mailbag tote over one shoulder and a small wheelie case at his side. Jean took the roller from him and pulled it inside. He followed, closing the door.

They faced each other, certainly not as strangers. The moment was so spontaneous that there was no time even to think what to do. His very presence sparked anticipation in Jean. There was an eerie quiet, the air charged around them.

"I didn't expect to be gone almost half the week."

"You were on assignment."

"By Tuesday all I wanted was to be back here. With you. *Here.*"

The declaration took her breath away.

"Really? Why?" she asked.

He looked puzzled. "Haven't you noticed I've been plotting and scheming like crazy to get us together every chance I could? I wanted to spend more time with you."

"Well…to be honest I wasn't exactly sure what your intentions were."

"No?"

"I mean, after that first meeting everything just sort of…kept going, and then…"

"Where did you think it was headed?" Patrick asked.

Jean met his gaze and blinked. "We seemed to be coming together. You know. Like when we were in high school. Except for…"

"Except for the hot, crazy kissing and holding each other. No, Jean. That was not the path to friendship. We were already friends. I'd hoped it was the path to something much more. Something new. Better." He took a small step closer, holding her gaze. "The night we got caught in the rain and came back here couldn't have been more perfect. I was hoping… Then I got that message and had to leave early. I'm pretty sure you were feeling the same thing about the two of us. Am I wrong?"

The question was not plaintive but needed a definitive answer.

"No," she said almost in a whisper. "I've been waiting to see if you noticed that this is not like when we were in high school. I'm not sixteen anymore."

"Still a little afraid of me?"

Jean shook her head. "I was never afraid of you."

Patrick let the mailbag slide from his shoulder. It landed on the floor with a thud. They both moved at the same time and, in one smooth stride, walked into one another's arms, their lips meeting and locking with an erotic intensity that forced their bodies together.

Jean could feel that, finally, there was nothing cautious or tentative about their actions. This was exactly what they'd both been wanting, and they were now of the same mindset. Their youthful history notwithstanding, the time was finally right to move past it. She was more than ready.

Their embrace was quickly infused with an urgency that made their breathing heated and heavy. The only other sounds were the quiet, moist meshing of their lips and tongue, of one low, broken whimper from Jean. It was not a sound of desperation, but surrender. She never thought to have this moment...*any* moment...with Patrick. His hand low on her back held her while he pressed his hips against her, his desire hard and obvious. He suddenly stood still, breaking the kiss, his slumberous gaze searching hers.

"Maybe I'm rushing this..."

Jean put her hand over his mouth, silencing him.

"It's been years, Patrick. That's not rushing. You never tried to kiss me when I was sixteen. You never handed me some lame line or made promises or played me. But I did wonder what it would be like if you kissed me..."

"I can do that," he murmured, bending toward her.

Jean knew that Patrick could not make up for lost time, but this was so much better because they had been forced by circumstances to wait. *Things happen when they're supposed to happen.* He pulled her back against his chest and picked up where they'd left off. The feel of Patrick, the taste of him, was intoxicating.

Patrick deftly braced one foot against the other to get his shoes off. Jean was already barefoot. She pulled down the side zipper on her black knit pants. Then she went to work finding the hem of his polo shirt and standing on tiptoe to pull it over his head. He had to bend to help her. Jean tossed it on her club chair. Patrick assisted the striptease by sliding his hands inside the waistband of her underwear and pants and pushing them down Jean's hips and thighs. She kicked her way out of the legs, standing momentarily bare from the waist down. She peeled off her silk print top and made swift work of removing her bra.

The removal of the rest of Patrick's clothing was quick and efficient. They allowed themselves to stare and study and appreciate the effect of standing naked before each other. Patrick was in full erection. Jean's breasts were small but sweetly perky and round. The nipples were engorged and stiff. Patrick shook his head, a bemused smile growing on his lips, silently taking in her beauty, unfettered and, yes, exotic. Her skin had a tawny, pale bronze glow. Jean's hair was mussed and wild around her face, falling into her eyes. He reached out to gently brush back the wavy strands from her face, his gaze settling for a moment on her full lips, parted and moist. They were beyond being coy about their need.

Jean took his hand and walked backward, carefully maneuvering around the love seat and into her bedroom. She hastily pulled the coverlet from the bed before sitting on the edge and scooting into the middle. She lay back wanton and open, her breathing causing her breasts to rise and fall. She raised a bent knee in an unconscious centerfold pose. She patiently waited while Patrick thoughtfully prepared himself before climbing next to her, immediately lying half over Jean as he began to kiss her again, deeply and with slow, thorough intent, until she appeared languid, the desire pooling between her legs. There was a roiling, spiraling buildup of tension in her body. She waited for Patrick to ease it away.

The room had only a bedside lamp turned on, allowing for them to watch each other's expression, the caressing of their hands, exploring of warm fingers in sensitive, tender places. Patrick watched with fascination the slight blush to Jean's cheeks and the warm glow of her skin.

Patrick's mouth held Jean totally captive until he knew she was so ready she might come just from his slow touch. But it was just a warm-up for what Patrick had in mind. While controlling her mouth with his, he shifted his body to the side, leaving Jean on her back, the length of her body exposed. Patrick let his hand gently massage a breast, rubbing the dusky nipple with the pad of his thumb. She broke the kiss to gasp, to moan quietly. But he didn't allow her a break, taking her mouth again, his tongue playing erotically with hers.

Patrick drew back to stare into Jean's face. Her hair fanned out like a lion's mane, her lips even fuller from his kisses. Her eyes were drowsy and sparkling with passion. Jean laid her hand along his cheek, brushed her fingers over his hard chest where the flat layer of hair felt like silk.

"Okay?" he whispered, his breath feathery and warm against her lips.

Her eyes drifted closed and she nodded.

Patrick lifted his body enough to move into position over hers. The weight of his chest and stomach melded them together, and Jean lifted her knees to make room for him to press even closer. His entry and Jean's maneuvering to meet him was exactly as nature intended. And as he'd always imagined. He held his breath and closed his eyes, savoring the moment.

Jean suddenly contracted her muscles, and he almost lost control as she tightened around his penis. Patrick grunted and gritted his teeth, willing himself not to give in to the sweet release he knew awaited. He moved slowly until they found the rhythm to rock and gyrate together smoothly. His hands gripped Jean's hips to hold her as he withdrew and advanced to her breathing. Finally, there was no help for the urgency that was building, no point in the continued heavenly torture until she drew in air...and held it. Her back arched, and Jean let it out in a long, sustained groan that ended in a soft sigh as she came, pulsing her release around him for long moments.

With heartfelt relief, Patrick let himself push a little deeper into her until the delicious agony of his own climax consumed him. Jean wrapped her arms around his back and held him close until the ride ended. He couldn't move, knew he was like dead weight on top of her. But she ran her hands through his disheveled hair, planting little kisses on his face, his shoulders.

Patrick smiled. The fantasy of what it would be like to be with Jean, like this, seemed too good to be true. It was a good thing that liking her so much, and his own overwhelming sense of what was the right thing to do, kept him from putting the moves on her in high school. It was a good thing she never seemed to show much interest in him beyond their study time together. It was more than amazing that Jean did now.

Patrick slowly withdrew from her, wincing as the last bit of pleasure was squeezed from him. He lay on his side and pulled her against him, kissing her forehead and smoothing her damp hair from her face.

"Wow," he croaked. "Who knew?"

He loved that she burrowed her mouth and nose against his chest. He could feel Jean smile against his skin.

Thank goodness that fate saw fit to bring them together again, maybe finally fulfilling some sort of unlikely destiny.

—

The phone was on silent, but it was the repetitive *wuzzz* of the cell phone that awakened Jean. She carefully fumbled on the nightstand until she located the device. There was no chance of slipping out of bed. Patrick's breathing signaled that he was sound asleep, but he was spooned closely behind her. He didn't move when she answered, trying to keep her voice quiet and low.

"Hello?"

"Honey, I'm so sorry. Did I wake you? Of course you went to bed. I guess you gave up waiting for me."

"It's okay, Daddy," she tried to whisper.

Jean knew her father especially loved when she still called him Daddy.

"Are you all right? I got really worried when I didn't hear from you."

"Well…" Seth Travis chuckled. "I'm here on business on someone else's dime. First, I got in late. I missed my scheduled connection out of Chicago. Then there was a screwup with my hotel. I was about to give up and make my own plans when they found me a room. A suite, actually. I did try to call. You weren't answering. I figured you got busy…"

Jean felt Patrick's rhythmic breathing against her neck, but he didn't awaken.

"I'm sorry. It wasn't plugged in. Sometimes I forget."

"Do you think we can still get together this weekend? I hate to come this far and not see you."

"Sure. When?" Jean asked.

"How about Sunday for brunch? Then I can head right out to the airport."

"Okay, where?"

"You can meet me at my hotel. Or I can come out to Brooklyn. I remember there are a couple of nice places near you. What would you like?"

"Daddy, can we talk...tomorrow night?" Jean whispered.

"Good idea. Again, sorry about tonight. Looking forward to seeing you, Jeannie. Love you, honey."

"You too, Daddy. Night."

The phone was suddenly taken from her hand and simply placed on the nightstand by Patrick.

"That was my father," Jean informed him.

"I got that. I take it you had plans with him before I arrived?"

"Yes, but he never called to confirm, and then you got here."

"I'm glad I got here first."

Me too, Jean sighed.

Patrick began nuzzling her neck, her ear, kissing her nape. Jean couldn't help wiggling against him as his gentle caressing became titillating and amorous. Immediately her body was responsive. His hands became busy, roaming to stroke and glide over her skin. His penis grew hard against her back. She drew in a deep breath, swallowed it. Patrick, fully awake, moved away, but only to ease Jean onto her back. He bent to clasp his warm mouth over a breast, to let his tongue tease around the nipple, causing it to stiffen. He stopped to regard her, his gaze questioning.

"What if your father had called earlier? Or showed up after all?"

"I...have no idea. And it doesn't matter right now..." she murmured, falling quickly into a euphoria of physical sensation.

"I guess it would have been awkward," Patrick theorized. His hand had gently begun kneading the soft flesh below her navel. His hand slid lower, the fingers trailing through the curly hair.

Jean's ability to focus was severely challenged, as she tried to respond lucidly while Patrick's lovely exploration between her legs became a serious distraction. Her hips began to move to encourage him. He leaned to kiss her, sabotaging her thinking even further. She was deep in the delirium of passion, her hips rocking against Patrick's fingers.

He pulled a kiss from her parted lips. "No. It doesn't matter right now."

Jean remembered nothing more as she reached for Patrick and a little cry was torn from her throat and her climax turned her body to undulating jelly.

Patrick barely waited until she'd recovered before settling himself between her legs, effortlessly sliding all the way home. It was his turn and Jean welcomed him. His own needs overrode any other coherent thought, and he began to move with great pleasure against her.

—

Jean awoke the next morning to find herself alone in her bed. It was a little before noon. It was quiet. But the bedroom door was wide open. She sat up, and every movement of her body attested to the activities of the night before…and early morning.

She closed her eyes, relaxing, letting a wave of contentment wash over her. And, just for a surprise moment, Jean conjured up an image of Ross, and a memory of them together in those heady days of late courtship and becoming engaged. She'd been happy then. She'd made the right decisions then. Until Ross had blown it up with a humiliating and stereotypical move. It had crushed her at the time, and as her mother so sagely advised, maybe she and Ross were never meant to be.

It had been more than two years since her broken engagement, and she'd enthusiastically chosen to break her intimacy fast with Patrick

Bennett. Jean smiled. She didn't have one single regret. She felt the rich emotional sweep of a second chance placed before her.

"Patrick?"

Immediately there was movement from the other room. In seconds, Patrick appeared in the doorway. He'd pulled on his briefs. His hair was a little tousled, and a light layer of facial hair sprouted on his jaw, chin, and upper lip. He gave her a slow, crooked smile, watching her as she arranged herself against the pillows, pulling the top sheet over her chest. She patted the space where he'd slept beside her.

"You're awake. It's about time," he mused, coming to join her.

"I had a very busy night," Jean responded, making him chuckle.

"We're not done yet. I have plans for us later today. I made a few calls to set everything up."

"That sounds like you're not going to tell me what those plans are."

"You're right. Now I know you're not a fan of surprises, but I can almost guarantee that you're going to love this."

"Um. We'll see."

He plunked himself down on top of the linens, sidling close to her. He lifted his arm so Jean could come even closer to rest on his side. She finally noticed he was holding a book. She twisted it so she could see the cover.

"That's my yearbook. What is it with you and my yearbook?"

With the book resting on his lap, Patrick began browsing through the pages. "I'm curious. I wanted to see if there were school pictures of you."

"Not many."

"Enough."

"Why are you interested now? You have the real thing right next to you." She glanced into his eyes.

He planted a quick kiss on her mouth. "Yes. At last."

"What does that mean?"

"Exactly what you think it means. Isn't it interesting that after all these years we find ourselves together? Don't you think maybe it's fate?"

"Or fairy dust?"

He laughed. "I like that."

He flipped through the yearbook pages.

"You were in the drama club?"

"Behind the scenes. I helped with costume changes between acts. I helped get a lot of the props."

"You should have been one of the actors onstage."

"Thanks. But I'm a terrible actress. I didn't want that kind of attention."

"Okay. I get that. You're better at other things. Thank goodness," Patrick drawled with meaning, giving her a warm, personal look. He turned a few more pages and pointed.

"That's Mr. Spencer. He's the math teacher who put us together so I could, maybe, get through the senior final exam."

"I have a surprise for you, Patrick. You would have passed that test without my help. You knew more than you thought you did."

"Maybe. But then I'd never have gotten to spend all that time with you."

"You didn't mind?"

"Not at all. I liked being with you. And, believe it or not, I actually did learn a few things. So…if I never said it before, thank you."

"You're welcome."

They kissed, a gentle sign of agreement.

"How come I don't see you in any of the senior prom pictures?"

"I was there."

"Were you?"

Jean heard the change in Patrick's tone. It was…anticipatory. It was curious. As if he was going to be told something he wasn't going to like. He'd already graduated. Why would he care?

"I went with a guy from my lit class, Jeremy. You wouldn't know him."

"Were you dating?"

Jean chortled. "Not Jeremy. Not anyone, really. The boys in my classes… I don't know if they were really interested beyond…you know…looking to score. Mostly more interested in knowing what I was. Like, they knew I wasn't white, and maybe that was important. Was I Latina? Was I half Italian or maybe part Pakistani? They couldn't figure out what box to put me into."

"Assholes."

"Ignorant."

"So, tell me about this guy you went to the prom with."

"Jeremy is gay. He got bullied, of course, but he was actually pretty strong. He could fight back and put up with a lot of horrible things said about him. The other kids learned to leave him alone. He had a boyfriend he wanted to bring to the prom, but…"

"It wasn't ever going to happen."

"Right. So he asked me to go with him. I always got along with Jeremy. I liked him. I said yes. The way I saw it we were both 'others.' He was a talented artist and very funny, and I thought it would be fun."

Patrick freed his hand so he could stroke her hair, press her head to his shoulder, kiss her forehead.

"How did that go?"

"Great. There were no problems. We danced all night. I think some of the other girls were jealous. My mom told me to invite anyone I wanted back to the house for breakfast the next morning, and that's what I did. Me and Jeremy and maybe three other couples. It was very cool, Patrick. I don't think I would have gone to the prom otherwise."

They were both silent as he continued to turn pages, Jean looking with him, reviewing the last year of school.

"I wished you'd gone with me," he said quietly.

"With you? Where?"

"To my prom."

"But you never asked me," Jean whispered.

"Didn't your mom tell you I asked her if I could take you?"

Jean turned to regard him, sliding her hand and arm across his bare chest to hold him lightly. "No. She never did. I only found out shortly after you won the lottery and she called me about the picture of the two of us that appeared in the paper."

He was confused. "And she never told you?"

"No. Maybe she thought that once she said no that would be the end of it. Why didn't you ask me first? I would have said yes."

"And what would you have done if your mother still didn't agree?"

"I would have found a way to change her mind. I would have gone with you anyway. Who did you take?"

Patrick closed the book and bent to drop it on the floor next to the bed. He turned to her, encouraging her to slide down with him until they were lying flat, side by side. His hand rested on the sheet covering her breasts.

"I didn't go. I pretty much knew before graduation that you were the only one I wanted to take. We'd spent a lot of time together, Jean. I feel I got to know a little of the real you. Not the school social version. I liked what I saw. I felt really comfortable with you, like you knew a lot about me too. I wanted to take you and be uncomfortable in a rented suit. I wanted to bring you a flower to wear on your dress or wrist. I wanted to come and pick you up at your house. I wanted your mom to see you were safe with me. No funny business. I wanted to hold your hand as we walked to my car…and for the whole night. I'm not a great dancer, but I knew I'd get to hold you during the slow numbers. That's what I wanted."

Patrick's fingers curled over the edge of the sheet and slowly began to pull it down. Her breasts were exposed, and Jean knew her nipples had stiffened with the growing desire stimulated by his words, his wishes.

"Patrick," she whispered but got no further. There were a lot of things she wasn't going to voice.

He kissed her gently, merely an introduction, a head start. He pulled the sheet away, laying her bare, and shifted atop her, wiggling to settle them both comfortably onto the mattress. Jean ran her hands through his hair, holding his head and forcing Patrick to kiss her in earnest.

Suddenly Jean heard a growl. She felt a quivering roll of his stomach. They broke the kiss and stared at each other and quietly began to laugh.

"The 'urri upps,'" Patrick murmured.

Jean nodded.

"But first…" he said, going back to kissing her and beginning everything it would take to bring them together again for another round of mutual satisfaction.

Jean reached as far as she could to help him out of his briefs and sighed deeply with the sheer joy of skin-to-skin contact again, of his penis resting on her groin, of Patrick lifting to seek her entrance, and then of the slow dance that came so naturally, and meaningfully, between them.

CHAPTER 9

Jean stood patiently while Patrick worked the texts, calls, emails on two smartphones. She'd never been fully aware before that he had two devices—three, if she counted his tablet—until inadvertently eavesdropping on a few of his calls answered her question. One was clearly a business phone, supplied by the station. It was not any different from the one the mayor's office issued to its management. She was management, and she had a phone. The second one was personal. And that was the smartphone Patrick was more likely to be talking on. His station staff texted schedule changes, last-minute announcements or events. But Patrick's personal cell was, to Jean's discomfort, alive and active with what she suspected were former, and maybe still present, girlfriends.

She and Patrick were now waiting outside her building—for what, she still didn't know. Patrick had been closemouthed and mysterious about this great plan he had arranged for them. And, of course, she trusted him. But so far, in just a few minutes while waiting, Jean now knew Patrick was fielding calls from other women. Just two weeks earlier, she would have accepted the flurry of outreach as his life, his business. After all, she and Patrick had only recently reconnected. But now things were different, at least in her mind. What a difference a few weeks made. They were now engaged in a relationship that had, beyond the fun and engaging ability to communicate and phenomenal sex, already changed the stakes for her. Jean was already aware that what she was starting to seriously feel for Patrick was no longer casual. But it was very possible that it was just that for him.

"I'm really sorry about that."

She turned her attention to Patrick, working hard to keep her expression nonjudgmental and glad that she was wearing dark glasses.

"Friend, foe, or work?"

Jean thought he might look a little sheepish behind his own shades, as he slipped the device into his pocket. "Someone I used to know."

"And dated?" Jean asked with what she hoped was mere curiosity.

"Yes," Patrick admitted. "Apparently there's a different definition of 'it's over' than when I say it. Or maybe I'm not clear enough."

"I don't think it's either of those things."

His brows shot up. "Really? What is it, then?"

Jean realized she'd backed herself into a corner. She could either be very serious or play her answer lightly. But how much would she be revealing of her own feelings either way?

"You're popular, steadily employed, reasonably good-looking"—he chortled loudly at that—"a fun date, and interesting conversationalist… and, maybe for some of your former flames, you're the one that got away. Or"—she put up her hand to stop Patrick from speaking—"or, they do get the boundaries and are just being genuinely friendly. They're happy knowing you. They want nothing from you."

Patrick blinked, staring at her as he considered the two options. He nodded and sighed. "Maybe it's a little of both."

"You're not flattered? Women are coming out of the woodwork after you. I'm aware of that."

Now he stared at her with what Jean knew was a serious consideration before shaking his head and reaching for one of the devices again and reading a message.

"No, I'm not flattered anymore. It's a little exhausting…and embarrassing. Here's our ride."

Jean watched as a private car slowed at the curb in front of her building. Patrick opened the back door and held it as she got in, climbing in
after her and closing the door.

"Is it pointless for me to ask where we're going?"

"Totally pointless." Patrick grinned. "But I'll play Twenty Questions
with you."

"Is there a prize if I guess correctly?"

"You can have anything you want, if you guess."

"That's pretty generous."

"That's pretty confident, because you're not going to guess."

The conversation didn't stay on her attempts to guess their destination, but it was surprisingly fun trying. Patrick was absolutely correct.
She would not have even come close to the right answer.

Their car exited the FDR on the East River at Thirty-Fourth Street,
with Jean's curiosity starting to get the best of her. She looked to Patrick
for any hint and found nothing but a calm demeanor and zipped lips.
He was torturing her and enjoying every minute. They were on some sort
of landing platform. A few hundred feet east, and they'd be in the river.

A stocky man of medium height walked to meet them as she and
Patrick exited the car. He was smiling broadly, his arms opening.

"Bro!" the man said with cheerful affection as he and Patrick hugged
briefly and went through a series of hand clasps and fist pumps as she
witnessed among males everywhere.

"Hey, man! Good to see you," Patrick said with equal pleasure.

"If you'd waited any longer to reach out to me, I'd have been on a
walker!"

The two men roared with laughter, as neither of them looked like that
was likely to happen. They were two fit men in their prime. Jean stood
watching the reunion, enjoying the display of friendship between them.

Patrick turned to her, extending his arm to urge her forward.
When Jean approached, Patrick placed his hand possessively around her
shoulder.

"This is Jean Travis. I think Jean and I have known each other almost all our lives."

Jean grimaced and smiled at the other man. "He's exaggerating."

"Well, since high school. Aaron Jacobi…a.k.a. AJ."

Jean shook hands with AJ as he welcomed her to the East Side Heliport. Only then did Jean realized there were several helicopters of varying sizes parked on the tarmac. Nearer the entrance to the highway was a low, almost hidden building that was discreetly labeled *Reception Lounge.*

"Welcome, Jean. Have you ever ridden in a helicopter before?"

"No. Is that what we're going to do now?"

Aaron glanced at Patrick. "I've been sworn to secrecy, so I'll leave Patrick here to fill you in." He shrugged. "He said it was a surprise. I'm just going in to officially log the flight, and we'll be on our way."

Jean watched AJ jog away, and turned to Patrick, who stood grinning like a Cheshire cat.

"Can we start the Twenty Questions over?"

Patrick shook his head. "Nope. But you have nine more guesses. Look, don't work so hard at this. Relax. Enjoy the experience. I promise it's not going to hurt and we're not leaving the country."

Aaron was back in a few minutes and walked them to a helicopter that looked like it was brand-new. Jean stopped in her tracks and glanced at Patrick, her mouth dropping open. "You didn't… Don't tell me you bought…"

He burst out laughing. "My garage isn't big enough, I don't fly, and it's a pure high to be able to rent now and walk away later. Besides, AJ has been after me, literally for years, to come fly with him."

"How do you know him?"

"Farm team."

"Do you know anyone you didn't meet playing sports?"

"Of course. You," Patrick said, his voice low, his smile warm.

Jean returned the smile but was glad her sunglasses hid the creeping blush. "And is he the only one of your friends who didn't go into broad-casting? And don't count me."

"I won't. AJ was not as passionate, or as talented, as some of us. When he didn't make it to the show, he shrugged, turned in his jersey, and joined the Air Force. He learned how to fly, finished a tour in Afghanistan, and came back to establish himself as a private pilot. Pretty cool, eh?"

"Yes, it is."

"So, I had this brilliant idea, called him, and he helped me put it together. And…here we are."

Jean looked around. "Patrick, we're on a tarmac inches from the East River. We aren't anywhere."

"Not yet."

AJ reappeared.

"Okay, folks, all aboard. Are you two sitting together in the back?"

Patrick again put his arm around her shoulders and rubbed her arm, glancing into her face.

Jean said nothing, looking at him. She was finally just willing to let whatever was going to happen, happen and unfold in its own good time. But her excitement was building.

"I want Jean to sit with you, at least for a little while. I want her to be able to see everything."

"All righty then," AJ said. He opened the cab door on the left side and provided a stool for Jean to use to climb into the copter. "Patrick, you take the bumper seat."

Then AJ got into the pilot seat that was on the right side of the craft. He told Patrick where to find two Bose headsets to help cut down the blade noise while they were in the air. They belted themselves in, and AJ got on his headset, communicating with the office. He started the engine, speaking and listening to instructions, reporting readings from his multiscreen console. Jean felt a subtle movement, and suddenly the craft lifted vertically into the air, rotated the nose north, and took off.

Jean held her breath. A silly smile spread over her lips. She could hear both AJ and Patrick through her headset. She now knew that without the headset the air noise would have been deafening. For several moments, she could do nothing but stare through the bubble windshield in front of and below her, watching the ground drop away and turning the city's landscape into a panorama. Before long, Jean realized they were flying up the East River, to the end of Manhattan, heading around the strait toward the Hudson River, and then north.

She felt Patrick's hand on her hair. "How are you doing?"

"Oh, Patrick…" was as far as she got.

"Pretty cool, right?"

"It's more than pretty cool," Jean said in awe. Beside her, she could detect AJ nodding in agreement.

Patrick said nothing more, leaving Jean to fully immerse herself in the experience. She craned her neck left and right and straight down, identifying buildings, neighborhoods, parks, and getting a perspective on what the city looked like from above. Within minutes, she realized they were flying over Riverdale, Yonkers, and quickly Tarrytown. Jean gasped, recognizing the neighborhood where she'd grown up. Her gaze searched for and found a focal point and then…identified her street. And then her house.

"Patrick, that's my house! There!"

Behind her, Patrick was chuckling. "Yeah, I see. This is a first for me as well. And there…I see my old house. The one with the double chimney."

"I found it."

But just as quickly, the copter had flown past, heading north along the Hudson River and the Hudson Valley. Conversation stopped, and she was glad so she could concentrate, absorb, and enjoy what she was seeing. Jean was breathless with the novelty of flight just several hundred feet aboveground, with the knowledge that Patrick had gone to great lengths to give her this experience. This was not a simple trick to impress her. This was an organized effort to give her pleasure. Patrick had actually done far more, as far as she was concerned. He had shown that he was learning a great deal about what pleased her, and he was going the distance to make sure he did that for her.

He was showing how much he cared.

It was late afternoon, and the sun was already in the west. The light had a warm yellowy-orange effect on the ground below, with just a few hours remaining until dusk.

The landscape eventually became more small town and rural. They passed over Albany, and Jean was stunned at how far they'd traveled in under an hour. The copter banked inland, west, and AJ once again communicated with a control point somewhere below. They were approaching Saratoga Springs. Soon they were over an airfield and lowering to the ground.

Patrick and AJ were quickly out of the copter, the blades still rotating over it and finally stopping. Her door was opened, and Patrick was there to help her out of the craft. He and AJ stood talking for a few minutes, laughing over some private observation, while Jean stood alone, bemused and giddy.

"Enjoy your adventure," AJ called out and then got back into the copter.

Patrick caught her hand, leaning to peer into her face. "Are you going to need oxygen? A drink?"

"I'm good, Patrick."

"Good. Because that was just the beginning."

Jean let herself be led and saw a luxury town car waiting just off the landing field. There was an older Black gentleman, the driver, waiting to greet them. Patrick introduced himself and shook the man's hand.

"Yes, sir. You're right on time. Welcome to Saratoga Springs. We have about a fifteen-minute drive. There are refreshments in the basket between the seats in back."

"I appreciate that," Patrick said.

Jean and Patrick got into the back of the car, and within minutes, they were being driven off the landing site onto a road. The driver chatted with Patrick, using the rearview mirror for face-time. She glanced at Patrick.

"What next?"

Patrick wagged a finger at her. "You'll have to wait and see."

Jean sighed, and settled next to him. She glanced out the tinted windows and nodded. "Okay," she responded simply. So far, it was proving to be so much better not knowing.

⟶

Patrick was feeling pretty proud of himself. That was, until a litany of possible complications that he hadn't previously considered made him break out in a sweat. What if Jean had been scared of being closed in, in a low-flying craft? What if she'd suddenly experienced claustrophobia? Or gotten motion sick?

"It's pretty here," Jean murmured.

Patrick sighed and relaxed. She *was* enjoying herself. "I thought you'd really like being able to find your childhood home."

She beamed at him. "Yes, that was special. I never realized we lived so close."

I did, he thought.

They chatted about the helicopter flight, and Patrick filled in Jean with more information on AJ.

"Have you remained friends with everyone you've ever met in your life?"

Patrick chortled and briefly shook his head. "Not everybody. Let's not forget a very angry ex-girlfriend who's suing me. Or an ex-wife who has accused me of ruining her Olympic chances. What else is going to happen?"

"Don't think about it. Don't look for trouble. You'll find it if you do."

"Yeah, you're right."

Jean turned to regard him suddenly through her dark glasses. "Can you at least tell me the reason for all the secrecy? I mean, I admit I'm loving it. It's like being on an active scavenger hunt. Really fun, but it's so…elaborate."

"As long as you're enjoying yourself. The thing is, I just wanted to do something that was fun. And different. Something I wouldn't have thought of doing six months ago. AJ's been asking me. Now it not only seems special; I get to do it with you. Maybe it seems over the top, a little wild, but I can afford it. I don't have to sweat the cost. It's taken me some time to get here, Jean, to figure out it's okay to have a lot of money. I want to enjoy myself. No pun intended, but I wanted you to come along for the ride."

She was quiet for a while, staring out the window before suddenly resting her hand on his thigh in an affectionate gesture. "I'm glad you asked me, Patrick."

When the town car turned onto the driveway of what appeared to be a stately, formal property, Jean's attention was once again piqued. There was a sign that announced the site as the Saratoga Spa State Park. Jean glanced at Patrick, but he was only sparing her the briefest look, a slight smile indicating that, again, he knew he was about to surprise her. She kept her silence, having already learned that he held his secrets—and surprises—very close.

The town car pulled up in front of a federal-style portico, with a small building behind the columns. The driver quickly got out to open the back passenger doors and to assist Jean in getting out. She looked around, trying to guess at the nature of the grounds, confused by the use of *spa* and *park* in the same title.

"This is good." Patrick nodded to the driver.

"I'll be right here waiting for you," the driver said without prompting.

"We'll be back in about forty minutes." Patrick turned to her, holding out his hand. She took it, already excited by the ongoing segments of the day's adventure. And she was feeling ridiculously happy with all of it.

"We're going on a tour that will tell you a little about this place."

"Okay."

His brows rose above his sunglasses, askance. "What? No questions? Have you given up?"

She grinned at him. "I know better. Questions are futile, and you're enjoying yourself too much, keeping me in the dark."

"I promise you won't be disappointed."

"I haven't been, so far."

The driver grinned at them and waved goodbye.

Inside the pavilion, Jean and Patrick were guided into a very small screening alcove with benches. As soon as they were seated, the lights dimmed and a video began. Jean was quickly caught up in the narration of the history of Saratoga Springs and its famous and therapeutic mineral waters. Jean was fascinated by all the ways the waters were reputed to be great for health, skin, digestion, and stress. She and Patrick briefly exchanged glances, and she knew he was thinking that, according to his mother, cuddling also served the purpose.

When they left the pavilion, they were given small disposable cups and a walking map showing the location of actual springs where they could, as the saying goes, "take the waters." They tried only a few, Jean sipping tentatively at the slightly salty, carbonated taste.

"How did you know about this place?" Jean asked. "Why Saratoga Springs?"

"My family used to come up during the summer. Not every summer, and only for a week. But it was pretty, and there're hiking and bike trails all over the place. My dad and I would go fishing; my mom loved the performing arts center."

"What about your sister?"

Patrick chuckled silently and shook his head. "She spent a lot of time flirting with all the cute guys who were summer help at the hotel or lying around the pool hoping to be noticed…"

"It's beautiful up here. I don't think I've ever been in this part of the state. And it's really not that far from the city, is it?"

"No," Patrick said, turning them back toward the entrance to the park. "I thought if you liked it up here, we might try out some other towns. We're not that far from Cooperstown."

Jean tugged on his hand. "That's where the Baseball Hall of Fame is."

"Right," Patrick said in some astonishment.

"See? I do know something about sports," Jean said proudly.

Patrick burst out laughing. "Sorry. Knowing about the Hall of Fame doesn't count. But I am impressed."

They got back into the waiting town car, and the driver, already having his instructions and Patrick's itinerary, drove not out of the park through the open gate, but farther into the interior. In less than ten minutes, they were approaching the Roosevelt Baths and Spa. They had appointments for the mineral baths, twenty minutes immersed in effervescent temperatures of 97 to 105 degrees. They were told that their skin would be smooth and soft as a baby's afterward.

"I guess I could have arranged a cruise for just us on the Circle Line around Manhattan"—Patrick laughed lightly—"and we are pretty much alone. I definitely wanted that."

Jean stared at Patrick for what he'd stated. She never would have thought of anything like this. Not even close. And certainly, she would not have had the means to pay for any of it. It wasn't the cost, whatever it was, that made Jean thoughtful; it was that Patrick had planned and executed a complex and, yes, costly adventure. And he had done so for her.

The baths were supposed to be individualized, to give each client maximum privacy. But Patrick had other ideas in mind. They left their things in lockers, were given plush robes and slippers, and were led to the bath facility. But the moment they had been left alone, Patrick deserted his private lair to sneak into hers. Jean gasped at first, at his audacity, but was tickled by his shameless and daring bending of the rules. And there was no question that it was infinitely more fun to be buoyed and weightless in the hot, steamy water in each other's arms. There was a lot of kissing and laughter, but they thought better of anything else for fear of being interrupted. Which did happen when an attendant came to make sure everything was all right. Panic ensued when Patrick was found to be missing from his bath, followed by sly laughter when another attendant figured out his whereabouts.

"I bet we weren't the first couple to get creative," Patrick said as they dressed. They tipped the attendants and left, once again getting into their private car.

Twilight had settle over the land when their last stop brought them to the Gideon Putnam, the second spa resort inside the park, where they had a quiet, intimate dinner out on the terrace.

Jean was not surprised when prosecco was served with dinner. She was not surprised when, as they shared a rich, gooey dessert, Patrick made a call to arrange for their helicopter transport back to the city. She was deeply moved when Patrick sighed at the end of their meal, smiled warmly at her, and said simply, "This was fun."

"I don't see how you can top this," Jean said in some wonder.

Patrick reached to lightly stroke her arm. "Want to make a bet?"

Jean shook her head. "I don't need to."

She looked out over the land, already shrouded in night, except where the sunlight was turning to royal blue below the horizon, a fantasy end to a perfect day. That was the primary reason for Jean feeling breathless and hopeful. She was always aware that Patrick, being Patrick, could be with anyone. The distant past—and present—attested to that fact. The awareness was never far away, with the constant incoming texts and messages and calls blowing up his devices, that he was popular...and desired. But he was here with her, with the once-blue sky now mostly a midnight black. And faintly, starting to appear overhead, the stars.

—

"I hope you have a good reason for throwing me over last weekend. Must have been quite a date. Anyone I've met?"

"Daddy, I'm sorry."

"Don't be, honey. I guess now we're even. One for one," Seth Travis said.

Jean could hear her father's amusement in his voice. She relaxed but left her office to continue the call in as much privacy as she could find.

"I will only say that the change of plans was so worth it. Sorry. You're not mad at me, are you?"

"Man, you do feel guilty, don't you? Honey, I could never be mad at you. I'm usually the one hard to pin down so we can spend time together. Don't worry about it. I'm probably going to be in and out of New York most of the summer."

"Will you be seeing Mom?" she asked, also trying not to be nosy.

"Probably. I have some things to discuss with her. You and I will get together another time. So, who is this guy?"

"I never said there was a…a guy."

"You don't have to, baby. I recognize all the moves. But I can tell you're not ready to talk about it. I'll stop teasing you."

"It's okay. You don't know him, I don't think."

"Are you going to give me anything to go on?"

"No. It's still too early. And…"

"You don't want your dad sizing him up before there's a reason to? Is that it?"

"Has anyone ever told you you should be a lawyer?"

Jean's father burst out laughing over the phone, delighted with the obvious comparison.

"Love you, honey. I'll talk to you soon."

"Love you, Daddy. Bye."

⌒

Patrick nodded and smiled at the executive assistant outside the station manager's office as he approached her desk. She never asked what he wanted, and Patrick offered no explanation for his sudden appearance.

There was no scheduled meeting or last-minute summons. The woman merely raised a brow of acknowledgment before turning to her PC.

"Go on in, Patrick. But he has an appointment in twenty minutes."

"Thanks," Patrick said. He opened the office door and entered.

The spectacled man behind the desk looked the part of a midlevel manager. He wasn't yet middle-aged but was already starting to paunch. His gaze held a perpetual stare of someone either expecting bad news or being asked to explain something he couldn't. Unlike more combative and ego-driven managers of the past, he'd learned the sure way to keeping his job was by not putting anything in writing he didn't have to, hedging his yeses and noes, and generally staying under the radar.

When he looked up and saw Patrick standing in the doorway, he blinked a number of times and, heavily, sat back in his chair in an attempt to look authoritative.

"Patrick. Hey. What can I do for you? You'll have to make it fast; I have…"

"JoAnn just told me. This won't take long. Five minutes, tops."

With that, Patrick pulled out a folded piece of paper from his pocket. He took his time opening it flat, all the while keeping his gaze on the manager. So far, the man looked curious, but nothing more. Patrick passed the paper over to him.

"I think this belongs to the station, to management, actually."

The man on the other side of the desk carefully reached for the paper and held it gingerly as if something offensive was crawling all over it.

"Are you kidding me?" Patrick asked, his annoyance and disbelief putting a sharp and bitter edge to his tone.

"I don't know what you're talking about," the manager said, slowly examining the sheet.

"I think you do. I didn't ask for any recognition for how great *REPLAY* has been doing. I didn't need an expensive dinner at an exclusive restaurant at which everyone there got to have dinner except me."

Patrick stepped even closer to the desk, peering down at the man, who was still reading every detail of the receipt, while trying to come up with a plausible response.

"I didn't ask to have the regional head of ESPN there to chat me up and tell me what he thinks I can do next for business. And I'm fucking pissed off that somehow, I got stiffed with the bill."

"Well, I can hear that you're upset."

"What you hear is me handing you this expense report and expecting to be *fully* reimbursed, immediately."

"You know I can't just authorize that. I have to…"

"You have to make me happy. I'm giving you the opportunity to make this right by the end of the week. It's not going to go over well if I take this over your head. I really don't want to do that."

The manager put the paper down flat on his desk and stared wide-eyed at Patrick. "No need for that. And I don't like to be threatened."

Patrick kept his voice even and smooth, but no less firm. "Take it any way you want. I don't really care. I'm going to assume the guys upstairs are not really interested in getting rid of me. Are you really willing to jeopardize all the good news with the bad news that I might be fielding offers?"

The man sighed, considering his position and his options.

"Patrick, take it easy."

"I'm going to go you one better. I'm going to give you the benefit of the doubt that no one was trying to screw me over."

"This was clearly an oversight. I'll talk to whoever set up that dinner. Of course you should not have gotten the bill for that. Just…just calm down. We'll get it straightened out."

"I'm glad you agree," Patrick said, his smile frosty and stiff.

"I'll have accounting push this through. You'll get a check by the end of the week. Soon enough?"

"I can live with that," Patrick said, turning easily to leave the office. He checked the time on his cell phone as he opened the door. "See, I told you. Under five minutes. We're done."

———

Patrick sat alone, for the time being, at a table in a corner in the depths of the tavern. He was frowning over two pages of a narrative he'd asked Pete Samuels to send him before they met. But Patrick was restless, his brows knotted as he considered yet another request for money—a loan—from someone he knew and liked. He'd ordered a drink while waiting for Pete, but the throbbing and gnawing at his temples told him it was probably not wise to drink. Patrick was not used to headaches. He wasn't used to ongoing stress and people, mostly friends and acquaintances, constantly asking for something from him. His problem was that he didn't know how to say no.

Jean had said to him at the start that it was okay to say no, to take time to consider the merits of each request and not automatically say yes because the request was coming from someone he knew. But Pete had been upfront from the very beginning about his need. And he might have asked even if Patrick had not won the lottery. Pete had no other talents beyond his ability as a running back in football. But his career had been short, if spectacular. He'd fallen victim to bad judgment, poor decisions, and massive overspending of his then very generous salary from the NFL.

Patrick had heard the sob story a dozen times over. Blaming everything from bad coaches to unexpected accidents and injuries to bad calls on the field. Nonetheless, Patrick empathized with Pete, not because of his bullshit excuses and lack of critical thinking, but because Pete was a genuine good guy, an *I got your back* kind of man he'd want on his team. This was different. Pete's playing days of glory had been over for almost ten years, and his gofer work deep behind the scenes of the station was purely by way of his friendly personality and former teammates wanting to protect him and help him out. But it was to Patrick that Pete had come for help. And he couldn't say no.

When his cell buzzed, Patrick immediately hoped it was Pete

canceling. But he recognized Jean's number, and although the headache remained, he felt, magically, revived.

"Hi, Jean. How are you?"

"I'm good. And you?"

He hesitated but was finally honest. "Working on a monster headache. Gin and tonic doesn't help," he joked. But there was no immediate response.

"Anything wrong?" she asked.

"Long day."

"I'm sorry. This is probably not a good time to…"

"No, no. This is fine. I'm glad to hear from you."

"You sound busy. I hear conversation."

"Not with me. I'm waiting for Pete." Again, it was a long moment before she replied.

"Is that the one with the bright son going to college?"

"Not yet. He's still in high school, but Pete asked me if I could…you know…help out a little with future tuition," he said, his voice trailing off.

"I remember. Patrick, I know you'll make the right decision."

"Thanks," he murmured.

"I won't keep you. I wanted to thank you again for the outing. I can't even begin to tell you how fantastic the whole day was."

"Your call is good enough for me." He briefly hesitated. "On second thought…how would you feel if I…came out later…if it's not too late?"

"Do you want to stay over?"

"Well…I don't want it to sound like I want… We should…"

Jean giggled. "You don't have to explain. I'll see you later?"

"Definitely," he promised, suddenly rejuvenated.

Patrick sat back in the banquette and sighed. He rubbed his temples, eyes closed, trying to ease the sense that his head was about to explode. He checked the time. Pete was not late, but Patrick wished he'd show up. It had been a difficult day. Natalie had tried reaching him again, but he'd not taken her call or any made from her in the past two weeks. And suddenly, out of nowhere, he'd developed an odd posse of bridge-and-tunnel groupies who'd become adept at finding him when he was in the city. He knew he'd have to have a talk with the station assistant assigned to his Instagram account and tighten the reins on what he could and could not post.

"Hey, man. I'm not late, am I?"

Patrick quickly pulled himself together. He opened his eyes to find Pete sliding into the banquette opposite him. Pete held out his hand for the customary bro clasp and greeting.

"You're good," Patrick said, signaling for the waiter.

"I'd like to know why the fuck ESPN had to put a goddamn studio in New Jersey. What a pain it is driving back in."

"Leasing there is cheaper than New York."

Pate cackled loudly. "Like they can't afford it," he said, shaking his head. "I know you don't mind 'cause you seeing some cute thing here in the city."

Patrick lifted a corner of his mouth in resignation. No point in denying it. Besides, his headache precluded excuses and sidesteps.

"You get that paper?" Pete asked.

"Yeah. Just reading it over again. Thanks for making it clear what you need."

Pete shook his head. "No, man. Thank you for meeting with me to talk about it. I'm a little ashamed, know what I'm sayin'?"

"Forget about it," Patrick said, scanning the pages again.

"Wait, wait!" Pete said suddenly, leaning over the table to Patrick. "You'll never believe who I saw last weekend."

"I give up," Patrick said at once. He wasn't in the mood for guessing games.

"Kate."

Patrick stopped, lifting his head sharply to regard Pete, who, given his expression, knew he'd succeeded in surprising the hell out of him.

"Kate. Katie?" Patrick murmured.

"That's right."

"Where did you see Katie?" he asked, not particularly pleased to be reminded of his ex-wife.

"Down in Philly, man. I mean, we didn't talk or anything. She wouldn't have remembered me anyway. I was in the car with my lady friend, my son, and two of his friends. We were at a stoplight, and I glanced out my window, and it was her crossing the street. Looks pretty much the same, but she let the blond hair go."

Patrick had no choice but to listen and was silent, waiting out Pete's report.

"She looks good," Pete said without being prompted, and almost with admiration. "But then Katie was always a looker, you know? She had a kid with her."

Again, Patrick's curiosity got the best of him, and he looked at Pete, expecting more details. "A kid?" he found himself asking. His mouth went dry.

"Yeah, yeah. 'Bout three or four. Little guy. And there was some man with them. Of all places to run into her. Philly, for Christ's sake!"

"That's where her folks live," Patrick filled in automatically. He took another deep breath, shaking off the past and the unexpected churning of his stomach.

Three or four...little guy.

Patrick swallowed, shuffled his papers. It had been longer than that since he and his ex had seen each other.

"Okay, Pete. Let's get to it. Let me tell you how I want to handle this. If you and I can agree on the basics, I'll turn this over to my attorney."

"Cool! This is dope, Patrick. Thanks, man."

CHAPTER 10

H i. I'm Ross Franklin."

"Patrick Bennett."

"Have a seat."

Patrick took the offered hand and liked that the grip was very firm but not aggressive. He was also pleased that Ross Franklin did not take the power seat behind his desk, but sat adjacent to him in the second of two comfortable chairs on one side of the office. There was a small functional table between them.

"It's nice to meet you," Ross said with a polite smile as he placed a small sheaf of papers on the table.

He didn't seem to be in a hurry to get down to business but appeared relaxed and willing to chat. The putting-the-potential-client-at-ease talk.

"This is going to sound lame, but I'm a fan of *REPLAY*. I caught your program last week. Do you really think the Giants are going to get the first-round draft pick this year? Who do you think they're seriously interested in?"

Patrick settled comfortably in his chair. The initial formality he always expected in a business meeting was not present. He gave Ross credit for not being officious. His interest in football talk was real.

"I'm not a betting man," Patrick responded. "I'm comfortable that I know what I'm talking about, but it is show-talk."

Ross nodded.

"I'm not sure the Giants organization is the best place for a top team prospect. If it turns out to be who everyone else is after, I'd say he'd probably develop best with the Eagles."

Ross's brows rose. "I hadn't looked at it that way, but that's a very interesting idea. And it makes sense."

"That's why I get the big bucks," Patrick joked dryly. Ross grinned.

Patrick tried to be subtle in his curiosity about Ross Franklin, studying him from the moment he walked into the office. He quickly knew two things. First, that the financial analyst appeared serious and organized and had done his homework. The second was that he had a strong, authoritative presence, was very professional and personable. And he was Black. Patrick hadn't expected that, but it didn't really matter. Jean had vouched for him.

"I hope you don't mind that I did a little informal background check," Ross stated.

"Not at all. I expected that you'd want to."

"I will say that you are in a very positive and, hopefully, satisfying financial place. You won't have to worry about paying your bills. Congratulations, by the way, on your lottery win."

"Thank you," Patrick answered simply. "Maybe. It's early yet."

"I understand it hasn't been all champagne and roses. You've probably already started to experience the good, the bad, and the ugly after your win."

"I'm starting to find out." Patrick glanced at the papers on the table. He detected a photocopy of an article. "You've been following some of the recent press about me."

"I have. And I will guess that much of it is distorted, written for maximum effect, and to sell papers. Not so many people read newspapers anymore."

"But they do browse the banners on their social media apps. The word still gets out."

"You don't seem to have lost any popularity."

"That I know of. It's still been…difficult."

"Of course."

"I'm still fortunate. Things could be a whole lot worse."

"So the last few months since your win have been an eye-opener."

"That would be an understatement. I need to gain some control. I'm trying to figure out, how do I deal with all the stuff coming at me because I won so much money?"

"I get it. But I was surprised to get your call."

"Why is that?"

"You're fairly high profile, Mr. Bennett…"

"Patrick, please."

"You could have gone to any of the top money management firms in my field. I've never had a sports figure come to me for help. Someone who's really in the entertainment end of public service."

Ever since his conversation with Pete, where he mentioned having seen his ex-wife, Patrick had been speculating like crazy about a possibility that was too mind-boggling to deal with in a single sitting. It had given him a few sleepless nights until he'd finally decided that he needed to pursue the information. But that wasn't part of what Ross needed to know or would even have to deal with.

"Jean Travis recommended you. That was good enough for me."

Ross was studying him, as if he was trying to look beyond the simple statement.

"How do you know Jean?"

"Beyond the surprise factor that she worked in the mayor's office and hosted the public announcement of the lottery win? Jean and I went to the same high school, different grades. Haven't seen each other since then."

"So…you don't really know each other well, do you?"

Patrick shifted in his chair, feeling the sudden need to be cautious in his response. He ran his hand through his hair.

"Small world, the saying goes."

"And getting smaller," Patrick murmured.

Ross continued to study him, pursing his lips. Patrick waited him out.

"Do you have any idea why Jean recommended me?"

Patrick's senses went instantly on alert. It was nothing more than the mention of a connection, but he didn't feel it was a simple question. And he didn't have an answer. He shook his head.

"She told me that you work with her father and that he was very happy with what you've done for him."

"Glad to hear that. I like my clients to be satisfied. I offer what I consider to be sound suggestions and back that up with statistics and annual reports. The client always makes the final decision about where to put their money."

"Good. So what do we do next?"

"Thanks for your confidence," Ross said smoothly. "Let's go through this initial interview session. I'm sure you have lots of questions for me. Why don't we start with basic background facts? Tell me more about your past career and financial situation up to right now. Next, I'd like to see copies of your salary arrangement with ESPN, and what the company has offered in terms of stock options, savings, and retirement plans.

"Then we'll move on to the seventy-five million dollars. That will be our next meeting. I'd like to get an idea of your future plans. Any major expenses coming up. Any liens against you—"

Patrick's knee began to bounce. He quickly caught the nervous movement and stopped.

"—that sort of thing. Has it fully hit you that you are obscenely wealthy?"

"I have my moments," Patrick said honestly, with an embarrassed grin. "And a lot of nightmares."

Ross laughed.

———

Jean heard the excited voices raised outside her office, down a length of the hallway to the left. She glanced up just as two department staffers walked by her doorway in the direction of the commotion. She turned to her boss, Brad, as he left his desk and headed for the door.

"What's going on?"

"I have no idea," he said.

She followed, glancing over his shoulder.

There was a small cluster of staff surrounding someone they all seem to know, chatting with the man with a great deal of familiarity, as if he was a celebrity. A quick tension gripped at Jean as the tall visitor turned his head and she recognized Patrick. After a few seconds he looked up, saw her and Brad, and gave a short nod and wave.

"Did I forget something? Was Patrick Bennett due in today for any reason?"

"Not that I know of," Jean said.

Brad moved forward quickly, his hand stretched out. "Hey, Patrick. Good to see you, man. I'm Brad Clark, PR director for the mayor. I have a serious bromance going with *REPLAY*. Great show."

"I appreciate that," Patrick responded in his engaging professional persona.

The men shook hands.

"I don't believe we had a chance to introduce ourselves when you were last here. Don't tell me you won the lottery again?" Brad looked briefly at Jean.

Patrick laughed easily, but Jean was happy that he didn't give her any particular attention.

"No, I think I've had my share of good luck for one lifetime. Sorry I didn't call in advance. I'm in the city for meetings. I stopped by hoping to see Ms. Travis, if she can spare a few minutes."

"Not at all. I'm in the middle of arranging a meeting myself, so I'll leave you two. *Ms.* Travis, you have a guest." Brad made a grand gesture with his hand to usher Patrick into the office. "I'll let you know when the mayor is leaving for Queens," Brad finished, leaving them.

Jean and Patrick faced each other. She immediately saw a kind of longing in his gray eyes now that they were alone. She tried not to let her gaze mirror his. One of them had to stay focused.

"Trying to surprise me again?" she said in a quiet voice.

"If it means you'll look at me the way you are now, yeah."

"I'm at work. There are people all over the place. The door is open…"

"I know you have a point, but…"

Patrick turned and leaned out the open door. He looked up and down the corridor. There was no one around and few sounds of any kind. He turned back to her and, taking her hand, maneuvered her behind the door while letting it stay open.

"Patrick…" she warned.

He placed a finger over her lips. And then he replaced the finger with his mouth, in a sensuously slow kiss that curled the muscles of her stomach as his tongue searched for hers. But Jean wouldn't let him draw her into an embrace. That was definitely playing with fire. The kiss would have to do for now. There was something deliciously illicit about kissing on the sly, behind a door. At city hall.

Anyone might walk in at any moment.

The mayor.

Their lips separated. Jean moistened hers, holding in his warmth. She moved back into the center of the room. She absently fidgeted with her hair. Patrick followed her, sweeping both hands through his own hair. He cleared his throat.

"I needed that," he murmured. "But I really do want to discuss some business with you."

"You mean, that wasn't just an excuse so we could canoodle in secret?"

"I know how to take advantage of any opportunity presented to me."

Jean gave him a half-sultry smile and returned to sit at her desk. "I'm glad. Sit down. What can I do for you?" His brows shot up at her double entendre. "I mean…"

Patrick grinned at her and then took hold of a very uncomfortable institutional-like chair and placed it as close to hers as the setting would allow.

He grew serious, and as long as there was still no one around, his expression and his voice became personal.

"It's been almost a week."

"It's been two days."

"It's killing me."

Jean smothered a giggle. "You'll survive. You said you have a Peloton. Work it off."

Patrick shook his head and sighed comically. "You're a hard, cold woman."

Jean's smile grew understanding and earnest. "I've missed you too."

"What are we going to do about it?"

"I don't know," she said. "But you can't stay over tonight."

"I can't stay over tonight. Seriously."

They were momentarily silent, dealing with the frustration of the situation and disappointment for the evening.

"So you had something you wanted to tell me?"

"I guess it could have waited. I took a chance coming to your office, hoping that…"

"Yes."

"…I could at least take you to lunch."

"That would have been lovely."

"I had a meeting this morning with Ross Franklin."

Jean smiled, pleased that Patrick was taking her advice.

"Really? How did that go?"

"Well, I think." Patrick shrugged. He didn't seem conflicted in any way about the meeting or Ross. "He knew quite a lot about me. It was a bit unnerving. Like he'd put PIs out on my trail. Like I'm an open book."

"I'm sure he never did that. He made sure he was prepared to see you. That's a good thing, isn't it?"

"Of course, but he managed to dig pretty deep."

"Anything for you to be seriously worried about?"

He lowered his gaze, frowning slightly. His jaw muscle tensed. "I don't think so. Just the usual foolishness of my testosterone twenties." His gaze held hers. "I'd also done my own research."

Jean swallowed, feeling heat infuse her body, flush her cheeks. "Okay."

"By all accounts he's got a great reputation in the field."

"I told you so."

"But there was nothing really personal. Like, is he married? Does he like sports? Is he gay?"

"I'm not sure any of that is relevant. You just want to make sure he's honest, has never been in a scandal or indicted for fraud."

"And I do have your say-so that he's an okay guy."

Jean looked down at her hands, unconsciously clenched into nervous fists. "You do. Maybe you should ask Ross if you could speak to some of his clients."

"I'll think about it."

Jean saw again his personal interest softening his gaze. The business part of his visit was over, but she still felt very vulnerable about information she'd not shared with him. He leaned toward her.

"Mind if I ask why tonight isn't possible?"

"I'm going out to Queens with the mayor in a little while. It's a neighborhood rally, and the mayor is throwing his support behind a candidate for city council. I set up all the local press and media, worked with community leaders. The mayor typically arrives just as he's supposed to speak, and he's out of there in under thirty minutes. Then I take care of reversing the process, making sure the copy is going to be positive on the news tonight and tomorrow. That sort of thing. What about you? Tonight?"

Patrick sighed. "I'm having dinner with 'the boys.' Brian and Pete and some of the crew. My idea. I think it's important to have real down-time to chill, talk off the record, tell dirty jokes or secrets. Women do it."

"Well, we're more evolved than the male of the species in all relationship matters," she teased.

Patrick narrowed his gaze. "You're going to pay for that. Here's a thought. I'm meeting the guys at eight or so. And I'm making sure it's Dutch treat…"

"I think that's a healthy idea."

"Any chance I can come with you out to Queens? I'd like to see the mayor in action. I'd like to see you do that thing you do when you're working."

"You can't be serious. It takes more time to set up and take down than what the mayor will have to say." He watched her and waited. "I…I don't know. I could ask Brad, if you're serious. But I don't want your appearance to turn the event into a photo op or unwanted publicity for you."

"Not what I intend."

"The mayor will not be too happy to have attention deflected away from him."

"Got it."

"Okay, I'll ask."

⟶

Patrick made it easy for no one to object to him tagging along with the city hall team. He had his own transportation and only needed permission to follow the mayor's caravan to Queens. He made no mention of Jean going to bat for him with her boss, in case anyone asked. He could see there was already a lot of speculation about what, exactly, was the nature of their relationship. He and Jean hadn't really defined it. In any case, it was too soon to go public. But the idea made Patrick realize it deserved serious thought.

What was their relationship? What did he want it to be?

It was one thing for him to deflect all the media speculation about almost every aspect of his life because that was the nature of being a public figure. But Jean had never bargained on becoming tabloid fodder. He wanted to protect her from that. Patrick lifted a corner of his mouth at the irony of the situation. The mayor's office and the mayor himself were *always* up for grabs for news copy.

Patrick did as he was told, and enjoyed that no one cared who he was and that he wasn't recognized. The anonymity gave him a kind of freedom that was hard to come by. Besides, he liked discreetly trailing behind Jean and watching her perform her duties as PR assistant director. She was great with the locals in the community, approaching people, smiling a genuinely warm hello, and introducing herself, then asking people *What do you think the mayor should be doing for your neighborhood?*

Jean wore a navy, sleeveless dress that buttoned down the front, paired with a thin red belt. It did two things for her: made her look professional so that she stood out and made her look down-to-earth...so that she *didn't* stand out when that was needed.

She smiled easily but, as was her way, never got too familiar, so the crowd also kept her at a respectful distance, so she could circulate and do her job. And she was just as communicative with her own staff, coordinating who they needed to work with from the community board. She made sure that everything was in order for the mayor's appearance, and spoke with the local precinct commander to make sure there was enough police presence to deter potential outbursts or protests.

It was a lot of responsibility for one pretty, small, amazingly self-possessed woman whose natural comfort zone was staying under the radar. Patrick admired Jean even more, seeing her on top of her game. He also felt a growing satisfaction, a contentment he got whenever he was with Jean. Patrick suddenly considered how important that had become for him.

"You with the mayor's office?"

Patrick didn't think the question was directed at him until he realized there was a tiny Asian gentlemen peering up at him from beneath an umbrella he was using to block the bright summer sun.

"Er...no. But maybe I can help you anyway."

"You look like you someone in charge."

"Thank you. Maybe it's my sunglasses."

The man stared blankly for a moment and then began to laugh merrily as the joke registered. He shook his head. "No, no. You tall. Tall, thin men always in charge. My wife say I not in charge. Too short." He began to laugh again.

Patrick joined in, enjoying the odd encounter. Then he saw Jean approaching, her gaze puzzled by the laughing exchange between him and the man with the umbrella.

"Here's just the person you need to speak with," Patrick said, indicating Jean. "This gentleman wants to speak with someone from the mayor's office."

"Someone in charge," the man corrected, beaming at Jean. "Too pretty. Not in charge. Not the mayor!"

And he was off again in a round of merry laughter.

Patrick met Jean's silent question. *What's going on?*

"I'm sure she can be of help. She knows everything."

"Ooh." The man nodded. "Smart too?"

"Very." Patrick smiled warmly at her. "I'll leave you two. Good luck," he wished the man. He raised his sunglasses so he could wink at Jean.

He walked away, circulating the area of folding chairs set up auditorium fashion, which was filling up with men, women, and children of at least half a dozen different ethnicities. Pop-up vendors and food trucks were kept at a distance from the gathering space and the podium set up for the mayor. Police barriers were also positioned to help control crowds and keep those not sitting from getting too close to the mayor, his staff, the press crews.

He purchased a cold drink from a woman selling frosty bottled water and canned soda from a cooler. He sipped thoughtfully as he realized he was finally beginning to relax a little after the meeting and interview with Ross Franklin and the continuing buzz in his head about his ex-wife. He took a long, cold gulp of his drink, trying to freeze out the troubling thoughts. He found Brad standing alone, reviewing messages on his cell phone and following an agenda on a tablet. "How's it going?" Brad asked absently.

"How often do these events take place?"

"If you're asking the PR office, too often. If you ask folks in the communities in all five boroughs, not enough. There's always someone somewhere who feels left out. The mayor is not paying enough attention to what's going on."

"True? False? A myth?"

Brad sighed. "There are eight and a half million people in the naked city…what do you think?"

"That you're probably not being paid enough for what you do."

Brad chuckled and glanced at him. "Care to put in a good word for the mayor's hardworking team?"

"I try never to get involved in family situations," he grinned. Brad chuckled again.

"So…how are you and our girl Jean making out?"

Patrick adjusted his glasses, glanced around at the gathering neighborhood people, the officials, and police, taking his time to assess the question.

"Is that idle curiosity, or a response to office gossip?"

Brad went back to perusing his two devices. "Okay, guilty. Sorry about that. Jean is really respected, and she works really hard. We all sort of feel a little protective of her, know what I mean?"

"Totally." He met Brad's questioning gaze straight on. "So I would never do anything to hurt that...or Jean. I know I have a profile and maybe even a reputation that comes with my profession. But if she's okay hanging with me, I think that says enough. We've known each other a long time."

"I didn't mean to imply..."

"Yeah, you did, and that's okay. I care about her too."

Brad nodded, then stared at him. "Look, I want to suggest something. The mayor thought it was a good idea to do some sort of charity event, the money collected going into our programs and services for the homeless. Would you consider helping us? It would mean putting your name on it as maybe a sponsor. That's all you'd have to do."

"What's the event?"

"A bike race... Well, it's not really a race. There will be a starting point, and the finish line will be at Battery Park. There will not be winners, but everyone crossing the finish line gets..."

"A T-shirt and a baseball cap."

Brad laughed, shaking his head. "No, no. That's so yesterday. You get a T-shirt and certificate, signed by *the mayor*. And snacks. It's a great cause and a good way to supplement what doesn't come from the city budget. There's always a shortfall for some programs. We do the best we can. By the way, the entire office is signed up to ride, if that makes a difference."

"And each rider or team can solicit sponsorship to see how much money they earn to contribute?"

"Correct."

Suddenly there were shouts and cheers and applause...and a short siren blast of warning from the top of a patrol car. The crowd was ordered to make way for several arriving black Escalade SUVs, carrying the mayor and his staff.

"I have to go," Brad said.

"I'll let you know," Patrick called after him, as Brad hurried away.

Patrick looked around, trying to locate Jean. Not seeing her, he made his way to the front and side of the area set up for the mayor to speak. He stood as far back and out of the way as he could. A Black officer approached, indicating that he should move along, that he couldn't stand where he was.

"No problem," Patrick said.

"Wait. Excuse me…"

Patrick turned back to the officer, who was studying him closely, a slight frown between his eyes.

"Hey. You're the guy from that TV show."

"Want to give me a better hint?" Patrick grinned.

"It's about sports. What's it called again? Oh man. I watch that show. It's…it's…*REPLAY*! That's it." He snapped his fingers a few times. "Patrick…Bennett!"

"Officer…" Patrick held out his hand.

"Jackson. Nice to meet you, man."

"Sorry I'm in the way. I'll go find a seat."

"You have a few minutes. Wow, if I'd known you were going to be here…"

"No one knows I'm here. I'm incognito."

The officer chuckled. "You need to work on that. I recognized you right away. I would love to talk to you about a Little League team I coach. My daughter's team. They could use a little help, if you get my meaning. How can I reach your people? I could send in a proposal or whatever."

Patrick blinked, trying to think fast. Ross had told him point-blank not to say yes to anything right away. Build in *let me think about it* time. He looked past the officer and saw Jean approaching.

"I tell you what, Officer Jackson…"

Jean stood next to him and smiled at the officer.

"Can I help with anything? I'm Jean Travis, from the mayor's office."

"Officer, if you get in touch with Ms. Travis, I'm sure she'll be happy to pass along your proposal to me. Will that work?"

"Awesome! Yes, sir, and thank you!"

Jean pulled a business card from the pocket of her dress and passed it to the officer. "I look forward to hearing from you."

The officer put the card away and turned to the security team surrounding the mayor as he made his way to the podium. There were sufficient cheering and whistles to constitute a real welcome. The mayor, shirtsleeves rolled up, sunglasses on, took his place at the podium. Jean looked at the time on her cell.

"He's right on time. Follow me," she ordered Patrick. "I'm holding a seat for you."

He smiled, getting a kick out of her take-charge persona. He hadn't seen it since the day he won the lottery and they'd walked right back into one another's life.

———

Patrick stood next to his SUV, answering the occasional question about the expensive car, casually perusing the crowds as they slowly left the announcement space and drifted off in all directions into the surrounding community. The food stalls and trucks were packing up, and the police barriers were being loaded onto an NYPD supply vehicle to be taken back to storage. He kept his gaze following Jean as she continued her duties in wrapping up the mayor's appearance in Queens. He had a little time to spare before heading to meet his guys for dinner. In that moment, he would have liked nothing better than to find a way to persuade Jean that they could spend the next few hours together. But he wasn't going to do that.

He watched as she went about doing what she had been doing all afternoon: chatting with several of the community board members and the candidate the mayor had come to support for a place on the city council. She gave directions to staffers, reviewed the itinerary with Brad for last-minute things to be done, and, finally, searched out Patrick and walked over to meet him. The business Jean was starting to turn off, and it was *his* Jean that met him next to his car.

He pushed his sunglasses to the top of his head so she could see his eyes, filled with his warm regard for her.

"Well done. I am in genuine awe."

"Thank you."

"I think you should apply for Foreign Service. Or the State Department. Maybe governor?"

She laughed. "I'm flattered, but no thanks."

"Do you have a few more minutes?"

She glanced toward the rest of her office entourage. They were just about ready to pile back into the company cars and return to city hall.

"Just a few. I have to ride back with them. I'm still on the clock."

He walked around to the passenger side and opened the door for her. Jean climbed in. Patrick returned to the driver side, turning on the ignition so that he could run the air-conditioning. They faced each other, and he let his fingers rest on her shoulder, intimately brushing the skin. They both held their inclinations in check.

"Who do I write the thank-you note to for letting me come today?"

"No thanks needed. I'm sorry I couldn't spend more time with you, but..."

"This is no different than when you came to see me in action at the station. It was a great experience, Jean, and very eye-opening."

"I was concerned you'd get bored."

"Not hardly. And I met some interesting locals. Who was that funny little man with the umbrella? What was that all about?"

She smiled. "Mr. Choi. He's a local force to be reckoned with. He's very funny. But he always gets what he wants by killing you with kindness and a smile. I like him."

"A natural politician. He knows how to work a gathering. What did he want?"

"To make sure his block association is given enough police and sanitation coverage for the Korean Day Parade next month. What was that about a proposal that officer is sending to me?"

"I didn't know what to tell him. I didn't expect a possible solicitation for support of his daughter's Little League team."

"His *daughter's* team? Girls rule." Jean grinned, causing him to laugh.

"I have a hard time saying no, and Ross gave me strict instructions on how to handle people approaching out of the blue wanting me to contribute to something."

"Good. He's got your back."

"Yeah. And then there's your office bike thing that Brad wants to get me involved with."

"I'll have to talk to him about that. He had no right…"

He gripped her shoulder, shaking it gently. "No, don't. It's for a good cause, and I haven't committed to anything yet. He said the whole office was signing up."

"Yes," Jean murmured, frowning.

"What's the matter?"

"I haven't been on a bicycle since I was twelve or thirteen, maybe." She nervously fingered her hair. Patrick grabbed her hand and held it.

"You never forget how to ride a bike," he teased.

"Easy for you to say. You're an athlete."

"If I sign up, maybe we'll ride together. It could be fun."

"Maybe," Jean said, looking into his eyes for more reassurance.

Patrick loved that she might allow herself to depend on him. He wanted her to trust him. He glanced out the windshield. The city hall staff was loading up cars to return them to the office.

"I guess you have to go," he murmured, turning back to Jean. She only waited, watching, until he made the first move.

He leaned in to kiss her, knowing full well Jean wanted him to. Easy task. He'd been waiting patiently all day himself. It was a potently intense kiss, their mouths and lips and tongues communicating far better than words ever could. She combed her fingers through his hair. He cupped the back of her head, holding her to him, kissing Jean with expertise—and need. Reluctant to let her go. Encouraging her to hold on to him as long as possible.

A car horn gave two short blasts.

Their lips slowly separated. They stared into each other's eyes.

"That's me. I have to go."

"I'll call you."

"Yes."

One more quick peck of a kiss, and she was out of his car, jogging gracefully to meet her coworkers.

CHAPTER 11

Good morning, everyone. We're here at what will be the start of the New York Cares Bike-A-Thon, as it's been billed. Organized out of the mayor's office, the goal is to use the Bike-A-Thon to raise money that will support the city's programs and services to help the homeless. For those of you well aware of this ongoing issue, the majority of people in homeless situations are women and children.

"It takes the loss of a job or a serious illness to plunge families into financial ruin, even losing their homes. With me is Jean Travis, assistant director of the mayor's Public Affairs Office, who will be one of the registered riders here today…"

Jean smiled and answered all the questions for the field reporter from one of the networks. She wondered if Patrick was watching. She knew he would have been here, part of the event, and she would have been more than grateful for his company, above and beyond his support for the event. He couldn't make it after all, and his excuse made perfect sense. It was a legal issue with his own network and terms of his contract. He could not be part of any public outreach venture that was not an ESPN effort. And there was a fine-print clause about doing anything during which he could be physically injured.

"Sissy," Jean had teased him when he informed her of the station's decision, even as her heart sank and her disappointment made it race.

"I'll cop to that," Patrick had said to her. "Jean, I'm so sorry. You know I'd be there if I could. If there was any other way…"

"You don't have to apologize. It would have been more front-of-camera and screen time for you. Your groupies could have raced to see who would be riding next to you…or they'd want to share their water bottles with you."

He had laughed uproariously. "I admit it's all very tempting. Other than the great cause this event is for, there is only one other reason I'd ride a bike on the Henry Hudson Parkway, down the West Side Highway, to Battery Park on a hot Saturday at the end June: you and me riding together."

Jean nodded and chuckled agreeably in all the right places, answered all the questions she knew were coming, mentioned all the people who needed to be named for the sponsorship and support of the mayor's initiative. The race was due to start in ten minutes, and her stomach was in a tight tangle of knots at the thought of riding for the next hour or more, some fifteen miles to the finish line.

"I see you're outfitted for the ride. Tell the audience about your gear."

As the camera came in for close-up shots, Jean pointed to the bright turquoise-blue T-shirt with *Mayor's Team NYC* printed across the back. In front was a simple slogan from the program, *Families First*. Over the front was her riding bib with her rider number. She was wearing biking shorts, a black baseball cap, and dark glasses on a neck cord, her hair pulled into a ponytail through the back closure of the cap. Jean pointed out her water bottle, also emblazoned with the team name. All the team registrants were using their own personal bikes or had rented them.

"And there you have it, folks. Everyone fully prepared to take part in this worthwhile event. And if you care to contribute to the bike event, you can go online to…" Jean finished her announcements.

"How's it going?"

She turned to Brad, who, despite his hefty size and weight, looked for all the world like he was about to take part in the Tour de France.

Jean grinned. "Is it over yet?"

Brad laughed. "Yeah, I feel the same way. You'll be fine."

She nodded. There were police officers all along the side of the starting line and would be for the length of the ride. There were volunteers also placed on the route to hand out water as the riders rolled by.

Jean jumped when a foghorn blasted into the air. A cheer went up, and slowly, hundreds and hundreds of bikers began to move. Spacing out, finding their balance and their rhythm, as the swarm of colorful bikes and riders began the journey. Jean let a good number of the more aggressive riders pass her, finding a space among families with children who were sure to be going slower. She wasn't going to race anyone. She just wanted to make it to the end.

Jean concentrated on steering the bike, watching out for death-defying teenagers and the occasional jock just showing off his maneuvering skills. She stayed as far to the right of the bike traffic as she could, just like slow drivers in the far right lane on the road. She was finally below 116th Street. She had a flashing temptation to take the exit and call it a day. Some of the elderly riders and those riding with children were given special dispensation if they simply got tired and hot and wanted to bag the rest of the ride. She had no real intention of giving up. She was tired but had finally gotten to a point where she found the leisurely pace she'd set for herself enjoyable.

Jean's cell rang and vibrated. She pulled her bike over and carefully came to a stop, safely out of the way. She fumbled with her smartphone trying to respond to Patrick's call, covering the earpiece with her hand for a tighter connection.

"Jean? Jean, can you hear me?"

"Yes, hi. It's me."

"Hey. How are you holding up?"

She chortled, using her forearm to wipe a trickle of sweat from her cheek. "Are we there yet? Can I go home now?"

He laughed. "What street are you closest to?"

She looked around. "I think I'm somewhere around Eighty-Sixth Street."

He whistled softly. "Still a ways to go."

"I know. I can do it."

"I know you can too," Patrick said with quiet encouragement. "Listen, just be careful. Take your time."

"I will."

"I'm waiting for you."

"You are? Where?"

"I'm at the finish line. I drove in from the station after my program this morning."

"Oh, Patrick..." Jean said, her voice cracking and filled with gratitude and much more.

"Can you keep that in mind? Can you stay focused? Keep your eyes on the prize."

She chortled. "You?"

"No, silly. The finish line."

———

A little later, Patrick tried again to reach Jean on her cell. The calls had been going to voicemail for about an hour. He doubled his efforts by adding duplicate messages in text. No response.

He began to pace, closely monitoring the bikers arriving at the finish line. Patrick worked at not letting his growing anxiety go off the rails.

Hundreds of riders had already reached Battery Park; the fastest, the most fit, those who insisted that it was a race that had to be won, met cheering crowds just an hour after the ride had officially begun. It was now ninety minutes into the event.

Patrick was beginning to form a plan. He'd figure out how to borrow a bike. He'd ride the streets up to about where he thought Jean should be by now. He'd explain to any NYPD officer who questioned him that his girlfriend hadn't reported in yet, and he was worried. Patrick didn't hesitate for a second over saying "his girlfriend" before just moving on. He'd come back to that thought later. He was going to secure a few bottles of water from the tent set up as Information Central and Administration, and he was going to get started on his own to find Jean.

Patrick thought positively. If anything serious had happened, everyone would have known by now. He'd already asked. Any accidents? Anyone hurt…or requiring an ambulance? No.

"It's a hot summer day. It's the weekend. No one cares when they get here," one veteran volunteer casually assured Patrick when he questioned whether anyone ever went missing in action at these events. "Maybe she got tired and decided to go home. It happens all the time. Relax. If she said she'd meet you here, she will. We've never lost anyone yet," she said, ending on a raucous laugh.

—

"Jean! Hey, Jean!"

The sudden shouting of her name threw Jean off momentarily, and her bike wobbled a yard or two before she regained control. She hazarded a glance to her left but saw no one she knew. In another minute, a streamlined racing bike pulled up next to her, its rider expertly maneuvering the speed and steadiness of his ride. Jean looked again. It was Brian.

"Hi…Brian."

"I didn't expect to see you, of all people, here."

"Well…that makes two of us." Jean frowned "I didn't have a choice. I'm with the mayor's office, remember? This charity event is his brainchild."

"Oh, right…" She watched as he pedaled a few feet ahead and then made a slow, arcing circle back to her side. "I hope you get paid overtime for dangerous work," he said.

He looked so fit and athletic in his spandex biker shorts and top. His hat, a tight-fitting cap with the brim turned upward; his eyes protected with expensive racing shades.

"How are you doing? Okay?" Brian asked.

"Yes. I...I'm fine. What are you doing here?"

"I live in upper Manhattan. Not that far from the GW Bridge. My cousin and his family wanted to do the Bike-A-Thon and asked if I'd join them."

"Where are they?" Jean asked, having regained her pace and balance on her bike.

Brian shrugged. "Who knows? Somewhere along the route. We agreed to meet at the finish line if we got separated. Why are you alone? Where's Patrick?"

They were going at a pace that suited her, and Brian had stopped doing figure-eight circles around her, settling into slow biking next to her.

"He said his contract doesn't allow him to take part in any physical activity where he might get hurt. He wanted to."

"He's right. But I'm not sure I would have let someone I maybe care about go off and do this event alone."

Jean picked up on his tone and felt herself responding with annoyance that Brian would be critical of Patrick.

"You're not in the same position he is. I understand why he couldn't."

He appeared to be staring at her through his dark, opaque lenses. "I think I would have bent the rules a little."

Jean was about to fire back with a more pointed answer about obligations, and integrity and honesty, when her bike hit an obstruction on the pathway, throwing her front tire to the left and causing the bike to tilt sharply to the side. In a panic, she realized she was going to hit the ground, the bike still in motion. She released the handlebars and put out both hands to break the fall. Her helmet slid forward over her eyes. Upon impact, Jean caught her breath, the instinctive reaction to getting hurt causing her mouth to go dry.

Immediately, Brian was off his bike, coming to her aid, as were several other riders near enough to witness her fall. Jean was hauled to her feet, voices around her asking if she was all right. Stunned by what had happened, she could do no more than repeat, "I'm fine. I'm fine." Slowly everyone drifted away as she tried to put herself to rights. She removed the helmet, her black cap coming with it, catching her breath and staying calm.

"Sure you're okay?" Brian asked, a hand cupping her elbow.

"Yes. I'm good."

He looked down the path. "Look, we're almost there. I can see the banner of the finish line. Maybe a half mile. Let's walk it."

She silently nodded. She and Brian walked their bikes for a while before he finally spoke again.

"So am I out of the running?"

Jean's insides twisted. This was the signal from Brian she'd been trying to avoid since the moment they first met. She looked around at the hundreds of bikers, the presence of police and curious bystanders, as if hoping for some miraculous response and solution to the tension between them.

"I don't know what you mean."

"I haven't been subtle about my interest in you. I really hoped we could get to know each other. I'd still like to take you out sometime. Let's see where that goes."

Jean swallowed and took a deep breath. She glanced briefly at Brian and back to the path. "I don't think so. I'm flattered that you're interested, but…I don't feel the same way. I can't imagine what I've done to make you think I would be, Brian."

"Sounds to me like you and Patrick really are more than just friends at this point."

"My relationship with Patrick is none of your business. And if you're a good friend and his colleague, you'll let this go. Besides, I don't believe for a minute that you don't have plenty of women you can choose from."

He chortled. "I'm not going to respond to that. I will say, Jean, that you're different. You know you are. I like that you don't come across with a show. You're not trying to prove anything to anyone. You're quiet. You're confident. You get noticed because you don't realize that's what's happening. And…you're so damned attractive."

There was a certain intimate inflection in Brian's voice that sent a shiver down Jean's spine, even in the sultry heat of the day. She looked ahead and was relieved to see that they were very close to the finish line. She abruptly stopped rolling her bike. Brian stopped beside her.

"I have a translation for that. I'm exotic, and you're curious. You're not the first man who's come on to me for reasons other than my charm and personality," she said sarcastically. "Certainly not the first Black man who's made assumptions about me. My looks are the result of family heritage. They're not magic or special, and I had nothing to do with it. Why are my looks the first thing that drew you to me?" Brian placed a hand over his heart, about to speak. She forestalled him. "I'm going to end this conversation, once and for all. I'm not interested in you in the way you want, Brian. Frankly, your interest is obvious and suspect.

"I know you're betting that I won't say anything to Patrick about this. You're right. There's no need to. You and Patrick are good friends. I believe that. I think you should remember that. I'm going to put this conversation between us under 'bad move,' okay?"

Brian stood staring at her silently. She could not see his expression, his eyes, behind the black lens of his glasses. He shook his head. "If I thought I could change your mind…"

"You can't. Period. The end. Please stop."

"You know, you're wrong about my interest in you. I'm sincere."

"Maybe. Like I said, the most important thing is that I have no interest in you."

Jean proceeded to roll her bike forward again, anxious to have the discussion and the ride over with.

Brian's name was suddenly called, and they both turned to a group of four bikers trying to get his attention. One adult and three young teens.

Brian waved. "You made it. I'll be right there." He turned back to Jean.

His ego was so large, so intact, that he didn't seem put off by her words. He gave her a slow smile, using charm.

"I had to try. But you've made yourself clear."

"Yes, but will that stop you from trying to pursue me?"

He once again straddled his racing bike and pushed off. "You'll have to wait and see."

———

Patrick checked the time on his cell, took a deep breath, preparing to execute his plan. He pivoted and nearly crashed into a small African American woman who was standing in his path, staring at him.

"Sorry," he mumbled automatically, trying to walk around her.

"Are you Patrick?" she asked.

He stopped and turned to her, frowning. "Yes, I am."

A quick, bright smile changed her face from watchful and serious to suddenly open and friendly. It was transformative, giving her brown features, her deep-brown eyes, a youthful appearance. She had the kind of smile that quite literally lit up her face. It was her eyes and her full mouth that finally connected with Patrick. They were familiar.

"I'm Jean's mother. Diana Chambers. Remember me?"

"Yes! Of course." He knew he was staring foolishly, studying her. She looked almost exactly as he'd last seen her…when she'd refused to give permission for him to take her daughter to his senior prom. "Wow! This is amazing. It's been a long—"

"Where's Jean?" she interrupted.

He saw the worry in her eyes.

Good question.

"I don't know," Patrick said honestly, watching the frown reappear on her brow. "She should have gotten here by now. I don't think I missed her. But I'm not getting through to her on her cell. You're here to congratulate her, too, I suppose?"

"She's not expecting me. I wanted to surprise her. It took forever to get here. I had to come by city streets because—"

"Yeah, the parkway was closed for the bikers."

"That's right."

Patrick took hold of her arms. As soon as he did, she seemed to become more composed. She gazed up at him for all the world like she expected him to make everything right.

Diana Chambers was not as tall as Jean, and he realized that if he were to see the two women side by side, he would not take them as mother and daughter. Diana Chambers was slight, dressed in print capri pants with a shell top. She wore a short-brim straw hat that shaded her small face. She looked too young to be Jean's mother.

"There are still a lot of riders out there. Jean is fine. She'll show up soon, I'm sure."

He looked around. There was really no place to sit.

"I'm okay," she said, seeing that he was trying to find a way to make her comfortable. "You don't have to fuss over me."

"I'd appreciate it if you'd let me," Patrick said. "Otherwise I'll have to answer to your daughter."

She laughed lightly, patting his arm affectionately. "I should have let her know I was coming."

"Probably. She's a little weird about being surprised."

"Even as a child. It's nice to see you again. I hope you don't still use that nickname. Trick?" She made a face.

"It was a great handle in school. My mom was very happy when I gave it up."

"Congratulations, by the way."

"Thanks," he said simply, knowing what she referred to.

As subtly as he could, Patrick kept glancing down the path from which bikers were arriving, still hoping to see Jean. His sunglasses hid his distraction from her mother.

"Did you ever forgive me? You know, for not letting you take Jean to your prom?"

"I was disappointed. But I tried to understand. I don't think I can speak for Jean."

"She only found out what happened recently. I thought you'd already asked her, but I caught her by surprise when it came up. I think it's fair to say she wasn't happy with my decision. Things were different back then."

He didn't respond. Was she talking about *her* time, or his and Jean's?

"It was amazing running into her again—" His thought cut off abruptly.

Patrick could see Jean was finally on the path, maybe a hundred yards away. There was a male rider giving her a brief goodbye wave as he pedaled away. Patrick blinked, following the rider until he met up with several other bikers and blended into the crowd. The rider was Brian. He turned his attention back to Jean. She was walking her bike. Had she blown a tire? Had the brakes failed? Her safety helmet was hung around the handlebar. She had a cloth event knapsack hanging by the strings from one shoulder. Her hair was disheveled, her ponytail a little cockeyed and loose.

Is she limping?

That was all Patrick had to see. He called her name. He released Diana Chambers and hurried into the oncoming participants, dodging bikes, riders, and walkers. He stopped in front of Jean, grabbing the handlebars of the bike, finally drawing her attention.

Her cheeks were flushed. Her eyes filled with relief…and, he thought, a rush of happiness at seeing him.

"Patrick…" she said in weak surprise, with a tired smile.

He spontaneously pulled Jean briefly against his chest and then let her go.

"Are you okay? What happened? I was about to come look for you…"

"I'm fine, I'm fine."

"Are you hurt?"

She looked bemused. "I…don't know. I fell. I think maybe I hit my knee." Jean released the bike to his support and looked at her hands and arms. There was a small raw abrasion on her arm and the heel of her palm. A dirt smudge on her chin.

Patrick muttered an oath under his breath, examining her injuries. "Come on. I want someone in the first aid tent to have a look at you."

Jean didn't object. Patrick took control of rolling the bike with one hand, while his other was planted in the middle of her back in support. He kept his pace to match hers, and they finally crossed together over the finish line.

"You made it! Good job." Several of the officials applauded, as had been done for every biker.

There were only a dozen or so well-wishers remaining, all strangers. Jean smiled gratefully at them.

"Jean!"

She glanced sharply at the sound of her name and found the woman waving at her from a crowded field of end-of-event men, women, and children.

"I didn't get a chance to tell you your mom is here."

"And my dad!" Jean added, turning in another direction.

Patrick had no choice but to follow with the bike. He spotted Diana Chambers, who was now standing next to a handsome, middle-aged man. He was white, with short, salt-and-pepper hair that had a tendency to self-part over his forehead. The man spread his arms and enveloped Jean, hugging her close for a long moment before letting her go. Jean turned to her mother, as Diana Chambers also wrapped her arms around her daughter, murmuring concern…as only a mother would do.

Patrick slowed to a full stop some feet away, mesmerized by what was clearly an unexpected reunion between Jean and her parents. It was all the more astonishing as he got to see exactly who Jean was, where she came from. She was not *an other*, but the combination of these two people who provided lineage, history, background, love, and beauty. That's what Patrick had always seen, what he'd known first of all. Jean was beautiful.

Her father separated himself from the cooing women and approached Patrick, hand outstretched.

"Seth Travis. And you're Patrick."

"Yes, sir. I'm glad to meet you."

"Same here. She overdid it," Seth said, motioning to the two women.

"I agree. I've seen Jean in action. She puts her whole self, her whole spirit into everything she does."

"Good observation." He turned back to Patrick. "You didn't ride with her?"

"Couldn't. I wanted to but…my contract with the network prohibits it."

"I see."

"I told her I'd meet her here, at the finish line. I was going to take her for a celebration and…and…"

"Sure. Of course. She didn't know I was coming into the city this week. I wanted to be here to root for her."

"How did you know about this?"

"Di told me. I wasn't sure I'd make it."

Patrick merely nodded. His mind was suddenly abuzz with dots and dashes he was trying to decipher about who knew what when, and from whom. TMI for now, but he was sure he'd work it all out.

"Look, I'm going to interrupt this lovefest and get Jean in to see one of the first aid staff. I think she should be checked out."

"Good idea."

Patrick trailed after Seth Travis and watched as he put an arm around his daughter, rubbing her shoulder, and steering her to him. Seth then stood next to Diana, and they both watched him lead Jean into the tent. Patrick signaled another volunteer and handed off the bike.

"The rider is with the team from the mayor's office. Think you can figure out what to do with the bike and helmet?"

"No problem, sir. I'll take care of it."

Patrick joined Jean inside. It was cool, and she was immediately handed a frosty bottle of water and ordered to sit on a makeshift examining table. She handed Patrick her knapsack and a pretty damaged smartphone. She would have to replace it. The doctor was a young African American woman from one of the local hospitals, volunteering for the day. She asked Jean a few questions while taking vitals, examining her bruises, and manipulating her knee to check for injuries or swelling. Other than some tenderness from the impact of her fall, Jean was, mercifully, okay. At the end of the examination, the young doctor leaned against the side of the table next to Jean to offer her assessment. She had the right bedside manner to be comfortable and friendly with her patient, while at the same time speaking authoritatively about Jean's condition.

"Just a few bumps and bruises. I suggest an ice pack tonight for your knee, and keep it elevated. That will prevent any swelling later. You're a little dehydrated, so plenty of fluids. Preferably not wine…"

Jean smiled weakly, exchanging looks with Patrick.

"If the knee still bothers you by Monday, you might check with your doctor about getting an X-ray. Overall, I'd say you're just overheated, a little banged up, and pretty tired. Go home and go to bed. You'll feel better tomorrow, but you're probably going to be sore. How long since you've been on a bike?"

"A very long time," Jean admitted. "I guess I'm lucky I only fell once and didn't do serious damage."

"Next time I suggest doing only half of one of these events. You want to be supportive of the cause, but not at the risk to your health and body."

"Hear, hear," Patrick murmured, high-fiving the doctor.

She stared at him.

"Are you Patrick Bennett?"

"You watch *REPLAY*?" he asked.

She shook her head, grimacing. "My boyfriend does. But I remember you. I pretend to be interested. You know."

Patrick grinned at her. "I know."

"I promise I won't tell anyone you're here."

"I appreciate that," he said, helping Jean down from the table.

They left the tent and stopped outside the entrance as they caught sight of Jean's parents. Seth and Diana were standing very close together, deep in a whispering conversation and not particularly aware of anyone else around them. But Patrick couldn't help but make note of what an attractive couple they were. Whatever had made it difficult—impossible—for them to consider marriage when they were young had perhaps become a non-issue with the years.

Seth was leaning a little over Diana, and she gazed up at him, smiling in her bright, open way. Patrick watched Jean for a reaction but he couldn't tell anything from her silence or her expression. He was also coming to full awareness that Jean was the product of these two people from different backgrounds who'd loved each other enough to have her. And Jean was someone he'd come to care for long before that reunion at city hall more than a month ago. Knowing as well that what he felt for Jean was significantly more advanced now than his high school fascination.

He touched her arm to get her attention. "Should I offer to take us all to dinner…or would you prefer bagging it tonight and going home?"

She hesitated, thinking.

"Or I can keep you with me, keep an eye on you tonight, and you can send your folks to wherever it is they have in mind. Your call."

Jean watched her parents in conversation before turning again to him.

"I should spend a little time with them. They both went to a lot of trouble to be here to support me today. You did, too, so…"

"Don't worry about me."

"I can't remember the last time I saw them together…"

Patrick didn't touch her. He didn't want to do anything to influence Jean's answer. In her amber eyes, he saw her ambivalence and a desire to try to please them all.

"I want to go home, Patrick," she finally said in a small, weary tone.

He placed a hand on her waist and gently squeezed. "Okay. Then it's settled."

She gave a barely discernible smile and nod of her head. Her hair was messy, with tendrils feathering around her flushed face. Her forehead and the back of her neck were damp, trapping strands on her skin. He wanted nothing more just then than to gather her close and say, *I'm going to take care of you.* Instead, Patrick spontaneously brushed hair from her face and fleetingly massaged his fingers through to her scalp. Jean's eyelids fluttered at his tenderness.

Jean turned to face her parents to address them, but her father, hugging her loosely, spoke first.

"Honey, your mom and I just had a conversation, and we've decided that the best thing for you right now is to get home and get some rest. As much as we'd love to have dinner with you...and Patrick, and catch up, I don't think you're up to it."

"Your dad's right, Jean. You're about to drop where you stand from exhaustion. Dinner can wait for another time, okay?"

Jean smiled. Slowly Patrick rubbed a hand up and down her back.

"Please don't be too disappointed. You both went to a lot of trouble to get here today."

"No sacrifice. You did all the hard work."

"They sure need to give you a raise, or something," Diana suggested. "Was this sort of thing in your job description?"

"Don't answer that," Seth advised his daughter. "Sometimes you do what you gotta do for the brownie points. Right, Patrick?"

"Absolutely. That's a very good lead-in to letting you know I'll take Jean home."

"That's sweet of you." Diana smiled.

"Not at all. My pleasure."

"I'll call you later, okay?"

"Call tomorrow, Mom. What are you going to do now?" Jean asked her parents.

"I'm going to take Di out for drinks and dinner."

"How long will you be in the city?" Jean asked, as her mother gave her a hug and admonished her to take care of herself. "Will I see you before you leave? What hotel are you staying at?"

Her father cupped her face and kissed her cheek. "I'm here until Tuesday. Maybe we can get together. I'll let you know. Your mom is putting me up tonight."

There was a quick, awkward choreographed dance of goodbye, more kisses and hugs and shaking of hands.

"I think you're in good hands, honey. I trust Patrick to be careful with you."

"I won't disappoint you, sir."

CHAPTER 12

Jean rode back to Brooklyn with Patrick after her parents had left them. It was so wonderful to be in his luxurious vehicle, just the two of them cocooned within the air-conditioned space...

"How are you feeling?"

"Good. Tired. I look a mess," she said, making a half-hearted attempt to smooth her wild hair.

"You look beautiful. Sexy, with your hair like that. When we get to your place, I'm kissing all your bruises. You know, to make them go away."

She laughed. "I'd enjoy that."

"Me too."

"Thank you for everything you did, Patrick."

"I want to stay in your folks' good graces. It's obvious they're protective of you. Glad I had a chance to meet them."

"I bet they have a ton of questions about you. Probably more about you and me," she ventured quietly.

He grinned broadly and then sobered for a long moment.

"Your dad lives in LA Your mom still lives in Tarrytown. Aren't you the least bit curious?"

"About what?"

"Okay, you don't want to speculate. But from my seat at the table, I'd say...they're not done yet. It's more than just being amicable and pleasant for your sake. There didn't seem to be any tension between them, considering."

"I noticed," Jean murmured thoughtfully. "I'm not sure I should make anything of it. Until my dad said my mom invited him to stay for the night. The way he said it. It's like it wasn't the first time. It may have just slipped out. Maybe he didn't mean to reveal so much. I don't know."

"It didn't look to me like they're trying to hide anything. Did you happen to catch the moony-eyed looks they were exchanging when we left first aid?"

"I did."

Patrick stared out the windshield waiting for her to continue. When she didn't, he pulled himself together.

"Okay, end of discussion. There's probably really nothing to talk about."

"I don't know what to say. I don't know how I feel. I spent my childhood praying for the miracle that would make us a whole family. That my dad and mom would come together in one place."

"And you'd live happily ever after," he added.

"By the time I was getting out of high school, it seemed less important. I was going off to college and becoming an adult, getting on with my own life. It was too late to wish for that kind of normal family. There were so many single-parent households all around me that it was no longer a *thing*, you know?"

"How would you feel if your parents are forming some sort of new relationship?" Patrick said.

"Bewildered. After all these years. Maybe they've somehow worked out that nothing matters anymore but how they feel about each other."

Patrick reached out and wrapped his hand around the top of her thigh. "That makes perfect sense. That's exactly how I'd handle it..."

For Jean, it was an intriguing recap that was just beginning to emerge into a new possibility, a new updated reality. Did her parents still love each other? Was she only wishing?

———

Jean sat watching Patrick's bent head as he studiously checked out the scrapes on her arm and her hand. He applied a healing ointment he'd found in her medicine cabinet. He'd already made up a ziplock bag with ice and had applied it to her knee, wrapping it in place with an Ace bandage. Then he'd placed a pillow under the knee, telling her to keep it raised, as per the doctor's orders.

"What do you think, Dr. Bennett?" she asked, resisting the urge to stroke his hair.

Patrick chuckled, wiping his fingers on a tissue. "Surgery is not called for at this time."

"I'm glad to hear that," Jean said. She was feeling happy but guilty. Happy that she was not seriously hurt, and she and Patrick had the evening together. Guilty that she'd chosen to stay with him over visiting with her parents. When had it come to pass that every moment mattered to her?

"Okay," he said, getting up from facing her on the side of her bed. He began gathering up the small cadre of medical supplies and headed to the bathroom. "I'm done. Want anything? There's more pizza."

"No."

She sighed, settling against her pillows. With closed eyes, she listened to him puttering around the bathroom, the kitchen. Familiar with her apartment, her home. Making a place for himself. Another happy thought. Jean could feel a wave of exhaustion begin to flow over her, softening her body, her mind. The bike event had done her in, but she was proud of herself for having seen it through to the end. She could feel herself slipping into a twilight zone just before sleep where she felt cozy, and safe.

She didn't move as Patrick carefully got into the bed, maneuvering close to her side until she rested partially against his bare chest. She was still on her back so her knee could remain in place with the ice pack. He was naked and warm and sturdy. He was whispering something sweet into her ear, kissing her neck, her shoulder, and tucking her head beneath his chin. His arms enclosed her, anchored her to him where she felt cherished.

"I thought I saw Brian earlier. It was almost at the finish line. He waved goodbye to you and met up with some other people."

Jean lay still, biding her time while she thought of an appropriate answer. Her conversation with Brian was more personal than she could ever hope to explain to Patrick. And it had nothing to do with him other than as the unspoken obstacle between her and Brian's misguided interest in her. How could she explain the dynamics of Brian wondering why she'd be more interested in Patrick, a white man, and not him, who was Black? How could she ever explain the racial history that put her in a totally different category of identity? Of having to defend herself against her own choices?

"Yes, it was Brian."

"I had no idea he was planning to participate. He never mentioned it."

"I'm sure you two don't tell each other *everything* you're doing outside of work. He said he was biking with family, cousins."

"Oh."

"We encountered each other near the very end. Less than a half mile from the finish time. So it's not like we had a lot of conversation."

"Was he with you when you fell?"

"Yes. My front tire hit something on the path. A rock, discarded garbage, who knows."

"Did he help you at all?"

"Well…he asked if I was okay. Helped me right my bike. That's when we decided to walk the rest of the way."

"Oh," Patrick murmured again.

Jean suspected he had other thoughts on his mind, more questions, but she wasn't going to add to Patrick's curiosity and open up a conversation that could lead somewhere she wasn't willing to go. She wasn't the least interested in Brian Abbott.

Jean was glad that Patrick didn't pursue the matter, settling down next to her with her in his arms. There was no need to move, and the otherworldly setting began to take over, sinking them both into a place that was either a fantasy…or a dream.

Sometime later Jean began to float above the internal changing scenes that had been her dreams when she felt Patrick's breath tickling her skin. During the night, she'd managed to discard the homemade ice pack, now melted. Her position had changed but Patrick still held her. He sighed deeply and uttered a soft moan. His hips pressed against her buttocks, his arousal bringing her into gradual awareness and readiness, drowsy but awake.

One of his hands rubbed and massaged a breast, and the other was positioned below her navel, encouraging her to push back to meet his growing urgency. It was suddenly matching her own. Jean was excited by the way their bodies swayed and undulated together, a precursor to a much deeper connection. She turned her head, seeking Patrick's mouth, his kiss, as if it was balm to her heated senses. Patrick rose to bend over her, to accommodate that need. He rolled Jean onto her back, her arms free to circle him, her mouth free and at a better angle to meet his kiss with a slow, sensual hunger that made her senses spin. She raised her knees, and Patrick shifted into place.

Abruptly he broke the kiss, stopped moving except to lift his body a few inches from Jean's. He gasped sharply.

"Your arm. Your knee. I'll…"

Jean cleverly distracted Patrick by kissing him, forcing him not only into silence, but back to the business at hand.

She whispered against his mouth. "Nothing hurts. Nothing…"

He believed her, instantly sinking back to her body, kissing her once again enthusiastically and maneuvering his way with ease to the very core of her.

It was lazy lovemaking. No rush to reach the end of the experience. They were enjoying the dizzy, erotic pleasure of being lost in each other.

———

They'd managed to pull themselves together and head out for a very late brunch before the café began setting up for dinner. It was the tail end of the Sunday crowd, and the place was mostly empty. As Jean finished browsing through the menu, it came over her that she was feeling a settled and calm kind of contentment. As if all was right in her world. She looked at Patrick, his head bent over the laminated card, and realized that so much of the ethereal feelings coursing through her had to do with being with him.

Jean could not pinpoint exactly when she'd let her guard down and come to believe that maybe—just maybe—she and Patrick were an item. After all, other people around them who weren't necessarily friends saw something between them that she and Patrick had not mentioned to themselves. The thought made her almost light-headed. Was this what it felt like when you knew you cared for someone and you became a different person than you were the day before? He had entered her sphere of being, and he mattered. There was a brief tightening in Jean's chest as she recognized the kind of open vulnerability that came with the territory.

It was also not lost on her that this was a new sensation and experience. She knew that, while she'd loved Ross for his qualities, his dependability, and was prepared to build a future with him, there was a clear and distinct difference from the certainty that was wrapping around her heart when she was with Patrick.

Jean blinked as the mist of her own fantasies suddenly vaporized and reality took over. And fear. It was that odd place in her heart where the desire to let herself free-fall into what she wanted to be true and the need to protect her heart from being shattered a second time clashed.

Patrick glanced up, and his own smile of contentment became quizzical as he returned her regard. He reached across the table for her hand.

"Hey. What's going on?"

Jean forced a smile and made a hasty attempt to cover her expression of self-induced doubts with one of wistfulness. "I was thinking that your treatments last night…"

His smile returned. "And this morning…"

"Worked. I'm still a little tender in places."

Patrick chortled and squeezed her hand. He braced his forearms on the table and leaned forward for a quick kiss. "I don't think all of that's from being on a bicycle for two hours yesterday."

Her mind cleared, her humor returned. She liked being reminded of just how good Patrick made her feel. She knew he liked being with her. There was no denying there was magic in his touch.

"Do you know what you want?" she asked, pointing to his menu.

He was still regarding her. His smile broadened. "I do. But I doubt it's served here."

Jean was left giddy with his implication.

"I think you're blushing," he said quietly. "I hope I did that."

Again, Jean couldn't respond, but she didn't have to, as a waitress appeared to take their order.

The meal was light and chatty and filled with easy good humor. Jean absorbed every minute, knowing that they had little time left before Patrick would have to leave to return home.

In the SUV on the ride back to her place, Patrick's conversation showed that his mind had already shifted gears and he was focused on his commitments for the next week. Jean listened quietly. At a red light, Patrick quickly read a text and followed up with a call. It was with Brian, whom Patrick identified in his greeting.

Jean ignored the conversation, drifting in her own thoughts and concerns. She didn't want to make too much of their sharing of time and space that, so far, had been pretty much on the fly. It was all satisfying, but she still felt incomplete.

"I'll get back to you…" Patrick was saying, ending the call.

Then, abruptly, he muttered an oath and hit his brakes.

Jean jerked out of her thoughts and forward against her seat belt. Patrick's arm shot out across her chest, holding her in place as added protection.

A sedan had cut in front of the SUV, and Patrick had barely missed running into the back of it. The car ahead of them started forward, slowly. Patrick resumed following, letting some distance build between the two vehicles. Now Jean was alert. The sedan seemed to be pacing him, and Patrick began maneuvering side to side, looking for an opportunity to change lanes and keep a safe distance.

He made his move to the right, accelerating, but the car ahead was quicker, getting in front again. Patrick applied his brakes but crashed into the back of the sedan. The impact was a loud thud and brief screeching of tires. Jean gasped, grabbing the open cuff near her door handle to hold herself steady. She heard the sound of plastic splintering and shattering. All around them car horns blasted as other drivers tried to avoid the accident.

Patrick put his car into park and put on his hazard lights. He turned to her, his eyes sharp and worried.

"You okay?"

Jean nodded.

"Get out of the car," he ordered.

He manually released the lock and was out of the driver's side before she could respond. Patrick hurried around the front of the vehicle and pulled the door open. Behind him, a small crowd was gathering. The two vehicles were spread over a lane and a half on the residential street, making it difficult for cars to drive past.

He didn't wait for Jean to climb out of the car but lifted her out by her waist. As soon as he released her, he had his cell phone out and opened the camera. He pivoted briefly to the sedan and began snapping photos. The car door opened, and a young man exited the driver side. Patrick quickly snapped the point of impact and the position of the two vehicles. He returned to Jean.

"I want you to go. Get to the next street or avenue and call for a car."

"I'm not leaving you. I'll stay. I'll…"

"I don't want you to get involved. I know why this happened. I'll call the police. I'll take care of it. Go!"

"Patrick, let me stay."

"Go home, Jean."

He took another moment to look searchingly into her eyes. She saw he was very alert, angry, concerned for her. "Patrick," Jean whispered, a final plea to stay with him. His thumb brushed her cheek, and his hand gently pushed her as he turned back to three young men who were exiting the sedan. Jean turned and maneuvered her way from the scene, away from the onlookers and gawkers, away from those holding up cell phones to tape or photograph the encounter.

Everyone was an instant reporter.

Jean reached the sidewalk and looked back to find Patrick on his cell. He was now videotaping the car he'd hit, as well as the three male occupants, young men in their twenties. Jean could tell by their gestures and the way they engaged Patrick in discussion that they clearly felt he was at fault and they were argumentative. Patrick put a hand up to stop their slightly aggressive attitudes and continued to make calls. He briefly looked around, as if to make sure she was no longer in sight. As his gaze swept the crowd, Jean repositioned herself so he wouldn't see her. She continued to stand in the background, watching everything unfold.

Only after a squad car arrived and two officers approached the scene, laconically, did Jean start to relax. One of them, apparently recognizing Patrick, walked right to Patrick and shook his hand. One of the three men from the other car involved could be seen photographing the exchange. Only then did Jean stop holding her breath and, feeling that the situation was under control, reluctantly went in search of an alternative way to get home.

Patrick called her thirty minutes later. She was just being dropped off in front of her building. Jean stood outside the entrance to take the call.

"Are you okay? What's going on?"

"I'm fine. The police are doing their thing. I called my insurance company, and I've left a message for my attorney."

She frowned. "Your attorney? Why?"

"I'll explain later. Are you home?"

"Just arrived."

"Sorry the day ended with a bang. No pun intended."

"I'm not laughing. I was worried."

"I appreciate that."

"What about the accident? Can you drive your car? Was anyone hurt? Patrick, I don't understand what happened."

"It wasn't an accident," he sighed.

"What?"

"The car can be fixed, and no one got hurt. Great lesson, though. I'm going to have to be more careful."

"What do you mean?"

"I didn't think all that much would change with the lottery win. But things have been happening that somehow make me feel like I have a target pinned to my back. Getting the Porsche for myself was not a smart idea."

Jean said nothing. She thought she understood what he meant.

"Look, I'm almost finished here. The car is drivable."

"Do you want to come back to my place?"

"I can't. I need to get home and take care of a few things. I'll have to have my car looked at, and I might have to get a loaner for a few days. Tomorrow is going to get very complicated."

"What can I do to help?"

"Forgive me."

There was no need for Patrick to give an explanation about why the incident between his SUV and a sedan occupied by three young men had not been an accident. The story appeared on the morning news as Jean was dressing for work. It was picked up by social media platforms and, in the tech language of the moment, went viral.

The broadcast headline read *Millionaire Misery*, subtitle *The Price You Pay for Being Rich*. These together told Jean exactly how the accident had come about and why Patrick was going to be sued. By virtue of being the driver of the vehicle that had rear-ended another vehicle, the accident made him the guilty party.

One accompanying photo showed Patrick on his cell, leaning against the hood of his very expensive Porsche SUV. Another showed him shaking hands with one of the responding officers. And the third image, just in case a reader had any doubts that the guy with the high-end car was at fault, the three young men were portrayed looking bewildered; they were just visiting from the suburbs and had gotten lost in Brooklyn.

The rear end of their midlist sedan was damaged, not built to withstand impact from the front of a vehicle that weighed 1,700 pounds more. The bigger news was that multimillionaire and popular TV sports anchor Patrick Bennett was being charged with recklessly driving his bro-toy that left three young men shaken. And one reporter found it necessary to point out that Patrick had been taken to task earlier in the summer when a former girlfriend accused him of cheating her out of a part of his lottery win. That story was resurrected, adding to an image of Patrick that infuriated Jean. He was not careless. He was not self-centered. He had not let his sudden wealth go to his head. She now had a suspicion that far more had happened than Patrick had admitted to her. He obviously didn't want her implicated in any way in his troubles. That didn't stop Jean from believing she should have been there with him after the accident. There was nothing she could have done to change the circumstances, but she would have been there with support and love.

Jean got through that Monday on text messages with amusing emojis from Patrick, but she knew immediately that he was more concerned than he was admitting. He'd been besieged for weeks for no other reason than his sudden good fortune. But his daily life was turning out to be more of a nightmare. Patrick might try to downplay the annoyance and the stress, and she admired him for the effort. But they were ever present. And Jean guessed that they were starting to take a toll.

She'd also recognized that, in his own way, Patrick was trying to protect her, keep her out of the line of fire of incidents that plagued him and the resulting publicity.

She took a chance and called him at the studio on Monday, knowing that he'd be at his usual routines and that the crew would protect him from aggressive reporters. But there was no way they could know for sure that she was who she said she was, and Jean had the sense she was being given the runaround by a string of handlers. Until Brian Abbott got on the phone, firm, cold, officious, doing exactly what he was supposed to do.

"Hello, Brian. It's Jean Travis." She waited, but there was no response at all. "Seriously. It's Jean."

She heard him inhale. "Right. Okay. Sorry about this, Jean. We've circled the wagons around our guy. He needs some space so he can do his job."

"I know. I just wanted to check in, make sure he's okay. I know this is not a good time…"

"Hold on," Brian abruptly cut in, and the line seemed to go dead.

He'd put her on hold. A full minute went by, and Jean was at the point of hanging up when the line opened.

"Patrick" came the voice. Like Brian's, it was firm, cold…and cautious.

"Oh…hi. I…I shouldn't have called. I was concerned and…"

"Jean! Brian didn't tell me it was you. He said it was a call I needed to take."

"I'll make it quick. I read the papers this morning. I don't understand how you knew what happened yesterday was a setup. "

He signed. "Someday I'll explain the basic ground rules of scam artists and how they pick their subjects."

"I don't think I want to know."

"I'm glad you called," he said in a voice she was more used to him using with her.

"I took a chance. I wanted you to know…"

"I know. I'm really glad Brian put you through. I'll have to put him up for a raise."

Jean smiled. "And thank him for me, for giving you the call."

"Yeah. I don't think you two ever quite hit it off, but he's always had my back."

"That's the only thing that matters."

"Thanks for calling, Jean. My day just got significantly better."

⌒

"Poor Patrick," Diana Chambers murmured, sipping her breakfast coffee as she browsed the paper and found another update on Patrick's troubles.

It was the very next weekend, and Jean had escaped the city to spend a night with her mother on Friday. She had taken a call from Patrick just as they were sitting down to eat.

Jean had excused herself from the table, fully aware that her mother, despite all efforts to the contrary, was quietly following the one-sided conversation, Jean's quiet responses. When she finished and sat down again, her mother smiled in a knowing way.

"How's he doing?"

"Who?"

"Seriously?" she quipped.

Jean shrugged. "It's hard to tell. I think Patrick's trying to put a good front on the situation. He seems more concerned that I don't think badly of him because of everything."

"Do you?"

"Of course not. I *know* him."

"I know all of the stuff that's happening to Patrick came out of left field. But he'll be okay."

"I hope so," Jean murmured, buttering an English muffin.

"He doesn't strike me as a man who would be so thoughtless, so indifferent to other people."

"That's because he's not."

"I'm sorry I misjudged him when he asked to take you to his prom. But to be honest, I was concerned that he was this cute white boy who might have been using you as an experiment. Understand what I'm saying?"

"Yes, of course I do. I was always a little skittish about what the boys especially were really thinking about me in high school. But I never felt that way about Patrick."

Dianna looked at her daughter over the top of her reading glasses. "Of course you'd defend him."

"What does that mean?"

"I think it's fair to say you like the man, Jean."

"I think it's fair to say I really believe him. Patrick is not capable of these terrible things. And the really unfair part is that all of this has happened since he won the lottery. Before that no one found it necessary to come after him, make accusations based on the…the…flimsiest of reasons. It's ridiculous."

"You're shouting, sweetie," Diana said in a soothing tone.

Jean took a deep breath. "Sorry." She cast a glance at her mother's always-peaceful demeanor.

"Did you go through anything like that with Dad? Wondering if there was an ulterior motive to his interest in you?"

Diana nodded, put her cup down, became thoughtful. "Absolutely.

I mean I liked him, and he was polite. It was a while before I realized he was maybe actively pursuing me, trying to get my attention in a personal way. By then I knew I was attracted to him. But I still made him jump through hoops to prove he was serious.

"Then it did become serious over the course of a year. And I began to ask what his family would think about his getting involved with a Black girl. He was honest, and that was hard for me. Your grandparents weren't thrilled either, but they understood better that it's my life. They hoped I wouldn't get hurt. Or used. Or embarrassed."

"What did happen?"

Diana became quiet with a faraway look for a moment. "Seth Travis loved me. And I loved him. That was never the issue. It was a much bigger problem beyond our control at the time. We tried to stay true to ourselves, what we felt for each other. But it got very hard, and very ugly." She smiled wistfully at Jean and playfully twisted strands of her hair. "Your father wanted us to get married, move somewhere we'd be safe. There was no such place. And then, I got pregnant."

Jean didn't speak. This was the most she'd ever heard about her parents' relationship. She didn't want to distract her mother from the tale.

"We had you and were pretty giddy. You were so beautiful. But it was obvious that a marriage wasn't going to happen. I had you to take care of. Your father was accepted into law school in California. I stayed on the East Coast so my family could help with you while I finished my master's. That's how we got pulled apart. That's how he became a long-distance father to you, but loving and attentive. Not the end of the story, obviously."

Diana patted her daughter's hand and deftly changed the subject. "You know, your father said that he liked Patrick. Now this was after only about an hour in his company, so take that with a grain of salt," she chuckled.

"Then why do you think he said it?"

"Well…like me, I think he noticed that you obviously hold Patrick in high esteem."

"We go back a long way, Mom."

"Yeah, but high school doesn't count. You have to grow up before you really get a sense of people, their integrity, their view of the world, the way they treat people. I trust your judgment because you've always been a little careful of who you claim as a friend. So...your dad and I hope your belief in Patrick isn't misplaced."

"It isn't," Jean replied, averting her gaze. She was not about to add any more as to why she believed so strongly. She knew she wasn't wrong.

The rest of their breakfast was spent on the subject of the new position her mother had been given as dean of students at a local college. The sudden mention of the local college reminded Jean of other recent news.

"Mom, you won't believe it. I got to see our neighborhood, our house from the air! I flew right over it."

"How did you manage that?"

So Jean had to relate the entire magical mystery tour with Patrick by helicopter. Diana's eyes lit up as Jean told the story. And as she finished, her mom grew wistful.

"That sounds like it was amazing fun."

"It was. A great surprise, and so thoughtful of Patrick."

"Um. Well...I hope you'll put in a good word for me and let Patrick know I'd *love* to come along for your next flight."

Jean laughed. "I'll make sure to let him know. And I want to say it was so great that you and Daddy showed up for the bike race. I think I forgot to thank you."

"I'm glad I came, but I was worried when I saw you limping over the finish line. You looked like such a sad little rag doll," Diana said wryly.

"Thanks, Mom."

"Come on, let's finish. I think we have about forty minutes before the next train to Grand Central. We'll have to hurry if you want me to drive you to the station."

They got up and began to clear the table in Diana's sunny breakfast nook.

"I have to ask you something," Jean said, following her mother into the kitchen.

"I'm listening."

"What's going on with you and Dad?"

The dishes were carefully placed in the sink, and Jean's mother began dismantling the coffee maker.

"I'm not sure what you're getting at."

Jean took the coffee carafe and the used filter out of her mother's hands and placed them on the counter. She tilted her head to peer into her mother's face. She knew she was onto something. Her mother was speechless. Her mother was *never* speechless.

"You don't? Really? Mom, I figured out a long time ago that you've probably never loved anyone else but Dad. Then last week when I saw the two of you together after the bike race, I knew something was going on. There have been signs. For months. For the last year."

Diana Chambers walked around her daughter, back to the dining table.

"Mom, please. I'm not mad or anything. If you and Daddy still have feelings for each other, that's great! It's also pretty romantic."

Diana smiled and faced her daughter. And Jean knew in that moment that she was facing not so much her mother, but another woman…who was in love. It was definitely an odd, disorienting feeling.

"We honestly didn't know this was happening, Jean. It was so strange, so unbelievable. After all these years, that Seth and I would circle back and find each other again. It's not like that first love we had for each other, but so much more now that we're adults. When we got together in college, we honestly didn't know what to do when I was suddenly pregnant, when our families had hissy fits about us getting married. And so many other unexpected things. It's…it's…"

Jean put an arm around her mother's shoulders and briefly rocked her to her side. "Okay, okay. You don't have to say anymore, Mom. I get it."

"Do you?" Diana looked at her daughter, beseeching. "I was afraid you'd be so upset. Especially because we never married."

"This is what I know. You and Daddy love me. I wanted us all to be together, but I never lacked for anything. You protected me and were both always there for me. Under the circumstances I was pretty lucky."

"And we're so proud of you."

Jean had about a million more questions to ask her mother, but having gotten a confession, more or less, about her mother's feelings, she was content that anything else would be revealed in due time.

———

Jean was sitting cross-legged on her sofa, working on the first draft of a presentation speech she had been invited to make to an undergraduate class in communications, when her laptop began to ring...like a telephone. She realized that someone was Skyping her, and she clicked to open with the caller. It was Patrick.

"Am I interrupting again?" he asked.

His smile was wan and seemed forced. Jean was immediately struck with how formal he sounded with her. Her stomach churned as she speculated if they'd somehow lost ground since the most recent events forced him into the news again.

"Hey. No, not at all."

"I know it's late."

"That doesn't matter." Jean searched his face on the inadequate instrument perched on her lap. They'd only managed a few calls, a dozen texts in the last few days...and she suddenly felt like there was a yawning gulf between them. "I'm glad to hear from you. I know you've—"

"I missed you," he interrupted.

Jean swallowed, blinked at his image. He looked so tired. And annoyed.

"Me too."

Patrick sighed, combing his hand through his hair. He'd cut it recently, and the look seemed to add several years to his features. That and a second layer of facial hair...as if he hadn't shaved in a few days. The light beard was groomed and trimmed. Was this a new look? The start of a disguise? Weariness? Jean acknowledged that whatever the reason, the changes also made Patrick look incredibly attractive.

"Where are you?"

"Still at the studio. Waiting for a car to take me home."

"What about your car?"

"Parked in my garage. It's a rolling billboard. I may have to think about switching it out for something less...pretentious." He smirked.

Jean could hear his frustration surfacing.

"Is the lawsuit moving forward? Are you able to get the charges dismissed? Like you said, the incident was a setup."

"Yes. No. That doesn't matter. My lawyer is taking care of it. Those guys really don't want their day in court. A first-year law student could blow their case apart. They want money. A settlement. That's what my lawyer recommends."

"It's so unfair," Jean muttered, touching the screen as if she could actually touch him.

"Unfortunately it's not about fair. It's about having good insurance and a willingness to cave just to close the case. That's essentially what I'm doing."

"I guess I don't have to ask how you feel about that."

He was shaking his head, his brows furrowed. "What I feel is that this is just a distraction. I'm concerned that it might affect my work for ESPN. But so far all it's done, like that issue with a former girlfriend weeks ago, is made people curious and boosted my show ratings! Go figure. My attorney tells me to let him handle things. Ross tells me to stay cool."

Jean nodded, blinking at the mention of her ex-fiancé. "Good advice. You've been seeing him?"

"A few times since our initial meeting. He's been really helpful on several issues. But he actually called me in to talk about this latest incident."

"What did he have to say?"

Patrick arched a brow and silently chuckled. "He said understand that this is a game. The purpose being how to separate me from my money. He said it's not personal but opportunistic. The lights went on. I knew he was right."

"So what's the answer?"

"Ross suggested setting up several kinds of funds, investments, shelters, et cetera. The idea being to make the money as invisible as possible. Also, not make it easily available. Then he said something really interesting. He said find a way to openly give back. And I've already started. He's also helping me with something that has nothing to do with managing money."

"Really? What?"

Patrick's brow furrowed deeply on his screen image. He slowly shook his head.

"I can't talk about it yet. Sorry to sound so secretive."

"It's fine," Jean assured him easily.

"I'm working with Ross on setting up something for Pete's son. Ross suggested I not offer to pay the entire four-year tuition for college, but give enough with stipulations about what Pete needs to do to contribute. And it might mean his son having to work part-time. Ross doesn't think it should be a total free ride."

"That all sounds fair, don't you think?"

"Absolutely. Remember I told you about the cop I met at the Queens event with the mayor? Well, I'm going out to meet with them and his daughter's Little League team to talk with them, maybe play a little ball. The leagues aren't ready for girl players yet, but I'll still talk about what it's going to take to get into the Major League someday. The emphasis is going to be on education and college. I'm going to offer to contribute money so the team can get proper uniforms and equipment."

"That's so great!"

"Yeah. After everything that's been going on, something like working with the Queens team feels really good."

Jean smiled at the screen. She held up her hands and applauded him. "Congratulations. It's a wonderful idea."

Patrick leaned forward, his face close to the screen. His features had finally settled down, the angles of his face softening into a real smile for her. His brows cleared and his eyes were suddenly really focused on her.

"Can I also get a kiss?" he asked.

It was so whimsical, so sweet. Jean was thrilled to hear the yearning in his voice. She laughed, leaning forward to air-kiss the screen. Patrick did the same.

"There," she said, as they gazed at one another through the digital display. "Does that help?"

"You have no idea how much."

CHAPTER 13

I want to thank everyone for the support and real team effort for the bike event. I've gone onto our Facebook page and did the math. The team clocked in at about eighteen thousand dollars given by all of your sponsors."

A roar, foot stomping, and applause burst out in the office as Brad used the megaphone made from a rolled-up booklet to make the announcement.

"I know it sounds great, but you guys are such slackers! You're welcome to go in and see what each of you managed to total, but let me just say that Jean wins. She personally came in at just over four thousand dollars! That's, like, almost a fourth of our grand total. Way to go, *Jean*!"

Jean grinned as the office again cheered.

"And to really put the rest of you to shame, Jean suffered a fall from her bike, got up, and continued to the finish line! Another big surprise, Patrick Bennett was there. He probably thought he was incognito, but someone noticed him. So…I'm not going to make a huge deal of his presence at the end of the Bike-A-Thon other than to say, I think he was there for more than the event. Am I right, Jean? I realize you two have become friends. I'll let it go at that."

There were wolf whistles here and there in the room. Jean was stunned that anyone else had paid attention, but also uncomfortable that Brad had publicly concluded that she and Patrick were a couple.

But really…what else were they to think?

Wasn't she already having dreams of the relationship with Patrick being far more than dear friends…now with benefits?

Everything eventually settled down, and Brad explained how some of the money would be used for homeless services, the biggie being housing.

Jean had forgotten all about the sponsors who'd signed up in support of her participating in the event, until her friend Annabelle Hampton contacted her to respond to the fact that Ross Franklin's name was on the list. So were her parents…and Brian Abbott! There was also an anonymous donor with the highest contribution of $2,000. Jean wondered if it was Patrick, but he'd never made any mention of being a sponsor, especially given the terms of his contract. And she wasn't going to ask. She already knew that Patrick was still trying to find a way of dealing with and appreciating his good fortune. He didn't feel the need to rub anyone's nose in it by boasting of his good deeds or giving some outrageous, over-the-top donation. Besides, everyone already believed he was being targeted because of the money.

Marin Phillips, the account executive she'd met at the dinner for Patrick, had called to congratulate her for the bike event. She had contributed but had done so in her late brother's name. Jean was very touched by her thoughtfulness, considering they didn't know each other well. Marin had suggested lunch to remedy that.

"Okay, enough of congratulating ourselves," Brad continued. "When we all return from lunch, we're having a discussion about planning for the July Fourth weekend. Be prepared with your list of ideas, potential problems, and their possible solutions."

The morning passed quickly, and just as Jean was about to leave for her lunch date with Marin, she got a call from Patrick on her new smartphone asking her to call him as soon as she could. As soon as he answered the phone, he launched straight into, "What are you doing this evening?"

"Going home after work. Why?"

"Can you meet me in the city? There's a meeting of anchors for some of the ESPN programs, and I'll be there. It's at a private suite of a Midtown hotel...not the one where they held that dinner for me. I've asked if I could stay there for the night when the meeting is done. I got a yes."

"You want me to come and stay with you?"

"That's the idea. It's perfect! The meeting will very likely end early. We could have the whole evening together."

"That sounds like fun, Patrick."

"I told you I'm very good at taking advantage of opportunities. I'd be crazy to pass this up. The suite is paid for anyway by corporate."

"I've never stayed in a hotel suite," she said thoughtfully.

Patrick burst out laughing. "I hope that isn't the only reason you'll come."

"How big is the bed?"

"King," he responded, restraining his amusement. "With about a dozen pillows."

"What about in the morning?"

Patrick sighed on the line. "I'm good until about noon. Then flying down to Philly for an important meeting. I'll be back by evening."

"I should be back downtown by ten. But I'll tell Brad I need to be a little late. Eleven?"

He didn't respond at once. "Are you okay with that? I don't want you to get into a thing with your supervisor. Too spontaneous?"

"A little."

"I'll have to do something about that. Will you meet me?"

"Yes, I will."

Jean arrived at the restaurant first for her lunch with Marin and spent the time making a list of what she'd need for the quick overnight with Patrick and work the next day. She could never deny her excitement at being with him, but more and more tried to keep at bay the unease of a relationship that didn't seem quite settled or organized. She wanted to be understanding of Patrick's unique situation. He was a public figure. Jean was beginning to wonder if there would ever be real time to form a solid, growing relationship. Was she just a warm, comfortable convenience?

Yes, she loved spending time with Patrick, loved the easy way they were with each other when alone. But they didn't seem to have a plan. She stayed away from the big *C* word: *commitment*. There had been no declaration of any kind, beyond the silent acknowledging of how much they enjoyed each other's company. How much they both obviously looked forward to it.

What kind of relationship, then, did they really have?

More importantly to Jean, where was it going?

She knew she was waiting for Patrick to make the first move on that front. She wasn't sure how she'd feel if she gave an indication of how she was feeling for him, only to discover that he might not feel the same. That Patrick admitting to something like that could break her heart was an understatement.

Jean had already gone through this with Ross Franklin. Her feelings for Patrick were much different because, as it was turning out, they weren't so new. She was feeling with Patrick somewhat the way she'd thought she'd feel with Ross. They were very different men. Both handsome, educated, and from a good family, both established and highly recognized in their careers, admired, and respected. They both looked incredible on paper, but in real life it was Patrick whose presence, whose persona moved Jean, stirred her, softened the woman she was in a way that reached out to her heart and her soul.

Recently that's what Jean saw when she considered her parents together. They'd loved each other once when they were very young and idealistic. She now knew that nothing had changed with age and time.

She still wasn't sure what to expect with Patrick. It was all so lovely at the moment. But was there a future in their *like* of each other, their clear attraction?

"Made it! I'm sorry if I kept you waiting."

Jean hastily closed the Reminders app on her cell phone and dropped the unit into her purse.

"I got here early."

Marin slid into her chair and put her oversize tote on the vacant chair next to her. She spread the napkin over her lap. "And you took the time to catch up. Why is it we're never caught up? Or is that just us women?"

"If I don't write it down, I might forget. We know what could happen then."

"We overschedule, overcommit."

They looked at each other and began to laugh. "It's good to see you again," Marin said.

"Thanks for reaching out first." Jean smiled.

She admired Marin's sophisticated but simple attire. She certainly looked the part of an executive who commanded attention and respect. Both professionally and personally, Jean thought. And Marin exuded confidence and authority.

For no particular reason, it briefly crossed her mind that Marin and Ross would make a great matchup.

"I was going to call you…"

"Don't worry about it. To be honest, if I hadn't seen Patrick last week when I stopped by the station, you'd still be waiting to hear from me."

Jean frowned. "I don't understand the connection. When you saw Patrick, you remembered me?"

Marin chuckled, picking up the prix fixe lunch menu. "I know I shouldn't, but at that dinner I did get the impression that…you know… maybe there was some interest between the two of you. Nothing specific, but you were there as opposed to anyone else he might have invited."

Jean's stomach tensed. "That sounds like he had a long list to choose from."

Marin smiled, averting her gaze. "He does. Or did. He's handsome, successful, and popular. He makes good money, and he's a nice man. What's not to like? That means all the pretty blonds, brunettes, and redheads are coming out of the woodwork to get his attention. Of course Patrick enjoyed the attention. He didn't have to work very hard, and the women were all pleasant, easy to please, and great for his ego. Look, he's a *guy*, you know? The thing is, Patrick is different. He has a conscience. He has self-awareness. He doesn't use people. His parents did a good job raising him," Marin remarked. "If you want my opinion, when he met you, he quickly realized there is a difference."

"That's nice of you to say," Jean responded, hoping that was a compliment.

"Now, that's all I have to say on the subject of Patrick Bennett and you. The rest you can figure out on your own." She chuckled. "I just wanted you to know he's wonderful. Believe me, if I thought he was a possibility when I first started with ESPN, I would have made a play. He was a gentleman, really friendly and helpful…and not interested."

"Well…I guess I'm impressed with your insights," Jean said, overcome with Marin's thorough assessment.

"I just wanted to get that out of the way. I like Patrick. But I also think you and I could be friends. I wanted to make sure we started on a clear playing field. Okay?"

"Okay." Jean nodded.

The lunch was fantastic.

~

The meeting had ended, and Patrick had been surprised by how much of the agenda had been devoted to the high public profile he'd suddenly attained through a series of unfortunate public incidents. The managing team kept repeating and assuring him that they couldn't be happier with the ratings and attention *REPLAY* was receiving. But there was most definitely a feeling that Patrick's money issues—as it was politely worded—needed to be handled.

Patrick understood exactly what that meant. How to separate his growing personal issues from his professional standing. Suggestions were offered, and in the end, he agreed to do what everyone believed was the best course for now. There was always the hope that focus on him would eventually die down and he could move on. Actually, the temporary solution couldn't have been more perfect, giving Patrick, unbeknownst to the studio, an opening for executing a few of his own plans.

Patrick didn't know whether to be annoyed with the studio for thinking *he* was the problem, or fall to his knees and thank them for offering a way out that answered more than one prayer.

He checked the time on his smartphone. Jean must be running late. Rush hour. Crowded subways…or lack of an Uber. There was no text or email from her, but hopefully nothing serious had happened. He tried to call her. It went straight to voicemail. But finally there was a text.

Unavoidable delay. Work. Hope to leave soon.

He sat on the long, modern Italianate sofa. It was hard and uncomfortable. He got up again, meandering to the panoramic windows, frowning out into the night. As luxurious and spacious as the suite was, with a drop-dead view of the Midtown Manhattan skyline, Patrick was beginning to feel slightly claustrophobic. He also felt an odd loneliness settle over him that was not only surprising but disturbing.

He wanted to be with Jean.

Suddenly it was imperative that they be together. He wasn't quite sure why he felt so strongly about this. But Patrick was coming to realize that he was decidedly restless when they were apart too long. He'd been feeling edgy, anxious, and a little impatient. He was counting on tonight with her to quell those sensations. His head was beginning to fill up with petty concerns, endless mental and emotional assaults.

Patrick began to pace again, hands thrust in his pockets. He checked his smartphone. Only five minutes had passed. In an abrupt move, he went in search of the suite key and left. Walking the long, silent corridor, as he neared the alcove bank of elevators, he heard the distinct *ping* that signaled a cab's arrival. He jogged, hopeful that it was Jean finally arriving. But an older couple got off. They acknowledged him with smiles and nods, and headed toward their room. Patrick stood in front of the empty elevator, disappointed and very concerned. Just as the doors were about to close, he stepped in and pressed the button for the exclusive bar and lounge several floors down.

It was moderately busy in the darkened space. Couples and foursomes were drinking and talking quietly, little clusters of beautifully turned out thirtysomething women, very likely looking for a hookup. Groups of men ignoring the women and discussing business...or pretending to. Patrick scouted the layout and chose a two-seat corner that allowed him a reasonable distance from other patrons, but facing the elevator bank.

He was well aware that a few of the women cast covert glances in his direction. Even the men gave him brief glances. But he was distracted because Jean had not arrived.

A waitress appeared, dressed in black and white, the straightforward and professional attire of high-end waitstaff. She wiped down the tiny bistro table.

"Can I take your order, sir?"

Patrick sighed. "Yeah. A beer, please."

She placed a cocktail napkin in front of him and walked away. Patrick didn't really notice when she returned fifteen seconds later with a dish of mixed nuts. Absently he began to pick at them. His beer was brought and he took a gulp. It was an anxious action, as if it might calm him down a bit.

He sent another message to Jean.

I'm in the bar and lounge on the 23rd floor. I'll wait for you here.

Patrick finished the beer, and the waitress returned.

"Another one, sir?"

"I don't think so. Gin and tonic, please."

She efficiently straightened the space of his table, refilling the nut dish and leaving to get his drink.

Patrick went back to looking at his cell.

"Excuse me. Sorry to bother you."

Patrick looked up. There was a man about his own age, standing with another male companion. The one who'd spoken held out his hand.

"You're Patrick Bennett, right?"

Patrick took the hand and smiled politely at the man. "Correct."

"I just wanted to say hi and your show is awesome. I think you're right on about the baseball season so far."

"Thanks. I appreciate that."

"Who do you think is going to make it to the playoffs?"

"Sorry, I don't want to speculate. It's still early, and a lot can happen before we get to September."

"Right, right. Well, thanks. Sorry if we bothered you."

"No problem. Thanks for stopping by."

The two men walked away. Patrick immediately pulled out his phone. There was another text from Jean.

So sorry! This is endless. Not looking good. I WILL call in a few minutes.

He began a response. Do you want me to...

"Hi."

Patrick contained himself and glanced up, looking askance at a very attractive woman standing right in front of him. She gave him no way of looking anywhere but at her.

"Hi back," he said with practiced ease.

"I see you're all alone."

"For now."

"Oh? Should I take that as an opening?" She flipped her long, black tresses behind her, only to have an alluring lock snake back over her shoulder. She tilted her head, smiling at him.

Patrick gave her his full attention. "I'm waiting for my lady." He felt a stunning relief at saying so. It was out there. Done. The acknowledgment actually lifted his spirits.

"Too bad," she said with winning charm.

Patrick smiled at her. "I don't imagine you'll be disappointed for very long."

"That's very sweet of you to say so, but...you're probably the most interesting man here."

"How would you know that?" he asked, pretty much guessing the answer.

"They're all business types. Serious, and a little nervous around me."

"Also, too bad. Is it okay for me to say they don't know what they're missing?"

She narrowed her gaze, clearly surprised. "You're different."

"I'll take that as a compliment." His phone began to vibrate. He held it up and pointed to it so the young woman could see. "My lady." He grinned.

The woman shrugged and gave Patrick a genuinely sweet smile as she turned away. "Lucky lady," she said.

"Jean? Is everything okay? Where are you?"

"Patrick, I'm so sorry. I didn't expect this to happen."

He could just hear a rumble of activity in the background. "I take it you got caught up in one of those infamous eleventh-hour meetings."

"Worse. I might have been able to excuse myself halfway through a meeting, but the mayor informed the staff that he was hosting a reception at Gracie Manson this evening for some dignitaries who arrived this afternoon and expressed interest in meeting with him. The mayor decided on a little social get-together. I had to work with his staff to make it happen. Very last minute. Very crazed. Even Brad couldn't get out of this one."

"What does this mean for tonight? How late do you think you'll get here?"

"It's winding down here, but I can't leave for at least another hour. Probably longer."

"So the probability is *very* high that we won't see each other later."

"Probably not. I was looking forward to tonight. I hope you know that. I hope you understand."

"Yeah, I do," he sighed.

"It's been pretty hectic. No point in going into details. Getting together would have been rushed as well. Watching the time right up until we both have to leave in the morning."

Patrick nodded to himself. Definitely too much like a quickie. "You're right. That wouldn't have been much fun."

"Or very comfortable."

"Probably not. I was hoping for a long evening and night, and an early morning with you. It is what it is. I better let you go. You're still working."

"I can't say enough how—"

"You don't have to, Jean. These things happen and it's no one's fault. I'm going to miss you," he whispered, his voice gravelly and sincere.

"Me too."

"Make sure they send you home in a car."

"They will."

"Send me a text so I know you arrived. I'll listen for the alert tone."

"Okay."

"Night, love."

Patrick hung up.

Jean gasped softly on his last words. She closed her eyes, resting her chin on her smartphone, letting them sink in.

The elevator stopped and the doors opened without a sound. The three men in the cab with Patrick waited until he'd exited first. His steps were slow, deliberate, almost like a death march, until they all four stood in an elegant, modern reception area. But there was no desk and no receptionist. As a matter of fact, for all intents and purposes, the floor seemed empty of life. Almost immediately, a young man appeared from an adjacent corridor holding out his hand.

"Hello, Mr. Bennett. My name is Randall Marsh. I'm Attorney Greenbaum's associate." Patrick shook the hand and silently nodded. "This way, please."

The young man, slender, professional, his posture erect and stiff with his own importance, began a litany of information for the four men following him. Patrick had already been told of the arrangements. He had already been briefed on what to expect. What he could, and could not, do when he entered the meeting room and the doors were closed behind him. He really didn't hear a word the associate was reciting or the response of any of the men behind him. He felt like he was the leader of the charge and they merely had his back. But his throat was dry, and his heart felt like it was trying to find a way of jumping through his chest wall.

He was scared.

Following Randall, the group turned a corner, into another reception area, smaller and more intimate. There was a couple seated together, holding hands. The audible inhalation of the female grabbed Patrick's attention, and he glanced in their direction, his gaze connecting with, first, the burly man clearly uncomfortable in his special occasion suit, and then with the woman next to him. Her eyes were wide, lashes fluttering in distress. She burst into tears and bent her face away, openly sobbing.

The level of her emotions was not surprising to Patrick. He thought of his mother's reaction when he told her of the recent revelations. She'd cried as well. Not with fear or guilt, however, as he was witnessing with the older couple, but with joy.

Patrick had only a moment to register his ex-wife's parents before being ushered into the well-appointed conference room. The small room seemed overly filled with more men. But at the table, a young, stylish woman dressed in crisp summer linen sat staring straight ahead. She didn't acknowledge his entrance, his existence actually, or any of the formal introductions. Patrick, as well, made no notice of anyone else in the room. Let the lawyers deal with the introductions. As he silently stared at Katherine Carmichael, his ex-wife, whom he had not laid eyes on in years, he felt heat rising swiftly through his body, blood pounding at his temples, until he began to sweat.

"Will everyone please have a seat? There's a lot of material to be covered and…"

No one realized that Patrick was rounding the oval table not to find a seat, but to place himself directly opposite Katie in a position of absolute confrontation.

Someone called his name, trying to get his attention. Someone was rushing around the table to his side, reaching for his arm. Two men rushed to flank Katie, as if to protect her. She never moved, but her eyes finally lifted to stare at him. He was genuinely shocked to see the level of anger and indignation reflected back at him. It infuriated him.

Patrick, without warning, abruptly bent forward across the table to brace his palms on the table right in front of her. She was momentarily startled but sat defiant, staring him down.

"Why?" he uttered, unable to keep the wounded feelings and bewilderment from his words. "*Why?*"

"He's *my* son," she responded coldly.

"He's my son too. There's nothing you can do to change that. Believe this, Katie. I'm not giving up my right to my son," Patrick got out through clenched teeth before he finally allowed himself to be coaxed into sitting. He would not shift from sitting directly opposite his ex, and so two of his attorneys each took a chair on either side of him.

"Don't worry," Patrick ground out. "I'm not going to go for her throat." He sat down amid so much tension and hostility between him and Katie that the nervousness of the legal teams was palpable as they struggled for some decorum and control.

Patrick let the lawyers talk over and around him. They were efficient and all on the same page as to the facts. They had legal DNA test results. They had the birth certificate and testimony from the ob-gyn who was Katie's doctor from the confirmation of her pregnancy to the birth of Nicholas Carmichael. That was the one moment where Patrick knew he might have lost all dignity and cried at the pain, the blind thoughtlessness, of what Katie had done. They had the legal separation papers and the final divorce decree. They had the dates, the places, as well as the evidence that they'd both violated the separation agreement just weeks before it would have ended and the divorce became an automatic conclusion.

"So it's our understanding, for the record, that Katherine Carmichael made no attempt to contact the biological father of the child, Nicholas Carmichael, to inform him of his status in this child's life?"

"Correct," one of Katie's attorneys said, his tone a giveaway to his belief that she'd handled the situation poorly.

"Any particular reason?"

The room went dead silent. Katie had the floor, and the opportunity to justify what everyone already knew she had no justification for.

"Patrick and I were divorced—"

"That decision had *not* officially come through yet," Patrick countered immediately. His lawyer touched his arm.

"You do understand that there is no question that Patrick is the father?"

"I didn't know that at the time," Katie said defensively. "I saw no reason to inform him of anything. We were done, as far as I was concerned."

"What you did was unbelievable!" Patrick raged.

"I wanted nothing more to do with you."

"Are you going to tell me what I did to deserve what *you* did? Because I don't think there's anything you can say that puts you in a good light."

"She is the mother of your child," one of the lawyers said sternly.

"You ruined my life!" Katie jumped up, shouting back.

"Okay, everyone calm down. Yelling isn't going to get us through this. And it's not going to change the facts."

Patrick stared at Katie, confused. "How did I ruin your life?"

"You did nothing to help when I was in trials, trying for a spot on the U.S. team."

"I had nothing to do with that. As a matter of fact, that was the year I was down in Florida after being signed. I was in training myself. There was nothing I could have done to help you. Nothing I should have done. That's what you had a trainer and coach for. That's what your dad said he'd do for you. He gave you the moon and the stars. All you had to do was show up and do the work!"

"You should have been there to help me."

Patrick's mouth dropped open. He bounded up, pushing his chair back before anyone could stop him. "Are you kidding me? Was I supposed to hold your hand? Run the track for you? Why was it my responsibility to make sure you qualified? Katie, your dad may have thought the sun rose and set with you, but you were in a competitive playing field. You don't get things handed to you. And *none* of that has anything to do with you not telling me I had a son."

"He doesn't know who you are. He has me."

"Well, that's going to change. Don't think I'm not going to fight you for the right to be a father to Nicholas. And don't think I won't sue to have his true last name put on his birth certificate."

"It's not going to happen!"

"It if takes the last penny I have. And I have a *lot* of pennies."

"Mr. Bennett. Ms. Carmichael. *Please calm down!*"

"Do you really think you can keep me a secret, or away from him, for the rest of his life? How do you think he's going to feel when it turns out you lied to him about me? That you denied him the chance to have a relationship with his father just because you were mad at me?"

"I'd make him understand what you did to me."

Patrick blinked at Katie and felt his anger and bitterness begin to dissipate. It was replaced with a profound pity for Katie. He realized that she was never going to be the kind of person who learned from mistakes and admitted when she was wrong or knew how to say she was sorry. And remembering how her parents appeared in the reception area, worried, concerned, and fully aware of what their daughter was capable of, Patrick was beginning also to feel more for them. They were not the problem. Their daughter was a profoundly unhappy woman who was comfortable holding others to blame for her own shortcomings. He had no intention of aiding and abetting her. And he had every intention of holding her culpable for the injustice she'd done to him and to their son.

———

Jean had been looking forward to the rendezvous in the luxury of a hotel suite with all the trappings…including room service! It would have been a fantasy meetup, and all they had to do was be together and enjoy themselves.

Even up to the time she'd actually been able to leave the mayor's reception, Jean considered taking a car down to Midtown to meet with Patrick. But it was nearly midnight, and even she had to accept the lost opportunity. And she was exhausted. It wasn't the end of the world, but she truly missed what the night might have been for them.

She knew that Patrick was going to be in Philadelphia the next day. And he'd called her from the airport in Philly and admitted that he was meeting with lawyers but didn't say why. He sounded distracted, like the call was an afterthought. What was going on?

Jean's heart sank. She found herself in a state of growing anxiety. She didn't really know where he was. Had he returned to the city? Was he in trouble again? Why was he meeting with lawyers in Philly?

They were off track. Disconnected. In separate universes. How could they do a flyby and catch up with one another? Or was it getting to be too late? Billy Joel had said it best: "'When you love someone, you're always insecure.'"

And that was the long and short of it, Jean decided. She was in love with Patrick, but their relationship was still unclear to her. She was at work and had to finally accept that it was a lost day. She couldn't concentrate. Had Patrick been so disappointed by their broken plans that he had established a cooling-off period for himself?

"Jean, can you come to the break room?"

Jean sighed and brushed her hair from her neck, briefly massaging the nape. She hadn't been sleeping well.

"What's in the break room? Please don't tell me a box of Dunkin' Donuts. I'm already on sugar overload from this morning's breakfast meeting."

"Nothing like that. Our intern just got engaged, and she's leaving at the end of the week for a full-time position at Hunter College. We got a bottle of champagne for a double celebration."

Jean went, relieved that the room was quite busy and filled with coworkers. She was able to join in the many good wishes, fond recollections, and anecdotes with reasonable cheerfulness before quietly withdrawing to the sidelines to watch. She was distracted, concerned about her own anxious state and what seemed to be her faltering relationship with Patrick.

Did it have anything to do with that stupid fake car accident or the ensuing lawsuit? Or the horrible attempt by a former college girlfriend who came forward with an accusation of sexual harassment? Or the Black soccer player who said Patrick discriminated against him by excluding him from a team interview, implying he wasn't a team player?

Or was it her? What had she done?

Jean navigated her way through the gathering and wished the young woman a last *very happy*, before putting down her unfinished champagne and returning to her office. It was a sad commentary on her life at the moment that her only plan for the evening was to order takeout and ensconce herself on her love seat with the Roku remote and her Netflix queue. Get through the night. Start over in the morning. Work. Repeat.

Jean screwed up the courage to try once more to reach out to Patrick. She sent a simply worded text.

Are you all right?

She gathered her tote, said good night to security as she pushed through the exit turnstile, and walked out the colonnade entrance. Jean looked up from putting away her security ID. Patrick was standing directly in front of her. His expression and features were hidden behind very dark sunglasses. His mouth was an unforgiving hard line. He was casually dressed in black slacks, a white camp shirt, and suede Adidas.

They stood silently facing off across a gulf of only eight feet, but Jean's sense of something being terribly wrong was only reinforced by Patrick's seeming lack of response to seeing her. She didn't want to be the first to speak. She didn't know what to say.

Patrick held up his smartphone for her to see.

"I just responded to your text. The answer is no."

"Want to tell me what's going on?" Jean finally got out. She hated that she sounded so plaintive.

Slowly, he closed the distance and seemed to glare down at her behind his imposing shades.

"We need to talk." Patrick nodded.

His tone was serious. Somber. That surprised Jean. She was resigned to the worse. But then Patrick reached for her hand, closing it in his firmly. Jean held on tightly. She took it as a sign. But was it going to be a good one?

"Where can we go?"

Jean blinked, glancing around.

"Let's go to Filmore's. You've been there before. It'll be quiet now."

Filmore's had been the venue for his lottery win after-party. Patrick opted to sit inside and had the waiter seat them near the window, but in a corner that guaranteed more privacy.

He removed his sunglasses, and Jean stared at his expression. He didn't look angry at all, but bone-weary tired. Done in. And agitated. Spontaneously she reached across the table and grabbed his hand.

"Patrick?" she quietly asked, trying to prompt him.

"What can I get for you?"

The sudden appearance of the waiter startled Jean. She swallowed the urge to shout at him to go away.

"Iced tea, please."

"The same," Patrick murmured, focusing on her as the waiter left.

She now noticed that his eyes were slightly bloodshot. He wasn't getting any more sleep than she was.

Jean sighed and spoke up. "You have something you want to say to me, don't you?"

"Yes, I do."

"I realize that things have gotten difficult, Patrick."

"They have gotten impossible," he blurted out with the first signs of anger. "Ridiculous."

She withdrew her hand. "Has something…happened?"

"That hasn't already happened? Yeah, it has. But I can't say if it's terrible. Depends. I…I don't know," Patrick murmured combing a hand through his hair. "Every time I think *I've got this, I'm on it*, the carpet gets pulled out from under me." He cupped his hands together and rested his mouth and chin against them. He glared at her over the top, his gaze distant and troubled.

"What?" she coaxed in a whisper, already prepared for the worst.

"We can't go on this way, Jean. I feel like I'm seriously losing control of my life. I think it's beginning to affect my work. Even the studio is becoming concerned. They want to do something about it."

She blanched, her eyes widening. She felt the heat of a blush rushing over her face.

"I get that…" She could barely get the words out.

"Here you go. Iced tea for two!"

She jumped. The waiter had startled her again.

Patrick set his glass aside. Jean stared into hers.

"So this is it. It's over. I guess the Force has not actually been with us after all," Jean said, managing humor and a shaky smile.

Patrick was staring blankly at her. "What?" He sounded puzzled.

"Like you said last week. No one's to blame. These things happen."

A furrow of confusion cleaved across his forehead. He reached out and grabbed both her hands, so hard her eyes rounded and her mouth dropped opened.

"Jean…*Jean!* What are you talking about? What do you think I'm trying to say? *No!* I'm not breaking up with you. I'm pissed off because we can't seem to plan real quality time together. Uninterrupted, leisurely, chill time together. Not a few hours that just dropped into our lap and we have to go for it or it disappears! I need more than that. I want more than that. Don't…don't you?"

She still didn't trust herself to speak. Her throat was about to close up with emotion. Her tongue was rooted to the roof of her mouth. She nodded. And she kept nodding until she could force it out.

"Yes, I do."

The allusion wasn't lost on either of them, and they both chuckled nervously.

Patrick abruptly pushed his chair back and stood up. His tight grip on her hands forced Jean to stand as well, and he pulled her into his arms. They hugged tightly. They stroked each other's back. Patrick was whispering something close to her ear, but Jean wasn't listening. She was burrowed into his arms and chest, a safe harbor. He pulled back just enough to capture her mouth, beginning to kiss with an intense intimacy. Jean broke the kiss, glancing quickly around.

"We're in a public place," she whispered.

Patrick's grin was resolute. "Ask me if I care." He began kissing her again. But it had to stop. They may very well not have cared that other customers were watching in amusement, but one man was bold enough to shout, "Take it somewhere private, Mac."

They came to their senses and sat back down.

"This is a preemptive strike," Patrick said, speaking quietly to her across the table. "Before things really get bad. Trust me, they will. To be honest, I thought you'd have had it with me, us, long before now and would call it quits."

"No, that's not true," she said, vigorously shaking her head.

"Good," he said on a great exhalation of relief. "Listen. It's all my fault. My life is a mess right now, and there's no end in sight." He stared at their hands clasped together, his thumb caressing across the top of hers. "There's something important I have to tell you about my trip to Philly. And I will, soon. It's just another brick in the wall. I'm honestly afraid to see what's going to happen next. But you're the *only* person I feel safe with, Jean. The only person I feel I can really trust. I'm not giving you up."

"Patrick," she said, "I don't believe any of it is your fault."

He raised her hand to kiss the fingers. "You're sweet to say that, but I have to accept some responsibility. From the start, as soon as I got the news I'd won all that money, I could have done things differently. I should have kept my mouth shut or left town for parts unknown. That's what I'm about to do."

"What do you mean?"

He finally sat back and drank from his tea, finishing nearly half of it like a man dying of thirst.

"My management team decided I'm getting a little too much attention. I'm a little too hot right now. Too high profile. The ratings are phenomenal, but it's the sort of attention that can turn against you in a heartbeat. Fans are notoriously fickle. They love you one minute, and then want to watch you drown in quicksand the next. The ESPN station is suggesting getting ahead of the curve."

"Doing what?"

"Blowing town for a while. I like the idea, frankly. I'm seriously in need of a break. Some downtime away from the public eye...and lawsuits."

"So what do they suggest?"

Patrick sighed, slouching in his chair, finally beginning to unwind.

"Well, the official line is that I'm going to be on assignment. Purpose and place undisclosed, of course. I'll be out in the field, maybe for a week or more."

"Okay."

"But the truth is, my plan is to really drop out of sight someplace where no one knows who I am and they don't care. I'm working on disappearing somewhere remote, in the middle of an ocean. The only people who'll actually know where I am is my mom and my sister in case of emergency, and you."

"That will be so great for you..."

"Jean, you'll know because I want you to come with me. That's what makes this whole idea so beautiful. We will be together. And no one will know where."

Again, she couldn't speak. After so many off and on days of wondering where she stood with Patrick, he had perfectly outlined the importance of her place in his life.

"Are you sure you..."

He groaned in the back of his throat, closed his eyes, and leaned across the table to press his forehead to hers. "I don't want to say that's a foolish question, but that's a foolish question. I haven't been so sure of *anything* in a hell of a long time."

CHAPTER 14

Jean heard not a sound from the rooms behind her, all of which had sliding doors that opened to the tiled deck, the beach just a few hundred yards beyond. There was the gentle swoosh of seawater lapping on the shore. No waves, no surf. She drew up her knees as she reclined on the lounger and peered from beneath the brim of her straw hat. The red grosgrain ribbon wrapped and tied around the hat trailed a bit from behind, tickling the skin at her neck and shoulders. Jean briefly closed her eyes, took in a long deep breath, and slowly exhaled.

Is this what heaven is like?

As she'd done since she and Patrick arrived in Turks and Caicos two days earlier, she sat looking out at a world that was not to be believed. She'd never been to the Caribbean before. On this eastern side of West Caicos, there were no speedboats with grinding, revved-up motors, no cruise ships off in the distance, no Jet Skis…no nothing. Patrick had said it was just what he wanted. Jean knew it was also what he needed. They both did.

It was time away from life in the fast lane, where nothing ever seemed to slow down. Time away from the kind of interruptions that couldn't be helped, but which hampered the time they had together. Time away from the crushing manipulations of perfect strangers. The fact that Patrick had insisted she travel with him on his bogus assignment did much to convince Jean his feelings for her were sincere. Ten days away could be time enough, she felt, to figure out where they were headed.

Patrick had taken full control of how they were going to drop out of sight by making all the arrangements. The studio would pay him vacation time, but Patrick paid for where he and Jean would stay and how they would get there. Jean enjoyed the private car service only because it guaranteed that they would be the only passengers. Unlike city cabs, the private car drivers weren't chatty. An excellent practice at 6:00 a.m. headed out to JFK. Taking a private jet for the first time seriously upped the ante! It couldn't get any better than being escorted through a tiny terminal and boarding the jet from the tarmac…with the pilot greeting you at the bottom of the steps.

This was unlike the helicopter experience, which was more intimate and basic, more down-to-earth in its own way. Boarding the Citation M2 light jet finally gave Jean a sense of what money could buy for the wealthy. And yet, she still didn't attach to Patrick the moniker of "super-rich," even though he was. The difference was, Patrick never behaved any differently. He'd only come to learn that having a lot of wealth meant he had access to more benefits and amenities. It didn't change who he was. But he was learning how to enjoy what he had.

The sun was already up when they took off. Just the two of them in what Jean had come to see as a *baby plane*. As soon as they were airborne, she could see the tension ooze out of Patrick's pores, leaving him so relaxed that in an hour, he'd fallen asleep. She let him. She understood what the past several weeks had been for him. And for her. She hoped that the time away would restore his balance and give Patrick perspective on his future. He woke forty minutes later to tell Jean all the things he wanted to do while they were on Turks and Caicos. *Nothing.* She didn't much care as long as they were doing nothing together.

She'd come to learn, however, that Patrick was very good at surprises. And even though he knew that surprises were not her strong point—they made her feel unmoored and helpless—Patrick's revelations were always fully that: wonderful surprises. They didn't land at Providenciales Airport but flew on for another fifteen minutes to Lettsome Airport on Virgin Gorda, BVI. While the pilot arranged for refueling, Jean and Patrick caught a cab to a beachfront restaurant called CocoMaya for lunch. It was open-air, with an on-the-sand lounge area—no shoes required—and an upper level that overlooked the sea and a beachside marina.

They were served fresh shrimp and salmon, salads, panko onion rings, and dragon board sushi. Patrick ordered prosecco.

"It's barely noon."

"Your point?" he asked, raising his brows above the sunglasses.

"Isn't it too early for that?"

He grinned woefully at her. "You don't get out much, do you?"

Jean shrugged. "I'm just not used to cocktails and sparkling wine at high noon."

The waitress served their drinks, and Patrick held out his glass so they could clink the rims. "We're not driving. Nothing to worry about."

Jean was almost delirious. She was never going to confess to Patrick that he made her feel special. *Princess* came to mind, except it was so corny and trite. *Special* was good enough.

"How did you know about this place?"

Patrick thoughtfully crunched an onion ring before responding. "I know a lot of people. And a lot of people I know do things like island hop in the Caribbean in the summer or fly to Europe for a weekend." He watched her for reaction.

"A great life if you can get it."

"Maybe, but not all the time. Then it loses its specialness if you take it for granted. What makes it so special now is that I can do some of these fun things with you, Jean. I'm really enjoying surprising you."

"Well, I'm not going to pretend I haven't loved every minute. But…"

"Yeah, I know. You'd be just as happy if we hung out in Prospect Park or did a foodie tour in Jersey City…"

She laughed sheepishly. "Busted."

Patrick looked out over the blue Caribbean, the breeze ruffling his hair. "You know, I think this is the happiest I've been in, like, weeks."

"Really?" she asked, tilting her head.

"Don't you know why?" he asked, turning his shaded gaze back to her.

"You're not at work? You don't have to wear a suit? Hordes of young women aren't camped out in your building lobby hoping to meet you?"

He silently stared, and Jean waited for a sharp and funny reply. Patrick shook his head. "We walked back into each other's lives. And suddenly mine began to make sense."

Jean couldn't think of a single intelligent thing to say. She didn't want Patrick to know she felt exactly the same way.

When they'd finally arrived that first afternoon, they'd left their luggage in the master bedroom and immediately gone for a walk on the beach, leaving their shoes behind in the grassy knoll below the deck. Patrick picked the direction, but it didn't matter. There was the sense of having stepped into another world, a time warp where deadlines, car services, upscale restaurants, ten-hour workdays, five-hour nights of sleep not only didn't exist, they had no meaning.

Once they'd explored the area and realized that, while they could see a number of expensive, private retreats around them, they could not hear their neighbors, Patrick put his arm around her waist and suggested, "Let's pretend we're the only people left on Earth," as they'd stood staring out to sea.

Yes, let's.

Jean had realized on their first full day that it was easy to become hypnotized by the setting. The pristine sand, the aqua sea, and the marine-blue sky with white clouds were soothing. Earth, sea, and sky… the edge of the world.

Jean repeated this to herself so as to forestall the inevitability of returning to their real world. On that first night, the housekeeper and cook from the management company prepared them an alfresco dinner of grilled scallops, asparagus, and corn, melon for dessert, and a wonderful pinot grigio that certainly suggested they were in paradise. But they informed the middle-aged woman, originally from the nearby island of Haiti, that they preferred to make their own meals for the duration of their stay. The kitchen had been well stocked. Jean knew that request must have been due to Patrick's desire not to leave the estate unless an emergency warranted it. He had completely shut down and he wanted—needed—to stay that way until they had to return home.

Afterward, that first night, as the dusk rolled in and they enjoyed the last of the wine, they relaxed in a stupor in sturdy beach chairs on the sand, tired and lulled into peace. Off to their left, they suddenly heard the high-pitched, excited babbling of a very young child, a little girl speaking in French. Eventually a young couple appeared, walking just far enough behind the little girl so as not to hamper her sense of adventure and freedom.

She trotted along on her short legs, holding a yellow plastic pail in one hand and blue plastic shovel in the other. The parents said something. The child ignored them, running as fast as she could and having an imaginary conversation. Jean and Patrick exchanged amused glances, watching the approach. The young child was almost abreast of them when she tripped and did a spectacular belly flop onto the soft sand. The parents didn't hurry to rescue her. The little girl did not cry. She laughed. Whatever had been in the pail had spilled out. She looked inside, then turned the pail upside down and shook out the rest of the contents.

Jean spontaneously got up and walked the short distance to the little girl. She crouched to her level. "Do you need help?"

Rather than becoming afraid or turning to run to her parents, the child regarded her with wide-eyed curiosity.

The parents were almost upon them. They stopped and said a friendly hello to Jean. They waved to Patrick, sitting lazily with his long legs stretched out, waving back.

"We are just a few houses down," the man pointed, speaking in perfect English with a French accent.

"We're here," Jean said, pointing to the house on the rise behind Patrick.

Jean turned back to the child. Without saying anything, she scooped sand into her hands and dropped it into the pail. The girl held out the shovel.

"*Ici.*"

Jean thanked the little girl, in English, and looked to the parents to see if they objected. Not at all, it seemed, as they watched the exchange.

Jean and the little girl took turns shoveling into the pail until it was full. But when the little girl tried to lift it, she grunted and heaved under the weight in a comical way that had all the adults smiling and chuckling.

"She is Lily," the woman said, pointing to the child. And then introduced herself and her husband.

Jean did the same for her and Patrick.

"Jean," the girl repeated, testing out the sound.

Jean nodded. "That's right." Then she spoke the French version of her name.

The couple and Lily became their only acknowledged neighbors. But only by chance did they see or have brief interactions with them. And it all was exclusively between Jean and Lily, the French parents more circumspect about being overly familiar with her and Patrick. There seemed to be an unspoken agreement that while they all liked one another, they were also all there for the same reason: to tune out and be allowed to enjoy their vacation.

Later, when she and Patrick lay in bed whispering in the dark, the night absolutely black beyond the open doors, he'd put his arm around her, coaxing her to put her head on his arm as they lay facing each other.

"You were amazing."

"What do you mean?"

"With that little girl. Lily."

"Isn't she cute?"

"So are you. I thought she'd be afraid because you're a stranger."

"Why? No one's afraid of me."

Patrick responded after several very long moments. "I am," he said quietly.

Jean chuckled, rubbing her hand across his chest. "Yeah right."

Stretching languidly, Jean put aside the book she'd brought with her. She hadn't managed to get past the first dozen or so pages, constantly distracted by the desire to stare out to sea and absorb as much as she could of this peaceful, stress-free place and being genuinely alone with Patrick.

Can we say divine?

Can we say magical?

Jean finally moved, rising from the lounger and heading into the bedroom, through the deck doors that were open to the warm air. She took off the straw hat and placed it with her sunglasses on the bureau. She quietly approached the bed. Patrick was still asleep. The top sheet had long since been kicked aside, and he was sprawled on his stomach, naked. She regarded him, privately enjoying the masculine build of him. He had not been an active athlete for many years, but he was still toned, fit, and well proportioned. Jean undid the clasps of the swim top and removed it, dropping it to the floor. She was stepping out of the boy-brief bottoms when she was thrown off balance as Patrick's long arm hooked around her waist and hauled her backward. She fell onto the bed next to him.

"Patrick!" she squealed.

He gave a low, throaty chuckle as he pulled her against him, throwing a leg over hers to hold her still as Jean wiggled and struggled fruitlessly. Patrick lay calmly, waiting for her to stop.

"You know you don't mean it." His voice was still gravelly from sleep.

Slightly out of breath, she relented and returned his drowsy, amused gaze. "You startled me."

"Are you mad?" he asked, merely curious.

"I should be."

They studied each other, as if the two of them together was still something of a surprise. Jean reached to stroke his cheek, her fingers rubbing through the short growth of facial hair. She now knew his habit of going for a few days in his off time without shaving. It gave Patrick a very different look. Wicked. Virile. Sexy. She liked it.

"What time is it?" he asked.

"Does it matter?"

He slowly grinned. "You're right."

"A little after nine."

"Nine?" he was genuinely surprised. "In the morning?"

Jean pinched him.

"How come you're up?"

Jean snuggled even closer, raising a bent knee to rest on his inner thigh. He let out a soft moan.

"It's so beautiful out. I didn't want to waste time sleeping. I'm usually up by six thirty anyway."

"That's indecent. And you deserted me. What if I'd had a nightmare? Who would comfort me?"

Jean rolled her eyes, suppressing a smile. "Oh, please. You're turning into a slug."

Patrick leaned in to kiss her nose. She wrinkled it. He moved his mouth lower, to her lips. Jean parted them to accept the invasion he pressed upon her. It was sweet and deep and aroused them both quickly.

His body reacted and Patrick rotated his hips, forcing her knee aside. Jean raised it higher, leaving herself wide-open at the core as she grew wet waiting to receive him. Yearning gnawed at her insides.

Patrick twisted his mouth over hers, massaging and stroking their tongues together, stimulating the kind of response that made her dizzy and limp with longing. He cupped his hands around her bottom, and she pressed her hips forward so he could find her. She broke the kiss, throwing her head back, moaning as Patrick slid smoothly inside her, his movement caressing the sensitive inner walls.

It was lovely to cuddle and thrust slowly together, to temper their breathing so there was no desire to rush. The cadence and movement of their joined bodies syncopated perfectly, the passion building gradually. A mutual urgency had Patrick twisting their bodies, putting Jean on her back. He grunted in relief as they were finally in a position to grant full sway and rhythm to their coupling. Patrick came first, Jean's light stroking on his lower back encouraging his response. Finally, his strong pulsing and thrusting forced Jean to the edge and over into a free fall of spiraling release. They were still and quiet, their bodies recovering, except for the low, breathy panting.

They couldn't move if their lives depended on it.

They lay entwined and dazed, their bodies languid and soft and damp.

They stayed that way for a long time, and Jean was happy to be locked in a sleepy, satisfied afterglow that was perfect just as it was. They dozed and fell in and out of dreams until they eventually awakened, replete and satisfied.

Jean found herself right where they'd begun: facing each other in unspoken contentment. It was almost frightening how happy she felt. Was it real?

"Do you ever wonder how did we get here?"

Patrick sighed, his gaze locking with hers. "Not anymore. I'm just glad we did. Why?"

Jean averted her gaze, smoothing her hand over his stomach, rubbing her cheek against the warm and hard muscles of his chest. "There was a time, after I'd left high school and was growing up, I imagined you always surrounded by gorgeous women. I felt that…"

Patrick smoothed her wild hair. He rested his hand on her waist. "What? That one of them would sweep me away? Or somehow ensnare me? Or I'd find them irresistible? Many of them were. But they also didn't last. We managed to get where we are because… I don't know. The time was right? Fate? Don't underestimate how attractive you are to me, Jean. I'm here. We're here."

"At least one of those women had something extra special. You got married."

He sighed, not responding for a moment. "Yeah, I did. Maybe too young. Certainly not knowing enough about anything. We loved each other at the time, probably for the wrong reasons. Then you start to figure it out, you know? You grow up.

"The way I see it now, by the time you and I met up again, I'd learned the difference between crazy, hot sex and…real feelings. I worked the booty calls out of my system a long time ago. I'm glad you and I had a second chance to meet again."

"That's lovely, Patrick. You're very persuasive," she whispered, staring into his eyes.

"I hope that means you're not going to kick me to the curb." He bent over her and began to nibble his way across her mouth.

Patrick drew in a breath to search into her eyes. "I think we need to do something. We have to get out of bed *now*, or we'll be here until we fly back."

"All right," Jean agreed. "What do you have in mind?"

Patrick thought for a moment and produced a wicked, sly grin. "Last one into the pool cooks dinner…and cleans up!"

With that, he threw the top sheet over Jean's head and scrambled off the bed. She squealed, trying to break free of the bed linen. She heard Patrick laughing.

Suddenly, there was a crash, and the chair next to the bed toppled over.

"Ow!" Patrick grunted as he tumbled over the fallen chair to the floor.

Jean took advantage, scooting from the bed and leaping over Patrick's prone body. She squealed when he attempted to grab her ankle but pulled herself free. She dashed through the open doors to the deck, racing around a line of loungers to the edge of the pool. Holding her nose, she made a childlike jump into the water.

She surfaced just as Patrick made a clean dive right next to her, cleaving the surface without so much as a splash, with beautiful athletic form. He surfaced, shaking water from his hair. In one long stroke, he reached Jean, pulling her into his arms and treading water to keep them both afloat.

"I win," he said boldly.

Jean tried to brush her thick, wet hair from her face, her ponytail pulled loose, sodden and heavy. She clutched at Patrick, an arm around his neck. Her bare breasts were flattened to his chest.

"You cheated!"

"I was hurt!"

His excitement and playfulness suddenly died down as he considered her.

"And it got me what I wanted," Patrick confirmed, a hand behind her head pressing Jean closer for a kiss that said far more than words ever could.

———

Patrick made sure his dark glasses were secure on his nose against the force of the wind. The motor of the small speedboat was noisy, blasting into the air and disturbing the tranquility of the islands as it skimmed over the sea. It was returning Patrick to the island where he and Jean had been staying. The young pilot, a mainland transplant from Texas, was shouting to be heard above the sounds. It was idle chitchat, and Patrick had mostly tuned him out. The last thing he'd expected since he and Jean had arrived on Turks and Caicos was to be asked to play the role of sports commentator. An urgent text from his manager had changed that.

His ESPN affiliate arranged for Patrick to conduct an interview at a jury-rigged studio set up in the tourist office of the main island. The subject was a famous Brazilian soccer player who happened to be staying at a nearby resort. The interview had only taken about forty minutes, but it was all the start and end setups that had nearly driven Patrick crazy.

He was anxious to get back to Jean. He stopped just short of thinking of their island as *home*, as if they were shipwrecked in paradise. They had one more day before heading back to the real world.

"How long you been here?" the pilot asked over the buzzing noise of his engine.

"Little over a week. Not long enough," Patrick mused.

"I know what you mean. Me and my girlfriend came for two weeks three years ago. She eventually went home. I stayed."

Patrick grinned. "Not prepared to do that. Maybe I'll buy the island to use for long weekend getaways."

The pilot laughed. "Only if you win the lottery or something."

The pilot didn't believe him. Patrick continued to grin, but it quickly faded.

It struck him that he'd not really had a vacation in…he had no idea how long. He did so much traveling anyway for the show, much of it never really felt like work. He'd become accustomed to hotel suites, expensive gourmet meals, overzealous waitstaff, the benefits befitting someone in his business—groupies—that he'd never really felt a need to "get away from it all." At least, not until recently, when his life took a screeching sharp curve to the left, leaving him battered by frivolous lawsuits, potential scandal, and a sudden appreciation for living under the radar.

Like Jean.

She had a very important position in the mayor's office of one of the biggest, most complicated, glamorous cities on Earth. And somehow, she managed to succeed with great skill and competence, and a high level of grace and charm. He'd seen her in action and how quick she was to adapt to any given situation, or person, without complaint. Patrick could easily guess he probably had the better salary, just for knowing a lot about sports.

On the other hand, Patrick had come to learn that being around Jean had other effects, like making him feel normal, finding ways to neutralize his sometimes chaotic life. All of that was really nice, but it was other areas that Jean touched on that were having the most impact—the in-depth conversations, teasing, and laughter. From the start, there had been lots of that. Patrick had suddenly realized it just that morning as he waited on the small dock built into the sand at the edge of the beach belonging to the property. A water taxi had been arranged to take him to the interview.

Jean had opted to stay behind. Having spent every moment together for a week plus, it had been unsettling to him that they were about to be separated, even for a mere three or four hours. He'd experienced a twinge of concern that this small fact bothered him so much.

"You're going to work, and I'll be in the way. There will be nothing for me to do."

"What are you going to do with yourself?"

She had given him a look. "I'm going to hunt for seashells. Then I'm going to do laps in the pool. Then I'll take a nap...or try to get past page twenty in that book I brought with me. I'm going down the beach to say goodbye to Lily and her parents. They're leaving today to fly back to Europe. I'll tell them why you're off island. "

Patrick had chuckled at her itinerary and then quickly cut off her list with a kiss. "Are you going to miss me?"

"You're not leaving for the Amazon, you know. I'll start dinner."

"I'll be back in time to help."

She smiled broadly, her nose dotted with freckles that had appeared during her time in the sun. Her skin was golden, like honey. "Okay."

When the boat had arrived at the dock and the pilot called out his name, Patrick pecked Jean one more time on her mouth.

Jean had been right, of course, and he didn't try to dissuade her from staying behind. But he'd felt a difference, a brief anxiety, the minute the engine of the small boat came to life, and the young pilot turned it on a course with sudden speed. The emotional sensation was instantly gone, but Patrick had taken note. He had waved at Jean, standing near the dunes in front of *their* house, watching her become tiny until her floral romper was just a splash of yellow under a straw hat and big, dark shades.

Now, the pilot cut the engine, and the noise abated as the boat swayed on the waves and floated next to the dock and the shore.

"I appreciate this." Patrick reached into his shirt pocket and pulled out a folded bill, stuffing it into the pilot's T-shirt pocket. "I'm home," Patrick said, pointing to the house just beyond the grassy dune. "Thanks for the ride."

Taking off his shoes, he swung his feet over the side of the boat and found the sandy bottom. The water level rose between his knees and up to his cargo Bermuda shorts.

"Thanks. See you next time." The pilot waved, expertly turned the boat, and sped away.

Patrick squinted toward the shore. Jean was not there. He made his way out of the surf, scanning both directions along the stretch of beach. He then headed up the dune to the short steps leading to the pool deck. He kept walking to the open doors to the master suite and stepped inside.

"Jean?"

No response. He put the envelope that held his program notes from the interview on the coffee table, dropped his shoes, and noticed that the outdoor dining table had been set for dinner. Patrick reversed his steps and returned to the dune, searching the shore once more. In the distance, he spotted three adults walking up to their ankles in the surf, two tall Black men, locals, and the shorter Jean in the middle in her distinct summery romper. He could just make out her laugh as the trio walked toward him, one holding a bulky wrapping.

And that was when the second realization hit Patrick. It completely turned his assumptions about him and Jean upside down. There were other men who walked the earth who recognized the amazing woman she was. He remembered that first night at the lottery-win party when he saw Brian Abbott's interest burn bright. And weeks later when Brian had played the gallant to Jean's damsel at the studio taping. Or being with

Jean during the mayor's bike event when she'd fallen. Now there were the local island men who had spotted all of Jean's glorious beauty and generous personality. Patrick felt a moment of insecurity.

Didn't Jean know that her place was secure in his heart?

Patrick blinked, watching her approach. The one man handed off the package to her. But all Patrick really saw was Jean beaming at him, half her face hidden by the wide brim of her hat and her dark glasses.

"You're back!"

The two men maintained their easy gait, but Jean walked a bit faster to hold out the bundle to Patrick. He looked at it and back to Jean, puzzled.

"Dinner," she said brightly. "Thanks to Kel and Remy."

Introductions were made, and Patrick silently listened to Jean's adventure of walking to a local market to purchase fresh fish for dinner only to discover that all the fresh catch had already been sold. Enter Kel and Remy, who had just finished dropping off their catch to several restaurants when they encountered Jean and her dilemma. Kel had promptly extracted a bonefish from the cooler on the back of their pickup, haphazardly wrapped it in wax paper and newsprint, and handed it to her.

Now, they seemed to have become instant best friends. Patrick was amused by the story and relieved that the encounter was no more than that. When Jean spontaneously invited them to dinner to share their catch, they politely turned her down.

"My wife kill me if I have dinner with another pretty woman," Kel announced, sending his dreads, caught atop his head, quivering with each animated movement.

"No fish." Remy shook his head, arms crossed and hands tucked into his armpits. "I vegetarian."

Patrick and Jean both laughed.

"We walk her back. Make sure no one take your dinner."

"Or your woman," Remy added.

"Thanks. Really nice of you. What do we owe for the fish?" Patrick asked.

"Nothing. Island gift to you and your pretty wife," Kel responded.

"Next time you come down, we take you fishing, yeah?" Remy added.

Jean fell into silence, caught off guard.

"Sounds like fun," Patrick put in. "Thanks for supplying dinner."

The two men said their goodbyes and turned to retrace their path up the beach. Patrick took the wrapped fish from Jean, and they headed up to the house.

"How did the interview go?" Jean asked.

"Good. The guy was really interesting. He's a world-class player with a World Cup team, *and* he has a degree in chemistry. Talked about maybe retiring in a year or two and taking over his family's vineyard. Seems to be doing well, making smart decisions." He turned to look down at her as they reached the open kitchen. "Glad to be back."

Jean returned his gaze with a warm, soft smile, reaching to caress his back through his summer shirt. "You know what they say about absence."

"Yeah, I do. And it does," Patrick said.

CHAPTER 15

Jean woke to the hint of light on the horizon before dawn. And an empty bed. She lay still for a moment before getting up and reaching for the short shift she'd discarded the night before, coming to prefer Patrick's habit of sleeping nude. It had been a wonderful feeling here in the tropics, but one she might not continue after returning home. Everything was different in the Caribbean.

Today was their last day. They were flying back to the city in the afternoon. They'd talked very little about it the night before, enjoying a very good dinner, thanks to Kel and Remy, and sharing a bottle of chilled prosecco.

Jean walked onto the deck and found Patrick in a lounger, his knees drawn up as he used his thigh to brace a writing tablet. His hair was ruffled by the morning breeze, but he'd not yet shaved off his facial hair that would have been a concession to his established TV look and a signal to the end of their vacation.

"Couldn't sleep?"

He reached out for her hand, encouraging Jean to join him on the lounger. "My mind switched to thinking about what has to be done when we get back. I'm making a list."

"I understand. Not much fun, is it?"

"No. But it will help me get back into the rhythm. I'll have to hit the ground running on Monday."

"Me too," she reminded him. "Can I ask what's on the list?"

"Program lineup for next week. Have Brian confirm all guests. Check if there are any meetings. The usual stuff."

"What's the unusual stuff?"

Patrick sighed, running fingers through his already mussed hair, only to have the breeze tear it up again. "Call my lawyer. There're still things on the table I have to handle," he murmured, his voice low and distracted. "And I want to check if anything else has come through while I was away. I need to meet with Ross about all the requests for money that I keep getting."

"I never realized that winning the lottery would create so many problems."

"I didn't either," Patrick said, putting his pad aside and placing an arm around her.

They were silent, each momentarily lost in their own thoughts.

"I have an idea for you to think about, if you won't mind."

"Of course I won't mind."

"Well...maybe you should consider forming some sort of charitable foundation. So any requests for money wouldn't come to you but go through the organization. You can hire administrators to manage the foundation, and you can serve as the founding CEO or COO. Maybe you can set aside money just for that but have your personal assets in different accounts.

"I don't really know much about how to do it, but the Rockefeller and Ford Foundations have been funding philanthropic giving for decades. I bet it doesn't touch their personal money."

"Wow," Patrick murmured thoughtfully. "That is a *great* idea. What made you think to suggest it?"

"It seems to me that a lot of what's coming at you has nothing, really, to do with you. It's all about the money you have. There are people working overtime to separate you from it. Why not make it easy…and worthwhile? You decide who you want to share your good fortune with. You set the ground rules, and you pick your target audience."

"Why didn't I think of that?" Patrick mused.

"You were too busy fielding curveballs."

He glanced at her with an arched brow and laughed. "You don't even know what a curveball is."

"Maybe not. Doesn't it have something to do with an unexpected turn of play?"

"Close enough," Patrick said. He regarded her quietly, his gaze suddenly drowsy. "That's the best plan I've heard from anyone the whole summer."

"You're welcome," Jean said, her voice low and warm.

"You know, I haven't given you anything since I came into such good luck. I think I knew you'd turn it down."

She became serious. "I would have."

"Why?"

She shrugged, resting her cheek against his arm. "I feel it would blur the boundaries too much between…" She stopped, trapped by anything she might say that would also assume too much.

"Where we are?"

Jean nodded.

"Where are we, Jean?" His voice was barely a whisper.

"Maybe…a very good beginning?" she asked, hesitating.

Patrick untangled himself and stood up, taking her hand to pull her up as well.

"I think it's a little more than a beginning," Patrick said, walking them back into the house.

He said nothing as he headed for the bedroom and then turned to Jean to pull her shift slowly over her head. She stood naked before him as Patrick held her gaze. He removed his shorts, and Jean caught her breath at the evidence of his arousal. Patrick's physical state had the same effect on her, and all she wanted just then was to be in his arms and feel safe in his embrace. Alone, together on an island, before they returned to the demands of their lives.

Jean got onto the bed to wait for him to join her, on her side watching his approach. He made it clear he wanted to lie atop her, and Jean sighed, settling on her back. She reached for him as Patrick pressed down on her to kiss her with a slow intensity, as if they had all the time in the world, even as they both knew they didn't.

He moved his mouth to kiss his way down her jaw to her neck and throat. Jean tilted her head back, loving the brush of his short facial hair on her skin. It was soft. She felt Patrick wiggle and undulate his body until he lay lower, his kisses trailing down her throat. He turned his head, and his lips closed sensuously around a breast, slowly licking and manipulating her nipple.

Jean drew in her breath and let out a long, quiet moan as he turned his attention to the other breast. A swirling of tension settled in her stomach, twisting and knotting lower in her core, where she felt a heat that seemed to melt her from the inside. Patrick moved again. Lower. Kissing her chest, her stomach. His beard tickled, and then the tickling turned to little tiny tongues dancing over her skin, building on the passion that was beginning to rage within her.

Patrick moved again.

What are you...?

And then she knew.

Jean drew in her breath again, deeper, holding it. Waiting for the touch she now realized she was waiting for. She drove her fingers into his hair, holding his head as Patrick finally reached his destination. His warm breath on her sensitive opening was immediately followed by his lips. A kiss. His tongue.

Jean felt like she was losing consciousness. She was swooning, falling into a delirium of feelings that rolled through her so strongly, she thought she might succumb and pass out. She began to pant, helpless to do more than let her limbs fall open, leaving her a wanton recipient of Patrick's knowing caresses.

Jean moaned again, not sure if she wanted this assault to go on and on or hoped it would finally explode from within, releasing her from the height of her pleasure to a safe landing. The latter happened beyond her control, her eyes squeezing tight, her chest heaving as the pulsating began, gripping her tightly for what seemed like forever. A soft whimper allowed her to breathe again, and her body went slack, splayed beneath Patrick as he crawled up her body and took her in his arms.

"Ooh, Patrick," Jean managed to breathe out, cocooning herself against his chest. Quite literally dazed and confused.

"I wanted to give you something special. And personal. Memorable. Just between you and me. Okay?"

Jean wasn't sure if she said anything or just snuggled closer. She heard a chuckle deep in his chest.

"I'll take that as a yes."

—

Ready to pack my bags. Are you coming?

Jean grinned at the text, amused and not surprised by the tone of exasperation from Patrick. Returning to the city had been more of a comedown than they'd expected. Almost immediately, they both were sucked into old daily routines. She was still holding onto the glory and romance of time away with Patrick, sure that something very solid had been built. But schedules and commitments quickly did her in. Were they back in the same old place? Had their feelings for each other changed? She knew hers were now locked in. She was in love with Patrick. But could she assume that the connection they'd made on the island meant Patrick felt the same way? It was frightening to realize her feelings. Jean felt more vulnerable than ever.

They'd managed one tryst, a matter of coincidence, just a day after they'd returned to the city. She happened to be at the same network for a PSA spot the day Patrick was on air promoting his fall schedule of programs for *REPLAY*.

With both their obligations done at the same time, they spontaneously decided to run away for the day. Brad had willingly given her the rest of the day. Patrick went unrecognized as they opted to stroll Central Park hand in hand, people-watching and laughing together at their playful take on the interesting activities they encountered, like the young guy skateboarding with his dog between his feet, or the Rollerblader doing fancy and amazing choreography to retro disco music. Or the older man sailing an elaborate reproduction of the *Titanic* on the boat pond. They had lunch at the Boathouse, and otherwise acted like any couple on a day out together. As it grew late, Patrick had called for a car and then turned to Jean to ask, "Your place or mine?"

She'd never been to Patrick's apartment, an oversight that seemed incredible now.

"Yours."

"Done," he said.

The evening turned out to be just as surprising as the day. Patrick's condo was spacious, with floor-to-ceiling living room and bedroom windows. The view over the Hudson back to Manhattan was stunning. He didn't make a big deal of giving her a tour of the place, but enough for Jean to see it was a very modern, high-end, masculine apartment that was attractive and nicely outfitted. Somehow it was lacking in personal touches, the messiness of single living, like articles of clothing casually left around, magazines, mail, mugs of half-finished coffee. There was commercial, framed artwork on the walls, and lots of photos of his mother, sister and her family, other family members…and Patrick with a variety of male pro athletes. And women Jean presumed to be good friends or more. Lots of blonds with Hollywood smiles. And this wasn't the first time that Jean wondered if Patrick had ever had an affair with, had ever dated another African American woman. The thought that she might be the only one raised old fears.

"It's very nice," Jean commented. She glanced out the window to the New York skyline. "You don't have a lot privacy."

"It's not like your place. Now you know why I'm happy staying with you."

"And that's because…" she coaxed.

He came to stand next to her, gazing down and shrugging. "I like your place better. I'm okay here for now. But this is an interior designer's dream. It's not a real home."

She chuckled, pleased that Patrick didn't treat her like she was a guest, but that didn't mean she had a place here. Patrick, however, behaved as if this wasn't a first time, it wasn't a last time, and it wasn't any big deal. He just wanted to spend the evening with her. He apologized, as always, when he had to selectively answer texts, emails, or calls, keeping them short. He clearly had developed a shorthand for business interruptions on his free time. She was impressed with the succinct way he handled them. Polite and businesslike. And when he was done, he was again the Patrick she knew and loved best.

Jean casually mentioned that she was being considered for a new job. Not in the mayor's office, but in the Department of Cultural Affairs. Patrick had poured her a glass of wine, gotten himself a beer, and sat next to her waiting to hear more.

"Good offer? Better position? Are you interested?"

"Yes. Yes. I'm not sure. I like where I am right now. It's crazy but interesting, with lots of different responsibilities."

Patrick studied her, thoughtful. He stretched his arm behind her on the sofa back, his fingertips rubbing along her shoulder and nape. "Would you take another job outside of the city?"

"I've never thought about that either."

He continued to stare as if expecting her to say more.

What?

"I've been thinking about doing something different, myself."

Jean recalled the speculation put forth by both Brian and Marin. "Really? Like what?"

He took a deep drink of his beer and put the bottle down. He brushed his hand through his hair, locked his hands behind his head, and sighed. "Don't get me wrong. The TV show is fun. But I can't see myself aging into it. The oldest living ex-ballplayer talking about the up-and-coming young Turks…"

She grinned. She couldn't yet see Patrick as old.

"I'd like to do something…serious."

"Any ideas?"

"Not a clue," he sighed. "Ross is a good sounding board for this kind of thing. Maybe he has some ideas."

She grew cautious and stared into her wineglass. Every mention of Ross from Patrick made her uneasy. She had long ago forfeited the chance to be open with him about her past relationship. But Jean had also never been able to rid herself of the feeling of impending doom.

Patrick reached for her hand. "I still think about The Island."

That's how they'd come to talk of their time on Turks and Caicos. *The Island. Their* island.

"We had a good time, didn't we?"

"Jean, it was a great time," he said seriously.

He tugged on her hand, and Jean suspected he now had something else in mind. She didn't object as she sidled closer to him.

"You look pretty hot in a two piece."

Jean smiled warmly. "I didn't get to wear it very often. Not that I minded."

He bent to kiss her briefly. "Glad to hear it. Any chance I can persuade you to stay the night?"

She kissed him back. "I'd love to. But I can't."

Patrick nodded in understanding. "You know I had nefarious motives in mind tonight when we came here."

"I didn't exactly kick and scream in protest. But I don't want to rush."

"Then consider this a pre-apology."

"What do you mean?"

"After Labor Day, the new fall show schedule kicks in. That means—"

"I know what that means. All hell breaks loose." She snuggled against his arm. "World Series, I think?"

"Football season begins," he murmured.

The comment suggested his field and area of expertise was a never-ending cycle of sports games. Jean's further thoughts were diverted when Patrick bent over her to begin kissing her. Sweet and teasing at first, but the sensual manipulation of her lips and tongue was quickly becoming a distraction. Jean caressed his cheek and broke the kiss. She silently smiled into his eyes, and he nodded.

"Right. Let's go have dinner. Then I'll drive you home."

And over a nice dinner with wine and a shared dessert, Jean absorbed the fact that the evening had been, strangely, an old-fashioned throwback. Plain and easy, just a lovely, straightforward date. Their first ever…

Jean reread Patrick's comical note that said so much. *Ready to pack my bags. Are you coming?* The reality of their lives, especially Patrick's, was more present than ever and seemingly harsher. Jean reread the short note, pleased that he'd included her in his getaway desire. But it wasn't going to happen. They'd only been back three days. Still, Jean smiled to herself at the invitation. She was tempted. What did Patrick have in mind?

"Finish that proposal?" Brad asked, walking quickly by her desk to his own. He didn't wait for an answer as he picked up his receiver to continue a phone conversation begun elsewhere.

His question was merely a reminder. Her getaway had been pure heaven. Returning to work was pure hell. It had taken her two days to catch up on messages, appointments, and commitments. And Jean had been forced to cancel meeting her mother for a preplanned day together. She turned to her desktop and tried to concentrate on the last few paragraphs of the dreaded proposal, a suggested citywide kids' forum on how to improve their neighborhood playgrounds.

Her mind drifted in an effort to find a balance now between not losing the intimacy she and Patrick had achieved together while away and the ever-present reality of their daily lives. They had demanding jobs. They lived in different states, although she gave Patrick props for being creative in finding ways to spend time together.

Just as she was leaving for lunch, her cell buzzed. It was Patrick.

"Hey…"

"So you're not a figment of my imagination."

She chuckled. "In the flesh. Alive and breathing. Thanks for all the lovely messages."

"I wanted to hear your voice."

"Are you saying you missed me?" she teased.

She was curious when he didn't answer right away. Jean was about to add something when Patrick finally spoke.

"You have no idea," he murmured.

———

"Take a look at this," Ross said, handing Patrick three ledger sheets with categories and columns uniformly laid out.

Patrick accepted the pages and took a moment to orient himself to what he was seeing. "This is a second-quarter report, correct?"

"Right. You'll see what you started with, the three funds we divided some of the money into, and where you are now."

"This is fantastic," Patrick murmured, quickly assessing the gains in the three accounts.

Ross sat back in his chair with the air of someone very pleased with his work. "Not bad."

"Are you kidding? Not bad at all."

"Now, don't go spending it yet. There are still taxes to be paid, and it's going to blow your mind when you find out how much. The economy can take a nosedive, or something else political might happen that could change those numbers in a heartbeat."

"And then what?"

"Well, we might not wait until that happens. The idea is to watch the market and anticipate when it might blow up. Then we move into safer products."

"Okay. Outstanding, Ross." Patrick nodded, examining the pages. He was about to pass them back to Ross, who waved them aside.

"Those are your copies. I've also shared them with your attorney and accountant. Of course they can contact me if they have questions."

"Good enough."

"So how was your vacation?"

"Amazing," Patrick said thoughtfully, a slight smile on his mouth. He felt a little dreamy just recalling some of the moments. "I didn't realize how much I needed to get away until I was away."

"I hope all the good stuff wasn't wasted just on yourself."

"You mean did I go alone? No. And believe me, there wasn't a single wasted moment."

Ross sat listening but made no further comment.

"The fact is, I went with Jean Travis."

Ross, again silent, merely pursed his lips, rocked back in his chair, and playfully spun his cell phone on the desk pad.

"You and Jean Travis are a couple? Nice. Congratulations. Sounds like it was a really special trip"

"Yeah, it was. You know, you just reminded me… I have an idea I want to run by you, see what you think."

Patrick then gave a brief synopsis of what Jean had suggested to him, of forming some sort of foundation. He especially liked it as a method for giving money to causes he believed in, while also avoiding the parade of sad sob stories and crackpot deals coming his way.

"Maybe we can take a share of my lottery winning and use it to seed the fund. And I guess there are lots of other things that have to be put in place to make it happen. What do you think? Does this make sense to you?"

Ross regarded him, studying him so closely that Patrick began to think Ross might think it an implausible idea.

"But if you don't think it holds water, I can—"

"No, no. Not at all. I was just thinking. To be honest, Patrick, that is one hell of a great idea. Do you know what kind of funding you want to do? What charities you want to support?"

"Not yet. That's why I wanted to talk to you about it. How do I set it up? What will it take? How do I find someone to be in charge?"

"Et cetera, et cetera." Ross chuckled. "Good thinking, though."

"Actually, it wasn't my idea. It was Jean's. She understands what I've been going through since the lottery win. She's been very supportive, and—" Patrick stopped suddenly, letting the rest of the thought drop. It was too personal.

"Yes, she is special. I always knew Jean was beautiful and very smart."

Patrick repeated Ross's remarks to himself, and it was like an echo in his head. In an instant, he felt himself physically disengage from where they were. Ross's voice droned and faded, and Patrick began to feel an odd pounding at his temples, in his chest. His mouth went dry. He looked at Ross intently, the man who was now his financial adviser, as if he'd never set eyes on him before. That was because he was suddenly seeing a new and different Ross. And he was suddenly seeing an aspect of Ross that, from the very beginning of their relationship, had made no difference to him at all. Suddenly, it was the elephant in the room.

"Hey! Dude, are you okay?" Ross reached out to him across the desk. "What's going on?"

Patrick blinked. He felt as if color was draining from his face at the same time that heat rushed over him.

"When were you going to tell me that you and Jean…that she and you…" He couldn't get it out.

Ross sighed. Defeat more than apology crossed his features. He clasped his hands, resting his mouth against them, peering over his knuckles at Patrick.

"I guess I just did," he said quietly.

No rancor. Just the truth.

"And you're correct. It's in the past. That means there's nothing between Jean and me now. That means it's over and has been for a very long time, even before you two apparently started seeing each another, or you and I agreed to work together."

Patrick's teeth clenched in an effort to stay in control of his exploding emotions. "Why didn't you say something? Wasn't your relationship with Jean, whatever it was, a possible reason me and you shouldn't work together?"

"What was I supposed to say? I was blindsided when you reached out to me and told me Jean Travis had referred you. The first thing that crossed my mind was, did you know about our history? Had she said anything to you? When it didn't come up, I decided to let it ride. I thought about the possibility that you knew and it didn't matter. I had no idea that you and Jean had any kind of hookup before you and I met. Obviously I was wrong."

Patrick moaned a profanity, leaning forward to rest his elbows on his knees and cover his face with his hands.

"Patrick...listen, man. I'm really sorry you didn't know. If you and Jean are together now, then the past is just the past. We all have one," Ross said in a feeble attempt at humor.

And, of course, Ross was right. In that moment, Patrick thought of two things. The time he and Jean spent together in high school, and the time they'd spent together since reuniting after the lottery win. Every single moment flashed in his head, until five minutes ago.

Patrick jumped up from his chair, startling Ross. "I can't discuss this right now."

"I think we should. I don't want you to leave here with the wrong impression, because I can already see that's where you're headed. If you decide we can't work together any longer, I'll understand. Hopefully, with no hard feelings."

"I don't want to know about you and Jean..."

"You won't. But here's the short version and the hardcore facts.

Three and a half years ago, we were engaged to be married. Three years ago, she broke it off. Until an unplanned meeting at a social function last May, we have not seen each other or been in touch in those three years. Standing by her daughter, Diana Chambers chose to take her investments with my firm elsewhere. But I continue to represent Seth Travis. That was his decision. End of story."

"And you think that's going to help?" Patrick said, incredulous.

"Not right away. But it should."

Patrick tried to calm down, to gather himself and force the burning anger and disappointment into a closed compartment in this heart. He took a long, slow, deep breath and just as slowly released it. He sat down, staring at Ross. "You don't understand."

Ross blinked at him, and his gaze narrowed. "Maybe I do. Better than you think."

"I don't believe—"

"You're a good-looking, personable white man who's involved with a beautiful and talented Black woman. I'm the Black man she was once engaged to. I understand perfectly. Your relationship with Jean is none of my business. I did worry about what might happen when the shit hit the fan, but that isn't my problem either.

"I like you, Patrick. You're a straight-up guy. I like working with you. In the social arena, I could see us becoming good friends. You know as well as I do that no one can work out how important my past with Jean is but you and Jean."

Patrick sat and listened, but there were too many things churning within him. Right now, he studied Ross, seeing only a Black man who once had a significant place in Jean's life.

Were they more suited to be together? Did Jean think about him replacing Ross? What place did he want for himself in Jean's life now?

Ross slowly leaned forward, reaching his hand across his desk to lay flat in front of Patrick. "I don't want to sound like I'm lecturing you, man. You certainly don't need that, especially from me. Right now you only have my side of the story, and it's all I can give you." Ross sat back and waited.

"I know you're trying to be honest with me…" Patrick said, his voice sounding very far away.

"Listen, if you want to change anything, end our agreement—"

"Not now, Ross. I can't think about that now. I'll get back to you."

"Whenever you want. And that foundation idea is on point. I recommend you give it serious consideration, Patrick, no matter how things work out between us."

With that, Patrick left. He walked through the office complex to the bank of elevators. He didn't respond to Ross's assistant when she said goodbye, too dazed with his own crashing spirits.

CHAPTER 16

It was late when the car dropped Jean off in front of her building. This was one of those nights when she really appreciated the perks of her position. Still officially on the job after 9:00 p.m., she got sent home like royalty. Jean tipped the driver and got out of the midsize Jeep Grand Cherokee. She absently planned an evening curled up on her love seat with a glass of wine in front of the flat screen. She could sleep in a little late in the morning.

The car was just pulling away when Jean stepped onto the curb and stopped abruptly in her tracks, recognizing Patrick at the entrance. A smile instantly changed her expression and then slowly began to fade. His gaze seemed disturbingly cold and closed as he watched her approach.

"Hi. What are you doing here? I didn't know…"

"I should have called. I just drove out. Took a chance you'd be home."

Jean studied his face with its unchanging expression. No hint of a smile or welcome. No sign that he was glad to see her. She almost didn't recognize the man who stood before her, wary and forbidding.

"Is everything all right? It's not your family, is it? Your mom…"

Patrick shook his head, momentarily averting his gaze as the question caught him off guard. "No, everyone is fine."

Jean went immediately from being concerned to taking control of the uncharacteristic and awkward greeting between them.

"Let's go upstairs," she said decisively, walking past Patrick and into her building. Already her mind was rapidly trying to assess the dynamics of the situation. She exchanged pleasantries with her doorman, who also greeted Patrick with a nod of recognition. Jean noticed that Patrick didn't respond. She began to feel a sudden tightening in her chest, unable even to guess what might be troubling him. She glanced at him as they waited for the elevator. He avoided looking at her, and her stomach sank. This was too much like his sudden appearance at her job when he expressed the need to get away...and he wanted her to come with him. Jean was pretty sure this was not going to be the same kind of scenario. He didn't speak, and she did not attempt small talk. His brows were drawn together in a dark storm cloud.

Was it her? Or was it him?

Once they were inside her apartment there were no more distractions, just the two of them in what felt like a Mexican standoff, but not of her making.

"You know your way around. Why don't you sit down?" Jean put her tote aside on the floor near the door. "Would you like something to drink?"

"No, nothing, thanks."

So formal. So stiff.

"I'll have some wine," she said, an excuse to escape momentarily to the kitchen where she racked her brain for a possible reason for Patrick's distance from her.

When she returned to the living room with her wine, Jean found Patrick standing in front of the occasion table, the top surface crowded with framed photos of people near and dear to her. She already knew that he'd looked through the images before, seemingly fascinated with the people in her life, past and present. There was no framed photo of him or them. There were not yet stars in her eyes.

He was holding a framed piece of paper. It was the note he'd written and left for her to find, just weeks after they'd met again. It was when he had to leave at the crack of dawn for a flight to the west coast for work.

"You kept my note." He seemed genuinely surprised.

"It means a lot to me."

"Why?"

Jean shrugged. "It was thoughtful. I found it...kind of romantic."

Patrick carefully placed the frame back among the others.

"Are you going to talk to me, tell me what's going on?"

She was pleased that her voice was strong and clear. But her heart was pounding. Could Patrick hear it?

He slipped his hands into his pants pocket, and then focused on her like a laser beam.

"Ross thought the foundation concept was brilliant. I told him it was your idea."

"Thank you." Jean was instantly alert. She wanted to place her hand over her chest, hoping to still the thumping agitation in the center.

"He said he always knew you were smart and beautiful."

Jean swallowed, keeping her gaze riveted to Patrick, trying to read his voice, his body language...his emotions.

"He told you, didn't he?"

Patrick shook his head. "I guessed about the two of you. He confirmed."

Jean carefully set the wine aside, trying not to spill any because her hand was trembling. "Okay," she whispered in a tone that acknowledged the truth.

He took a step forward. "Why didn't you tell me? Say something? *Anything!*"

"I thought about it but didn't think I needed to. What did an old relationship have to do with you and me when we met up again?"

"It would have been nice to know that it was over, for one thing. Especially after we began seeing each other. Especially when you recommended Ross as a financial adviser. Don't you think there was a little conflict of interest?"

She stiffened, angered by the implication. "My only interest in suggesting Ross was to direct you to someone I knew you could trust. It was all about you. I don't benefit in any way."

"Yet you came to believe you couldn't trust him, right? For whatever reason. He told me about the engagement, that you broke it off. So how was I supposed to feel about working with a man that you'd cast off? That you once..." He turned away, pacing.

"I don't know," she admitted flatly. "I...I was concerned that my past relationship with Ross might seem... I wondered if I should tell you, Patrick. It didn't work out between him and me, but he's a very honest and principled *businessman*. That's what I hoped you would see in him. And, to be honest, when you and I did start to see each other, I didn't feel it was any of your business. We didn't have that kind of relationship at first."

"And now?"

"Now is a different conversation. I don't think we should go there. What you have to know is that I *never* would have gotten involved with you if Ross and I weren't done. Dead and buried."

He glanced at her, a question in his expression. "Why did you break it off with him?"

"I'm not going to talk about it."

"That means it was important."

"When you break off with someone you used to care about, of course it's important."

"Did he hurt you?" His voice was low and quiet.

"He disappointed me."

He took another step closer. "I didn't ask him what caused the breakup. He only said it was your decision. Like you, I guess he felt it was also his private business. Okay, I get that. But then...when I thought about it..."

"I think I know what you thought. You started comparing yourself to Ross. Why? There's no contest. And I'm not the prize in the middle. He made a serious judgment error about me, who and what I am. Don't you do the same."

"I'm trying not to. I want to believe what we have together. Our relationship now."

"We've *never* talked about our relationship. What is it? Where is it going? Yes, we have a great time. I think…we're good together."

"Solid chemistry between us. Don't forget that."

"You've never said anything about *us*. I don't know if there is an *us*." Jean sighed and turned away from him. "It's so frustrating, not knowing if maybe…there's something about me. Do you understand what I'm saying?"

"I think so. It's the same feeling I had when I found out about you and Ross. That maybe his being Black had more meaning for you. The fact that you're half Black never mattered to me at all. Not in high school, not now. And that's why I'm here. I need to know. Did I miss something? Did I assume too much?"

Jean didn't hear him come up behind her but didn't resist when he carefully slipped his arms around her, drawing her back against him. Patrick gathered her close, his chin resting just above an ear.

"I admit I felt jealous when I found out about you and Ross."

"You're both very different men. I'm not going to make comparisons. That would be unfair to both of you."

"Yeah, it would be. And I like him." Patrick paused, then went on. "Jean, you're right that we've never had a real conversation about us. Maybe I've been taking a lot for granted. Maybe I let what I want get in the way of what you want. I have something to say about that."

She felt him sigh, leaning back against his chest.

"How could you not know that I'm in love with you?" He sounded bewildered.

Patrick's voice was a smooth whisper, his warm breath fanning the side of her face. Jean's stomach muscles curled, and she felt a rush of emotion that caused a welling of tears. She blinked them away.

"Learning about you and Ross took my breath away. I realized I should have told you how I felt, have felt about you for a long time."

Jean shook her head, and she turned in his arms to face him, resting her palms on his chest.

"I was hoping...but I was afraid to. I did my fair share of thinking about all those women lined up in your past. Many are showing up again, trying to squeeze themselves back into your life. It's not exactly an image that I fit."

"Thank goodness."

"I'm glad you said it first, Patrick. It would have been awful if I confessed I love you, only to find out you didn't feel the same."

"Not a chance. Now you know. As for what's next...let's talk about that later. I think it's going to be an ongoing conversation." His hand cupped her cheek, his thumb under her jaw lifting her face. "For the moment I have something else in mind. Can we just hold each other?" he asked, almost sheepishly.

He kissed her with a slow command and purpose that was almost reverent. Jean slid her arms around him to hug closer. She tilted her head to meet his lips, pressing with a sweet, deep urgency that immediately sparked arousal and tenderness in both of them. She felt the urge to cry with relief and joy. Hope and happiness.

Patrick broke the kiss, looking deep into her bright eyes and waiting for her to take the lead. Jean headed for the bedroom with Patrick following. They silently disrobed, stopping once in the process to clasp and kiss and stroke and caress each other with a mutual ache of longing.

On the bed, they lay facing each other, kissing and stoking the passion. It was like a new discovery, their light, reverent touch titillating, electrifying each other. They didn't want to rush, finding pleasure in the extended foreplay, in exploring new territory with daring and passion.

Their lovemaking escalated to the only possible finish. The ride was dizzying as they responded to each other, mindlessly headed to the edge of a precipice without falling over yet. On her side Jean lifted her leg over his, leaving the path open for Patrick to shift and position himself. He placed a hand on her hip, holding Jean steady as he undulated, thrusting slowly into her.

They clutched each other tightly, breathing deeply, moaning softly, moving in syncopation. The sensations spiraled through their bodies in an exhilarating climb, falling over that edge in free fall as they climaxed in tandem. It was all born of being in a safe place where they could just love each other.

———

The magic spell continued for a few weeks. It was time in which Jean's hope grew to near mythic levels with each FaceTime call and text from Patrick, every day, weekend, *any* time spent together. No different from what he'd been doing all along, but now with more meaning and promise. In between claiming time for themselves that was not work centered, Patrick had finally met with his son. The space between him and his ex-wife remained planted with explosives that had to be navigated. The different family configuration was a difficult work in progress.

And Patrick found creative ways to always remind Jean that he loved her. He sent flowers. He arranged a VIP seat for her at the U.S. Open in Flushing Meadows, introducing her to one of the nation's top-ranked Black female tennis champs at courtside. Somehow, Jean managed a thirty-second conversation with the very public, popular, and talented woman in which she didn't make a stammering fool of herself.

Everything cemented her belief that she and Patrick might actually have a future together, although it was too early still for that subject to be raised. They'd both gotten used to the chaotic cadence of their relationship, thrilled when they could spend time—a night, a weekend—together. They were handling the inevitable separations and interruptions with more confidence. Every time Patrick called with some hastily concocted plan, there was never any other answer to give him but yes.

Jean had sometimes taken to watching *REPLAY* on a Sunday, not because she hoped to glean any understanding of sports statistics, predictions, or players, but because she so enjoyed watching Patrick work his expertise, and his charm, with the television audience.

There were moments when she felt like she could levitate, float on the delicious sense of well-being that had come with the admission between her and Patrick of their mutual love. That she was in love with Patrick also solidified a connection and the feelings that had withstood the test of time.

And then one day, not long after they'd made their mutual confessions, Jean was hurrying back to her office after lunch with Annabelle, who'd wanted to gossip about the latest scandal involving an acquaintance. As they were saying their goodbyes, Jean's cell indicated the posting of several texts all at once. She decided they could wait until she reached her desk. But then she encountered Brad on his way to a meeting. In passing he mumbled, "Sorry about the latest reports. It certainly has been a tough summer for the guy…"

Jean had been so confused by the comment she didn't respond.

At her desk, she turned her attention to all the texts and several voicemail messages. The very first message directed her to a news link. As did the second. Jean turned to her PC and opened a search engine. She randomly picked a network. The top story headline read in bold type: *Multimillionaire TV Sportscaster in Baby Daddy Drama.*

Jean began reading and got no further than Patrick Bennett's name, which appeared in the first sentence.

Her skin flushed and she felt overheated. Her mouth went dry. She kept reading the first few sentences over and over. Patrick…popular TV personality…served with papers…sued with request for child support… ex-wife…a son, almost five…

Jean skipped down to see if there were any quotes in response from Patrick. *No comment at this time…being handled through our attorneys.*

It was already public, and she'd had no idea.

Further down in the report was the revelation that, apparently, Patrick had no previous knowledge that he had fathered a son with his ex-wife until almost a month ago. She had chosen not to inform him, leaving open the question of why she was coming forward with paternity claims and a lawsuit now.

Jean felt herself crashing. She left her office, trying to avoid any coworkers and questions she could not possibly address. The news was stunning enough. But she couldn't help but wonder what Patrick was going through. How was he handling the news?

How could such a situation have happened?

She left the building to get fresh air. It was raining, which only added to the general aura of scandal and gloom. The news was a life-changing surprise. Jean stood behind one of the massive columns fronting city hall and texted Patrick.

I'll call you tonight. There's a lot going on right now. Are you okay? Want/need to talk? I'll come to you. She hesitated a moment and added a final line: Hugs and kisses.

Patrick got the messages. And the voicemail. He didn't respond to either. Jean was the first person who came to mind when his initial suspicions were confirmed in a basic PI report before he and Jean had gone away. After that awful meeting between him and his ex, he wanted to destroy something. And then he wanted the comfort of Jean's arms. He and his attorney were working out a custody arrangement to present to family court, so it was bewildering that Katie was now making public a situation that put him in the worst possible light…another wealthy man dodging responsibility for his child. No exonerating facts. He had been speechless, unable even to conceive that his ex-wife had kept such a personal and important fact from him. He had a son.

Patrick considered Jean and how she might take the news. Would it change her mind about him? Them? Other than his own family, Patrick hoped she'd be in his corner. Unfortunately, he was becoming used to unexpected revelations. That didn't mean that she had to. What if this latest complication was one too many? What if…

It was mind-boggling to believe that his ex was capable of such duplicity. Did she hate him so much that she'd withhold life-changing facts from him?

Yet he couldn't envision having a child. His lifestyle in the last five years had not lent itself to that possibility. He'd been very responsible in his relationships. Being married had been different, and there had also been an unspoken assumption that their careers were, at that time, more important. He was doing well in baseball, having just signed a new league contract. Katie had made the finals for the U.S. Olympic team. She'd scored a bronze medal her first time and was training for a second shot at gold. She didn't make it. She'd somehow convinced herself it was Patrick's fault because he hadn't supported her enough. She filed for divorce. Within a year, she was off the radar in the competitive sports world. She was angry, uncommunicative, unreasonable.

And now they had a child together.

Patrick didn't call Jean because he didn't know what to say to her. There was no question that she was deeply concerned, that she was reaching out to him. And he needed her. But he'd been advised by a cadre of attorneys, his accountant, and Ross that he needed to be very careful about who surrounded him who might, even inadvertently, compromise his delicate position, especially where a custody fight was likely to evolve. The court of public opinion may be unfair and shortsighted, but it held clout that couldn't be denied and might lose him sympathy. He might not do well when pitted against a divorced woman who, once married to a high-profile personality, was a single mother raising a child alone.

It was never going to be lost on Patrick, nor would anyone allow him at this point to forget, that he was a millionaire dozens of times over. He had means and the wherewithal to affect the outcome of a lot of things going on in his life. And anyone else's.

But the truth was, Patrick was feeling not only powerless but disillusioned. It seemed that the only steadying force in his life was Jean. In his heart, Patrick had to face a painful truth that she was the one being shortchanged. And he was the one to blame.

———

"Hello?"

There was a deep chuckle on the line. "You sound like how I feel."

"Oh, Patrick…I'm so glad to hear from you. I thought—"

"I love you, Jean."

She slumped back against the sofa cushions. She closed her eyes, so much relief rolling over her that she felt weak. "Ditto," Jean croaked, her voice breaking.

"Sorry I haven't called. I've been told to maintain a low profile until the lawyers and family court come to a decision."

"I know. I've been following the reports. Believe it or not, my mom seems to know a lot more about what's going on. My dad is a close second. I'm just feeling so…so…"

"I know. I know. I think about our island a lot these days."

She grinned. "Our island. That does have a nice sound."

"The alternative is to run off and join the circus."

"Circuses are out of style."

"You know what I mean."

"Yes, I do. How are you? Are you getting any sleep? Are you eating?"

Patrick laughed. "Now you sound like my mother. I have to say she seems really happy to know there's another grandchild. She always knew my sister would marry and have a family. I was the wild card."

"How do you feel about it? I mean, knowing you now have a son."

He sighed deeply. "I don't know yet. I feel like a lot of people lately have been playing Whack-A-Mole on my head. I guess I'm a little weary. I had to go down to Philly to meet my son, Nicholas, for the first time. My ex didn't want him taken out of the state. The local court rejected that," he chortled. "I'm too angry with what she's done to be forgiving and generous. Maybe that will come later."

"How did it go?"

"Well, they had us in the judge's chambers, just me, Katie, and Nicholas. Nico. The judge made some opening remarks or something. To be honest I wasn't listening. I was busy staring at this kid. I suppose he'd been told I'm his father. I don't know if that means anything to him. Seeing him for the very first time, though, felt kind of exciting. I really wanted to try to make a connection."

"Just think how hard that was for your son, Patrick," Jean sympathized.

"It was surreal. This little human being is part of me. He's a cute little guy, Jean. Later I showed a photo of him to my mom. She started crying. She said he looks just like me and my sister when we were his age. That kind of surprises me. There's no question he's mine. I really never doubted it. Katie and I didn't part on good terms, but I don't believe she'd try to pass off someone else's kid as mine. Maybe she's been really cruel, but I don't think she's evil."

"That's very understanding of you."

"Not understanding. Just dealing with the facts. I don't hate her, but I am royally pissed. I didn't want to do or say anything that my mother wouldn't be proud came from me. I feel the same way about you. What *you* think matters to me. We haven't seen each other in, like, forever."

I miss you so much, Jean thought plaintively, swallowing the well of emotion that rose in her throat, brushing away an errant tear she couldn't prevent from falling. She swallowed hard. "I'm okay. Worried about you. Was he afraid? Did he seem curious about who you are?"

"Not at first. It was clear Nico didn't know what he should do. We were introduced by the judge and then…nothing. So Katie spoke quietly to him. Then, all of a sudden, he walks across the office and stood right in front of me. And he looks at me with these incredible chocolate eyes, and he says, 'Are you my daddy?' Right then and there, he had me." His voice cracked.

Jean listened to Patrick's recital, trying to envision the scene and a mini-me of Patrick. But that was harder.

"I said, 'Yes, I'm your father.' Then I didn't know what to do. Should I try to hug him? Should I shake his hand?"

Jean mewed at the poignancy of that moment.

"The kid comes closer and holds out his arms. Luckily, I didn't embarrass myself. I hugged him. And he let me. So I'm sitting there, and no one else is saying a word, and Nicholas and I are holding on to each other. Jean, I have to tell you…it was an incredible feeling."

"I'm so glad Nicholas wasn't afraid of you."

"But I was very afraid of him. If he'd refused to have anything to do with me, I didn't know what I was going to do."

"And now?"

"Lots of details to work out. For now, Katie is ordered to let me have Nicholas one weekend a month. We're staying at my mom's, so she can get to know him, and she can run interference if he has a meltdown… and I become catatonic with fear." Jean chuckled quietly. "The visitation time increases when it's clear he has no problem with me and doesn't mind the time away from his mother."

"I guess you did a victory lap after that."

"I did one better. I went out and had a couple of drinks."

She laughed again.

"I tried to come to see you, Jean. I needed to be somewhere and with someone that made sense."

"Why didn't you say something? When? What happened?"

"I know I have to be careful. But I thought I could sneak out to see you anyway. I drove out to Brooklyn and found about a half dozen people hanging around your building. They all looked suspiciously like press. I knew I'd be recognized so I didn't try to go in or talk with the doorman. He'd remember me. So I called to see if you were upstairs. I got the answering machine…and your cell voicemail."

"I figured out about the reporters a week ago. They tried questioning me when I got home one night, but I told them they had the wrong person. I don't think they believed me, but they didn't challenge me. Since then I've been entering the building through a side door that leads to the recycling area and the laundry room. Outsiders don't know about that."

"Very cloak-and-dagger," Patrick said dryly.

"It would have been fun to have a clandestine meetup with you. We could have snuck through the back alleys and gone to Julio's for pizza."

"That was my game plan exactly. Didn't work out."

"Will you try again?"

"You can count on it. I'm consulting with my lawyer and Ross on some kind of permanent settlement for my ex. I've only had Nico twice, but I think it's promising. He holds my hand sometimes when we're out. He asks a lot of questions. He sometimes volunteers information about his mother. I admit I like getting those insider scoops.

"I knew about Nico before you and I went away. I hadn't met him yet. I wanted to tell you so badly about him, but I was so afraid of doing something to screw up the plan. And I didn't trust Katie not to try to stick it to me if I didn't follow the court's instructions, so…"

"I understand. Don't apologize."

She heard him moving around. She couldn't tell if he was lounging on his sofa or in a chair, or if Patrick was in bed. It was an intimate call without the intimacy. Jean closed her eyes and just listened.

"The very first time I had him for a weekend I woke up on Saturday and found Nico next to me in my bed. That was kind of…kind of…"

"Sweet? I think the word you're looking for is *sweet*."

There was no response, until… "I don't think so. Not sweet. It wasn't sweet. It was…awesome." His tone was filled with elation. "Jean?" His voice dropped to a whisper. "Can I come out?"

She slowly began to smile in relief. "It's almost midnight."

"And your point?"

"Okay."

Jean was glad, and she was also realistic. Their lives had changed,

Patrick's in particular. Maybe he understood that better than she did, but Jean wasn't going to fool herself into believing that there was a happy-ever-after ahead of them, over a rainbow. Patrick had instantly acquired lifelong responsibility. She knew he would absolutely rise to the occasion. She knew in the depths of her soul that Patrick loved her, and she loved him. But that also did not guarantee a life together built on their love. She had only to think of her own parents, their circumstances, and the decades before they could fully enjoy each other. Jean tried to allay the creeping fear that she and Patrick could find themselves on a similar merry-go-round. Could she settle for that?

To her astonishment, Patrick was at her door in forty minutes. Her standing by the entrance waiting for him felt normal, comfortable, and left Jean feeling that they'd already established a routine and understanding that was safe and loving.

They kissed at the door, hugged briefly, and Patrick entered, putting his leather mailbag on the floor. He bent to pull off his sneakers and sat slouched on the sofa with his legs stretched out. Jean went into the kitchen and returned with a bowl of popcorn and beer. She curled up next to Patrick, the bowl between them. The conversation was idle and fairly meaningless. It was just that they were together, and that was all either wanted.

"I'll probably have indigestion in the morning," Patrick joked, slowly munching and regarding her.

"I don't want to be a complete pill, but beer isn't going to help either." He silently nodded in agreement. "Tell me more about Nico," she said.

Surprised, Patrick blinked. And then he shook his head. "I'm glad you're interested, Jean, but I don't want my son to always take over the conversation."

"Tell me something funny about him. Tell me something that sur-prised you."

Patrick chewed and thought. And then a smile played around his mouth. "So Nico and I and my mom went out for breakfast that first Saturday morning…"

"After you awoke and found him sleeping next to you."

His smile grew, becoming warm and whimsical with the memory. "Yeah. And my mom asked Nico if he knew how to cook. And of course he shook his head and said he was too little. And she asked if he liked brownies, and his eyes grew into saucers and he says, 'Yeeeaaahhh!'" Patrick imitated him, making Jean chuckle. "My mom says, well, I'm going to need your help because I'm going to make some brownies, and I need you to lick the bowl. I don't think he quite understood what that meant. But later, Mom actually had him mixing and stirring and eating samples after they were done. Nico said to her that if she needed him, he could come again and help lick the bowl."

"Aww," Jean cooed.

"Don't do that," Patrick said, his voice cracking. He shifted position and averted his gaze.

Jean realized he was actually becoming emotional over the incident. And she knew it was already a story that was going to become legend.

They tired of the popcorn and took everything to the kitchen. Again, almost in silence, comfortable in the way they navigated around each other, they went into the bedroom to take up the places they'd made for themselves together. They undressed each other. And Jean was not at all surprised—she was content—when the lights were out, and the ceiling fan turned lazily overhead, and they loosely embraced with deep sighs.

"So this is the game plan," Patrick croaked quietly. "We cuddle, and we go to sleep. In the morning…we rock the boat. What do you think?"

Jean giggled. "I like it. And no cheating. No waking me up in the middle of the night to—"

Patrick silenced Jean by leaning over to lightly kiss her. "I don't promise, but I'll do my best." He yawned. "Love you."

Jean sighed, her happiness revived…and her hope for the future.

"Night. Love you too."

CHAPTER 17

Jean didn't for a moment begrudge Patrick the wonderful discovery and unexpected addition to his life, his family. But she could no longer pretend to herself that she didn't feel somewhat left out as a result. It was doubly ironic that, almost the moment they'd finally confessed their love for each other, Patrick was pulled away and engulfed in, arguably, an even greater love—that for his newfound son.

Was she being monumentally selfish? Or painfully insecure?

Who was to blame for Patrick's heart having been captured by a five-year-old with big brown eyes and a winning personality? It simply meant that, understandably, he was faced with a different set of priorities. It was no longer clear to Jean that she was on that list.

He'd already told her that, eventually, he would have to get a bigger place so there was more room for a rambunctious, active little boy. He'd have to come to civil agreement with his ex about schools after kindergarten. Private? Boarding? Patrick could well afford it, but he'd shared with Katie that the right public school would better prepare his son for a diverse world and learning how to navigate it. After all, the system had done very well by the two of them. Summer vacations? Holidays? Who would get to have Nico when?

And when would Jean get to have Patrick?

Jean liked that he trusted her judgment and could talk openly with her about the growing number of parental issues popping up in his life. She knew it was a privilege. She knew he'd arrived at a point, after the stresses of the summer—and a lot of extra money—where the list of people he openly brought into his circle had shrunk. She had reminded him that she had no children and was inadequate at giving any kind of advice. He'd laughed.

"Consider it training."

Her mother had counseled her. "It will all work out. It always does."

"Forgive me if I don't find that reassuring."

"Okay, I get it. You're in love with him. You're on uneven ground, and it keeps shifting. I know what that's like."

"Weren't you angry or scared when Dad and you couldn't marry? Or even be together with me?"

"Sure. I wanted Seth to step up to the plate. He loved me, and I never doubted that. But time and history and our folks were formidable obstacles. And I haven't even counted on the unforeseen and nasty surprises. Not that I'm taking Patrick's side, but try to look at his circumstances from his point of view. Seventy-five mil, give or take a few hundred thousand, doesn't make up for the aggravation of the real world and day-to-day life. I guess some people revel in that kind of excitement; he clearly does not."

"Sorry, but you do sound like you're on his side."

"I hope you know I'm always on your side. But I understand his. And so did you until Nico…is that his name?"

"Nickname. It's Nicholas."

"I like it. Until he came along and pulled the carpet out from under your feet…and Patrick's. Find a way to deal with it, Jean. Try not to let your heart get broken. Try not to give up on your love for Patrick. It will all work out."

In the middle of the night, Jean tried to. But it was hard. And it was painful. And it was lonely.

And everyone seemed to know.

A few nights after the surprise sleepover with Patrick, Jean went to a party at Annabelle's. It was noisy and crowded in Annabelle's small Upper West Side one bedroom, but entertaining with her usual mishmash of unrelated friends. Annabelle loved bringing diverse people together.

"Girl, I haven't seen you in ages. Always happens. Bring a guy into the picture, and all the girlfriends fill with lust and get dreamy-eyed."

"I don't know what you're talking about."

"Oh, yeah you do. Anyway, all the newspaper reports about your Patrick talk about a beautiful woman connected with the mayor's office who has been seen out and about with said Patrick during the summer. And obviously you missed a photo of the two of you having a cozy dinner at some tiny dive in the East Village. Thought no one would notice? Please."

"Is there a lot of talk about me?"

Annabelle smiled kindly at Jean. "Look, I know you're kind of a private person, so all of this is probably not making you very happy. It might be a lot easier if this Patrick would openly admit to the relationship and let it fly. What's the worst that could happen?"

"Right now, a lot. You probably also know about his son. The one Patrick only learned about recently."

"Yeah, I heard. Does that bother you?"

Jean sighed and sipped her wine. "I'm very happy for Patrick."

Annabelle stared at her. "That wasn't the question I asked."

Jean managed not to give a direct answer, and Annabelle dropped the matter, caught up in being hostess to her disparate group of friends and acquaintances.

Yes, Jean had missed the photo Annabelle referred to. But she'd caught a clip of Patrick heading into the offices of the lawyers representing him. He'd looked cool and calm behind super dark shades, casual business attire, but not the formality of a suit. He did not wear a baseball cap or lower his gaze or hide his face behind a newspaper. He was fully accepting of the public scrutiny and curiosity about the most recent upheaval in his very public life.

Then there was the afternoon when Jean had seen a still shot of him covertly escorting a little boy, his son, into a waiting vehicle to whisk away to a place unknown.

But at least she'd finally seen Nico.

Patrick sat on a panel at Brooklyn Academy of Music. The subject was athletic greats who never got the attention they deserved during their playing days. Patrick had arranged for Jean to attend as his guest. Not as a rep for the mayor's office, but as his lady, as he'd taken to referring to Jean.

When the panel and Q&A were over, the panelists had been escorted into an alcove to sign autographs. Patrick excused himself. On the alert, Jean had followed as he'd explored a lone corridor and found an unlocked and empty theater. Patrick pulled her inside with him and into his arms. It was not crazed groping, like teenagers, but a true romantic embrace of a man and woman who cared deeply for each other and had not enough time to show it. There was a sweet kind of desperation to them sneaking away to hug and kiss, and it made them laugh at the absurdity and necessity.

"We have to stop meeting like this," Patrick groaned, pulling kisses from her lips and not giving Jean a chance to respond.

But she didn't disagree.

His uncertainty and fear about what he was learning about a five-year-old were poignant to Jean. And it was wonderful to do nothing more than hold each other for real comfort. No other action needed.

—

Patrick had gotten a pass from ESPN to host the girl's little league event. When the sports clinic Jean and Brad had helped to arrange for Patrick finally came about, it had never occurred to her that he might bring his son along. That was how Jean first met Nico.

The day was organized to last no more than three hours, due to threatening rain. Besides the kids, there were also parents, and a discreet group of reporters and photographers that Brad had arranged for. It was a great photo-op event, and she and Brad wanted to use the day to promote similar community events in the city. There was a rumor that the mayor might show up, but Jean knew that wasn't going to happen.

She'd milled about at the start with some of the parents, casually questioning them about this workshop for their kids with a former league baseball player and TV star. Jean witnessed the kids' excitement, but they were too young to think much more of Patrick's appearance than that he used to play pro baseball.

When Patrick came out onto the diamond, a small little figure trudging right behind him, she sat up straight, staring at this child who was Patrick's. She could not fully describe the feelings that coursed through her, that twisted in her chest and seemed to constrict her heart. But Jean experienced an emotion that went far beyond the love she felt for Patrick.

Patrick was easy and open and accessible to the kids, parents, and coaches. He introduced his son. He started out talking to the gathering about professional sports and what was needed to fulfill dreams of playing in the big leagues. He told them how it was discovered when he'd already started college that he had a talent for baseball. Patrick told the girls' team that they were starting at the right age. He put the kids through simple routines and exercises, ostensibly to see what they had, but it was just to keep them moving and busy. For a while, Nico mixed with the much bigger kids, trying to keep up. Jean could see that Patrick carefully kept an eye on the child, until it was clear that Nico's attention and energy were failing him, and he stopped.

Patrick went to his son, crouching down beside him, questioning him for a few minutes. Jean could see the boy either nodding or shaking his head at the questions. Finally, Patrick stood, looking around the field and seating benches. And he spotted her. Jean spontaneously gave a half wave in acknowledgment. Then, Patrick pointed her out to Nico, and after a few more minutes, he stood watching as the youngster made his way to the stands and joined her in her otherwise-empty row.

Nico sat right next to her, his feet not quite reaching the ground.

"My daddy told me to sit with you."

"Oh, okay. My name is Jean. What's your name?"

"Nicholas. But everybody calls me Nico."

"I like that. Can I call you Nico?"

He nodded silently.

She tried to watch what was happening on the playing field between Patrick and the Little League team, but Jean was very conscious of Nico's presence next to her. She was solidly aware now that this child was Patrick's. She accepted that Nico was a forever presence in Patrick's life. Jean didn't know if she ever would be.

Nico suddenly shrugged and raised his hands. "I can't see."

Jean focused on his comment and looked around. The benches were all ground level, and not stadium seating. He was too short to see past the many rows in front of him.

"Maybe if you stand up…"

Nico pushed himself off the bench and stood in front, leaning back on the edge.

"Is that better?"

"No," he said plaintively, shaking his head.

She looked around for another solution, a different vantage point. She glanced at Nico, with his thick, dark, tousled hair, not unlike his father's.

"Would you like to sit on my lap?"

"Okay," he said readily.

Without any help or further encouragement from Jean, Nico climbed on the bench and then swung his leg over Jean's lap, plunking himself down.

"Now I can see," he said triumphantly.

"Good."

For a long time, he watched the action on the field, occasionally fidgeting and shifting his position, making comments or asking questions. Jean had to make up many of her answers. Nico sometimes began a conversation that seemed to be mostly with himself or hummed a tuneless melody. Every now and then, Jean automatically reached to put an arm around him to hold him steady but didn't. She could no longer concentrate on Patrick or what was going on with the team. She was only acutely aware of this small creature comfortably seated on her lap. He was warm, active, unexpected, and he fascinated her. Other than brief visits to cousins on her mother's side who'd begun to marry and have children, Jean never had an opportunity to be around small children.

Jean wondered how Patrick was managing with this new, even more significant change in his life. How was he feeling, having to adjust to acknowledging a son he had no previous awareness of? She didn't want to make up the story. After all, she had no idea what it must be like. Had Patrick fallen in love with this child, or was he still trying to find a place in his heart for this small stranger?

She realized when Nico was getting tired, losing interest in the activities that he wasn't a part of. He yawned and stretched and, abruptly, relaxed back against Jean's chest, his head and curly hair just inches below her chin. Now she did allow herself to loosely place an arm around him, holding him in place. She searched out Patrick, but in that moment, he was physically engaged in a demonstration for the team. He was distracted but clearly trusted she and his son were both okay together.

Patrick was instantly surrounded by more than a dozen little kids when the afternoon was finished, who each wanted to high-five him as they were led away by parents or older siblings. He stood talking with the coaches, laughing and engaged, and now and again casting a glance toward Jean and Nico. Finally, after shaking hands with everyone, Patrick consented to pose for pictures with anyone requesting more of his time. The photographer from Jean's office and a young reporter in particular continued to take pictures and interviewed Patrick for usable quotes.

People were still making their way from the park when he approached. Nico had been very still, but Jean wasn't sure if he'd fallen asleep or was just happy sitting quietly.

Patrick briefly massaged her shoulder from behind before bending to look into his son's face.

"Hey. Ready to go?"

Nico's response was to nod silently and wiggle from Jean's lap. Over the top of his head, Patrick exchanged a silent and grateful glance with her. A corner of his mouth lifted in a smile.

Jean followed them from the seating area to the entrance of the park. She had brief words with the two staffers from her office, telling them they were free to leave. Patrick pulled a new, unused baseball from his pocket and handed it to his son.

"This is for you."

"It's mine? Thank you!" Nico said with the kind of reverence only a small child who loved surprises could manage with charming sincerity. He clutched the ball, staring at it and rotating it in his hands.

Patrick turned to Jean. "I didn't know you were going to be here."

"Brad gave me the assignment to set this up."

"Thank you, Brad." Patrick grinned. "Thank you for staying. I didn't have a chance to introduce you to Nicholas. I hope it was okay to send him to sit with you."

"We managed on our own. We learned each other's names."

"Sounds like you're already friends. I'm not surprised."

Jean watched him, watching her. She knew he was trying to gauge her thoughts, her feelings. In a frustrating sense, it felt like they were back to the beginning of their relationship. All the summer blowups had been annoying but manageable. Patrick's latest situation was complicated. And permanent.

She didn't know what to say to him. For the moment, she only knew how she felt, and her confusion was compounding her anxiety and helplessness. She was in love with Patrick, and that absolute truth was contributing to feeling in limbo. A major part of their connection had been clarified, had been a balm. But a future seemed more distant than ever.

Jean's gaze turned to the little boy, who was tossing his new ball and mimicking base running. He was getting fidgety again. Nico approached and patted Patrick on the leg to get his attention. "Can we go, now? I'm hungry."

"I bet you are," Jean said with understanding.

"Come with us," Patrick said suddenly.

Jean looked to Patrick. She shook her head. "You don't get that much time with him, Patrick. You're still getting to know each other. I'll be a distraction."

"I don't get that much time with you either. Don't you think that's crazy?"

"What I think is that it can't be helped."

"I disagree, and I have a plan to do something about it. For right now, I can offer pizza with me and Nico, and we'll take you home."

Jean turned her attention to Patrick's son, who was patiently waiting. "Is it okay if I have dinner with you and your father?"

He shrugged. "I guess so."

"Jean is a very important friend of mine," Patrick added.

"Okay," Nico said on a deep sigh.

"Then let's do this."

Patrick led the way to his Lexus RX 350, for which he'd exchanged the Porsche Cayenne. Bottom line, Patrick had told her, he only needed a smart vehicle to get him from point A to point B. It didn't have to be exotic…or obvious theft bait.

Nico skipped beside his father, asking questions about anything that caught his attention. Patrick would glance down at his son as they walked, making gestures to illustrate his answers. But Nico would interrupt to ask, "What does that mean?"

Jean smiled. Patrick was still learning how not to talk down to him, how to find the language that a five-year-old understood, while also trying to be entertaining. He was making an enormous effort. Jean was impressed and empathetic. She admired that Patrick wanted to do the right thing. Every now and then he said something that made Nico burst into loud, childish laughter.

She trailed along behind them, vacillating between eavesdropping and following her own thoughts.

Patrick secured Nico into his car seat. Jean got in on the passenger side. "Where do you want to go?" she asked.

"To our pizza place," he said, as if she should have known.

Julio welcomed them. He teased and joked with Nicholas, adding a basket of garlic knots to their order...and serving him with a double scoop of ice cream for dessert...all on the house. Patrick tried to give as much attention to Nicholas as he did to Jean. But Nico won on that score. Jean was not surprised, and she was fine with that.

She believed that Patrick loved her. He had gone to extraordinary lengths to demonstrate his feelings. There were parts of his real life that trumped their hearts, where love not only had to show itself constantly, but where it also could prove to be not enough.

Jean carefully observed Patrick's valiant effort to be attentive to his son, this new, small being who was his natural ward and responsibility, while also wanting to maintain a relationship with her. It had taken the better part of the spring and summer to cultivate their love, to grow it, and that could still wilt on the vine with a lack of attention and care.

Now and then Jean thought of her parents' history and the things that had kept them apart for decades. She didn't want to go through that. She didn't want history to repeat itself.

After Patrick had paid for the dinner and thanked Julio for his kindness to Nico, they all got back into the Lexus. Patrick had to get him back to Philadelphia to his mother the following day, while also having a deposition to give the coming week. It was only a fifteen-minute drive to Jean's building. Nico had fallen asleep on the way.

Patrick pulled in front of her building and turned off the engine. Neither she nor Patrick said anything. And Jean found herself suddenly reluctant to get out of the car. Patrick looked over his shoulder to study his son, slumped a little to the side, already deeply asleep. He turned to Jean. "I'll walk you to the door."

She opened her door to climb out. "You don't have to. I'll be okay."

Patrick ignored her. He took a final look at his sleeping son, then followed Jean to the entrance a short ten feet away, from where he could still keep an eye on the vehicle. She was about to pull the door open when he took her arm as he also stepped to the side, away from the overhead entrance light, a little bit in the shadows. It was just late enough that Patrick wasn't concerned about who might pass by or enter beside them.

And he didn't wait for her to protest his next action. Surprise was his best weapon, and he used it. He pulled Jean into his embrace. His hug was a crusher for a long moment before he drew back and began to kiss her. He caught her as her head lifted to look at him. Patrick closed the distance to capture her mouth, press open her lips, and thrust his tongue to stroke against hers.

Jean moaned softly and gave in immediately. Patrick softened his attack, knowing that he now had her full attention. *It isn't fair*, Jean thought crazily as she welcomed his advance, his knowledge of her need, as he began to fill it. It was physical. It was emotional. But Jean was not ready, by any means, to concede to him. He couldn't have everything. He couldn't always be right. He couldn't always be met with challenge and adversity and still come out a winner.

Where did that leave her? she wondered plaintively. Was the only answer to not having her heart broken to walk away?

Was it her father or her mother who had walked away? Had they given up at the same time, accepting defeat against outside forces and history? Was she fated to experience the same?

Jean turned her head, breaking the kiss.

"Patrick," she whispered, her forehead pressed against his jacket.

"I know. Believe me, I know," he said just as quietly.

She shook her head. "I don't think you do."

"Then tell me."

Jean hesitated, struggled. Gnawed her lip to keep from speaking. "You've been through a lot this summer. *We've* been through a lot."

He sighed, rubbing her back as if trying to soothe her.

"I don't want to add to that, Patrick. I'm also figuring out what might be best for you, for us."

"What does that mean?"

"You can't be three places at once. Something has to give. Right now, neither of us knows what the future holds. But it's very clear what your responsibility has to be, first and foremost, Nico."

"And you. I'm not going to let us come this far, to know we love each other, just to have us fall apart." He reached for her hand and held it flat to his chest. "What do you feel?"

"Your heart. It's beating very fast."

"Why do you think that is?"

She tried to search his eyes in the dim light shining from the entrance. Jean shook her head. "I don't... Are you afraid?"

"Yes. Of losing you. I'd hoped for a better place, a better time to do this. I'll make it up to you. I told you I have a plan. Will you marry me?"

Then quickly, Patrick placed his thumb over her lips.

"Don't say anything right now. I want you to think about it. I want you to be sure. Will you do that?"

She stared into his eyes, listened to the underlying plea in his voice and the inherent bravura and fear. Her knees felt wobbly, and her heart also began to race. Jean pulled his hand away.

"Yes, I can. I'll..."

He covered her lips again. "That's all I need to know for now, Jean. Remember that I love you."

He hugged her close again. Jean could feel a subtle tremble in his breath as his mouth pressed to her cheek. She hugged him back.

"And I love you."

Jean pulled out of Patrick's arms, pivoting to enter her building quickly. She didn't look back, and the door swished closed between them. She didn't want him to see her tears.

CHAPTER 18

"You can wait in here. Mr. Franklin will join you in a moment."

Jean thanked the receptionist and took a seat at the oval conference table. It wasn't a large room, with the capacity for only eight people around the table, and it had no windows. The fourth wall, however, with the entrance door, was floor-to-ceiling glass. She recognized that it was functionally designed to eliminate the distraction of the outside world beyond the window, while allowing the occupants to be seen and monitored from the corridor.

Maybe it was Ross's intent that they could be seen at all times. His office would have been too private. There, she would be least comfortable alone with him, as opposed to being seen by office staff passing by. But Jean didn't necessarily feel safe in the conference room either.

Getting the call from Ross had caught her off guard. They had not spoken by phone in three years. They had exhausted the need for conversation on his part, and the desire on hers. Running into one another at a social function early in the summer, while unexpected, had not been disturbing for Jean. But she was still not totally clear why Ross had requested that she meet him at his office.

Jean was still creating her scenarios and possibilities when he pushed through the glass door.

"Sorry I kept you waiting. Impromptu corridor meeting with a colleague on my way here. Thanks for coming."

Ross sat down. His little speech gave her a chance to scrutinize him and see him without the hordes that had surrounded them at the reception.

He pushed back comfortably in the leather high-back chair. He placed a tablet on the table at an angle easy for him to read.

He finally looked at her directly, but Jean could tell nothing by his expression. He didn't appear to be the least bit nervous. Ross also had no trouble meeting her own wary gaze or offering a faint nondescript smile.

"It's good to see you."

Jean didn't respond to his greeting.

"Thanks for coming in. I especially appreciate this when I really didn't give you a lot to go on about why I wanted to see you."

"Curiosity got the best of me," Jean said calmly.

"However you came to agree, thanks."

Ross pushed a button on the tablet, and the LED screen came to life. He glanced briefly at it and then back to her. His elbows rested on the chair arms, and his hands were clasped together in front.

"First of all, I want to thank you, Jean."

She frowned slightly, having no idea why he felt the need.

"You recommended Patrick Bennett to me as a client. That was incredibly...kind of you. Of course I'm curious why, given our recent history," he added carefully.

Jean shifted in her seat and it swiveled slightly with her movements. "I wasn't being kind, Ross. I was trying to be practical and useful to Patrick. He was a little overwhelmed when he came into so much money last spring. I felt that you would be a good fit. There was nothing personal in what I did. I felt that your kind of business expertise was what he needed. I knew you'd be honest and fair...with him."

For a moment, Ross actually looked embarrassed, but that quickly cleared from his features. He unclasped his hands momentarily, spreading them before bringing them together again.

"Well, I still thank you. And I thank you sincerely for that trust. I know it must have been hard."

"I had no problem with it," Jean said formally but without any rancor. "I'm glad the arrangement seems to be working out."

"Yes," Ross said thoughtfully.

Jean nodded silently.

Ross shifted. He glanced at the tablet. "I also wanted to let you know that your idea for a foundation is really smart thinking. So I appreciate your contribution to the conversation."

"Will you help Patrick set it up?"

"As much as I can. I'm researching and talking to people who have more knowledge than me on the subject. I also have a friend who works with a traditional foundation that's operated for decades here in the city. He's offered to guide us. I don't suppose you also have a title for the foundation, other than the obvious Patrick Bennett Foundation for...? There's been no decision on what the foundation is for. What will be its mission statement?"

"I haven't given it serious thought, but I always felt the Millionaires Club had an original and catchy sound to it."

"The Millionaires Club," he repeated, testing the sound of it. "Then, as a club, there is a possibility for more millionaires to join? We might have to define what we mean by 'millionaire' to start."

"Yes, I think so. There are so many wealthy people who might want to be a part of something like this. You know, the idea of being philanthropic. Giving back. And it's not a new concept. Patrick didn't earn his sudden wealth, and he's very aware of that. He was lucky. So it seems smart and generous to want to share. It wouldn't take much to come up with a list of social needs that would benefit from private-sector investments."

All the time she spoke, Jean realized that not only was Ross listening closely to her, but he was making notes on the tablet, occasionally nodding at something she said that he agreed with or found important.

He asked questions, and their conversation continued on the subject for another thirty minutes.

"This is a really good, simple synopsis of your idea. I won't use any of this, or your name, until I can formalize the concept, get a proposal written up, and run it past Patrick's attorneys and the people here."

"I don't need credit for this."

"Well, we can talk about that later. And I'll discuss with Patrick. But thanks for your thoughts on this, Jean." He took up his original position, sitting back in his chair, hands clasped. "I have something else I'd like to talk to you about. It's more on a personal level."

Jean immediately became cautious, even more so than when she'd first arrived at his office. She leaned forward, preparing to stand. "I don't think…"

Ross put out a hand calmly to stay her. "It's not about you and me. I like to believe we've put that to rest so we can both move on, okay?"

She settled down slowly, but on the edge of her seat.

"This is about Marin Phillips. I think you know her?"

"Marin?" Jean repeated, surprised. "Yes, I know her. Well…not really. I first met her at a dinner party. She's an account executive with ESPN."

"Patrick's company."

"Correct. We sat next to each other and chatted during the evening. I liked her. And then we got together for lunch some weeks later. We'll probably do that again. I can see us becoming friends."

Ross nodded, watching her. "I met her at another party a month ago. I thought she was very attractive and very sharp. And not automatically defensive. I asked her out. We met for brunch on a Sunday. You know… lots of people around, kept it light and open. She talked about Patrick briefly, in a coworker kind of way, although she's on the business side of the network. Nothing at all personal, just the connection. And she spoke about having met and liked you at that party you mentioned."

"I don't know her well at all, Ross. She's a new acquaintance."

"I'm not asking you to give up any secrets. I liked her. I was immediately attracted to her."

Jean chortled nervously. "I hope you're not asking me for advice."

"I am. I honestly am asking you if you think I should pursue my interest. How do you believe she might respond? What should I be careful of? You know me well enough to be able to make a judgment that I'll be comfortable with."

Jean stared at Ross, stunned that he would put such a responsibility on her. That he would even want to. She was forced to dig into her memory banks, to conjure up the Ross she'd first met and had been attracted to because of his masculine good looks, his smarts, his good manners and sense of humor. His seductive courting of her, even their satisfying lovemaking that altogether made him a very worthy suitor. That their relationship had a spectacular flameout no longer affected her. She'd long ago lost emotional feelings for Ross Franklin. But he was not a horrible person. Just human and imperfect like anyone else.

"You really do like her, don't you?"

"Almost immediately when I first met her."

"I will say this. She's a friendly person and easy to be with. She's smart and a good listener. She's very observant. She will give you the benefit of the doubt. If you've had one easy, pleasant outing with Marin, I think she'll definitely be open to more opportunities to get to know you."

"We left it at 'I'll call you.' I didn't want to seem too…"

"I get it. My only real advice to you, Ross, is to be a lot more thoughtful about her than you were inclined to be with me. Don't do her dirt if you're really interested. Don't play her. You only get so many chances to prove you're not a jerk. And…and I know you can do better than that."

"I just screwed up royally with you. I shamed myself," he confessed honestly.

There was absolute silence as they faced each other. Jean's countenance was calm and composed, clear and confident. She didn't blink.

Ross regarded her, and she began to see regret and a visual apology that meant more to her now than the mea culpa he'd attempted so long ago. Jean took in a deep, affirming breath. She was in love with Patrick Bennett, and Ross's feelings didn't concern her.

This time when she made to stand, Ross didn't stop her. It was only as she walked past him to the door that he called out, but he didn't touch her.

"One more thing, Jean. As long as I was bold enough to ask your opinion, I'd like to offer one of my own. Patrick never mentions or talks about his relationship with you. But I know there is one. And I know it's extremely important to him. I'm going out on a very thin limb by offering that I believe he's really in love with you. Of course I don't know your expectations. And I know his life has gone off the rails a number of times this summer. My opinion is, he's been pretty good about dealing with it. So…my unasked-for comment is, whatever is going on in his life, don't give up on him. I think he's worth the effort. Far more than I was."

"What makes you think that I would give up?"

Ross sighed, stood tall, and looked into her eyes. "I know you've found yourself caught in dramas where you've had to worry if a Black guy is seeing you as a Black woman or someone who's half white. Or if a white guy wants to think you're white or he's experimenting because you're Black. And there are the ones who think they want you, but then go after someone else who's exactly the opposite. Pretty confusing to keep track of. I've been guilty of one of those possibilities. There's no ambivalence with Patrick."

Jean swallowed, genuinely moved by Ross's support and deeply appreciative that he recognized her desire for a true love that she deserved.

—

"How did you find this place?" Diana Chambers asked her daughter once they were seated in the quiet, upscale restaurant in the Flatiron District of Manhattan. She looked around, appreciating the muted beige design and accessories. Almost plain, but elegant and simple. It was a Tuesday night and just before the dinner hour, so it wasn't crowded or noisy. It was actually possible to have a conversation and not have to listen to anyone else's.

"My friend Annabelle told me about it."

Diana squinted through her glasses at Jean. "You mean that crazy lady you used to work for when you were in college?"

Jean laughed. "Annabelle is not crazy. She's just colorful and larger than life."

"Maybe not crazy. Just off the wall?"

Jean shook her head. No point in arguing with her mother. "Annabelle says her goal is to eat at all the top places in Manhattan in five years."

"Then what happens?"

"I have no idea. Maybe by then she'll have no money? Or she'll move out of the city before she gets halfway through her list?"

"Maybe she'll finally get married to someone..."

"Who will appreciate her unique personality. Annabelle is a lot of fun. She's stylish and original, and she's been a really good friend to me."

"I hope that means she likes you just the way you are," Diana commented. "You can tell her that I like her suggestion for this place. I hope the food fulfills the promise of the setting."

Jean chuckled again. She was happy she got the call suggesting that they meet for dinner in the city. In truth, Jean was happy to be rescued from a night of soup and salad...and too much introspection. She hadn't been sleeping well and was struggling to stay positive and hopeful. Patrick was always on her mind...in her heart. He'd reached out to her, and she had opted not to respond, afraid that she would give in and agree to anything he wanted. Jean was determined that any further discussion, any decision, had to be on her terms. Maybe she was cutting off her nose to spite her face, but...

Jean looked up from the menu to find her mother studying her. Her gaze displayed curiosity and concern. "What?" Jean asked.

Diana shifted her gaze back to her own menu. "You look a little tired and restless. Is everything okay?"

"Of course. I mean, the job has been kicking my butt this summer. It's been super busy with not a lot of time off."

"But you did take that week to go away with Patrick."

Jean quietly sighed to herself. She didn't want to go there. It was hard enough agonizing over her belief that she needed to regain perspective on Patrick and their relationship. The problem was, she couldn't figure out to what purpose. Just so she could be right? Just so she could feel she was in control and not losing herself in Patrick and the soap opera that was currently his life? Just so that she'd stop feeling afraid?

But if their relationship ended, would she really feel any better?

"Yes, I did. It was a wonderful week, Mom. I had a great time."

Diana stared at her daughter. "And?"

"What do you mean, *and*?"

"You haven't mentioned Patrick. Are you still seeing him?"

"When we can," Jean answered truthfully, although the admission made her feel empty and sad. "You know about his son. It's taking a lot of lawyer time to figure out joint custody. His ex-wife is still being rather difficult. Like she still wants to punish Patrick. I don't really understand why."

"What do you think will happen?"

Jean shrugged, wanting to drop the subject. She could already feel her insides twisting into knots. "I don't know, Mom."

"But you do love him?"

Her mother's voice was low, understanding, and maternal. It now had the kind of soothing undertone that could break her, make her want to curl up in her mother's lap, like a wounded child, and cry her eyes out. Jean was not about to let that happen, as much as she could seriously use tender reassurance...and a good night's sleep.

"I don't want to..."

Jean looked up and over her mother's shoulder. She stared at the man with the dark, graying hair and recognized her father.

"Daddy? What are you doing here?" She looked with suspicion to her mother, who pretended as much surprise as herself. But there was no way her mom could pull off the subterfuge. Jean knew full well that the only way her father could have known where they'd be was through her mother.

"Don't I get a hug?" Seth Travis approached with his arms outspread and a happy, satisfied smile. He'd surprised his daughter, leaving her speechless.

Jean got up from the table and fulfilled her father's request. They hugged as if they had been apart for years. They hugged in the way Jean needed, to feel comforted and made whole.

Could he feel her shaking and her despair?

"Hey, I'm glad to see you, too, honey," he chuckled quietly. He slowly pushed her away so he could peer into her face. "Sweetheart, are you okay?"

"I'm just so happy to see you. Mom too. But you're not going to get away with trying to make me believe this was a coincidence. What's going on?"

Seth pushed her back toward her seat and took the empty one next to Diana. As Jean was settling into her chair, she would have to be blind not to have seen the warm, welcoming gestures and greetings that passed between her parents. Her father patted her mother's shoulder. Her mother placed a hand over his, and they held tightly. Seth sat down and turned to Diana to kiss her a brief hello. But it was not just a friendly hello. What Jean was witnessing she knew was the simple and sweet expression of love.

"So now that you've both gotten me here under false pretenses, I want to know what's going on."

Seth smiled like a Cheshire cat. Diana appeared not only to be blushing under her warm brown countenance, but also appeared young, giddy, and content.

Seth sat holding Diana's hand. Before answering his daughter's question, he took the time to gaze at Diana, and Jean felt like she was intruding on a very tender, private moment between the two of them.

There was no question anymore that her parents were in love. *Still* in love with each other.

Seth faced Jean, now that the hellos had been said between everyone. "I'm here to see you and to spend some time with Di. I'm planning to move back to New York."

"Seth is staying in Tarrytown with me while he's here. He'll be back and forth for a while during the transition."

Seth smiled at Diana. "I want your mom and me to spend more time together."

"Time together...to do what?" Jean asked.

"To make sure about our feelings. To plan the rest of our lives, hopefully together. And to make sure you're okay with our plans."

"I have no say in your plans. Anyway, you can't make them based on what I want. I've thought for a long time that you two were in love. Maybe you've never stopped loving each other."

"We had to rebuild a lot," Seth responded. "But I think it's fair to say we feel like we have a second chance, and we have no intention of beating around the bush." He reached across the table and took Jean's hand. "I've always loved your mother. I'm not going to fight it any longer. She's been far braver than I have about dealing with the bad timing we got caught up in all those years ago. Having you helped us a lot, because we loved you so much. You connected us forever. In a way you made it a lot easier for us to try again, Jean."

Jean looked back and forth between her parents, both of whom were practically glowing with joy and hope.

"Well, to be honest I suspected this was happening. You two are like teenagers. It was impossible for you to hide your feelings, and I spotted the clues at the start of the summer. As a matter of fact, so did Patrick. He even asked me how I felt about it."

Her mother looked suddenly apprehensive. "How do you feel about it? Are we being foolish? Are you angry that we want to get back together after all these years?"

"I'm happy that my parents love each other. I'm lucky that they love me enough to come full circle and become the family I always wanted us to be. But I feel I have to ask, what took you so long?"

Fortunately for Jean, her father laughed at her question before she could lose it and break down in front of them, spoiling their moment of glory. Her father leaned across the table to kiss her with paternal affection.

"Thank you, sweetheart."

She rose from her seat to go to her mother, to hug and kiss her, and to say, again, how happy she was for both of them, and for herself.

Diana Chambers cupped Jean's face and kissed her forehead.

"Don't think I'm not aware that you're going through something with Patrick. I'm so sorry I can't help you, love. I hope everything will work out. I hope he's worthy of you."

"He is, Mom. And I do love him."

"Be patient, honey. We guys don't always get it right away. I'm betting on you and I'm betting on Patrick. I know you'll figure it out."

"I hope you're right, Daddy." She hesitated, glancing back and forth between them. "Are you and Mom thinking of…you know, getting married?"

The look exchanged between Seth and Diana was so magical it left Jean breathless. This was what true love looked like. No barriers, just believing in each other with their hearts and souls.

"That was always our plan. There have been too many detours along the way, but it's been written in the stars since before you were born. It just took time for our destiny to catch up to us."

CHAPTER 19

think we're making progress. The custody agreement will be drawn up in its final form. You each can have your attorney review and direct any further questions to the judge in family court. I will continue to act as mediator, if you will."

The attorney at the head of the table closed a folder, and he signaled to the transcript reporter that he could leave the room.

Patrick did not so much sit in his chair as begin to feel his body slump. Every time he had to meet with the lawyers and his ex-wife, Katie, his body became stiff and awkward, wired with stress and anger at the loss of five years in his life, robbed of the chance to bond immediately with his son.

He glanced at Katie, seated two people away from him, on the other side of the table, making it possible to avoid chance eye contact. She had changed since their divorce. Her once-blond hair was now, more or less, its natural color of light brown. She no longer had the lean, taut body of an athlete, but she was slim, now an attractive adult who had come into her own. Watching her, one wouldn't conceive that she was capable of being mean-spirited or plotting to get even with anyone for any reason. And that was one of the things Patrick had to deal with when it was revealed that he had a son.

He sighed and momentarily closed his eyes as the lawyers continued to chat and pack up their briefcases. He'd begun to make peace with the situation. When he'd first met Nicholas, the appropriate professionals had been present to try to manage any anxiety on the child's part, or of his parents, who initially faced each other with barely concealed, hostile glares, although each for very different reasons.

Meeting his young son had vanquished Patrick's tightly held anger against his ex and immediately softened his heart. Nicholas had been quiet, understandably, and wary at first. Thereafter, he seemed to accept readily that this man he'd met was his father. Together, the two of them had felt their way from being strangers to a comfortable place where Nicholas was okay being alone with Patrick and began to talk more openly with him. Patrick stopped trying so hard to figure out how to be a father in a few weeks.

The only glitch had been Nicholas's second weekend stay with Patrick at his mom's house. Suddenly, just after they'd had dinner, the child had become weepy and cranky...and he wanted to go home to his mother.

Patrick had panicked. What was he supposed to do? What if Nicholas didn't stop crying and threw a fit and could not be consoled? Patrick spoke gently to his son as the boy buried his face in his hands and cried into a sofa pillow. His mother had not been much better at consoling the child.

"Okay, if that will make you feel better, Nico, I'll take you home. But we have to wait until tomorrow. It's too late to drive you back tonight. It's dark. I promise, after breakfast in the morning, I'll take you to your mother. Okay?"

Nico had begun to calm down at once, satisfied with the promise. "Okay," he said in a shaky voice, wiping his tears on the sleeve of his shirt.

But two things had happened. Patrick had awakened early to find that his son had made his way to his room again and climbed into bed with him to sleep. Then, after breakfast, when Patrick suggested they get ready for the ride back to Philadelphia, Nico had said with a vigorous shake of his head, "I don't want to. Can I stay a little while longer?"

From that moment, they were a father and son easing their way to a bond that was just a few years behind schedule.

Patrick sighed and sat up in his chair. He wanted to leave and go home. He'd been thinking of Jean. He was filled with anxiety, not about Nicholas's future but his own. He had become deathly afraid that he might still lose Jean, her love, and her presence in his life. He didn't want to consider what that would be like if it happened. Patrick now knew it could happen.

"Is there anything else anyone has to say before we close shop? Please remember that the official signing of all documents will take place ten days from now. Next time we'll accommodate Mr. Bennett and meet in his lawyer's office in Manhattan," one of the attending attorney's instructed.

Patrick stood, picked up his portfolio, said a brief good night to the room at large, and checked if there was still enough time to catch the last flight back to New York...or if he wanted to go so far as to hire a private car to drive him, as opposed to staying overnight. He left the room and headed for the elevator, juggling his options. Which would be the fastest?

"Patrick, can I talk to you?"

Surprised and wary...and impatient to get going, Patrick nonetheless turned to Katie. She approached, equally wary, Patrick noticed, but also with determination. He didn't say a word as they faced each other. But she met his gaze and didn't avoid what she found there.

"I know how you feel, and I don't blame you. I know you must hate me for not being honest with you. To say I'm sorry won't cut it."

Patrick let her talk. He was taken aback by his ex-wife's sudden confession and mea culpa. He tried to look kindly on her, and he couldn't. Not yet. Did she really understand the damage that had been done?

"And...I also want to say I'll cooperate with Nico being with you when you want. You and I can work out extra visitations not in the agreement. We can keep our attorneys informed."

"Okay." He nodded, distant and cool.

Katie seemed to struggle with her next words. As a matter of fact, she seemed to be gearing up for something was that really difficult for her to say. "I also want to thank you…really thank you, Patrick, for offering to rewrite the alimony settlement. What you've increased it to is…is… I can't even say how generous you've—"

He cut her off. "I can afford it. And I didn't really earn it. The way I see it, you're the mother of my son, and I want to make sure you have what you need to raise him well. We both need to be invested in that."

She nodded, again appearing contrite and accepting of his lack of warmth. "I agree." She met his gaze again. "My parents never liked what I was doing, not letting you know I was pregnant. I couldn't believe that I was, after the divorce. I was angry, immature… No excuse, I know."

Patrick pushed the button to summon the elevator.

"Let's move on, Katie. No matter what, Nico is *our* son, together. He is going to be the glue that will help us work to do right by him. That's all I care about."

"He likes you. He gets home and all he talks about is what his daddy did, and where you went, and what he eats. You should know that, the last time he came home to me after a weekend with you, Nico wanted to know right away when he could go back."

Patrick felt a constriction in his chest. It was squeezing out profound relief and hope.

"Thanks for letting me know that. I've been…" Patrick stopped, afraid of how his confession might come across.

Katie grinned knowingly. "Scared shitless. I think you're doing great, considering. I hope that, maybe, someday you can forgive me."

"I'm working on it," Patrick murmured, as the elevator arrived. He held the door. "Coming?"

"You go on. I'm waiting for my lawyer."

"I'll see you at the signing."

"Get home safe," she added at the last moment as the door began to close.

For the moment, Patrick didn't have any particular feeling about Katie's admission and wishes. He didn't want to be bitter, but he wasn't going to pretend that all's well that ends well. No one owed him anything, and he could never get back the time lost with his son anyway. His life could hardly be said to be a tragedy. It could be stated fairly, however, that there had been a series of unfortunate incidents that had tested him. But all the good stuff far surpassed even that.

The good stuff included Jean. It had all begun with Jean.

He'd found out what a beautiful, caring, steady, amazing woman she was. He'd fallen in love with her. He wanted a life with her. His son was the ultimate surprise, but Nico would be his son forever no matter what. He couldn't imagine life without Jean anymore.

———

Jean was just about to leave her office for the day when a brief item was announced on network news on the flat screen. She was stopped in her tracks when she caught the name Patrick Bennett spoken by the anchor. The news had been following the case of sports commentator Patrick Bennett and the legal complications he was currently engulfed in having discovered the existence of a son. A video piece showed Patrick leaving a law office. He was immediately surrounded by a bevy of eager reporters who were seeking salacious details to make the continuing story more interesting than it actually was. Jean was pleased to see Patrick remain cool and calm, true to the kind of man he was. He was gracious and answered reporter questions smoothly, not saying anything that amounted to a usable quote for the news at six and again at eleven.

The second thing Jean noticed was how very tired Patrick appeared. She suspected he was reaching his limit, worn-out by the incredible personal revelations, good and bad, that had been thrust upon him.

Patrick stepped into a town car and firmly closed the door.

Jean thought quickly, realizing suddenly that Patrick was out there dealing with all of the public scrutiny by himself. There was never anyone by his side, never anyone supporting him emotionally. In and out of courthouses and law offices, out on a limb, braving a sea of reporters, still doing his program, and smiling to an audience that had no idea of the toll the summer had taken on him. Alone.

"Oh my god," Jean moaned quietly to herself.

She raced back to her office, to her cell phone, grabbing it to punch in a number. Her thumb fumbled over the keypad. She tried again. It went through and the line began to ring. On the third ring, he finally picked up.

"Hey…"

"Patrick?"

"Yeah."

"Oh, Patrick," she tried to say with deep sympathy and feeling. But no sound came out. Her throat seemed clogged and incapable of letting air through. Jean swallowed and took a deep breath. "Where are you?"

"At the airport in Philly. Just about to board my flight for New York. Is something wrong? What's going on?"

"To Kennedy or LaGuardia?"

"Newark."

"Come to me when you land."

"What?"

"Come here."

"Jean…why?"

"Because I asked you to," she said softly.

He didn't answer. The silence went on so long Jean began to think it was already too late. They had missed a moment when the time and distance wouldn't have mattered. They would have thrown caution and common sense to the wind and made it happen.

"You want me to come to Brooklyn." It wasn't a question. Patrick was still trying to understand her request.

"Yes."

"Tonight?"

"Yes."

"That's crazy. It'll take a long time. And… Jean, I'm…not in good shape."

"I know. That's why I want you to come. Patrick, everything is going to be all right. Just please come home." She didn't mean to plead, but her pride simply didn't matter just then. It was all about her heart. And his.

"Okay. Okay, Jean. If you want me to, I'll be there."

"I'll be waiting," Jean said.

Hurry!

———

The moment he'd committed to Jean's request, Patrick felt like fresh air had been pumped back into his lungs. He became fixated on figuring out how to get to Brooklyn from Newark International as fast as humanly possible. The destination was not just to be with Jean; he realized it was an instant way back to her heart…and she'd left the way open for him. By the time the plane had reached altitude, it was already descending, preparing to land. The trip had been less than an hour. Patrick knew the airport well and was out of the terminal in ten minutes. No need to order an Uber; there were plenty of cabs at the taxi stand.

On the flight, Patrick had already Googled that the quickest route from the airport to Jean's would take less than thirty minutes by car. It was ironic that he had to travel within a mile of where he lived in Jersey City, to the Holland Tunnel into Lower Manhattan, and the Battery Park Tunnel into Brooklyn. When the cab pulled up in front of her building, Patrick immediately experienced profound relief. He was finally back where he belonged.

———

Jean hurried home after work to prepare.

She could not contain her impatience for Patrick to arrive. She kept looking out the living room window to the street in front of her building. Every black sedan rolling slowly down the street had her poised to dash to the elevator to meet him in the lobby.

It was astonishingly early when the doorman buzzed to let her know someone was asking for her. He'd send him up.

Jean's insides twisted with the knowledge that he'd made it to her. But she was suddenly very anxious about how they'd greet each other, even though her apartment had always been their rendezvous location by default.

She went to the door, her hand trembling as she held on to the knob. She closed her eyes and took deep breaths, knowing that the next few minutes when they met were going to be critical. Jean had summoned Patrick after having held him at bay, afraid that there was no room in his life for her. Now she was ready to welcome him because, no matter what, the only thing that mattered was loving him.

She pulled the door open and stood there, just as the elevator arrived. Patrick stood inside the cab, and her heart turned over to see the face of the man she loved, emotionally battered and worn down. Jean knew she was responsible for some of it. Was she going to be able to make Patrick understand that fear and insecurity had driven her to try to protect herself? Could she convince him that fear and insecurity, and love, might also save them both?

Patrick seemed to take forever to cross the landing, to walk through her entrance and into her open arms. They embraced slowly, carefully, as if to savor the moment of seeing each other again. He didn't seem angry with her, as Jean had suspected. If anything, it felt like an odd resignation from Patrick. As if there was no other option. As if he also realized he had to come when she called. This was where he most belonged.

They hugged in the doorway. It seemed to be enough for the moment. Until she leaned back to study his face. There, Jean found a man who needed unconditional TLC and a place to feel safe. She placed her hands on his face, holding it to make Patrick focus on her.

"Are you okay?" she asked quietly, concern woven into her voice.

"Now that I'm here, I think so."

"Then, come on in."

He carried only a small weekend duffel Jean took out of his hand. He shrugged out of his short black leather jacket…the one she'd first seen him wearing at the lottery announcement. That occasion now seemed like forever ago. She set his things aside. He stood waiting for guidance and instruction from her. It troubled her to see Patrick numb with exhaustion and passive.

She stood in front of him again. "When was the last time you ate anything?"

He frowned. "What day is this?"

She told him.

"It was lunch yesterday."

"I'm going to get you something to eat. And then you're going to bed to get some sleep."

She turned to head into the kitchen, but Patrick caught her hand and pulled her back to face him. "What do you have in mind?"

She laughed lightly, so happy to have Patrick to herself, so happy that he'd come willingly. "Does it matter?"

He shook his head, deftly drawing her into his arms. Patrick held her, rubbing his cheek against hers. "I guess not. Thank you. I'm so glad I made it here."

She closed her eyes and surrendered to his embrace. "Are you still mad at me?" she asked.

"I was never mad at you, Jean. I was afraid you'd given up on me."

She pressed a kiss to his chest through the opening of his shirt. "We can talk about all of that later. I want to get some food into you and then get you to bed." Jean could feel him chuckling as he hugged her, nuzzled her, kissed her face, hampered her attempts to break free.

"That's the best offer I've had in weeks. You're going to feed me and take me to bed. I'm feeling better already."

Jean stopped wiggling and looked at him. "I'm sorry I couldn't be of more help to you."

He sighed. "You've done more than I could ever have hoped for. You've given me more than I think I deserve."

"I'm glad you came, Patrick. I was afraid you wouldn't."

He stroked her back. "I hit rock bottom today. There didn't seem to be an end in sight. I felt like I was on a merry-go-round that was never going to stop. I was afraid...I'd never have this again," he whispered close to her ear. His breath tickled her skin.

"Me too. I called because I couldn't be there with you. So I brought you to me. I wasn't sure you'd come," she ended.

"My lady calls, I come. Sorry if I babbled. I couldn't believe it was you. I didn't sound like an idiot, did I?"

Jean looked at him again, stroking his face, which had twenty-four hours' growth. She so loved the look that a little facial hair gave him. "You sounded zoned out, to be honest."

She felt him sway slightly against her. Jean tiptoed to kiss him and pushed Patrick away. "I'll fix you something. Go in and make yourself at home."

In the instant they stood staring at one another, Jean's words sank in.

"After I finished your call, I did feel like...I was coming home."

"And here you are."

With that, they separated, and Jean scavenged through her kitchen to see if there was enough of anything to make a simple meal for Patrick. It was very late, and she settled on an omelet, avocado toast, and decaf coffee. Nothing that would give him heartburn or nightmares.

She called him to the small dining nook in the living room, instead of the table for two in the kitchen. He reappeared in a T-shirt, black cotton knit pajama bottoms, and bare feet. He looked comfortable, but no less tired.

"Sit here. Eat," Jean commanded, indicating a chair. "Is it okay if I leave you for a little bit? Or do you want company?"

He gave her an amused grin. His eyes were slightly bloodshot. He took her hand. "I'm not afraid of the dark or being alone. As long as you're not planning to leave for China, I'm okay."

"I'm here."

With that, Jean walked away to see to the other ways she could make him comfortable, give him space to recoup in peace. She wanted to show Patrick he was not alone. And he didn't have to be ever again. While he ate quietly in the dining area, she put out fresh towels for him, put away her few personal things spread around her room. She took out her tablet and quickly composed a message to Brad telling him she was taking a day off. Something personal had come up. Jean returned to the kitchen to clean the coffee maker and set it up again for the morning. Or afternoon. Whenever Patrick would arise.

Then, she began to prepare herself for the night, vanity and love driving her to make sure her hair wasn't a bird's nest of tangles and wild curls. In the bathroom mirror, she stared into the face of a young woman deliriously excited about being with the man she loved and once again sure that they could have a future...and make it work. Jean had only to recall the extraordinary turnaround with her parents to let her hope reign supreme.

She and Patrick could do this. It was no longer defying the odds. It was simply making it happen. Together. They could love each other and be happy.

Jean heard dishes being placed in the sink and followed the sounds. She encountered Patrick as he exited the kitchen.

"I didn't wash anything."

"Don't worry about it. I'll take care of it in the morning."

He approached, again bemused. "You're taking care of me."

"Somebody has to step in and make sure you don't crash into a wall. I don't do this for everyone."

"Glad to hear that."

"You don't need this all the time. I just knew right now you needed something a little extra."

"We'll have to talk more about the little extra sometime."

"Okay." Jean pointed to the bedroom door. "Go to bed."

"Yes, ma'am," Patrick said, his voice becoming gravelly with the need for sleep.

Jean turned out all the lights, made sure the front door was locked, and joined him in her room. She found Patrick removing the lounging pajama bottoms and the T-shirt. He kept on his jockey shorts. He got into bed and more or less collapsed, spread-eagle.

"Move over," Jean ordered in a quiet voice. He obeyed, making room for her. She lay flat, trying to get into a position that wouldn't disturb him during the night.

Patrick had other plans.

He rolled onto his side facing her. He put his hand around her waist and easily pulled her close. The movement forced Jean to roll onto her side so that they were spooned together. He held her close to his chest, and Jean could feel his heart beat against her back. She moved her legs to experience the silky feel of the hair on his legs against hers. Their toes played footsie for a moment before relaxing. Patrick's forearm, resting on the mattress, became a warm and firm pillow. He sighed deeply, and Jean knew he was on the verge.

She offered no more conversation. They both needed a little peace and quiet.

"She apologized," Patrick suddenly whispered into the dark.

"She who?"

"My ex. Katie. She apologized for keeping Nico from me."

"We'll talk about it later."

It was silent again. Until…

"She said that Nico talks about me a lot. He likes coming to visit me."

She didn't respond. She wanted Patrick to sleep and just let it go for now. Of all the insanity that was thrown at him since the spring, news about his son had been the most challenging, the most surprising, and the most hurtful. But it was going to work out.

"Shh. Go to sleep."

The silence grew.

"I love you."

It didn't make sense to cry at this point. But Jean swallowed, knowing she was about to.

"I love you more," she managed to get out, her voice reedy and broken.

And then they were both instantly asleep.

Jean woke up in the middle of the night to discover that she and Patrick were still melded together in the same position. But she was beginning to cramp. She eased herself out of his arms and turned to face him. He was clearly deeply asleep, his breathing even. She shook his shoulder.

"Patrick. Turn over."

He moaned and stretched out his legs.

"Patrick."

He sighed and rolled over so their positions were reversed. Jean closed the space between them, resting her arm across his waist. After a moment, Patrick reached for her hand, urging her even closer and threading their fingers. He mumbled something she couldn't understand.

"Go back to sleep."

"Don't leave."

She did hear that.

The thing that happened next was, while dreaming, Jean had the titillating experience of holding a bird in her hand, its wings fluttering and brushing over her breasts and the nipples. She released the bird and it flew away, but the mildly erotic sensation remained and only seemed to get stronger. In the dream, she could feel her reaction centering, traveling through her body down to her stomach, her groin, releasing a gentle heat.

Jean moaned, shifting to ease the caressing assault on her body. The dream was fading, but her breasts still felt oversensitized, tender, yearning. Her eyes fluttered open, and she became fully aware of Patrick half covering her body with his, his lips planting moist, little featherlight kisses on her breasts. She moaned again, closing her eyes and letting herself become fully enveloped in his foreplay. She combed her fingers into his hair, holding his head to her so the kisses could continue. Patrick had somehow managed to remove her night shift, leaving her naked except for her panties. She undulated against him. He was already completely naked.

"Patrick," she whispered, her emotions heightened by being awakened to lovemaking.

He stopped to lift his head. Jean could see he hadn't been awake that long, but he had awakened with a great raging need.

"Good morning," Patrick said, shifting upward to lie completely on top of her.

He kissed her with so much slow, immediate passion that Jean thought they both could burst into lustful flames. The weight of him made her feel safe and loved. She thought she could die right then and there of total happiness.

Jean responded to him in kind, shifting her legs to make room for him. He nestled and rested in position. They continued to kiss and stroke each other slowly and languidly. He slipped his hands under the band of her panties, curving around her buttocks, forcing the fabric down her thighs, maneuvering the underwear to her knees. Patrick let her figure out how to wiggle out of them, while his hands transferred to her breasts and one slipped lower to stroke between her legs.

Jean went limp. Mindless. Helpless against the overwhelming attack on her nerve endings, the very tender center of her body.

They were a tangle of arms and legs and hands and fingers, as she returned the favor to him, while she had the presence of mind to give Patrick what he needed as well.

He pulled his lips from hers to hug her. "Is this what you meant by a little extra?" he growled close to her ear.

"Is it helping?"

"Oh yeah…" Patrick said, sliding effortlessly and slowly into her warm body.

No talk was possible after that. There was just shifting of their bodies on the linens and that rhythmic dance of lovemaking. There was their breathing mixing into the wordless language of love. There was, with great effort, murmured endearments, encouragements, exclamations of delight.

After Jean's release Patrick turned his attention all to himself, and with her help of small kisses and light stroking of her hands and fingers in all the right places, he soon followed. They lay still, panting. That slowly turned into steady breathing until they were both asleep again in each other's arms.

Jean was up first the next morning, curled on the sofa with her laptop, checking to see if there was a message from her boss. There was, confirming that he'd received her email about taking a day off. No problem. Nothing of importance on their office agenda for the day.

She read one from her father who was back in LA continuing his arrangements for the move to the East Coast. There was one from Marin.

Guess who I met? I think we're dating. Or is this just a hookup? No response necessary. Hope to see you soon.

Jean smiled at that. Lots of good things suddenly seemed to be happening for a lot of folks. She certainly counted herself among them.

There was shuffling from the bedroom. She listened for a moment and knew that Patrick was finally waking up. She looked at the tablet clock. It was a little after ten in the morning.

"Jean?"

She put aside her devices and quickly headed for the bedroom. She'd found and dressed again in her night shift. She climbed onto the bed and back into Patrick's arms, snuggling down against his chest. He kissed her forehead.

He let out a mighty yawn.

"How did you sleep?"

"I always sleep well when I'm with you."

She smiled, brushing her hand across his hairy chest. "Why is that?"

"What I think is that I feel completely safe here. I'm away from my world and in yours. Not a work thing, but a man and woman thing. I haven't given this a lot of scientific thought, but I'm happy when I'm with you. That's the short explanation."

"What about the longer one?"

Patrick placed his free hand behind his head and closed his eyes. "Not now. I think we'll have time later for that. At least, I hope we will."

She tilted her head to gaze at him. "Ask me again."

"What?"

"Ask me again."

After a moment, Patrick turned his head sharply to blink his understanding. "Will you marry me?"

Jean smiled, stroking his chest again. "Yes."

She could feel his body completely relaxing, like air being let out from an inflated object.

"Seriously?"

"I want to marry you."

"What made you change your mind?"

"I didn't change my mind. I always wanted to say yes when you first asked me. But...I was afraid there wasn't much room left in your life for me. I knew that, first and foremost, there was Nico. That was obvious. I just wasn't sure that you would love me just as much. Almost as much."

"Jean," he moaned, with regret and frustration. "You have been the best thing to happen to me since I don't know when. I felt that way about you right after I graduated, but that was because I liked you a lot, you weren't like the other girls, and you kept me on track to graduate. You should be sainted."

She laughed quietly. "Let's not get crazy."

He turned to face her. "So you mean it? We'll get married."

"Yes, my love. Do you think Nico will mind?"

"First of all, he's a kid. I doubt he quite understands the concept of marriage. But he seems to really like you. I was sure he would. I kept thinking of that little French girl on the island."

"Lily."

"Yeah...Lily. She took to you right away. She made you her play-mate, and you were so good, so natural interacting with her. Even her parents were impressed with your instant connection. That's what I saw with you and Nicholas. I'm not worried about the two of you."

"Is...your ex okay with your custody arrangement?"

"I think so. We'll see what the future holds."

"Has she remarried? Does she have someone else?"

"You know, I never thought about it. I guess, for now, her love life is not at the top of my list of concerns. If Nico ends up with a stepfather, I'll see how it goes. What about your folks? Anything new to report?"

"Well...my father is moving his practice back to New York. He's going to relocate."

"Okay, I can figure out the rest. He and your mother are in love. They're being open about it and going for all the marbles. I applaud them. 'Don't postpone joy.' I'm not sure who said that, but I'm a true believer."

"I asked my father if they are going to get married. I never did get a yes or no, but I believe it's going to happen."

"Are you okay with that?"

"Very okay with that."

"What about us?"

"We're different. Or maybe not. We have this weird school background, but when we met again, we were starting over…"

"Yeah, but not totally from scratch. We were able to skip steps two through five, I think."

Jean laughed.

"I think the next time your dad is in town, we should take them out to dinner and tell them about us."

"That sounds lovely."

"I hope I didn't become a jerk and complain all summer, especially after coming into so much money."

"Patrick, you didn't complain. I think you were confused and you were a little scared. It was like *Now what do I do?*"

"Yeah, maybe." His gaze was filled with warmth, satisfaction, and love. "You know what? All that green stuff is not bad to have. We're going to have fun, but I want to be smart. Ross is all over the foundation idea, so I'm good with that.

"The thing is, Jean, none of it would mean a lot to me now, if I didn't have you. I have your love. That means everything. That's what really makes me a winner."

"The two of us is a big win for me too. Sorry, no money comes with it."

He kissed her with great gentleness. It seemed to seal their commitment. "I like this. Let's do this every day of our lives."

"Make love?" She grinned.

"Well, yeah. That too. I was talking about kissing each other every morning when we wake up. And at night before going to sleep."

"That's a great tradition."

"I thought so."

There was suddenly an odd grumbling coming from beneath the covers. They looked at each other and grinned broadly.

"The 'urri upps'!" they said simultaneously and chuckled.

"Last one out of bed and into the kitchen makes breakfast!" Patrick challenged.

There was a wild, mad scramble on the bed, but Jean had learned one of his tricks on the island, and she was on the side of the bed closest to the door. She jumped off the bed, ran through the door, dashing around the end of the sofa and into the kitchen. She turned around, leaning back against the sink, grinning triumphantly.

"I win!"

But Patrick was sauntering toward her, naked, tall, and handsome, well rested. Not in a hurry, and not even trying. He trapped her against the sink, his hands braced on the edge on either side of her.

"Of course you do," he said.

And then he kissed Jean again and again.

ACKNOWLEDGMENTS

A HUGE, heartfelt appreciation to Alexandra Gil, JD, MLS, for supplying the law student's POV to my story. Also, thank you to Alexandra for the many amusing insider anecdotes of her three years. After many years in the field, she then received her MLS to become a librarian in New York

ABOUT THE AUTHOR

Prior to breaking out in the mainstream, Sandra Kitt was considered the foremost African American writer of romance fiction and was the first Black writer ever to publish with Harlequin. Sandra is the recipient of a Lifetime Achievement Award in Contemporary Fiction from *Romantic Times*. Romance Writers of America presented Sandra with its 2002 Service Award, and the New York Chapter of RWA presented her with a Lifetime Achievement Award. In 2010, Sandra received the Zora Neale Hurston Award.

A native of New York City, Sandra holds bachelor's and master's degrees in fine arts from the City University of New York and has studied and lived in Mexico. A one-time graphic designer and printmaker, her work appears in corporate collections, including the Museum of African American Art in LA Sandra is a former managing director and information specialist in astronomy and astrophysics at the American Museum of Natural History in New York and has illustrated two books for the late science writer Dr. Isaac Asimov. In 1996, Sandra wrote the last show script for the Hayden Planetarium, narrated by Walter Cronkite. A frequent guest speaker, Sandra has lectured at NYU, Penn State, Sarah Lawrence, and Columbia University and was an adjunct professor in publishing and fiction writing.

Sandra Kitt's first mainstream novel, *The Color of Love,* was released in 1995 to critical acclaim from *Library Journal, USA Today,* and *The Black Scholar* and was optioned by HBO and Lifetime from a script by Sandra. The anthology *Girlfriends* was nominated for the NAACP Image Award for Fiction in 1999. *Significant Others* and *Between Friends* appeared on the bestseller list in *Essence,* and Amazon has named *Significant Others* among the top twenty-five romances for the twentieth century.

A MILLION TO ONE

Bestselling and beloved author Sandra Kitt is back with the Millionaires Club series!

Beck Dennison doesn't know who the beautiful woman at his stepfather's funeral is, but he's determined to find out more about her—such as, exactly what was her relationship with Everett Nicholls? Mourning the loss of her mentor, Eden Marsh is shocked to realize she's attracted to the handsome stranger who tries to comfort her. And that's only the beginning. Beck and Eden discover surprise inheritances are in store for them both. Can this be the start of something wonderful, or will money and suspicions tear them apart?

"Sandra Kitt writes beautiful stories about fascinating characters I would love to know in real life. *Winner Takes All* is romantic, tender, emotional, and compelling."

—RaeAnne Thayne, *New York Times* bestselling author, for *Winner Takes All*

For more info about Sourcebooks's books and authors, visit:
sourcebooks.com